CAPTURING VICTORY

Driven Hearts Book 3

NIKITA SLATER

For my grandma.

*She raised strong women who raised a generation of strong,
independent women. 1930-2018.*

CHAPTER ONE

Ivan strode next to his man, his smooth expression in no way communicating the irritation he felt. "This is the third time you've failed to secure the hacker's services for me," he said, his voice glacial. He climbed the stairs to the helicopter pad, Keane pounding the steps behind him. "I'm starting to wonder if I should employ someone else for this task."

The other man knew better than to defend his actions. He simply stated facts, spitting out the words in his Irish accent. "This fuckin' hacker you want... this XSource..." Keane said the nickname with such disdain that Ivan nearly smiled despite his annoyance, "... has made it disgustingly clear in downright insultin' terms that he wishes to remain a free agent with no contractual obligations. Despite your more than generous offer."

Ivan lifted a brow and turned to his head of security, looking at him through the lenses of his darkly shaded sunglasses as they stood on the deck of his yacht waiting for the pilot to complete preparations for his flight into Athens. "I've been insulted?"

The giant, red-headed tattooed Viking throwback looked more uncomfortable than Ivan had seen in a while. Not since Keane had been caught quite literally with his pants down in the middle of a night raid during one of their Saudi arms deals. They'd planned everything meticulously down to the last detail, yet somehow the meeting date had gotten switched and their team hadn't been notified. A trigger-happy pup on Keane's team jumped the gun and opened fire on the men coming into their camp, nearly starting a war with their allies. The big man, viciously and with extreme prejudice, showed everyone involved why he didn't enjoy a) newbies with attitude on his team, and b) date and/or time switches with minimal effort at notification. Ivan would bet the few Saudi's his man had left intact to take the message back to their employer had never made that mistake again.

Keane's lack of tolerance for bullshit was the *only* reason Ivan was allowing his failure at retaining the hacker to pass. If Ivan's security expert couldn't find the son-of-a-bitch with quick efficiency, then no one could. It was why Ivan was, sadly, going to sacrifice his favourite cat burglar to get his hands on the little fucker. Unfortunately, Katie's usefulness had waned and the hacker's progressively crude insults couldn't be allowed to pass. An example would have to be made.

Keane pulled a tablet from his back pocket, tapped the screen and handed it to Ivan. Ivan took it and glanced down impatiently. He didn't have time for this. He wanted to board his helicopter, get the Athens function over with and travel home where he could relax in solitude. He despised these trips necessary though they were for both business and personal interests. He was about to hand the tablet back when an image on the screen caught and held his attention.

Hundreds of tiny... what were they called... bit cube maybe?... robots danced across the screen. They were meant to look like they were from the 70s or 80s. They marched in ever tighter circles until they formed a hand that waved at him. He knew exactly what was coming next well before it occurred. Yet, still he watched, fascinated, as these tiny robots moved and oscillated on the screen, appearing to leap between decades as they transcended technologies. The carefully controlled icy façade that Ivan spent so much time cultivating cracked and he actually grinned as the hand moved, appearing to leap off the screen using 3-D technology as it gave him the finger before the tiny robots fell apart on the screen and scattered in every direction.

He had the final answer to his request for the hacker's services. It was too bad Ivan didn't take no for an answer.

As the last robot danced off the screen he handed the tablet back to Keane, his smile fading. He strode toward the helicopter. "It really is a shame that we'll have to exterminate such talent." He climbed on board and shouted, "Bring me the hacker. I want to cut his head off myself."

Breathe.

Every particle of her being urged her to run. To escape to her safe comfortable basement in the lovely, anonymous seaside resort town where she'd taken up residence. A place not readily traced unless one were extremely technologically savvy and able to command satellites at will. People like her. She'd purposely chosen her home for its remote location and spotty internet access. It concealed her global movements.

She snatched a champagne glass from a passing tray and pressed the crystal against her shaking lips. She knew it was a mistake to drink. She hadn't eaten anything all day due to nerves and rarely imbibed alcoholic beverages. She hated crowds. She more than hated crowds. She was absolutely fucking terrified of them, jumping at every sound, every touch. Expecting a bomb to explode and kill them all. She knew she was paranoid, but when a person lived through that kind of hell, she could be forgiven a little paranoia.

That and she was waiting in tense misery for the moment Ivan Vogel or one of his henchmen recognized her and pounced. As she gulped the sparkling wine, she reminded herself that they didn't have a clue who she was and couldn't possibly recognize her in the sea of faces.

She'd made the, perhaps very bad, decision to attend the Athens fundraiser in hopes of facing her enemy in person despite preferring the anonymity of the web, her home. At least it had become her home, her independence, her hidey hole, her secret lover and the place where she soared in silence. But she'd made the decision, this one time, to step from her comfort zone and confront her enemy. The man stalking her across the globe, determined to steal her independence and force her into his service.

Oh, she wasn't stupid enough to confront him face to face. Not by a long shot. She wasn't even close to that brave. She was the mouse that hid in a corner, nibbled on her bread crumbs and kept her head down like a good little genius. She just wanted to see him, see what he looked like in person, how he handled himself in public. Understand how her enemy worked, how he operated. Then maybe she stood half a chance of escaping his clutches intact.

She took a hasty sip of her champagne and then coughed as the bubbles hit her throat. What was she thinking? She shouldn't be there at all, let alone drinking in a crowd near a predator like Ivan Vogel. If he knew she was only steps away, he would snatch her up and whisk her away. No, she needed to be clear headed if she were going to win this war. She placed the glass on a nearby table, lifted a hand and pressed the edge of her sari against her cheek, covering her face and taking a few steps closer to her prey.

The crowd kept drifting in between them, blocking her view of the notorious international arms dealer. She wrinkled her nose. It was such a crime that he was allowed in public, rubbing elbows with the rich and famous when he was the shadiest of them all. And there were some pretty awful people in the room. She'd seen the president of at least one brutal military-run regime who would hopefully soon be facing war crimes. To her left there was a prince with a penchant for teenage boys. On his arm was his extremely made-up wife, dripping with jewelry and furs.

She stood on tiptoe trying to catch a glimpse of Vogel. It didn't help that she was shorter than most of the people around her and hadn't bothered with heels. Having never worn them in her life, she didn't think this function was a good place to start accessorizing just in case she had to make a quick getaway. She shifted around the beautifully dressed people, slipping in and through the crowd, trying not to touch anyone. It wasn't that she was agoraphobic. She just really preferred to be by herself. In her own space. She rarely socialized unless it was online. With one exception, and she hadn't seen him in a few years.

The press of people was starting to get to her, her breathing was becoming elevated and her pulse erratic. She knew she was seconds away from totally disgracing herself in front of a huge crowd of the world's elite including princes, sheiks, businessmen and women, the extreme wealthy, the list went on. She needed to get out of there. But first, she needed to face her enemy. Squaring her shoulders, she pushed through the final few people separating them and directly into his path.

She hadn't meant to actually draw his attention. Unfortunately, when a person virtually falls on a man of Vogel's stature in a place with all the world's beautiful people where tickets are invitation only and cost $2000 each, she was bound to draw his notice. XSource assumed she would either be shot by his security or immediately escorted from the premises since her invitation was fake, albeit a clever fake. Instead, she found her hand taken in a firm grip.

Ivan had been deep in conversation with the crown prince of Algeria when she made a less than smooth beeline directly into his path. Her scarf chose that moment to disengage from her shoulder and drift between her legs, tripping her up with embarrassing efficiency while baring a healthy swath of her stomach at the same time. Without breaking conversation, he reached out and took her hand, saving her from an embarrassing fall and helping her straighten, his eyes flickering rapidly over her. His gaze was coolly assessing, dismissive at first glance, and then more careful as he looked her over again. She couldn't help but stare up at him, drawn by the intense strength of his handsome profile while at the same time completely repelled by the aura of destructive power surrounding him. It very much reminded her of someone else she knew.

Her heart skipped a beat and then started thundering like crazy. She tugged on her hand. Now that she'd seen him up close she was totally fine with getting the heck out of there, putting her comfy clothes on and never, ever doing anything this stupid again. In fact, she was probably going to write a manual on how to not do things this stupid in future. Rule #1: don't search out the international criminal mastermind that you digitally gave the finger to who is also hunting you across the planet in hopes of either employing you against your will or murdering you for giving the aforementioned finger to.

She was about to completely lose her shit, punch him some place vulnerable and start running when he turned to face her, giving her his complete attention. His chilling gaze searched every inch of her before piercing her eyes with obvious intent. She was to be his next meal. The breath caught in her throat and she blinked several times. How had she never noticed how utterly, sinisterly handsome Ivan Vogel was in the few pictures she'd managed to dig up of him? Was it because he never completely faced the camera? He was nearly as reclusive as she so there were few pictures for her to study.

He stood nearly a foot taller than her, at around 6'3" if she had to guess. His tuxedo did nothing to hide broad shoulders and long, muscular arms. His face was the most intriguing thing about him though. It was all broad angles and harsh lines put together in a terrible, handsome package. She knew he was in his late thirties, but his steel grey eyes and his icy expression, surrounded by thick, dark hair made him look ancient.

He took a step toward her, closing the gap. Then he did something he shouldn't have done in a public place with so many different cultures mingling, with a woman he didn't know. He took the edge of her scarf, still clutched tight in her fist, and tugged. She didn't realize she still had a death grip on it. She held tight. Instead of yanking it from her grip and taking the risk of tearing the delicate fabric, he took her small fist in his large hand and pulled it down, revealing her face completely.

She tilted her chin down, as if too shy to show her face in public, which was ridiculous considering the gorgeous pink and gold sari she wore bared her entire midriff. He took her jaw between his fingers and tilted, searching her face for a moment. She struggled to keep the emotions from her eyes; the fear, hatred, anger... and recognition. She must have failed on some level because she saw a flash of surprise reflected in his own cool grey gaze.

She quickly jerked her face away and took a step back, then another. She knew if she didn't act quickly he would recover from his momentary surprise and grab her before she could leave. He had no idea who she was, but if he was intrigued, he wouldn't stop until he found out. She knew that Ivan was a man that always got what he wanted. It was how he'd became so rich.

Rich, ruthless... and deadly. She'd done as much research on him as he'd done on her. There was a damn good reason she'd refused to work for him. He didn't allow people to leave his employment. Not alive anyway. And she had no plans to get involved with a man like that. It was bad enough that she'd gotten mixed up with the likes of Soloman Hart and Roman Valdez. At least those two mobsters were on a completely different continent from her and currently not attempting to hunt her down.

The last thing she heard as she turned to rush through the crowd was Ivan's deep voice, "Find out who she is and bring her to me."

Not fucking likely.

CHAPTER TWO

He was closing in on the hacker, but the tech genius was making him angry; very angry. And things that made Ivan angry tended to die slow, painful deaths. He hated playing games of cat and mouse. He preferred to lay his cards on the table, do his business out in the open with guns and steel. Which is why he dealt mainly in weaponry; he understood armaments. He didn't like the world of sophisticated technology, though he certainly wasn't a technophobe. He understood the use for computers, technology and the internet and was happy to exploit them any way he could, which was why he'd wanted the brilliant mind of XSource on his payroll. But he couldn't stand the covert nature of internet crime; especially when it was keeping his prey from him.

Ivan would have been more at home in the wild west, hunting his victims on horseback, taking and conquering through sheer strength and force of will. But he'd been born in a different time, forced to channel his intelligence down a different path, hitting the international market, trading in arms deals across borders, building a private army of mercenaries and highly intelligent minds that worked beneath him to help him amass power and fortune through underworld profiteering.

When his phone rang, he nodded at his secretary, allowing her to pick up the call that would set his plan in motion; the capture of XSource. He turned away and watched the harbour, ignoring the initial back and forth as his various teams connected on the operation. He knew he was expending ridiculous amounts of money and resources on this capture. But the people closest to Ivan, the few that knew him best, knew that he was a bloodhound. He never gave up. Whether it was a business acquisition, an arms deal, an art thief or a hacker, he would hunt to the ends of the Earth, until he had what he wanted within his possession. Then he would play God, decide what to do with his new property; keep it or crush it.

When his people, scattered throughout the world, seamlessly co-ordinated themselves, he asked, "Where is he?" his voice cool, betraying none of the irritation he felt.

They'd just turned on their cat burglar, luring her into a clever trap in Mexico and handing her over to Roman Valdez, leader of the Valdez cartel in return for a location on the hacker that Katie Pullman used for her thieving jobs. They'd ensured she would definitely need the hacker's services on this one to get into a specialised room at the hacienda where the painting she was supposed to steal was kept.

Silence greeted his demand. It took patience he didn't have to keep quiet and not interrupt his people while they digitally knocked down the hacker's attempts to cover his tracks. Ivan locked down the urge to pace his office and shout further demands. He was a man of action, but this was not his time to shine. This was the reason he spent copious amounts of money employing people all over the world. So he could have the things he needed... and wanted.

And right now he wanted the hacker's head on a platter. He needed to step aside and allow his people to track the hacker using the sophisticated resources he purchased for these jobs.

After a long moment of silence, he could hear Katie scuffling with Roman and screaming through the phone connection, "Source, get out now!"

This was quickly followed by one of his own people from the command center. "We have him pinned down. He's in Portugal."

"Where in Portugal?" Ivan asked coolly.

Several seconds passed and then the answer came through clearly. "Quarteira. A small coastal fishing hub."

"Keane?" Ivan demanded over the connection. "Who's closest?"

Keane replied immediately. "We have a man in Lisbon, he can be there within the hour."

"Not good enough, he'll go to ground by then," Ivan snapped, pacing his office. He could feel the tension rolling off his secretary. "What else?"

Five more seconds passed then Keane said, "Know a guy in Cadiz, Spain. I've used his team for some jobs in that region. Can either chopper in or boat across the water, fifteen minutes if he goes now." Keane hesitated and then added, "Mean fucker though. Can't guarantee the package'll get to you in one piece."

"Do it," Ivan said. "And Keane?"

"Yes, sir?"

"The package will arrive intact."

Few words were exchanged while Keane engaged the services of his mercenary contact in Spain. The man was indeed rough around the edges, but quick to leap to action when a generous contract was immediately laid out. Ivan did not negotiate. He offered. His offer was accepted, both parties moved forward with their contractual obligations. It was really too bad the hacker failed to understand.

He closed his eyes and continued to practice patience, counting down fifteen minutes to the second as Salazar's team took a military commissioned craft across the Gulf of Cadiz to Quarteira.

"They've landed," Keane's voice came across the line. "They're in the vehicle and movin' toward the signal. ETA, two minutes."

Ivan allowed himself to feel the first stirrings of satisfaction since he began closing in on his prey. Soon the hacker would be within Ivan's power, begging for mercy. He would quickly find out that Ivan had none.

"Sir," Keane's voice came through the speaker, cool and professional. "We have the hacker, we have XSource."

Ivan allowed the corner of his lips to curl slightly in satisfaction. "Excellent."

"She was preparin' to run."

She? A woman?

He turned to his screen, the smile leaving his face. "Show me."

An incoming message popped up on Ivan's screen. He tapped it, sitting down for a better view. He was stunned when her image filled the screen. He recognized her, of course. She was the lovely woman in the pink sari he'd attempted to converse with at the Athens ball two weeks before. Even in the overly bright light cast on her squinting features by the camera phone, he could tell it was her. Thick, dark brown hair swirled around her shoulders, forcibly hunched forward from the man standing behind her, holding her arms behind her back.

Suddenly a bag was shoved over her head, blocking her from view. He watched with disinterest as she fought her captors, screaming and kicking until someone slapped her in the side of the head so hard she was knocked off her feet. When she was righted, it was clear the fight had drained out of her. She leaned limply against one of the men her small hand clutching his forearm like a lifeline.

Ivan felt a tweak of annoyance at the way these men were handling his merchandise. The hacker belonged to him. No one else had earned the opportunity to punish her. He wanted to tear the bag from her head and shoot every man in that room for touching her. But she was still several thousand kilometres away from him. There was little he could do, but calmly, coolly wait for her arrival.

Salazar spoke to his men in rapid Spanish. "Load her up. Take as much of the equipment as you can. Don't damage anything."

Once the woman was taken from her shadowy basement home and out of view, Ivan placed his fists on the desk and leaned, making absolutely sure his next instructions were clear. "Keane."

"Yes, sir."

"No one touches that woman again. Understood?"

"Understood, sir."

Ivan ended the call, turned to his computer and ended the video feed. He trusted that Keane would make sure his instructions were followed. He glanced at his secretary. She was looking at him, her expression empty and serene, exactly as she knew it should be. She was to have no emotion while in his presence. She lifted her tablet and waited on his next instructions.

He turned his back on her, squared his shoulders and emptied his mind for a moment, attempting to centre himself; release some of the emotion boiling up. "I need you to make some changes for our guest. Circumstances have become different. She'll be staying for a longer period of time than I was anticipating. Make sure a cell is prepared for her right away. It is to be comfortable, but there will be absolutely no technology in or around her room. That includes light switches, plug-ins, anything she can get her hands on. It all needs to go."

"Yes, sir," Anna said, her fingers flying over the tablet as she gave his people real time instructions. They would have a few hours to prepare the room to his specifications.

"I'll be leaving for home sooner than expected. I'll have to finish the Ukrainian deal, so Thursday I'll leave. Arrange it." Though he wasn't facing her he could still feel her hesitation. "What is it?" he asked coldly.

"Wh-what about Mr. Kadir? You were supposed to meet with him on Friday about the..."

Ivan turned to his secretary of six months and stared at her, his grey eyes expressing his distaste for her lack of foresight. She swallowed, her face slightly pale. She nodded.

"Of course, sir. I will cancel your meeting and reschedule," she said in a slightly higher voice.

He jerked his chin in a nod. "If he's not willing to reschedule, let Keane know. He can take care of the situation." They both knew how Keane would take care of the client. Anna made a note, keeping her eyes averted. "That's all for now. You may leave."

She uncrossed her legs and stood. Though no part of her body language conveyed relief at his dismissal, he could feel the emotion coming off her in waves, see it in every line of her sleek, professional body as she moved toward the door. She was a beautiful woman, had even tried to flirt with her new boss upon meeting him, a few weeks into the job. Instead of harshly rebuffing and firing her, as he'd been tempted to do, he'd instead given her time to get to know him. Given her time to look beyond what he knew was a classically handsome face to the monster within.

He knew who he was. He'd made deliberately, terribly

immoral decisions simply to keep business flowing smoothly. Each step forward he'd taken into the darkness throughout his life had been a strategic decision. He'd never questioned the path he was taking, never thought twice about the stain on his soul. Nothing mattered to him except the power, the gain and the ability to crush anything that might be able to crush him first.

Thus, his pretty little secretary learned quickly not to flirt with her new boss. Not in an office where more than one person had disappeared, where being fired could too easily take on a permanent meaning. Instead, she took extra pains to blend in, do her job seamlessly and with the utmost respect. So far Ivan was mostly satisfied with her performance.

He sat down at his desk, pulled the computer monitor closer to him and expanded the frozen picture of his hacker until it filled the screen. The terror and anger in her dark eyes filled his chest, his heart and his lungs with... something. Some kind of feeling. He sat watching her for several moments, tracing her features, bare of make-up and artifice. He touched the screen, outlining her cheeks and lips with a fingertip before tapping her right between the eyes. He sat back in his chair and closed his eyes, breathing in and out, attempting to rid himself of the feelings, to centre himself once more.

He sat up abruptly, his eyes flying open. He knew what they were, the feelings he was associating with the woman, the hacker. For the first time in a long time, rather than feeling apathy, he felt anticipation, excitement... and desire.

CHAPTER THREE

"Lovely."

The deep voice echoed through the darkness, penetrating the warmth of what she'd come to think of as her dungeon. She turned, heart beating erratically, knowing it was finally time for her to meet her captor face-to-face.

It had been two days since she'd been taken. The men who had stormed into her tiny, underground place in Portugal and put a bag over her head had hustled her into a car, sped her through the rainy streets and then onto a private aircraft. When she tried to fight and wrestle the bag off her head, a man had wrenched her arms back and ruthlessly zip-tied them. When she'd screamed curses and begged her captors to let her go, the same man had pressed a gun against the side of her head and told her to stop speaking or die. She had chosen silence.

Though she had no idea where she was, she knew who had taken her and why. Katie Pullman's last call had held a chilling warning. Her voice had screamed out for Source to run. There was only one man connected to Katie with the resources to hunt someone as digitally invisible as XSource.

Source had done her best to heed the blond cat burglar's warning, erasing sensitive files and throwing necessities into a bag at hyper speed.

She hadn't thought there was any chance Ivan's people could be so close. He must have a truly stunning amount of resources all over the world to be able to grab her in such a small and insignificant place. There was a reason she'd chosen the small seaside town in Portugal to hang out. It wasn't for the seafood. The place was gloomy as fuck.

She thought when she arrived at wherever she was that Ivan would confront her and demand again that she work for him. At least that's what she hoped the plan was. Knowing what a cold-blooded bastard Ivan Vogel was, he might have just brought her here to torture and kill her for turning down his incredibly kind offer of employment. Instead, she'd been left alone for two days, imprisoned in some kind of old-fashioned dungeon with stone walls and barred windows while she awaited his arrival. Granted it was a comfortable dungeon, warm with a large cozy bed, reading materials and plenty of food. But still...

Now it would seem her captor had arrived. And he was in the mood to inspect his newest acquisition.

"You are a pleasant surprise," he drawled in flawless English, though she still detected an accent. He stepped through the shadows toward her. "I was led to believe you were a man."

He stopped so close to her she could feel the heat from his body. She'd stood up to greet him, not wanting such a predatory man to have any kind of physical advantage. Not that it mattered, he was still almost a foot taller than her. She shuddered as his grey eyes roved hungrily over her despite the shadows, taking in every part of her. Instinct screamed at her to back away, but pride held her still.

"Of course, had you been a man, you would be dead," he said easily, as if he'd been informing her of the time.

She bit her lip to stifle the whimper that threatened to break free. "And why is that?" she asked, attempting to infuse strength into her husky voice. She didn't speak often, preferring her own company.

His lip lifted in a cold smirk. His face looked like it was sculpted from granite, hard and masculine, with barely any emotion except what he allowed. His body was built from the same rock as his face, all sharp planes and hard muscles with long, masculine limbs. She'd thought he was a handsome man when she saw him at the Athens ball. Now?... now that he held her fragile life in his ruthless hands, she wasn't convinced.

"You refused to work for me," he said simply, his eyes never leaving her face.

"And no one has ever refused you before?" she asked sharply. "I somehow doubt that."

His brow lifted in surprise, as though reminding her of her precarious position. A small shudder rippled down her back. She needed to remember who she was dealing with and somehow rein in her impulsive tongue. There was a reason she was a hacker. She preferred not to develop the social skills necessary in dealing with the masses. She didn't like interacting with people or giving them the required responses to their inane conversation.

"No one refuses me for long, little Miss Source," he drawled her nickname out as though teasing her with it. "And you withheld services from me repeatedly. Refusing my advances, despite my ever more lucrative offers."

He stepped closer to her as he spoke, purposefully using provocative language. He lifted a finger and ran it over her cheek, testing the softness of her skin. Her eyes flared wide and the breath strangled in her throat. She stumbled back a step, but her legs hit the edge of the bed. He stepped closer, trapping her against the high bed she'd been sleeping on for the last two days.

"P-please," she whispered, terrified of the big man. She'd heard so many horrific stories of the international arms dealer over the years. He worked in and out of the shadows. The one story she should have listened to when he first started pursuing her a year ago was that Ivan always got what he wanted. "I'm sorry."

He looked down at her, lifting his hand again and touching it to her cheek before drifting it down her throat and then her arm. He lifted her hand and brought it to his face, caressing the back with his lips. Her skin was only a few shades darker than his. Her hand looked so small and delicate in his much larger hand. His tongue darted out to touch the back of her fingers.

"You are sorry you didn't come to work for me?" he asked against her hand, pressing the soft skin against his hard jaw and then rubbing his rough cheek against her. "A little late for apologies, don't you think?" His sardonic gaze flickered around her prison before settling back on her face.

She could barely breathe, let alone keep her thoughts straight when he touched her like that, yet she knew she had to force her brain to work. This man was brutal, intelligent and deadly. She was way out of her depth and almost completely alone in the world. There was no one who would miss her if she disappeared forever. Except, perhaps, for her friend Katie, now in the clutches of the Mexican cartel. She needed to use her head and get out of this with her principles intact.

She raised her chin and said in as clear a voice as she could manage, "No. I don't work for organizations, only for myself. What I'm sorry about is that you're the kind of guy who won't take no for an answer."

His fingers tightened painfully around hers. She tried to jerk her hand away, but he refused to let her go. His eyes blazed down into hers for a moment and she feared he would just give into the fury and get rid of her. She knew Ivan wasn't used to denial of any kind. He could buy, bully and steal anything he wanted. He was one of the most powerful men in the world.

Well, he couldn't have her.

He reached for her so quickly, she thought a blow was coming and cried out. Instead, he sank his hand into her hair and jerked her head back until her face tipped up toward his. She gritted her teeth against the pain. His eyes flashed in cruel approval. Her chest lifted and dropped as she breathed rapidly, standing stiffly against him.

"What's your name?" he demanded, his cold, dark eyes searching her face as though he could pull the answer from her.

She wouldn't give him anything. She would lie to him, give him one of her aliases. She hadn't said her real name in years, preferring to bury herself under layers of false identities. When the last of her family had died, so had her real identity along with any sense of belonging. She opened her mouth to give him one of her most used false identities, Pari, but she must have hesitated too long. Or maybe he saw the flash of dishonesty in her eyes.

Suddenly, he seized her by the throat, lifted her off the floor and slammed her down on the bed. The fluffy quilts softened the blow to her back. He came down heavy on top of her, straddling her flailing limbs. She would have screamed, except he was choking the breath from her body. His actions were so swift and precise she didn't stand a chance. He had her arms and legs completely pinned and her throat in a tight grip that she knew would leave bruises later.

Tears rushed to her eyes as she stared up at her cruel

captor. He didn't even look angry that she had been about to lie to him, just slightly irritated, as though he expected it and was put out at having to mete out discipline.

"You don't want to lie to me," he said, his deep voice glacial.

A tear escaped from her eye and ran into her hairline. She nodded. She could feel his erection pressing into her belly where he was straddling her. He wasn't completely unaffected by their little struggle, but he didn't seem to notice or care. Neither his actions nor his expression indicated he was about to ravish her. Or maybe that was wishful thinking?

He eased his grip on her throat and gave her an expectant look.

She licked her lips and whispered the name she hadn't spoken in six years, "Jaya."

Genuine satisfaction suffused his features, giving his angular features a softer cast. "Victory," he said.

He didn't mean that he was victorious over her. Her name meant victory in Hindi. And somehow he knew that. Though she hated him with every fibre of her being, a small part of her couldn't help but be impressed.

"Yes," she whispered.

His eyes cut to hers. "You think you will be victorious, little hacker?"

She glared up at him, hating the way he played with her. She was ill-equipped to deal with a man like him. He was sophisticated, a world traveller. An international criminal and an arms dealer. She might be international in her own way, but she lived in basements and cellars in small towns, in places no one ever heard of, so she could stay off the grid, hiding from people like this psychotic villain.

"You tell me," she snapped, arching her back in an attempt to dislodge him. He was so much bigger, all she managed to do was buck her body up into his and show him the curve of her full breasts against her T-shirt. "You're keeping me in this dungeon for no good reason. Either let me the fuck go or let's get on with whatever this is! Because I'm telling you right now, I won't be working for a criminal like you."

He raised an eyebrow and chuckled at her audacity. She got the feeling it was a gamble with him. Either he would laugh at a person's hastily spoken words or he would take offence and murder them swiftly and without remorse. He rolled off the bed, leaving her where she lay. He watched her as he adjusted his clothing, the amusement fading from his face.

A muscle twitched in his jaw as his eyes darkened with something she couldn't define. "And I'm telling you, little Jaya. I will be keeping you... until I get what I want."

As his eyes roved over her prone body she suddenly didn't think Ivan wanted her hacking services at all anymore. She rolled onto her side and pulled a pillow against her stomach, giving him her back. He clearly didn't intend to let her go and she didn't have anything else to discuss with him.

She waited until he walked away and closed the door to her dungeon before she allowed the tears to fall.

CHAPTER FOUR

Jaya spent the next few days trying everything she could think of to get out of her prison. She hardly slept on the big, comfortable bed, constantly expecting her evil captor to come back and finish what he'd started when he crushed her into the mattress and held her down. She paced back and forth picturing everything he might do to her, her agitated brain playing out the worst possible scenarios.

There was zero technology in her cell. Not a single computer, cable, TV, radio or camera. There weren't even any light switches or plug-ins. They'd been removed and boarded up. She thought a pervert like Ivan might've at least installed a camera for his viewing pleasure but no such luck. If she had a camera at her disposal, she might have been able to rig something to enable an escape attempt. So either her captor actually respected her technological abilities to the point that he wasn't even going to trust her with a single piece of modern equipment or he really was this technologically unenlightened. Jaya was on the fence; her opinion of the man could go either way.

The only thing left in her cozy little dungeon suite,

besides the bed and washroom stuff, was a bookshelf with a selection of period novels that she would never in a million years have touched. The authors included Mary Shelley, Jane Austen, Charlotte Bronte, Sir Walter Scott, Henry James and others. Either Ivan was extremely well read and enjoyed authors that were long dead or he somehow knew she was woefully undereducated in the arts. She did decide to keep a book called Tess d'Ubervilles by Thomas Hardy near her bed just in case she needed to defend herself. It was the heaviest of the selection left at her disposal, but so far no one had touched her except Ivan.

After her initial I'm-going-to-be-raped-and-murdered-at-the-hands-of-a-madman panic began to subside, her superior intelligence started to kick in and she began looking for ways out of her cell. The bars on the windows were impenetrable and the door was solid steel with absolutely no give. It didn't take long for her to realize that her best bet was going to be mealtimes. This seemed to be when her prison cell was at its most vulnerable. Problem number one; the giant red-headed guard who stood beside the door while a servant brought the meal in. Problem number two; the giant red-headed guard with the semi-automatic rifle attached to his side like it was his firstborn.

There was absolutely no way Jaya was getting past him in one piece. And unfortunately the look on his face suggested he would enjoy an escape attempt since it might break up the boring five minutes it took him to supervise meal drop-off. She thought about throwing the tray in his face and running past him, but again, there were two problems with that idea. First, she was assuming the person serving her food would do nothing while she ran, and second, she was pretty sure scary red-headed guy wouldn't be distracted by a little flying food. Oh, and third, he looked like a shoot first and ask questions later kind of guy.

If only she could get past him. As soon as she got her hands in the security system, which would be easy from outside her cell, she would own Ivan's little lair and bring them all down. She just needed out!

So, she started working on plan B. Dig her way out. She grabbed a plastic knife from her food tray and hid it in the washroom. Just in case they actually checked the tray she snapped the fork into little pieces and tore up the paper plate and napkin, as though in a fit of anger, hoping to misdirect anyone who might check for the knife. The servant had merely glanced at the tray, picked it up and left.

Jaya grabbed her plastic knife and, sitting on the counter in the washroom, began digging at the little wooden panel covering where the light switch would have been. It was somewhat difficult since the area was dark and shadowy, with little light filtering in from the barred window in her bedroom. She was gratified when it started to lift from the wall. Just as she thought, it'd been mostly screwed right into the drywall instead of a wooden two-by-four. After using the knife to lift it up, she managed to wedge her hand in the side and yank it completely off.

"Yes!" she whispered to herself and squinted into the dark hole. "Now what do we have in here?" She reached her hand in, feeling around for wires. She sighed in disappointment when she felt nothing but empty space. They'd clearly thought to gut the entire thing.

"Exactly what I was wonderin'," said a voice from behind her in a deeply accented Irish drawl.

Jaya jumped and would've fallen off the counter if a large hand hadn't shot out to steady her, wrapping itself around her arm and pulling her right off her perch. She yanked her arm from the grip and steadied herself against the marble top. She swallowed hard, wetting her suddenly dry throat, and edged sideways in an attempt to get away from the towering red-haired, tattooed man, who was now filling the doorway of the washroom.

"What *do* we have here?" he murmured, looking down at her. His face was completely shadowed so she couldn't tell from his expression what his mood might be. But it couldn't be a good thing that he'd found her digging into the wall. "Is our wee canary trying to find a way out? Gonna fly home?"

She shook her head and kept edging until her back hit the glass wall of the shower stall. He remained in the doorway, thank god, his arms crossed over his massive chess.

"Truth now, and maybe I won't tell the boss what you were up to," he said.

She nodded quickly, immediately understanding that this man was the lesser of two evils. "I was going to see if there was some kind of wiring I could get my hands on, then trick you into coming in here and maybe zap the shit out of you, steal your gun and get out of the dungeon. Once I'm on the outside, I'm golden."

He didn't say anything for a moment and then he threw his head back and laughed, the sound booming off the walls of the small space. "Well, I'll give you credit for creativity, canary," he said wiping tears of amusement from his eyes. "But it'd take a helluva lot more than anything that wall has to put me on the floor. And even if you got this gun from me, baby, she wouldn't work. She's fingerprinted to me. Boss has the best in weaponry supplied for his men."

Jaya was surprised. That kind of hardware was extremely expensive and hard to come by. "S-sorry," she said.

"No you're not," he replied, but he didn't sound annoyed.

She shook her head. "Okay, I'm not," she admitted. "Of course I'm going to try to escape the first chance I get. Wouldn't you? Can I please see your gun?" She couldn't believe her boldness in asking, but she was actually curious. She'd taken some weapons training in her teens and played a lot of first person shooter games. She knew guns, and more importantly, she knew sophisticated tech. This particular gun sounded unique.

She could feel his shock rather than see it, but he pulled the weapon off his shoulder and held it out. He didn't relinquish his hold so she took it in her hands, clutching it lightly, her fingertips on either end. She leaned in closer, automatically edging past him toward the light in her room. He moved a little allowing her by, his hand still firmly on the gun. She barely noticed his proximity, she was so absorbed. Instead she muttered to herself, "An assault rifle, semi-automatic of course, but nothing I've ever seen in simulations or pictures before." She tipped it over. He allowed her, shifting his grip, watching her face carefully. She quickly found the fingerprint identification just along the flat surface above the trigger so it wouldn't interfere with a security situation. "Impressive," she breathed, then she looked up at him and said, "You're a lefty, Irish. And the boss cares enough to have weapons made specially for you. You must be important."

He looked startled for a moment and then a myriad of emotions crashed across his rugged, bearded features. First anger, which had her handing the gun hastily back and stepping quickly away, and then speculative calculation as his gaze swept over her from head to toe and back again. His look wasn't exactly sexual, but it was thorough. She felt as though he was seeing her for the first time, though he'd entered her dungeon bedroom many times in the past few days.

"You ain't stupid, canary," he growled, shortly. "There's a dress on the bed for you. Boss wants to have his evening meal with you. Get dressed and I'll take you up." She nodded, her eyes wide on him and the gun he slung back over his shoulder. His pale blue eyes swept her one last time. "Just a word of advice. Step carefully around Mr. Vogel. The things I tolerate are not things he will find nearly as amusin'."

She stared at him wondering if she'd somehow found an unlikely ally, and whispered, "I understand. What's your name?"

"Keane," he growled, then added sharply, "Get changed and don't take long." He turned on his heel and left, slamming the door shut behind him.

She turned and looked down at the bed, despair filling her. Spread out across the blankets was a beautiful gold and white-trimmed sari, golden sandals adjacent to the outfit. The entire thing set out like that, the bars on the windows, the lock on the door, her not having any kind of choice, even Keane's warning... she felt like a slave with no idea of her ultimate fate.

CHAPTER FIVE

Ivan watched as Jaya approached, gliding toward him like a golden goddess. He was relieved that she'd chosen to wear the sari he'd sent down for her. It was beautiful on her, golden with lace trimming. One of her shoulders and part of her smooth, brown stomach was left bare. His own stomach clenched in response as she rounded the large pool area brightly lit by lanterns, and continued her path toward him, flanked by one of his men. As she approached he heard the soft jingle of the metal beads on her sandals and wished her sari would allow him to view her feet and ankles. So far, every part of her that he'd seen was perfection, though he'd never craved a woman built quite like Jaya. In fact, nothing about her and his reactions to her was preceded by experience.

It wasn't like him to care about such things as women's apparel or an individual woman's comfort, but there was something about this particular woman that made him care. He didn't want her to feel discomfort. Nor did he want to visit her in her prison cell. He didn't want to get to know the facets of her character in the confines of the stone walls he'd imposed upon her. For some reason, he wanted her to see the man rather than the ruthless arms dealer who'd kidnapped her with every intention of ending her life. Now he was on new ground. He'd never put himself out to be kind to a woman.

"Why are you doing this? What do you want from me?" she demanded, eyeing him as she stopped next to him, her head barely reaching his chin. It was clear that she was frightened, but still she spoke to him in such a way. She was a brave little thing. Perhaps this was what intrigued him about her? But then, he'd met and killed braver women.

Indeed, why was he doing this? He didn't need to 'date' his captive. She was wholly under his control, he could easily fuck and dispose of her when he tired of her. He'd done much worse in his life, so the moral issue shouldn't pose a problem. Yet, for some reason he felt compelled to wine and dine her. He was attracted to her and something about their situation made him uncomfortable. Those dark eyes of hers, both world weary and innocent, saw right through him, pierced him when no others could. They didn't chastise him. They simply looked through him. It was as though, once she'd taken a thorough look at the Athens ball, she'd dismissed him for good, turned around and walked away. And not even kidnapping her could force her to acknowledge his presence in her life.

He gave her an honest answer. "I don't know yet, Jaya." He took her arm and led her to the table across from the pool deck. Her guard melted into the shadows but remained within the vicinity. The table was lit by lanterns as well as candles in bowls filled with water and white lilies. As he seated her, he leaned down and said against the side of her head, enjoying the silky length against his cheek, "But your safest course is to follow instructions and indulge me. I'm not a man to be crossed and you've tried my patience beyond what I would ordinarily accept."

He was gratified to feel her shiver before he stepped away from her chair and made his way around the table. He wasn't pleased at the length separating them, but he would accept the space for now. The table had been prepared to perfection at his specifications, each dish had meaning to her culture. Or the culture he believed she'd been born to. He would allow her some time to see him as more than her captor before he began pressing his suit. Now that he saw her dressed similar to the way he'd seen her in Athens, looking lovely and soft, he knew for sure he wanted her. But the thought of just taking her, raping all that loveliness, ruining it... didn't sit well.

A servant filled his glass with a rich, red wine and then stood stiffly at Ivan's side tilting the bottle so he could see the label; it was a Chilean Errauriz La Cumbra Syrah. He sipped the spicy red and nodded his head before waving the man toward Jaya. She smiled nervously and held her glass out for him to fill.

Ivan stiffened. Thus far she hadn't once shown interest in a single member of his staff or security, yet she was smiling at the man serving their table. He watched and ruminated as she lifted the delicate crystal to her lips and took a tentative sip. Her eyes widened a little and she took a longer drink, her full bottom lip curving against the glass. His stomach clenched in response. For a man used to controlling both himself and his environment, he was finding he had a distinct loss of control around Jaya.

"Where were you born?" he asked so suddenly that she nearly lost her hold on the glass.

She set it down on the table and looked at him. "Why does it matter?"

He clenched his teeth. He wasn't used to people withholding answers from him. But he knew getting anything out of this woman wouldn't be easy. After all, she'd spent the better part of a year evading his best attempts at finding her.

He would have to resist the urge to use his usual methods of persuasion. But he wasn't going to banter with her all night. He wanted answers and he was going to get them. "Speak, Jaya, or this meal ends in your hunger and an even smaller cage."

She stiffened and sent a glare down the length of the table that should have scorched him in his seat. "I was born in Mumbai," she snapped.

His dick perked up at her heated look and the blood flowed thicker in his veins as though their banter, their body language was all a dance that would end in his conquest over her. Perhaps this was all new to him, having patience, but he thrived in the arena of battle.

"And where is your family?" he asked, fingering the stem of his wineglass, watching her every move with the sharpness of an apex predator. Sure enough, she flinched.

"Dead," she said through gritted teeth.

The same servant who had brought their wine returned with a cart. On it were several dishes including tandoori chicken, chole bhature, butter chicken, biryani, litti and naan. Her eyes skimmed the food and her mouth opened in appreciation, her former ire forgotten as the delicious smells rolled toward her. She needed no urging. She quickly began filling her plate when the cart stopped next to her.

Ivan watched in amusement as she spilled a spoonful of rice on the tablecloth and ignored it in favour of grabbing another tandoori drumstick. She grabbed a handful of naan and said, "I'm done," to the hovering servant. He smiled at her indulgently and rolled the cart toward Ivan.

"My dad hated ethnic food," Jaya said, shoving a big piece of potato into her mouth and chewing. "He used to order pizza all the time and wanted my mom to make hamburgers and French fries. We almost never ate this stuff." She took another big bite and closed her eyes while she chewed and swallowed. "But I've missed it. This is actually really good."

She'd just offered him something voluntarily and the knowledge of her willing disclosure felt somehow valuable. He wanted more, but he didn't know how to get it out of her. Watching her eat, watching her speak without rancor or fear in her voice was... stunning. He now knew exactly why he was doing this. So he could have moments like this; could have her voluntary participation in whatever it was he wanted from her. Without tearing his eyes from her, Ivan dished up his own plate.

"What happened to them?" he asked.

Her eyes snapped open and the peaceful moment she had been enjoying melted away. Ivan felt the man standing next to him stiffen. The cart rattled. He could feel his annoyance begin to rise. The other man should not have eyes, let alone feelings, for Jaya.

When she didn't immediately speak, he pressed her in a cool voice, "Jaya, what happened to your family?"

"They died," she said flatly.

"Yes, you said that already. What happened?" he demanded.

"I don't talk about it," she snapped.

The cart rattled again, and Ivan turned his head to the side to look at the man who had well past served his purpose. The man cleared his throat and hurried away, taking the cart with him. Ivan turned back to Jaya and raised an eyebrow leaning his elbows on the table. "You do now, sweetheart."

"I'm not your sweetheart!"

"Start talking, Jaya, or find out exactly how uncomfortable life can become," he said coolly, taking another bite of his food.

She glared at him and stabbed a vegetable with her fork. She didn't put it in her mouth though. "Is this how you treat all your dates? I'm surprised women go out with you," she sneered, her cheeks darkening with emotion. "Then again, you probably have to kidnap them to get them to go out with you."

He shrugged. "Actually, I rarely ask about a woman's family and if I do, I couldn't care less about the answer. With you, I do care. So, please indulge me, if you don't want to find out where my patience ends."

She sat in her chair breathing heavily for a moment, clearly struggling with her need to defy him. Eventually self-preservation won out. Staring stonily past him she said in a flat voice, "They were killed in an embassy bombing. The few people that survived the bombing were killed when gunmen went in after and... and took the building. There were no hostages left alive."

He nodded, not surprised. He thought it unlikely that she would have living family given the way she'd survived and lived the past several years. "How many of your family were killed?" he asked. "How were you spared?"

She didn't bother withholding the information now that he'd gotten what he wanted from her. She continued to stare past him as she spoke, her fork held stiffly in her hand as though she'd like nothing better than to stab him with it. "Most of my family died in the bomb – mom, dad, two brothers and a sister." There was no inflection in her voice as she spoke, though he suspected her inner turmoil was intense. "I was at a hotel with my grandma. She was sick and my mom wanted me to stay behind and take care of her. I w-was annoyed because I wanted to go with them. I thought the embassy would be somehow exciting."

He didn't think she'd meant to divulge how she'd felt. Survivor's guilt. She thought she should've died with the rest of them. Up until that point he'd listened to her with his usual dispassion. Then she turned those dark eyes on him, that velvet brown gaze that looked right through him and she said, "My grandma died of a massive heart attack that night, only hours after we found out about the bombing. She couldn't handle the thought of losing her only son and three of her grandbabies. So, she left me alone in the world."

A piercing shaft went through his chest and his fist clenched against the table as he imagined her pain. Glass shattered behind him. The servant dropped something on his way back to the table. Jaya jumped, her gaze flying past Ivan's shoulder. Ivan didn't bother turning to look. He knew what'd happened. The man had been listening to her, watching her. She'd touched him with her pathetic story, just as she'd somehow touched Ivan.

"How old were you?" he asked, his voice cool.

"Twelve," she answered picking at her food.

"Impossible," Ivan snapped. "You can't have been that young. Who took care of you?"

She shrugged. "No one. I took care of myself."

"How is this possible?" he asked, staring at her. "You were practically a baby. You weren't taken in by family or friends? You just... what? Wandered the streets of Mumbai until you grew up and became a hacker? No, I do not believe this, Jaya. Tell me the truth."

"I am telling you the truth!" she snapped. "I had no more family left, or none that I could get in touch with. But I was self-sufficient. I'm a genius, Ivan. I didn't just *become* a hacker as you call it, I was always gifted this way. I look at technology and I just know how it works. I've always been that way." She stared at him, her expression a cauldron of emotion. "What about you, Ivan? Did you just become this way overnight? Or were you born with a gun in your hand? I think something shaped you to become this way. What was it... what's your accent, Ivan? Bosnian? Croatian? What, you don't like talking about it?"

He stiffened, anger finally overriding the desire and curiosity he'd been feeling toward his dinner guest. He stared back at her, his icy expression the only warning he gave for her to stop speaking. She didn't heed him.

"If I had to guess again I would say you were shaped into this soulless monster through war," she continued, charging forward, heedless of the boundaries she smashed through. The servant who'd become instantly smitten with the pretty hacker wasn't heedless though. He stood next to Ivan, his mouth open in horror, obviously terrified for her as she ploughed recklessly on. "What happened, Ivan? Did your neighbours murder all of your people and now you take your revenge on others as a way to control the world around you because you couldn't control your childhood. Is that what happened?"

Ivan picked up his wineglass and took a sip, the only emotion visible was the slight tremble through the stem. He set it carefully down and asked, "Where did you find this information?" She couldn't possibly have guessed. She must have come across it somewhere else.

She closed her mouth and stared at him, her face paling slightly as she realized exactly how far she'd just gone. What she'd just said to a notoriously vicious international arms dealer. He stood slowly, unfolding his tall body from the chair and then straightening the sleeves of his dress shirt before making his way around the table toward her. Her eyes widened and her mouth opened slightly in fear as he approached.

"Talk, now," he demanded.

The servant hovered behind Ivan as though he could somehow save Jaya from Ivan's wrath. In a move so swift that the servant didn't see it coming, Ivan picked up a carving knife from the table, grabbed the other man by the jacket, slammed him against the table and sank the blade deep in his neck, slicing right through in one quick motion. He made sure to sever the carotid artery so the man would bleed out quickly and save them unnecessary screaming.

Jaya stared down at the man's face, which was less than two feet away from her dinner plate. Blood poured from his neck and soaked into the white tablecloth while he flailed helplessly against the side of the table. Ivan watched Jaya during the entire episode, judging her capacity to handle this side of him. Her face had drained of colour and she looked as though she was about to either vomit or faint. As the servant ceased struggling, his body growing limp against the side of the table, Ivan tossed him away and dropped the knife back on the table. He stepped toward Jaya.

She stood abruptly and tried to back away from him, stumbling into her chair, terror creasing her features.

"Don't move," he growled.

She froze, her breaths coming out in whimpers. She bowed her head and refused to look at him as he stepped up to her. He tilted her chin and stared down into her face. Even frightened, she was so fucking beautiful it made his black heart ache. This evening might have ended in disaster, but there would be others. He'd ensured it by caging her in an impenetrable fortress.

He leaned down, bending his neck to adjust for his height and pressed his lips against her trembling mouth in a chaste kiss. "Sleep well, my Victory." He turned and strode away leaving her to the care of her bodyguard.

CHAPTER SIX

The bodyguard left Jaya just inside her room, closing the door behind him and locking her inside. Never in her life had she felt so frightened, so lonely. Even after the bombing she'd been surrounded by well-meaning people. Now she was left completely alone, isolated and helpless in the clutches of a remorseless killer.

"Oh god," she moaned and grabbed her head, shaking it as though she could get the horrific image of the dead man out of her head. Besides her grandmother, she'd never seen a dead person up close before, let alone someone killed so horrifically.

She could barely catch her breath, her chest was squeezing itself tighter and tighter. And her limbs were shaking, about to collapse. She rushed to the bed and climbed on top, wrapping herself in the blankets. Once she started to warm up, once her shivering was under control, the crying started. She pulled a fluffy pillow into her cocoon and hugged it against herself while she sobbed out her fear and panic.

As the storm of tears subsided and the hours passed, it became clear that she was going to be left alone in her prison to contemplate what had happened. She pushed the panic away, took a shower in the pristine washroom, in the dark, and changed into a pair of sweatpants and a T-shirt. Then she put her powerful mind to good use. After all, she no longer had access to the things she was used to having around to keep herself occupied.

If Ivan wanted to go to war with XSource, then he would find her a capable opponent, even without her toys. "Time to wake up and fight back," she told herself as an image of the dead man's face flashed through her brain. She didn't want to end up like him when Ivan's use for her ended. Or when she tried his patience one too many times.

The next few days became an exercise in gathering intel. Jaya was used to having technology at her fingertips at all times. She had to practice patience, attempt to control her emotions and reroute her impulses so she could take in more than she was giving away each time she was taken from her cell. Twice more Ivan insisted she dine with him. At first Jaya had sat, stiffly terrified that there would be a repeat of their first evening. However, Ivan had been on his best behaviour, simply sharing a meal with her.

Conversation had been stilted and minimal as though Ivan were distracted. Each time he'd sent another sari to her room with instructions that she prepare to meet him. After their second meal, Jaya found her annoyance rising. She wasn't able to gather much information during her outings. A guard came to pick her up and escort her to Ivan, then curtly turned away to pretend he wasn't there during their meal. Then they'd sit in virtual silence while Ivan studied her across the length of the table as though attempting to decipher a particularly difficult puzzle. Jaya was starting to think of these meetings as some of the weirdest dates she'd ever been on. And she'd been on some pretty bad dates given her tendency towards antisocialism.

This was their third night together, her third summons. She impatiently pulled on the sari, barely glancing at the shimmering green fabric in the mirror before yanking a section strategically across her bared belly. She slid her feet into the matching flats and stomped to the door to wait for her escort.

Jaya strode across the pool deck, the place she was beginning to associate with seeing Ivan. It was where his man brought her whenever she was summoned. She glanced around, annoyed, searching for him. He was usually out here before her, waiting for her arrival. She was about to ask the guard where Ivan was when she spotted his tall, dark-haired form clearing the stone staircase opposite her.

She crossed her arms and glared at him as he approached. His own gaze roamed over her, as though he were starving for the sight of her. She knew he didn't like this growing dependence he seemed to be developing for her, because his frown was almost as fierce as hers by the time he drew close.

"You have something to say to me?" he asked.

"How long are we going to play this game, Ivan?" she demanded, and before he could ask her to explain she continued her tirade. "Where you summon me from my cozy little dungeon with all its wonderful amenities, force me to dress in traditional Hindi clothes and drag me into your exalted company as if I'm here for your amusement, which, based on what I've seen so far, has a fifty percent chance of ending in my death. Because I have to say, this is starting to get old."

The clench of his jaw and flash of his eyes told her she'd angered him. She half expected him to retaliate physically, the way he had with the servant during their first "date." Instead, he did what Ivan did best, he used words like poison darts, each one burying themselves in her skin. "You will watch your words, Jaya, lest you find your dungeon shrinks to the size of a cage and your amenities need be bought with favours rather than simply given by my grace. Your present *coziness* can easily be remedied. Never forget that."

She shuddered and bowed her head, giving him a slight nod. For the most part, she'd lived on her own for many years, free of interference. She used her quick, intelligent mind to absorb and learn everything she could about the world around her to avoid situations like the one she was currently embroiled in. There was a reason she never worked for organizations or governments. Jaya didn't want to have to account for her words or actions; she wanted to live free. She knew what it was like to fall victim to the hatred of men.

Now she was finally caught. Crushed under the heel of a criminal mastermind, a man who was simply curious. A man who would probably forget about her the moment she stopped amusing him. She glanced past him at the table. This time, instead of food, there was a chess board laid out, all the pieces in place.

"Ar-are we playing chess today?" she asked him hesitantly.

He didn't say anything for a moment, simply studied her face as she warred with herself. She really did hate Ivan. He'd stolen her freedom, murdered someone in front of her and bullied her every chance he got. Yet, he was an extremely intelligent man, the head of one of the world's most powerful criminal organizations. The thought of pitting her mind against his was... exhilarating.

He strode to the table and pulled a chair out for her. "Come, sit," he commanded.

Jaya took the chair he offered, shivering slightly when he ran his long fingers through the thick fall of her hair. His people had provided her with a hairbrush but no ponytail holders. She had asked, but her request, like most of them, had fallen on deaf ears. His people looked through her, like robots, only responding with slight nods when she asked for something they could actually provide. After the death of the waiter, she understood why. Interest in her could be fatal.

Ivan took the seat opposite her and sat with a relaxed posture she couldn't hope to emulate around the terrifying man. The table they were sitting at wasn't their usual dining table, but a smaller version. They would be able to reach the chess pieces easily. The white pieces were facing her. Before Ivan could prompt her, Jaya reached for her queenside knight and moved it over the pawns and onto the board.

He arched an eyebrow and for a moment she could swear he fought not to lift the edge of his lip in a smile. "A bold move, Jaya," he said, his voice almost chiding. "I wouldn't have expected it from you."

"And why is that?" she asked coldly.

He moved a pawn, clearing his queenside rook for easy movement. A common first move. "You've spent most of your life moving in the shadows, running and hiding, perfecting the art of protecting yourself at all costs." His grey eyes snapped up, pinning her to her chair. For a moment she feared he saw everything and terror unlike anything she'd felt swamped her. Would he reach for a knife? Gut her like he'd murdered that servant on their first night together? He continued, "You set defenses up all around yourself, hide behind your computers and your programs. At the expense of real life experiences."

Jaya glared at him and moved a pawn away from her castle. "Real life is overrated. It got me kidnapped."

"Perhaps your lack of real world experience is what prompts your bold play," he murmured as he studied the board. "I wonder, Jaya, are you so bold in other forms of play? I admit, I'm intrigued by the thought."

"While nothing about you intrigues me," she snapped in a rush, her face heating as she allowed anger to control her words. She knew better than to provoke him, but she hated how he controlled her every move, how he attempted to learn things about her, to predict her. He was right, she did hide in the shadows, set up defences. And he was also correct, on an ordinary day she wouldn't play a bold game of chess. But Ivan was pissing her off, pushing her, making her unpredictable.

He ignored her outburst, instead he continued to move his pawns, creating a defensive barrier around his king. They maintained silence while Jaya played recklessly and Ivan played cautiously. She was beginning to think Ivan was playing differently than usual as well, luring her in with his cautious textbook moves before he showed his true strengths. The hallmark of a true predator; patience.

"Tell me more about your family," he asked in a musing voice.

Her head snapped up from the chess board and her concentration scattered. She stared at him for a full minute before she could find her voice. "Why?"

He stared back, his expression coolly disinterested. He lifted an eyebrow and glanced at the board. "Your move, Jaya," he said chidingly.

She barely looked at the board as she moved a piece and slammed it down. "I don't like to talk about my family. You know that," she said gritting her teeth and trying to control the tears that rushed forward. They were tears of frustration more than anything because Ivan was using her dead family as a way of getting a reaction from her, of rattling her. He was a formidable enemy and she was weakening under the onslaught of his quick mind. And the sad part was, Ivan didn't need to do much to rattle his victim. A word here or there sufficed, and he was winning the war through a ruthless psychological campaign. Ivan was turning out to be a master manipulator, one that Jaya might admire if she wasn't so wholly under his power.

"Nonetheless, I want to know about them," he said,

taking one of her pawns off the board with his rook. "Or more accurately, I want to know how you look and how you sound when you talk about them."

She clenched her fist in her lap. "That's some Silence of the Lambs creepiness right there, Ivan. Maybe you should work on sounding less psycho when you talk to women. Then you wouldn't have to resort to kidnapping to get a date."

His eyes narrowed. "This isn't a date. If it were, you would finish the evening in my bed."

"You keep threatening me, yet still we continue this sick poolside parade," she snapped, her heart pounding furiously. Though he hadn't moved and everything about him portrayed cool disinterest she could *feel* searing, angry heat pouring across the table and washing over her. He wanted to attack her, tear into her. Perhaps beat her, perhaps fuck her. Or maybe both. The more she was getting to know this man the more she was learning about his contradictory nature. She suspected few got close enough to find this out about him.

"Start talking or we *will* end this date the way I've wanted to for a while," he said, his tone as steely as the grey in his eyes.

Jaya shivered and reached shaking fingers for the board, moving another piece while she thought about what to tell him. Ivan wanted her badly and he wasn't making a secret of his intentions. She knew that he wasn't holding back out of any desire to make her more comfortable with her situation. A man who could ruthlessly kidnap and keep a woman, then subject her to the things Ivan had done and threatened Jaya with wouldn't care about her comfort. No, Ivan didn't like the idea of anyone having any kind of control over him. So he was spending time with her, trying to figure out what it was about Jaya that drew him to her. What scared Jaya was the thought of what Ivan might to do to her if he decided she had too much control over him. Because there was something about her that drew him and she didn't want to be around when he decided what it was and what he wanted to do about it.

She took a deep breath and began speaking while he debated his next move. "My brother was the youngest at nine years old, then I was the next at twelve, my two sisters were fifteen and sixteen. I always wanted to be treated like my sisters but was often too young to go out with them so got left behind with my grandma. My brother was the baby and indulged, which was pretty common. He was a sweetheart though and loved to share. He used to come into my room to play with my toys because he liked mine better. It used to annoy me, but now I wish I could go back and share better with him. My dad was strict, but not authoritarian by any means..."

Ivan snorted, "So he isn't where you got your severe dislike of organizations."

She glared at Ivan and continued speaking. "My mother was awesome. She could yell like nobody's business when she was mad about something; usually one of my sister's coming home late or someone messing up one of her rugs. But mom also cooked better than anyone I knew and loved having people over to eat. She shouldn't have died the way she did. None of them should've. They were just... just applying for passports. We were going to travel..."

She couldn't stop the tears now as they spilled from her eyes. Her hands fell into her lap and she glared at the chess board, no longer interested in playing. She didn't want to jump through Ivan's hoops anymore.

"Your tears only make me hornier, sweetheart," he said, smiling coldly. "Keep crying. In fact, why don't you pull your chair closer." He reached out and slid the chess board closer to his side of the table. "Come here."

She swiped angrily at the tears dripping down her face and

bared her teeth at him. "You're a sick fuck!" she snarled. "You know that, don't you, Ivan?"

The only evidence that her outburst hit the mark was in the slight tightening of his muscles. His smile never slipped though the grey in his eyes became even more glacial if that was possible. "Just for that," he said coolly, "you can get on your hands and knees and crawl to me. Then you can finish this game sitting on my knee. Apparently, you need to learn your place."

"And where is that?" she asked, her ire growing with each exchange they had.

"For now?" he said, eyeing her with little more than casual interest. As though she held his attention for the moment but could be easily discarded once she no longer amused him. "A slave."

Jaya knew she should be outraged, and part of her definitely was. But her opinion of Ivan had sunk so low that she expected little else from him. She stood and stepped away from the table, her fists clenched tightly against the soft folds of her sari. He waved his hand, gesturing for her to move away from the table. As she did he pushed his own chair back a few feet and spread his legs, resting his arms in a relaxed position. She knew better though, Ivan never relaxed.

He lifted one arm and pointed two fingers toward her stomach, "Remove the wrap," he said, waving his hand imperiously.

Breathing heavily through her nose and using jerky motions, Jaya took the wrap section of her sari off. She allowed it to drop to the stone tiles. She lifted her chin and stared at him, trying to convey every ounce of contempt she felt for him in one scorching look. If the heated look he gave her in return was any indication, she both succeeded and failed at getting her message across.

He nodded toward the ground. "Now the shoes."

She kicked the shoes off, knocking them viciously to the side.

"On your knees."

The words were emphasized with pleasure dripping from each one. Reminding herself that this was all a game to him, a power play to get under her skin and rattle her, she lifted her chin and dropped to her knees, wincing a little as she hit the stone. She leaned forward onto her hands and arched her back, her hair falling in a wave on either side of her face.

"Now crawl, Jaya," he said huskily. "Show me what a good little slave you are."

She glanced up at him. His voice sounded different, as though he were struggling to control it, keep it as cool as always. She was affecting him. Gritting her teeth, Jaya started crawling toward him, ignoring the tug of her skirt as it caught against the rough stone with each movement she made. What did she care if the delicate fabric tore? He could just get her a new one from his seemingly endless supply of Indian women's clothing.

He shifted his chair even further from the table, closer to her and patted his knee. Jaya stopped crawling and dug her fingers into the stone tiles. She pulled her lips back in a growl and thought about launching herself at him, maybe punching him where he was vulnerable. She swayed forward, closing the space between them until she was kneeling at his feet, glaring up at him. He leaned over and braced his elbows on his knees until his face hovered over hers. She tried to cringe away from him, crawl backwards but he grabbed the hair at the back of her head, tangling his fingers in the thick mass.

Using her hair to guide her, he forced her up higher and urged her further between his legs until their lips were only inches apart. Her heart nearly jumped out of her chest and her skin crawled as if it was on fire. Though she didn't want to touch any part of him she also really didn't want to get any closer, so she grabbed his thighs and braced her arms. He yanked on her hair until her head twisted. He leaned down, his lips grazing the edge of her jaw. He didn't kiss her exactly, but he ran his mouth over her, touching the skin of her chin, the curve of her cheek and finally the shell of her ear. A tiny sigh slid from her lips before she could stop it. She wanted to hate his touch. But, while his caress invoked terror, the slightly rough rasp of his chin sliding across her also felt good.

"Such a sweet little slave," he murmured in her ear.

Jaya jerked against his hold and then cried out sharply when pain streaked through her scalp. She twisted sideways and swung her fist toward his face. Ivan caught her hand easily, grabbed her around the middle and yanked her into his lap. She had less than a second to struggle when she found herself swung forward. She screamed as the table rushed at her head, the image of the dead servant flashing through her brain, but Ivan swiftly turned her to the side so she was simply restrained with her back to his chest and her arms locked behind her back. Her hair was tangled in his fist so her head was forced back against his chest. She was held completely immobile, but unhurt.

Frightened, breathing heavily, Jaya kept her mouth shut, knowing if she angered him further she could very well be risking her life. Though she was panting, her breaths bursting from her mouth in wild gasps, Ivan wasn't even remotely winded. He simply leaned against her, mastering her until she calmed down, as though he were breaking a wild animal. After a few moments she gradually began to relax in his hold, her breathing evening out. The heat from his chest seeped into her back, warming her... and somehow reassuring her that he wasn't going to brutally murder her. At least not yet.

He shifted her against his chest, his grip on her arms loosening ever so slightly. Then he moved a swath of hair from her face and neck, smoothing it back. She tensed but didn't fight him as he petted her hair. Finally, he leaned down and said in her ear, "Are you ready to finish our game?"

She nodded quickly. "Yes, Ivan."

He ran his thumb behind her ear, pressing it gently into the hollow just underneath. Shivers coursed right down her neck and through her spine. She lifted her shoulder in reflex to shrug him away, but he simply cupped her arm and ran his thumb across the bare skin of her shoulder blade.

"So tempting to make you call me master, to see you force that word past those stubborn lips," he said, his voice back to its cool cadence. "But I do so enjoy hearing my name come from those pretty lips. I wonder what it will sound like when you scream it?"

And Jaya wondered if she would be screaming his name in a bed or a torture chamber, because with Ivan she suspected it could go either way. "Please, Ivan, I'll be good," she begged. "Can you let me up?"

Her shoulders were beginning to cramp and she despised the intimacy he was creating between them. The faster they finished this farce of a chess game the faster she could go back to her dungeon and try to plan an escape.

"You will sit quietly on my lap and play the game?" he asked. "No more outbursts."

"I'll be good," she said, trying to sound as if she meant it.

He eased her off the table, untangling his hand from her hair and gentling his grip. Jaya shook her head a little, amazed that she was unhurt. His hold had been tight, but he hadn't ripped any of her hair or even bruised her arms. In fact, he'd been incredibly careful, skillfully taking her down without so much as disturbing their chess game, despite her struggles. Though the thought had occurred to her before, it became starkly apparent now, that this man could do absolutely anything to her, quickly, ruthlessly and she would be helpless to defend herself.

"Sit, Jaya," he said, resuming his own seat and pulling the chair back to the table.

Gripping the edge of the table she lowered herself gingerly onto his lap. He took her hips in his large hands and moved her until she was settled with her back against his shoulder. Then he pulled the table closer so they could both reach the chess pieces. Jaya expected to feel uncomfortable, and part of her hated the way he held her trapped between him and the table, her legs between his. But she wasn't exactly uncomfortable. His thigh was hard and muscular, but not rigid against her ass.

"Your move," he whispered, his breath touching her shoulder, making her hyper-aware of their proximity.

She glanced at the board, uncaring of the outcome of the game so long as it ended soon. She reached for a pawn, but his voice stopped her. "If you throw the game, then we'll play another and another until I'm satisfied I conquered you in a fair game. I want to see you fight for your life, Jaya."

She gritted her teeth, closed her eyes for a second and moved her hand from the pawn to her queen, changing her original move. Ivan was always several steps ahead of her, picking through her thoughts, blocking her strategies. When she set the queen down, trapping his rook in a corner, he splayed his hand across her belly, running his thumb over the bare skin.

"Good girl," he murmured. "The win will be so much more satisfying for the fight."

Sick fuck, she thought to herself, trying to keep the words from bursting forth. She shifted in his lap, trying to find a better position. His body stiffened for a second, his hand tightening on her stomach. A vibration seemed to go right through him, like a small jolt. The tension released slowly and he reached for the board without studying his move the way he'd done when she was sitting across from him. Her mouth nearly fell open when he moved his rook out of the path of her queen... and into the path of her castle. She raised an eyebrow and held her breath, wondering if he would notice his mistake. He pulled his hand back from the board and settled it on his thigh, right next to her knee.

Keeping her face averted, Jaya smirked. Perhaps she *should* be courting his attentions, apparently the distraction made him careless. She swept his rook aside with a flourish. He said nothing but continued to play as though he hadn't lost an important piece. Jaya continued to shift in his lap, occasionally brushing her arm against his or tossing her hair back against his shoulder. She could tell by the gradual stiffening of his body that she was affecting him.

Within minutes she had the upper hand. Several of his pieces, including both of his castles and a knight were in her possession. In fact, she was a little disappointed. Ivan had shown better strategizing than this in every aspect of his life. How was it possible that she could dominate him on the chess board? Finally, she was setting his queen up for a fall, when he murmured, "Watch your back, sweetheart."

Taking him literally, Jaya looked at him over her shoulder, frowning. He reached over her and took her white queen out with his pawn. Her mouth fell open. She'd been so busy trying to maneuver him into a corner she stopped paying attention to one of his least important pieces. She should've known better. Once her queen was gone, he systematically took out each one of her pieces before she could recover from the loss, then he pushed her king into a corner. It was a hard-fought game, but she suspected the conclusion had always been foregone. Ivan didn't lose and he didn't get distracted, not even by his captive.

"I am not so much of an amateur as to be taken in by a beautiful face and curvy body," Ivan said coldly, taking her king, though the move was unnecessary as the game was already over. He'd done it to prove a point, to show her she was truly beaten. His arm tightened ruthlessly around her stomach and he pulled her back against his chest, speaking rapidly in her ear, his accent more pronounced than ever. "Every move I make is a calculated step to force your hand, to force you to show me what you're made of, Jaya. I'm learning everything I can about you, and you are making it so easy with your childish plays."

"Ivan," she gasped, her voice barely a whisper. "I can't breathe!" She gripped his arm in both hands and pulled, trying to get him to stop squeezing. Despite the cold delivery to his message, he was rattled. Something about her shook him up.

He released her, moving his arms so abruptly that she nearly fell off his lap. She reached for the table, gripping it and sucking in deep breaths of air. She turned her head to look at him, her dark hair spilling across her back and arm, the sun beating down on top of them. Tears of anger sparkled in her eyes. "You may be a manipulative asshole who's learning everything you can about me using disgusting, degrading methods," she snarled. "But I'm learning about you too, Ivan."

"You think so, little girl," he said, his voice cutting like ice. She knew he was close to the edge, knew she shouldn't be pushing him.

"Oh yes," she said, her desire to strike back making her reckless. "Your accent tells me you're probably of Balkan descent, not from Switzerland, where you like people to think you were born." His face grew stony and if she had an ounce of self-preservation she probably should have quit speaking right then. "Given your age and shitty attitude, I would say late 70's, Bosnia. I'm guessing, given the style of the times, you were likely somehow involved in uprisings, rebellions, mass killings, all that good stuff. But what side were you on,

Ivan? Did you fight for independence, for your country's right to be free or did you help hand it over on a platter? Is that what turned you into this cold, unfeeling monster?"

She would have said more, but Ivan exploded out from underneath her, shoving her against the table. She turned and brought her arms up to defend herself, positive he was about to murder her, but Ivan was striding rapidly away, leaving her and the scattered chess pieces for his man to deal with. Staring after his departing back she realized that Ivan just gave away more than he ever had before. Without words, he confirmed her guess.

CHAPTER SEVEN

I t wasn't working.

He was spending time with the woman and he still couldn't figure out what it was about her that he wanted. Couldn't figure out why he cared. She wasn't an enigma, wasn't special. She was easy to read. Like a clock, he knew exactly what made her tick. He could predict down to the last detail what motivated her, what enraged her, what saddened her and what made her happy. She should be boring. Another useless, pointless, slightly skilled sheep.

But she didn't bore him. She fascinated him. And though he could predict her every move ten steps before she made it, he still wanted to watch her take those steps. Because they were the most beautiful, sexy steps he'd ever seen a woman take and he was somehow utterly and completely obsessed. Obsessed with her mind, obsessed with her body. Obsessed with everything about her.

And because Ivan was an arrogant bastard that spent over a week mentally dissecting and tormenting the woman, he'd created an enemy. She feared and despised him, wanted no part of him. Now he needed to figure out how to manipulate her into caring about him. She was vulnerable, should crave companionship and acceptance after all these years of fending for herself. Perhaps the way to her heart was through a softer approach.

Ivan looked toward his security man. "Keane," he barked. The other man looked up from the security report he'd been going over, outlining ways to strengthen the island's defenses without drawing attention to their hardware. "You know much about women?"

Keane's expression went quickly from bland to alarmed. Clearly the last thing he wanted was to give his notoriously ruthless boss woman advice. He cleared his throat and leaned back in his seat. "Uh, not really," he said hesitantly.

"Well learn fast," Ivan said coldly. "Because I want Jaya to warm up to me and I don't think, given the way things have been going, that her emotions are leaning that way."

Keane snickered. "You ain't kiddin' about that."

Ivan shot him a look that wiped the laughter from his face and told him he'd better get working on the immediate problem of making Jaya soften up. Keane slumped in his seat and looked completely stumped. He was definitely a fuck em' and leave em' kind of guy. Ivan was partially responsible for that. Under his employment, women weren't allowed on the island unless they were there to cook or clean and the men were under strict no fraternizing or die instructions.

"Ah, fuck me, boss," he growled, his Irish accent even more pronounced than usual. "Don't women like pretty, glittery things, like clothes and jewels and shit?"

"I've given her all that," Ivan said dismissively. "She doesn't care. She could afford clothes and jewels well before we picked her up. She chose not to spend her money on frivolous things. What else do women like?"

Keane looked as though he'd rather be eating a bowl of

live grenades than having this conversation. "Cats!" he burst out, relief lighting up his bearded face.

"What?" Ivan asked, his lip curling derisively.

"I once dated this looney little bitch that had five freakin' cats. Nearly killed one when I got up in the middle of the night to take a piss and stepped on it. She shot me in the arm with my own damn gun before shovin' my naked ass out her back door and then throwin' all my fucking clothes out the window. Bitch cared more about her cats than anything else," Keane grumbled and rubbed his arm. "Women like cats."

Ivan was pretty sure not all women liked cats based on Keane's single experience, but he gave the idea some merit. Jaya had spent the majority of her life alone, running for her freedom. As far as he knew she'd never stopped long enough to form any solid attachments. Perhaps she would enjoy the company of something small and helpless, something dependant. Something that might bond with her and banish some of her loneliness.

The sneer playing around his mouth slowly softened. Yes, he would get Jaya a kitten. Give her the gift of a bond. And perhaps she would appreciate his present so much she might soften her attitude toward him. He thought about tasking the job to someone else, but the idea was distasteful. No, he would find the beast himself. He would have it flown in that very evening and give it to her with his own two hands. He wanted to see her face when she opened his gift and realized that he was capable of more than bloody vengeance.

Without looking up, he said, "Dismissed." He was no longer interested in the security reports; he had a cat to find.

Jaya didn't bother turning around when the door to her dungeon opened. It would be her evening meal delivery. She continued doing what she'd been doing for the past several hours, tearing pages out of Walter Scott's Ivanhoe in an attempt to teach herself the art of origami. She'd deemed the book unreadable with a stupid title and thus the best choice for paper cranes, butterflies and whatever else she might be capable of. At the moment her bed was littered in failed attempts. Maybe she should request a book on how origami worked. Apparently it was a lot harder than she thought.

"You've ruined my book," Ivan's voice drawled from behind her.

Jaya twisted around so suddenly her finger slid along the page she was tearing, cutting painfully into her skin. "Ouch!" she yelped and automatically stuck her finger in her mouth. She narrowed her eyes at Ivan as he approached her. She scrambled off the bed, not wanting to be at a disadvantage around him.

The book fell to the floor, landing on her foot. She pursed her lips in annoyance as pain shot through her. She was beginning to hate Ivanhoe almost as much as she hated the real Ivan.

He frowned, his icy façade cracking. "Are you hurt?"

She ignored his apparent concern and, taking her finger out of her mouth, pointed at the box under his arm. "What's that? Finally giving me a laptop? I've only asked about sixty times, but no big deal. I know these things take time, especially when they have to ship it UPS to an evil crimelord's secret lair. I promise not to use it to escape," she said sarcastically.

The man hadn't given her so much as an electric toothbrush or a flashlight. There was no way he was giving her a laptop. Besides the box under his arm was the wrong shape and size. It was perfectly square, about a half a foot wide and high. It was white with a red ribbon and a bow on top, like something you might see in a movie. It was probably another ridiculous sari he wanted her to wear for yet another episode of the bachelor billionaire's kidnapped date.

Instead of answering, he dropped the box on the bed and reached for her hand. His fingers felt rough against her skin. She was surprised. She assumed he ran his evil empire from an office and let his minions do all the heavy lifting. She studied him while he examined her ridiculously small cut. He had shown amazingly fast reflexes on several occasions and she really didn't think the appallingly easy way he'd dispatched the poor serving man had been a fluke. So Ivan was incredibly skilled at hand-to-hand combat, which meant he trained to become that way. And he probably trained often. The promise of hard muscles beneath his well-cut, expensive clothing weren't fake either, she'd felt against her body during their chess match and that time he'd held her down on the bed.

She sighed and rolled her eyes, tugging uselessly at her hand. "Really, Ivan? After everything you've done to me, you're this concerned over a little paper cut?"

He dropped her hand, the frown that had been furrowing his eyebrows smoothing into his usual sculpted expression. "There's the Ivan I know and hate," she murmured, stepping back until her thighs met the edge of the bed. "I was worried you might be growing a conscience."

He reached for the box, scooped it up in a large hand and thrust it at her. "Take it," he snapped.

"And if I don't accept your generosity you'll put me in a cage, blah, blah, blah." She accepted the box, curious despite herself. She nearly dropped the damn thing when it made a horrific yowling, pleading sound. "What the fuck, Ivan, it's alive!"

"Yes, and I'm not entirely certain how long it's been in there, so you may want to unwrap it," he said coolly.

"What the fuck!" she screeched again, wrenching the bow

off the box and tearing the top off. Inside was a tiny, shivering ball of striped grey and white fur with wide, terrified eyes. She carefully reached into the box and pulled the kitten out, cuddling it against her chest, then lifted accusing eyes to Ivan. "You monster!"

He lifted his hands as if to say, 'what did I do?' but before he could say a word, Jaya stepped into his space and started yelling, "How could you possibly think it was a good idea to stuff this poor, tiny little creature in a box for god knows how long? What kind of cruel monster are you, anyway? You thought it was a good idea to give me something that was living? Is this your idea of a new torture technique? You're just going to take it to the next level, are you? Get me attached to this poor helpless little cutie and then tear it away. Well... well, it's not going to work!"

"It's not?" he asked, looking genuinely baffled for the first time since she met him.

"No!" she shouted, clutching the kitten under her neck.

"And why is that?" he asked, beginning to look a little more cautiously optimistic. Especially now that she'd opened the box and wasn't outright rejecting his gift.

"Because I refuse to fall for your sadistic tricks," she snapped. "You can just... just go away. We don't want you in our dungeon right now."

His lip twitched and he gave her a brief nod. "I will leave for now, Jaya. But I am coming back and I expect a friendlier reception."

He turned and walked away, leaving her alone with her small shivering bundle. Before he reached the door, she called out to him. "Ivan."

He half turned to her and raised an eyebrow. "Yes, Jaya?"

"We will require a litter box, a supply of fresh litter and kitten food," she said in a voice that made it clear her terms were non-negotiable.

He nodded. "They'll be sent down with your supper."

She turned her back on him, focusing entirely on her new companion. She barely heard the door bang shut and for once the sound of the lock engaging didn't send a shaft of near-panic straight through her. Jaya set the kitten gently down on the bed and climbed in after it. They studied each other for a moment and when it became clear that she would have to make the first move, Jaya reached out and picked the creature back up, cuddling it against her chest.

She had no idea how old it was, having no experience with animals, but given its size she thought it must be very young. "Did that evil, horrible, villainous human take you away from your home too?" she asked. When the kitten didn't respond, she kissed it and said. "Because he really is the worst, so I believe he's capable of tearing kittens away from their mommies." She glanced down at its wide, frightened eyes and murmured, "I'll be your new mom. At least until we find a way to escape and we can find your real cat mom."

The kitten made a sound. Jaya pulled it away from her neck and held it out so she could examine it. "What was that?" she asked, cocking her head to the side. "You think we should find a way to kill Ivan on our way out of this place? Wow, you are a bloodthirsty little thing."

Its eyes started to close and within seconds it fell asleep in her hands. And just like that, she knew she'd fallen for Ivan's devilishly manipulative plan, whatever it might be; she was in love with his beastly gift. She sighed and tucked it into her lap, running her finger soothingly over the top of its head.

"Alright fine, if you insist, we'll murder him," she murmured with a grin. "But I'm calling you Hatyaara, or Haty for short. If you're going to act like a killer, then we'll give you a killer name."

CHAPTER EIGHT

Haty changed everything for Jaya. For the first time since childhood, she had a companion that belonged solely to her. The possibilities in her new buddy were both inherently wonderful and terrifying. In the days that followed, she bonded with her new furry friend, carrying her around everywhere, talking to her, planning with and feeding her; cleaning up after and scolding her. Haty quickly became attached to Jaya as well, hopping along after her, dogging her every footstep and using her tiny claws to climb her new mama when she wasn't paying enough attention. But Jaya was also terrified for her new friend. Ivan could too easily use the kitten against her. Threaten Haty's life or hurt her in retaliation, maybe use her as a way of getting Jaya to submit. Or what if Haty just got sick and died? Jaya didn't think she'd survive that scenario either.

She contemplated the fluffy critter as it batted around a ball of string that she'd unravelled from her pillowcase. "What am I going to do with you?" she asked. The kitten did what she usually did, ignored Jaya in favour of her current activity.

Jaya studied the tiny creature, which was thriving under her constant attention. Her little belly was rounding from a nonstop supply of high-fat kitten food and her paws were growing bigger by the day. After Jaya showed Haty to the litterbox once, she took to the sand like a duck to water, kicking it everywhere. Her request for a broom and dustpan had been granted, along with some newspaper to help keep the spread of litter to a minimum.

"One day we're going to have to have the grown-up girl talk, Haty," Jaya said, lolling idly against the edge of her bed and gazing at the kitten. "I'll leave the choice up to you, but I've heard the responsible thing to do these days is spay and neuter. I think since you're a girl, you'll get spayed, but I'm not sure. Although, if this is what you look like as a baby, can you imagine what your baby kittens would look like! Damn, girl! Anyway, we have a few more months before we need to have that talk," she said in her best parenting voice. "But I would like to talk about the amount of treats you've been begging for. And you really need to stop making eyes at the guards. They are *not* our friends."

Jaya jumped when the door to her dungeon slammed open, hitting the wall. It wasn't her supper time and the servants were usually a little more respectful of her space. She scrambled off the bed as Keane stalked in. It was a damn good thing she'd decided to start changing in the washroom in case of moments like these. She frowned at him.

"Boss wants to see you," he grunted.

She so badly wanted to say, 'your boss can go fuck himself,' but Keane was twice the size of anyone else and had an aura of psychotic bloodthirstiness that made her keep her nastier comments to herself. Given Ivan's evil tendencies, she wasn't at all surprised that this guy seemed to enjoy a level of prestige in the arms dealer's organization. She nodded and silently followed him out the door. She was confused. She wasn't given a sari to wear and she wasn't being shown to the pool area. Instead she was led through a series of wide stone hallways. She stared around her, trying to stamp every twist and turn on her mind while she hurried to keep up with Keane's long strides. They climbed a set of stairs and followed another long hall. This one had open stone archways that showed a gorgeous view of the ocean. Jaya gaped at its raw beauty as they passed, nearly slamming into Keane's back as he stopped moving. Looking up, she realized they'd stopped in front of another door, this one was wooden, weathered, like an antique. She was beginning to suspect she was actually inside of a castle.

Keane used his bulk to open the heavy door and waved her through. "He's expecting you."

Jaya stepped into what could only be Ivan's personal office. It was big, lovely and sparse. Like the man himself, until a person got a glimpse inside his twisted head. Ivan stood next to one of the open windows with his back to her. When she entered he turned, his face smooth and cool. For just a moment though, the mask slipped, and she saw a flash of longing mixed with fury. Then he shuttered the expression and stepped toward her.

He didn't bother with his games this time, no preliminaries. He got directly to the root of her summons. "How do you know the things you know about me?"

"What?" she asked, confused.

"Don't play innocent," he said sharply, stepping toward her. "You will weigh your words carefully when you are in here, Jaya. When we are outside, by the pool, we play the game, but in here you give me the answers I want or you will suffer the consequences. Now tell me what I want to know."

"I don't know what you're talking about, Ivan!" she said backing away from him.

"You know exactly what I'm talking about. You know

things about me that no one else knows. Things that have been buried so deep, you leave me no choice but to either bury you or keep you."

Jaya gasped, her hand flying up to cover her lips. She should never have let her temper get the better of her, never have let Ivan know that she knew about him. Now he might guess her secret. And the moment he did, she was a dead woman. He stalked toward her.

"Tell me!" he snarled.

"It was a lucky guess!" she cried.

"No!" he shouted, his voice booming unexpectedly in the airy room. She flinched. "You couldn't have guessed all that based on a perceived accent. Impossible. I've collected all your stuff from Portugal, had my people pick it apart with a fine-tooth comb and they've found nothing. All your stuff is encrypted to hell and back. Now you'll give me access and you'll tell me what I want to know."

She could feel the blood draining from her face. Really, she should be surprised Ivan hadn't demanded this of her sooner. But she absolutely couldn't allow him access to her data. He'd tear it apart, not only discover her secret, but gain access to all of her former clients. He could use that information against everyone she'd ever worked with. Some of them probably deserved to be stripped down and torn apart, but the majority most certainly didn't deserve to have a man like Ivan come after them.

Despite her terror of the towering, enraged man, Jaya lifted her chin, crossed her arms and said, "Absolutely not, my database holds confidential information. Neither you, nor anyone else, will ever be allowed access."

He laughed coolly, cruelly. "You think not?"

She shook her head and stuck to her guns. "I'm the best, Ivan. There isn't a person on this planet that can hack my encryption codes."

He nodded his head thoughtfully and then stepped up to her. "Yes, it would seem that my people agree. You are the best." He ran a finger down her cheek and then circled her throat. He didn't squeeze, but he held her pinned, trapped like a butterfly, awaiting his torment. "Even the best can be cracked."

Her eyes widened. She knew he didn't mean the encryption, he meant her personally.

His eyes lingered on her face and lips. "How to do that without destroying all this perfection?" he said, almost to himself. "There are so many techniques that would give me what I want quickly but would mar all this beauty." He ran his fingers down her hair and arm. She shuddered, her stomach rolling at the implication of torture. He cupped the back of her head. "But do I want to crack this incredible mind wide open and look inside?"

Jaya licked her lips and then stopped when his eyes followed the movement. "I don't know, do you?" she whispered.

He didn't say anything for a moment and then a flash of disappointment crossed his face. That one look sent a shaft of terror through her heart. Somehow, she knew she wasn't going to be sent back to her cozy little dungeon to carry on with her kidnapping undisturbed.

"Last chance, Jaya. Tell me what I want to know."

She stared up at him, struck once more by how handsome he was. She could feel herself beginning to weaken. Not because of his sheer male beauty. No, simply because Ivan had been taking care of her. In his own twisted way, Ivan had been providing for her needs, basic and otherwise. For once in her life, Jaya hadn't been forced to fend for herself and, as insane as it was, a part of her liked it. Sort of like being on vacation, with the downside being she was under the care of a psychotic evil crime lord.

She shook her head and said, "No."

"Very well," he said coldly. "Your cage has just shrunk."

CHAPTER NINE

"Pssst, Haty," Jaya whispered.

The kitten scampered to her, fitting easily through the bars. She scooped the small bundle up and held the purring creature against her chest, settling back against the pillows of her makeshift bed. Her prison had indeed shrunk... to the size of a cage. It was just high enough for her to stand up and long enough for her to lay down. She was only allowed a thick cushion and some blankets to lay on, along with a few of Ivan's books. She wasn't sure why he kept giving them to her. She certainly didn't read them.

She was let out of her cage a few times a day to attend to her basic needs, to shower and to change. Otherwise, she was left alone to contemplate her new reality. Her cellmate didn't seem to care about their predicament. Mostly because Haty was still small enough to fit through the metal bars.

"I don't know why you like his bed better," Jaya sighed, rubbing the kitten under her chin. "He's an asshole and he snores."

"I don't snore."

Jaya sat up so fast she startled Haty, who yowled in protest and ran straight through the bars to Ivan. Without slowing his long strides, he scooped the animal up in one hand and tossed her up on his shoulder. Haty dug in and clung to him as Ivan made his way to Jaya's cage. She glared at him, making sure he knew via the fire in her eyes that she was not impressed with her new bedroom inside his bedroom.

"You know," she said heatedly. "It takes a sick man to keep a woman in a cage in his bedroom."

He shrugged carelessly and crossed his arms over his broad chest. She tried not to gaze at his bulging biceps. It didn't help when Haty slid from his shoulder, down his arm to settle in the crook of his elbow for a snooze. Jaya really didn't think Haty understood the concept of supreme evil yet. From the moment they were moved to Ivan's living quarters yesterday, Haty took to Ivan as though determined to make him her new daddy. The big man didn't exactly return the cat's affection, but he didn't reject it either, just accepted it as his due.

"I don't play by any standard rules, sweetheart," Ivan said, his tone bored. "You need to stop forgetting this or you'll end up hurt. For now, my fascination is all that's keeping you alive. Stop testing my patience and you may continue to breathe a little longer."

Her mouth fell open and for a moment she was speechless. She knew he was an evil bastard, knew he played horrific games, but he'd never threatened her life so blatantly. Either this was a new game or he was tiring of her constant resistance. She curled against herself, bringing her knees up to her chest and hugging them. His sharp eyes caught the movement. He dropped Haty on his giant bed, with its fluffy white duvet, and crouched next to Jaya's cage, only a few feet from the bed.

They stared at each other. Oddly, some of the antagonism, the power struggle that always waged between them, seemed to drain away. She saw a flash of something like regret in his face. He leaned against the bars and watched her intently. "You are the most alluring, most unique woman I've ever met," he said, his voice a little rough. "And I don't understand why."

Jaya tried hard to keep her feelings close, to not give him anything, but when he looked at her that way, spoke to her that way, stripped bare, it was like he wanted... no needed something from her. It was too hard not to give him something in return. Perhaps if she gave him a crumb of the honesty he was looking for, he might relent and let her out of the cage. She loosened her arms, climbed to her knees and crawled toward him.

She stopped about a foot away and watched him, her eyes searching his features while she spoke. "You scare me, Ivan."

He dipped his head in a nod, his grey gaze devouring her as though she were his next meal. "I know. It's better this way, better you fear me."

Tears filled her eyes and she blinked, not wanting to cry in front of him. She didn't want to show weakness, because she hoped, no, she needed to use this moment to negotiate with her captor. She sensed that, for once, his agile brain wasn't on the hunt, that he was willing to give her some leeway, some insight into his complicated mind.

"I'm terrified that you'll decide I'm not worth it, that you'll have me killed at any moment," she whispered, searching his face for a hint of compassion. When she saw nothing but cold, bottomless grey, she slumped back on her heels, her shoulders bowing. There was no getting through to him. Not a remorseless killer like Ivan Vogel.

After what felt like endless minutes he finally spoke. He didn't give her what she'd been hoping for, didn't promise not to kill her, but he gave her something he probably never gave anyone else. An admission. "I wanted you here in my space," he said gruffly. "I wanted you where I could see you, smell you, breathe you in all the time. Not just the brief moments you were paraded out on the pool deck. But I had no reason, no excuse. So I made one up and here you are."

Jaya's mouth fell open again. She needed to process this information, figure out how she felt. At the moment, she was feeling only confusion. "B-but why didn't you just take me? You own everything around you? You can do anything you want. I don't understand."

Fire seemed to leap into his eyes creating a storm of emotion unlike anything she'd seen on his face before. She tried to back up, but he was too fast. He reached between the bars and grabbed her arm, yanking her against the solid metal. She yelped and reached out to grip the bars, stopping herself from being painfully jarred.

Though his face was still several inches from hers, she could feel the intensity, see the vein in his forehead stand out and the pulse in his neck jump in agitation. His carefully tended mask was slipping. It was falling away, showing her the monster and the man that lay beneath, and he hated it. Her heart picked up speed until it was thundering, and he nodded as if reading her thoughts.

"I should have had my men kill you," he said, his voice rough with all the emotions he'd been hiding from her. "Then we wouldn't be here. You may prefer death over what I'll do to you by the time I'm finished, Jaya. Because this is uncharted territory and the only thing left inside me is blacker than pitch."

"Please, Ivan," she begged him. "You're scaring me."

He ignored her. "You want to know why I haven't touched you yet? Why I haven't taken you and fucked you?" She shook her head, her whole body quaking now. "Because I don't know what will happen once I've had you, Jaya. Maybe this obsession will break. Maybe I'll have you killed after all. Or maybe this feeling will only grow stronger. And then what? I chain you to my side for the rest of your life and you belong to one of the worst, most hunted sons-of-bitches on the planet."

Tears dripped down her cheeks now. She was powerless to stop them, frozen in his hands, terrified of his next move. "D-don't, Ivan. Please just let me out, let me go. I'll d-disappear. Like you never met me."

His lips curved up in a terrible smile and she knew what his next words were going to be before he even spoke. "It's far too late for that, my lovely captive."

He yanked her hard, up against the bars. She cried out as her cheek hit the metal, but he swallowed the sound in a kiss. His tongue invaded her mouth, capturing, conquering her as though she were virgin territory he was intent on discovering. When she didn't open wide enough for him, he gripped her face in both hands and dug his thumbs into her cheeks, forcing her mouth wider. He plundered the tender recesses, taking everything she refused to give.

Jaya gripped the bars as though her life depended on it. She couldn't move away from his assault, though she tried. She began to weaken under the onslaught until she was sliding down the metal, away from his brutal kiss. Ivan growled against the loss. He reached as far as he could between the bars, took her by the waist and yanked her back up, smashing her against the unyielding metal.

"Ivan, please don't," she whimpered and tried to turn her face away from him. He ignored her plea and kissed her stinging, swollen lips. This time he tempered the brutality, licking and nibbling, attempting to coax a response from her. Jaya moaned and turned her face to the side, laying weakly against his arm. She hoped that he would stop soon and leave her, prayed that he wouldn't open the door to her cage and finish what they'd been dancing around for weeks.

He cupped her face and tilted it against the bars, more gently this time, so he could kiss her wherever he could reach.

He pressed his lips against her cheek, her chin and her forehead. He twisted her head to the side and explored her ear, then groaned against her when it became clear he wanted to continue a path down her neck but was prevented.

"Want you so fucking bad, Jaya," he mumbled against her. "I should just end this for both of us and take you now."

Jaya shivered at his words and the rush of heat that shot through her. Though she despised him, his kisses enflamed parts of her that usually lay dormant. She flexed her fingers against the muscles of his side and suddenly realized that she had reached through the bars and was clutching him, holding herself up using his rock-solid body. She snatched her hands back with a gasp and Ivan released her. She rocked back so hard that she fell on her butt, hitting the edge of her cushion and scattering the books that were on her blanket.

Ivan sat back on his heels for a moment, watching her intently, his eyes going from dark and stormy to ice grey. His breathing evened out before hers did. His gaze flickered to the books scattered across the bottom of her cage and landed on the one closest to her.

"Wuthering Heights," he said coolly. "I thought you might enjoy that one, its dark and romantic, like you."

She glared at him and made a production of using her sleeve to wipe her mouth. "I don't know what you're talking about, I'm no romantic." Her gaze flitted down to the book. The copy looked old and well used, as though it had been read several times. "And I don't like reading."

He stood and looked down at her, his own gaze dispassionate. "I don't care how you pass your time, but you may want to consider cracking that one. Find out what happens to Cathy when she crosses the man obsessed with her."

"Fuck you, Ivan." Jaya snatched the book up and threw it at the bars. It hit one and rebounded, falling harmlessly to the floor.

"You'd better hope not, sweetheart. I don't think either of us wants to find out what happens after I've fucked you." He strode from the room, slamming and locking the door behind him.

Jaya slumped against her bed and turned her glare on the tiny bundle of sleeping kitten laying in the centre of Ivan's giant bed, completely oblivious to the fireworks that just went off all around her.

"You could at least scratch his eyes out for me!" She scowled and reached for Wuthering Heights.

CHAPTER TEN

"Shut the light off, I want to go to sleep," Jaya demanded, doing her best to be as annoying as possible.

New strategy.

Annoy Ivan until he sends her back to the dungeon. At least she had more space down there, she got to go out to the pool patio once in awhile and she didn't have to suffer through Ivan's presence during the night. So far her strategy wasn't working even a little. Ivan seemed incapable of being annoyed. He was like a robot, turning his emotions on and off, ignoring her most of the time and then deciding when to pay attention to her.

Jaya lay on her back counting the bars of her cage. Twenty-five across the top, thirty-three along each side. She'd abandoned Wuthering Heights almost as soon as Ivan entered the room, not wanting him to catch her reading the book he recommended. He was right though, the dark gothic romance did appeal to her. The vivid scenery and character drama helped her mentally escape from her own predicament. And she so badly wanted to see if Cathy ended up with Heathcliff. She doubted it, given Ivan's earlier comment. But for some reason Jaya found herself as helplessly attracted to the dark, villainous character as Cathy was.

Rolling onto her side, Jaya thrust an arm under her head and stared absently out the open balcony doors leading outside of Ivan's bedroom. She could smell fresh sea air, like her home in Portugal only it was a slightly different scent, more humid. And she seriously doubted she was anywhere near Portugal. In her time with Ivan she'd seen very little of his home, or wherever he was keeping her, beyond the dungeon room, the pool patio and her current cage. When she'd arrived there was a bag over her head.

"Ivan?" she asked softly. "Where are we? Like where on a map are we located."

Her tone of voice must have captured his attention because he looked up from the book he was reading and, for the first time since entering his room that evening, gave her his attention. She glanced out the window into the dark night, a question clear on her face. He seemed to understand. He sat up, swinging his long legs over the edge of his bed and leaning his arms across his knees.

He studied her for a moment before answering. "We're on my private island, a few hundred kilometres northeast of Jakarta, Indonesia."

Her jaw dropped in surprise. She'd known they must be on some kind of coastline, had even batted around the idea of an island, but had not in a million years considered that she'd been brought this far from her home. She thought back to the terrifying ordeal of her kidnapping and frowned. It couldn't have been more than a few hours. She'd been moved from a van to a helicopter and then the helicopter to an aircraft of some sort. Her head had been covered through most of the trip so she hadn't known where she was going, not that she could have oriented herself had she been able to see, everything had happened in such a dramatic rush.

Ivan must've caught the drift of her thoughts because he interjected. "You were brought here on my Citation X, one of the fastest light aircraft available. It took eight hours. You were given a sedative; you probably don't remember much of the flight."

"I was not!" she protested, frowning. "I would remember being sedated."

He studied her dispassionately. "It was done under my orders."

Jaya squeezed her eyes shut and thought back to that horrific day. She'd been shoved around and grabbed so many times, it was actually quite likely someone had managed to drug her without her knowledge; poked her in the arm with a needle while hustling her from vehicle to vehicle. And that would explain how she'd managed to lose several hours of flying time. But the thought of being alone and incapacitated in the company of so many immoral, rough men was utterly horrifying. She simply couldn't go there. Instead she opened her eyes again, took several deep, calming breaths and concentrated on the sea air.

There was a reason she'd chosen Portugal for her home, beyond her need for privacy. She usually chose small out of the way places in seaside towns to settle for a few months to a few years at a time before moving on. She was trapped by her own insecurities and thus used the ocean for escape. It always felt so wild and free to her. When her small home and internet community became stifling she would wander down to the beach and breathe the air into her lungs, feel the sand between her toes and think about how small she really was in comparison to mother nature.

"Can I please go outside, Ivan?" she asked tentatively, hopefully. "Just for a few minutes."

He watched her intently, devouring the hope on her face and sucking the need for freedom from her. Gradually she watched the cold calculating Ivan that she'd spent weeks battling with take hold. She knew what his answer would be.

Still, she had to try. "Please, Ivan," she begged, curling her legs underneath her so she would look as defenceless as possible. "I'll be good, I just want to smell and feel the fresh air on my skin."

His lip curled up in a cruel semi-smile and he stared coldly down at her for a moment then shook his head. "A slave doesn't need fresh air."

She clenched her fists in the bedding and glared at him thrusting her chin out. "The moment my cage door is open, I'm out of here." They both knew she meant figuratively, as in, as soon as the opportunity arose she would attempt escape, since she was let out of her cage a few times per day. Her guards were always present though, never allowing her the opportunity to escape.

He nodded, his eyes flicking back to his book. He reached for it and settled back on the bed. "I've no doubt you will try."

Jaya lay back on her bed and fumed until he finished reading and begin his bedtime ritual. She tried really hard not to peek when he rolled off the bed and strode toward a walk-in closet. She sighed in defeat and allowed herself to linger on the deeply tanned skin of his back, stretched taut over sculpted muscles and moving in beautiful concert as he yanked his T-shirt over his head. She bit her lip as he hooked his thumbs into the waistband of his sweatpants and started sliding them down just before disappearing into the other room. She got to see a tiny bit of ass and then he was gone.

Jaya realized that she'd pushed herself up on an elbow to get a better look. She fell back with a groan and covered her face. "Pull yourself together. Don't drool over the criminal warlord."

"You need something?"

Jaya pulled her hand away and looked guiltily up at Ivan who was standing right next to her bed on the outside of her cage. Her eyes widened when she realized he was wearing nothing more than a pair of tight men's boxer briefs. And they left *nothing* to the imagination.

Without thinking she blurted out, "Why on earth do you need to resort to kidnapping women? Look at you! Holy hell, Ivan, you are built! You should be dating Scarlett Johansen or some other super hottie, not locking someone like me up in a cage." Then her brain caught up with her mouth and she felt her face begin to flame. She was thankful then for her darker skin tone.

Ivan merely raised an eyebrow, looked down at her for a moment and then turned away giving her a stunning view of his backside. He turned the light off, saving her further embarrassment at her inability to tear her eyes from all that spectacular male flesh. She'd been in the same room with him the evening before but had been so freaked out and upset by her new prison that she'd buried herself under the blanket and ignored him.

Now it felt like every move he made, every breath he took was a shock right through her system. Like she was somehow attached to him. To her captor. How had this happened? Was it Stockholm? Because she was dependent on him for her survival? She thought about it and then decided there was no way she had that particular syndrome because she still intended to leave first chance she got, and she was going to knife the asshole too if she got a chance.

Feeling better, Jaya yanked her blanket up and made herself comfortable by tucking it between her legs and under her chin. She was about to drift off to sleep, Haty snuggled warmly against her stomach when Ivan's deep voice reached out to her through the darkness of their shared bedroom.

"I think you're very beautiful, Jaya," he said, his voice

sounding oddly husky. "I've wanted you from the moment I saw you in Athens and the feeling has only grown stronger. I've fought it and I've failed."

She held her breath, squeezing the blanket hard against herself and staring into the night. She sensed he had more to say, but he hesitated. It was so unlike Ivan. He always seemed to know what he wanted and where he was going. Ivan was ruthless and deliberate. But navigating his actions seemed to be a slippery slope into the unknown.

"I don't know what to say to you, Ivan," she whispered honestly.

"Don't bother," he said gruffly.

Because anything she said wouldn't change the outcome. Wouldn't change his mind. He was still going to keep her locked up in a cage, possibly forever. The unspoken words hung heavy in the room, separating them with more than metal bars. She clung to the blanket as though it were a lifeline, feeling the weight of Haty against her. She forced her mind away from the bleakness of her imprisonment toward thoughts of freedom. She knew her world was narrowing around her, mentally and physically. Ivan's patience was running out and she had nowhere to run. The only thing keeping her going, keeping her from giving in to compete despair was the knowledge that she could and would escape the moment fate gifted her the opportunity.

"Go to sleep, Jaya, there's nothing you can do," Ivan's deep voice touched her through the blackness, sending a chill through her despite the warmth of the evening.

CHAPTER ELEVEN

"Ivan, wake up!" Jaya shouted, her voice breaking.

It didn't matter. She'd called to him at least a dozen times, he didn't acknowledge her. At first, when she realized he was deep in the grips of a terrible nightmare she'd said his name softly, thinking to jar him out of it without fully waking him. But as the dream progressed and she'd been forced to watch him thrash and twist on his bed in the clutches of one of the most frightening night terrors she could imagine, she began pacing her cage and calling to him with increasing volume.

Jaya gripped the bars of her cage and stared around trying to figure out what to do. She could barely make him out in the shadowy room, his tall form lit by only the dim moonlight filtering through the curtained windows. She squinted at the corner she'd seen Haty run toward. The kitten had slipped through the bars and gone for cover when Ivan's nightmare began.

Jaya's gaze snapped back to the bed when Ivan shouted something in a language foreign to her and then thrashed so hard she thought he was having a seizure. A pillow hit the floor between the bed and her cage. His arms came down viciously on the bed, bouncing the whole frame against the floor. His voice was urgent as he shouted what sounded like a name and then he seemed to become desperate, almost screaming at the phantom person. It was clear he was fighting some invisible enemy and was losing the battle. She couldn't watch anymore. She'd never seen anyone self-destruct like this while they were asleep, it was heartbreaking.

"Please, Ivan!" she yelled.

Still he continued to groan and hit the bed as though trying to murder it. Finally, Jaya bent down and picked up Wuthering Heights. Reaching through the bars she hurled it as hard as she could. She was surprised when she actually hit him, the book smacking his shoulder and sliding onto the mattress next to him. He woke with a start, reaching underneath him and pointing a gun at the empty room. Jaya shrieked and hit the floor of her cage, thinking she was about to get shot for her good deed. When no bullets broke through the heavy silence, Jaya peeked up through the fall of her hair and the arms she'd wrapped around her head for protection. Ivan was standing over her, his gun at his side. Somehow he'd slipped silently from the bed and crossed the space between them. She couldn't see his face properly, but she could feel the intense storm of emotion still surrounding him.

"Jaya." His voice was rough when he said her name.

"Are you okay?" she whispered.

He didn't reply. Instead he walked to the door of her cage and punched in the code. He jerked the door open and stepped inside. It was the first time he'd entered her tiny space. She could see his eyes now, they were intense and focused completely on her as though she were a target that he'd set his sights on. Shocked, Jaya scuttled backwards as he took the three steps that closed the distance between them, his gun held tense at his side.

"Ivan!" she cried out when he reached for her, his hand gripping around her arm and pulling her upright.

He yanked her against his bare chest, his arms wrapping tight around her. She gasped and froze when she felt the gun touch the side of her head. But she quickly realized he wasn't threatening her, he was seeking comfort. He was so used to handling weapons that he probably didn't even realize how uncomfortable she was with the touch of his gun against her face. She shivered and closed her eyes tight so she wouldn't have to look at the cold, terrifying metal that could easily end her life in a split second.

"Relax, Jaya," he said quietly. "I won't hurt you."

For some reason his words helped. She knew he didn't mean them long term. Ivan was an evil bastard, he wouldn't make a promise he couldn't keep. He wasn't going to hurt her in the next few hours. Or at least that was how she was taking his statement. She nodded slightly and allowed her body to melt against his. There was no point in fighting him. He was much bigger, stronger and faster. He was also giving her a temporary reprieve from fear. Something she desperately needed. So they stood there in her cage and held each other, offering comfort.

"Come to bed with me." His breath touched her hair and his deep voice caressed her in a way that felt better than it should have. She stiffened in his arms and tried to back up. He tightened his hold, not allowing her to leave his embrace. She froze when the gun clipped the edge of her ear and pressed hard against her temple.

"P-please take the gun away, Ivan," she asked, her voice shaking. "It's scaring me."

He immediately dropped his gun hand, moving the weapon away from her. It touched something inside her that he hadn't been using it to frighten her, that he truly hadn't realized what he was doing. She thought he would step away from the cage and shut the door with her inside. He didn't. He took her by the arm and pulled her with him when he stepped out of the cage. He walked to the bed, checked something on the gun and slipped it back into its place under the mattress. She shivered and tried backing away.

Ivan didn't even look at her when he turned, gripped her by the waist, picked her up and tossed her on the bed. Jaya landed in an ungraceful heap, her nightshirt rolling up her thighs. She let out a startled yelp and grabbed for the edges, yanking it back down.

Ivan climbed on top of her, caging her in and pinning her to the mattress. She gripped his shoulders, clamped her legs together and stared up at him, panic surging through her. "Ivan, what are you doing?" she gasped into his face.

"I'm holding you," he muttered, pressing himself hard against her and burying his face against her neck.

Jaya had no choice in the matter. She was helpless beneath him, forced to take the weight of his heavy body. Though once she took a few gulping breaths, filling her lungs, she realized he must not be pressing his full weight on top of her, because he wasn't completely crushing her. In fact, once she calmed a little and thought about it, she realized, the way he curved one arm around her back and cupped her neck in his broad hand was actually quite comfortable, almost protective.

She allowed herself to relax a little more and soak in some of the warmth and human contact he was offering. She couldn't remember the last time someone had touched her without it being an accident. She allowed her mind to drift back to better times when she had people in her life that cared for her. Apparently, Ivan was thinking along similar lines.

"Never touched anyone like this before," he mumbled

against her. She felt the warmth of his breath against her neck and shivered. Her hair was a curtain fanning out across the pillows and separating his face from actually touching her skin. Ivan pulled his hand out from beneath her head and began delicately brushing her hair away from her skin. Her shivers increased at his soft touches, sending goosebumps rushing down her arms and side. Just as she began to fear that he would take advantage of the intimacy of their situation he slid his hand back beneath her head and buried his face in her neck, pressing his lips against her throat.

Jaya took a deep breath in, feeling every particle of air going in as it filled her lungs. Her nipples peaked as sensations rippled through her. All because the gentle touch of his mouth against her skin felt so incredibly good it started to melt her inhibitions. She could feel moisture gathering and knew she was getting wet for him. She bit her lip to keep herself from whimpering and giving her arousal away.

To take her mind off the awakening fluttering up and down her body she asked, "Do you want to talk about it?"

She fully expected him to say no or snap at her for bringing up the subject. Instead, he flexed his fingers against her waist and spoke into her hair. "Was dreaming about my family, about death."

She nodded. She'd known it was horrific, probably a memory of some kind. She got nightmares too. She hadn't actually witnessed the violence against her family so she only had her imagination to haunt her. "Were they killed?" she asked tentatively.

He nodded. "My country was at war with itself following the separation of another nation. Our government was crumbling under the pressure. I joined the rebellion, though I was still barely more than a boy. Invaders came to our village under the guise of government soldiers." His voice took on a cold, vicious edge as he spoke, his accent more noticeable than ever. "They lined up our people, my family included and slaughtered them. They had no mercy. No one was spared."

"But you survived?" Jaya asked.

"I wasn't in the village," he growled. "I was waging war on the border. When word of the massacre reached our unit, I abandoned my brothers and made my way back. There was nothing left, just burned out shells where homes used to stand and a mass grave. The soldiers called it an uprising, but it was nothing less than an ethnic cleansing."

Jaya began shaking so hard her teeth chattered. "What did you do?" she whispered, staring up at the shadowy ceiling. Somehow, she already knew the answer. Something had led Ivan down the dark path he was on.

"I discovered from a source in a nearby town what had happened and who had committed the atrocity." His voice had calmed, become more matter-of-fact. She recognized this Ivan, knew the true horror was still coming. She suddenly wanted to crawl out from under him and go back to her cage. "It took time, but eventually I found them and took my revenge."

"You killed the soldiers that murdered your family?"

"And as many of their families as I could get my hands on," he said, tightening his arms around her as though sensing her need to run from him. "Even at the age of fourteen I was a formidable enemy."

Jaya gasped and nearly choked when he crushed her against him. Terrifying images of him as a teenage boy hunting and murdering his prey flickered through her brain. "Why are you telling me this?"

"Because you make me want things I shouldn't want, Jaya," he said against her neck, once more sending a cascade of shivers over her sensitive flesh. Why couldn't her body get the message that she was absolutely, unequivocally terrified of this man? She couldn't help the moan that slipped from her lips. She turned her face away from him, but the move only gave him better access to her throat. He took advantage, pressing his face further against her. The rasp of his unshaven jaw felt even better than his lips. She could feel her panties heating up along with the crazy pattering of her heart. "And I think you want them too."

"No, Ivan," she whispered against the pillow, but she didn't try to move away from him. Her mind still rebelled at the thought of wanting her captor in such a way. "This is wrong. I want to go back to my cage now please."

"It doesn't matter what you want," he said, shifting his body more heavily on top of hers. "You're my slave, every part of you belongs to me."

His words were like a bucket of cold water. She froze beneath him. "Fuck that!" she snapped. "Let me up!"

He gripped her jaw in his hand and forced her to look up at him. "Watch what you say to me, Jaya," he growled down at her, shifting his body more heavily on top of hers.

"Or what?" she hissed up at him, her face aching around the clench of his fingers. "You'll torture me? You'll lock me up? What more are you going to do, Ivan?"

She saw the flash of something truly awful go through his eyes. They were so close to hers that she saw everything. She opened her mouth to cry out, to deny the punishment she saw for herself in those depths, but he slammed his mouth over hers, swallowing her scream. She twisted beneath him, but he captured her wrists and held them easily in one of his large hands, reminding her of how much weaker she was. Reminding her that she'd spent a lifetime trolling the internet while he'd honed every part of his body from his muscles to his mind. She was no match for the marauding conqueror, bent on taking his captive and teaching her how to be a proper slave.

Though she tried her best to fight, there was no possible

way to fight a man like Ivan. He was too broad, too skilled and too perceptive. He countered each move she made almost before she made it. She was left gasping and pinned to the bed with nowhere to go. He shoved himself between her legs, thrusting them apart and pushing his hips between. She whimpered into his mouth, giving him the opportunity to push his tongue deeper inside and vanquish new territory. She was swamped in sensations and helpless to fight him off. She could do nothing but feel. Feel his weight on her body. Feel him touch every part of her, invade flesh that hadn't been stroked in a very long time.

And her body continued to betray her, continued to peak with excitement, to drip with arousal, though she was terrified of the man holding her, forcing her desire. She took her hands, the same that he'd chained with his, and shoved in an attempt to force him away from her. He growled, tore his mouth away from hers and yanked her wrists over her head. He held them in one hand and reached between their bodies to pull her T-shirt up her body, exposing her stomach and then her full breasts.

Jaya's eyes widened, and her whimpers turned to a cry. "Ivan, please!" she yelled up at him. "Not like this!"

"What then?" he growled, reaching between them, his fingers seeking her panties. "What the fuck do you want from me? Tenderness? Not in my bed, Jaya."

"Stop!" she shouted, throwing her head back into the pillow.

He took the opportunity to bite her neck, not hard enough to hurt, but enough to make her feel him. To draw out the arousal he'd been playing out on her sensitive skin. She cried out and twisted against him as his fingers found their way into her cotton panties and glided along the folds of her vagina. She knew she was well past wet for him. There was no denying her arousal.

He pressed his lips to her ear and snarled, "You want me."

She turned her head to look at him, uncaring that her nose touched his cheek. "I hate you," she hissed, trying to inject as much venom as she could in the words.

He pressed one long, thick finger inside. She was tight from years of abstinence. It burned. It hurt. Her stomach clenched with butterflies of anticipation. It felt so damn good she would have bowed right off the bed if he wasn't laying on top of her. "You're tight as fuck body says otherwise," he said, his voice deepening.

"I don't care what my body does," she answered, her pussy clenching around his finger. She squeezed her eyes shut. "Please, Ivan. Please stop," she sobbed, turning her head into his shoulder.

Something about her plea seemed to reach him. He removed his finger and pulled her up until they were both sitting. Jaya blinked, tears gathering in her eyes. Her body was both buzzing and hurting. She could feel the sexual tension still flowing through Ivan. She wanted to strike out at him for daring to hurt her this way, for holding her captive and making her feel so helpless. Making her worry about imminent rape now on top of everything else he'd done. The sexual frustration, combined with fear and anger made her feel reckless.

"Fuck you, Ivan. You know what you want from me, what your twisted, evil mind wants? Why you can't just let me go?" She was crying, and she couldn't even catch the tears because he'd clamped her wrists together in a brutal hold. Her legs were curled beneath her, her T-shirt hiked up past her hips. Her tears dripped onto their hands. The words were spilling from her lips fast and harsh. "You want a connection; a human connection. And for some reason you think you'll get that with me. But you know something, Ivan? We'll never connect."

His fingers squeezed her wrists until she thought the bones might snap under the pressure. She moaned in pain. "And why is that?" he asked coldly.

She gritted her teeth against the agony shooting up her arms and said in as chilling a voice as she could manage, "Because I was being kind when I woke you from your nightmare, I didn't want you to suffer. Because I understand what it's like to close your eyes and see your dead family. I have nightmares about mine being blown to pieces all over the Indian consulate. There's nothing left but blood splatter. Do you know that? No, you don't. Because instead of letting me comfort you and commiserate, like a normal human, you called me your slave and tried to rape me." She tugged on her arms and cried out in pain when he finally released her. She cradled her arms against her chest and edged toward the opposite side of the bed, her eyes glued to him. "And that's why you can never have any kind of human connection, Ivan. You're an animal."

They stared at each other for a moment. She didn't dare move, though she desperately wanted to escape him. She sensed he could go either way, that he wanted to drag her against his body and savagely finish what he'd started a few moments earlier. But something was stopping him. Maybe something in her words. Sympathy perhaps for what she saw when she closed her eyes at night. She didn't know what kept his hand from reaching for her and she didn't care as long as he didn't hurt her again.

"Go," he ordered harshly.

It was all she needed. She rolled off the bed, rushed around the side like a demon was chasing her and flung herself into the cage, slamming the door shut. She collapsed on her small bed and yanked the blanket up to her shoulders. She pressed shaking fingers over her face and tried to calm down. She knew he wouldn't change his mind and come after her. Ivan didn't do that. Still, she nearly leapt right off the bed when she felt something land next to her.

Haty let out a tiny mewl of annoyance when Jaya jerked back. Then she settled her soft little body into her usual spot against Jaya's stomach, determined to get comfortable for the night. Jaya forced herself to relax and reached an arm out to stroke the kitten's soft head when Ivan's deep voice reached out to her from the darkness.

"How far did you get in Wuthering Heights?"

She thought about denying that she'd been reading the book at all, but she knew he would see through the lie. She would only diminish herself in his eyes if she didn't answer him, play his game. "Heathcliff has left to seek his fortune. Cathy is spending more time with the neighbors," she said, trying to keep her voice normal but knowing it sounded breathless and sad.

"You want to know what happens to Cathy?" he asked, his voice more of a demand than a question.

Jaya bit her lip and stared hard toward his bed, trying to make out his form. What was he doing? Was this another game? "Tell me," she said softly, knowing she would regret it. Ivan never did anything nice.

"She dies." Ivan's voice was cold and calm, but still urgent, as though he wanted her to understand something important. "Ultimately, Heathcliff's obsession kills her."

CHAPTER TWELVE

Jaya decided to keep reading anyway. She wanted to find out for herself what happened to Cathy. She suspected Ivan wasn't telling her the whole truth about the unfortunate heroine's demise. So after a fitful sleep she woke to find Ivan already gone, rolled over and picked up the book. Apparently, he'd pushed it back through the bars while she slept. Perhaps encouraging her to continue her newfound literary pursuit.

Though it vexed her to give him anything, she *was* actually enjoying the book. With Haty ripping around the bedroom, running energetic circles and killing imaginary bugs, Jaya read comfortably, enjoying the morning sunlight filtering through the open balcony doors. She had just reached the part when Heathcliff returned to Wuthering Heights only to find Cathy married to another man when a servant entered the bedroom, followed by Keane.

"Psst, Haty," Jaya hissed urgently. She didn't trust the giant redhead and the man knew it. She could tell by the vague smirk playing around his thin lips. But he kept his eyes averted, his beefy arms crossed over his broad chest, tattoos popping and rippling all up his arms while Haty ran to Jaya. She scooped the kitty up and held her against her chest while sitting cross-legged on the mattress. She watched him warily, but he didn't move as he stood by the door and ignored both her and the servant while the servant approached the cage with Jaya's breakfast.

She was so used to the routine she accepted the food without thought and ate, setting aside what she couldn't finish. As usual, she had a brief thought that she shouldn't be settling into the routine of captivity, but it took too much energy. Especially when she was immediately hustled through the door, toward the washroom for her daily shower.

As Jaya took her shower, scrubbing her body, she thought about her feelings toward her captivity. She was bored, that was for damn sure. She was used to having the world at her fingertips, her agile brain constantly on alert for a new project. She was worried about Ivan's next mind-fuck. But... she wasn't stressed. She was eating and sleeping better than ever, her meals were well-balanced and she wasn't constantly terrified of the bogeyman breaking down her door and murdering her in her sleep. Because he'd already broken down her door and stolen her away.

She ran her hands over her body, feeling some of the new curves that were already starting to develop from the regular meals Ivan's people forced on her. She'd been enjoying a healthy selection of fruits and vegetables, meats and breads rather than her usual fare of whatever she remembered to grab in between jobs and whatever her pantry might happen to support at any given moment. Computer geeks weren't exactly known for healthy eating habits and Jaya was definitely of the breed. She regularly forgot to eat and when she remembered, she usually discovered an empty fridge.

Jaya slapped the shower handle off with a vicious swipe and stepped out of the state-of-the-art floor to ceiling marble shower stall. She was definitely growing complacent if she was having thoughts like these. After all, Ivan nearly raped her the night before. They were in a constant tug-of-war and she never knew which way she was going. If she became too satisfied under Ivan's care, she'd wind up dead.

She dried herself off, brushed out her thick hair and pulled on a pair of black leggings and a red sleeveless shirt she'd chosen from her wardrobe. There was a soft, warm breeze flowing from the open windows that she could enjoy from her cage.

"There you go again," Jaya growled at her reflection, taking a swipe at herself. "Enjoying your damn captivity. Maybe you should pick out your grave stone while you're at it, stupid."

She stomped back into the bedroom and into her cage, throwing herself down on her bed. She refused to look at either the servant or Keane again. Usually, once her needs were cared for, they would leave at this point in her morning anyway. She curled her arms beneath her chin and glared moodily toward the open balcony doors, wishing she could go outside.

"Do you require anything else?" the servant asked.

Jaya raised an eyebrow and twisted her head around. The servants didn't speak to her. She thought it was pretty clearly not allowed. She opened her mouth to reply, but Keane snapped at the woman to get out. She looked terrified for a moment, her gaze jumping from Jaya to him and then back. She bobbed her head at Jaya and then scurried off.

Jaya turned and shot the man a glare. "You're an asshole."

He gave her a nasty grin. "Might be an asshole, but I ain't caged up like a little canary."

"Fuck you," she snapped.

"You wish." He winked and flexed a bicep at her.

Jaya blinked and then started laughing. "What are you,

like thirty-five? Is that the most mature reply you can come up with?"

He chortled in response showing a ton of shark-like teeth. "It's all I can give the boss's lady."

"Oh my god," she giggled and rolled her eyes.

He nodded and left, closing the door behind him. It took about two minutes after that for Jaya to realize that she never actually heard the click of her cage door when the servant had locked her back in. She gasped and flew to the opening, reaching for it automatically. Her hands shook as she took hold of the bars and pushed, swinging the door open. It wasn't locked. It wasn't even latched. The servant had forgotten to close her inside.

"Oh my god." Jaya's voice was hushed now as her brain flew. She had to force her scattering thoughts to organize. She was a highly intelligent woman, used to working rapidly through problems, but she'd been locked in two rooms for days on end, her brain slowing in the process. "Okay, I can do this." She snapped her fingers and glanced around for her cat. "Psst, Haty."

The kitten looked up from her dish, where she'd been eating her crunchies, and immediately abandoned the food to scamper over. Jaya bent over to scoop her up. She stood part way between freedom and caged captivity and worked the problem. The urge to simply run was so great she had to sit down on Ivan's bed and take several slow, steady breaths, so her brain could function properly.

"Okay," she whispered out loud. "They won't be back for hours, that gives us lots of time to plan." She glanced around the room and began mentally stockpiling and discarding each item her eyes fell on, based on its usefulness. She nodded sharply, stood up and headed for the closet, intent on finding a bag of some sort. "We're out of here, Haty. No more cages for us."

"What the fuck?" Keane grumbled, his thick red brows pulled together in a frown. He stood next to a monitor with his hands braced on his hips, watching the hacker scale the outside of the building with a makeshift backpack slung over her shoulders. "She didn't even try the door. Look at her, that woman is not built for climbing."

Ivan stood frozen, watching the same set of monitors as his men. To anyone else, his icy exterior would appear normal, as though he were dispassionately watching the evolution of their experiment with the hacker unfold. But the sight of Jaya clinging to the outside of a sheer stone wall over-looking a cliff ending in crashing surf far below as she forced herself to steadily climb toward the roof with some kind of sack tied to her back, had his guts clenched and burning in both terror and fury. Two emotions he hadn't felt this strongly since childhood. Had he pushed her to this point of desperation? That she would choose escape via the roof was smart. That she would risk her life in such a way was reckless. He was going to spank her ass like there was no tomorrow and shrink her cage to the size of a pair of handcuffs. He didn't know or give a shit why he cared, but this woman would never again be allowed to put herself in danger.

"She knows there are cameras in the hallway. Probably saw them when she was escorted to my room. She's taking the risk that there won't be surveillance on the roof," he muttered, his eyes glued to the drama unfolding on the screen. She was inching her way toward the top, a good ten feet over her head. Keane was correct, Jaya was not built for climbing. She didn't have the upper body strength and her generous hips and breasts were getting in the way. He wanted to call the whole thing off, haul her to safety and lock her back up, but it was too late. If they tried to approach her, they could startle her off the wall. Besides, she was doing surprisingly well, taking her time, ensuring her foot and hand-holds were solid as she pushed her way steadily upward.

"She's wrong. But she's a smart little cookie, ain't she?" Keane said in a voice that had far too much admiration for Ivan's liking. He also didn't like the way his second watched the monitor with such sharp interest. "Is that sack of hers moving? Did she take the fucking cat with her?"

Ivan narrowed his eyes. The bag on her back was indeed squirming around, causing Jaya to shift dangerously. She braced herself against the wall and said something over her shoulder, which seemed to calm the movement. Sweat broke out on his forehead. Not only was she risking her life, but she was doing it with a three-month-old cat that could cause them both to plunge to their deaths at any moment. Her punishment was growing more and more severe with every move she took away from her gilded cage.

He held his breath when she reached high over her head and grabbed the roof ledge. She was shaking so bad now he could see it through the cameras installed on the opposing cliffs. Somehow she managed to pull herself over the top, crawl away from the plunging precipice and collapse on the rooftop tiles. He released a long, slow breath and eased the tension in his muscles. He felt as though he'd made the climb along with her, and he knew exactly what it felt like, having scaled the cliffs beneath her with his men in training exercises. He closed his eyes and when he opened them, refocused his mind back on the task. The point was to see what his hacker captive could do. And though she'd taken a terrible risk, she was smart. She knew her best bet at escaping his island was leaving via the outside of the building.

"She's back on her feet," Keane noted, the admiration in his voice growing. "Heading for the first obstacle."

"I can see that," Ivan said icily, his gaze never leaving her.

She looked tiny against the backdrop of his castle-like mansion, built with the highest tech security available and constantly updated.

They had created a series of scenarios when they'd decided to set Ivan's bird free. He wanted to see what she could do, how far she could get. Though logically he knew he would eventually need to utilize her considerable skills, emotionally he wanted to tear the room apart, murder all of his men, go find the woman and punish her for every perceived infraction she was currently committing. She was his slave, his captive, his caged canary, as Keane liked to call her. Allowing her free rein aroused every dormant instinct within him. Threatened to release the beast he kept carefully hidden so he could make ruthless, cold-blooded decisions without remorse or regret. The woman was changing everything.

"She can't get off the island," Keane said quietly from beside him as if reading his thoughts.

Ivan calculated how long it would take him to reach his sidearm and take the man down. Would Keane resist? He was intensely loyal, but he was a psychotic and unpredictable bastard. It was what made him such an excellent second-in-command.

"Perhaps not," Ivan snarled from between gritted teeth. "But she can cause some damage while searching for a way out. Both to herself and my property." He tapped the screen where she was currently sitting cross-legged on the ground next to something he didn't recognize. "Does someone want to tell me exactly what that is she's messing with and what she's doing with it?"

There was a flurry of action in the room while five grown men tried to figure out what the thing on the west wing of the roof was and what it could possibly do. Ivan was starting to get really angry at the level of incompetence he was seeing when one of his tech guys mumbled, "Oh oh."

"Just tell me she can't hurt herself," he snarled, reaching for his gun and resting a hand on the sidearm for reassurance. It wasn't going to help the situation, but someone was going to die if Jaya got hurt during their idiotic experiment. They had assured him that every scenario had been thoroughly checked and that it was extremely unlikely she would go to the roof. His people had been wrong. She had outsmarted them. Now he was sorely tempted to kill them all and start over with a new, more intelligent team.

"I think she's messing around in an electrical panel," the same guy said, clearly sweating. "I don't think she can hurt herself..."

"Stop thinking and start telling me exactly what's happening," Ivan said, ice dripping from every word.

"I think..."

Ivan pulled his Glock and shot the man. He pushed the body away from the monitoring station and turned to the room. "Anyone else 'think' or does someone want to tell me exactly what she's doing." A few of the men took steps toward the door.

"Don't even think about it," Keane growled. "No way off the island." He glanced dispassionately down at the body and nudged it with his toe. "Guy was warned. Now it's your turn to give the boss some answers."

One of the technicians stepped forward and said, "She's attempting to disable the camera systems and possibly the general electrical systems."

Keane chuckled. "Smart girl."

"Keep your thoughts to yourself, Irish," Ivan snapped. He turned his cold gaze back to the tech guy. "I get the cameras, but what would the electrical systems do? And how could she possibly shut them all down using one panel? I was assured by the extremely expensive security and building specialists I hired that my systems would be separated in the eventuality of a hostile takeover or similar scenario."

The guy nodded. "I believe…"

Ivan twitched, the gun hand that was relaxed next to his leg tensing in readiness.

The man cleared his throat. "I mean, there's a high likelihood that she's isolating and disabling a specific system."

"Which one?" Ivan growled, asking the next obvious question. He was definitely going to have to get rid of these idiots and find smarter tech people. They couldn't anticipate their way out of a cardboard box.

Rather than answering, the guy dropped into the chair that had been occupied by the now dead man and began typing. He brought up a series of blueprints, first for the building, then for the electrical systems. Ivan leaned in and read them along with his man. He nodded and had the answer at the same time the tech guy said, "Alarms and lights."

"Would she know what they're for or is she just causing havoc in an attempt to draw our attention elsewhere while making a run for it?" Ivan asked.

The tech guy shook his head. "She knows exactly what she's doing."

Just as the words left his mouth, Jaya glanced over her shoulder, her eyes touching a camera she couldn't possibly see since it was nestled on a cliffside several metres from her position. Seconds later the video feed shut down cutting her from view.

"Amazing." The techie now sounded as admiring as Keane. "So incredibly fast."

"Get it back," Ivan snapped. The guy knew better than to argue. He set to work attempting to either fix or bypass whatever Jaya had done to the security feed. "There must be back-ups," Ivan pointed out. "I insisted on them when the whole system was installed."

"There are, but they'll take a few minutes to get up and running."

Ivan looked at Keane and tried to keep the worry from his voice when he spoke. "I want eyes on her. I know we told the men to keep their distance, but the situation has changed. I don't want her up there alone, she could slip and fall." Keane nodded and radioed to his men, telling them to get to the roof. Ivan turned back to the monitoring station about to ask where they were at with the video feeds when the lights in the room went down. The room was windowless so they were left in the dark for about thirty seconds before the back up lights kicked on.

"Brilliant," the techie muttered and started pounding the keyboard so hard the desk creaked. It was clear he was trying to beat Jaya to something.

"Talk," Ivan demanded. "Tell me what she's doing."

"She's blinding us, sir."

"For what purpose," Ivan growled, pacing like a caged animal. It occurred to him that she was doing to him exactly what he'd been doing to her. Cutting off his senses one at a time and taking away his power. "Tell me what she's up to."

Keane stepped between Ivan and the technician. "Let the man work, boss," he growled, holding up his hands when Ivan looked as though he'd get physical. "Might I suggest that he will update you as soon as he knows something."

Ivan breathed heavily through his nose and jerked his head in a nod, turning to stride across the room, pacing the length. The room, which was more than large enough to contain six grown men before, now five and a body, seemed the size of a shoebox. He wanted to punch something. He wanted to leave, stalk his home until he found her and lock her up tighter than before. Ensure she never escaped him again. Never put herself in harm's way again. He couldn't abide the idea of Jaya running free, attempting to leave him. No matter that he'd been the one to sanction the experiment. He wanted her locked back up immediately and all her toys taken away.

"Fuck me."

Ivan whipped around to look at the man who'd spoken. Camera feeds were flickering to life, but they were completely screwed up. Some feeds didn't register, some were completely blacked out and some were crossed with ones they shouldn't be.

"She found her way into a separate security feed," one of the other techs said.

"Does that tell us where she is?" Ivan asked, trying to sound like he wasn't about to murder another of them.

"Possibly, there are only so many access panels on the roof."

Before the guy could explain, Keane's radio interrupted. "She's not on the roof anymore."

Ivan took a deep breath and reminded himself that this was a good thing. At least she wasn't at risk for falling. "Exactly how many electrical panels does she have access to now that we don't have eyes on her and she's no longer on the roof?"

The first guy checked the original blueprint, cleared his throat and said, "Uh, around two dozen, give or take."

Ivan gritted his teeth and snarled, "Send men out to those panels. They are to detain her without touching. Any man that lays a hand on her dies."

"Yes, sir," Keane said and then relayed the order to his men. He turned back to Ivan. "Andrew says there're power cuts all over the building and they've been locked out of certain sections. Somehow she's gained access to our security system."

Ivan was equal parts angry and deeply impressed with Jaya. She was turning out to be a formidable opponent. He might be able to dominate her on the chess board, but she was quick on her feet. He would bet half his empire she'd been waiting for this moment. Maybe even guessed he would test her eventually. She probably sifted through dozens of potential scenarios in her brain until she settled on the one that would seem most unlikely to him and be difficult for her to manage, but not impossible. And she had nothing but weeks of time to lay around, first in a dungeon room and then a cage, and think about how best to escape when he presented her with the opportunity.

Ivan's cock twitched in appreciation of the woman who finally decided to show him her hand. He suddenly realized that she probably could have maneuvered an opportunity for escape far sooner. He frowned. Why wouldn't she have taken the chance to run when he wasn't expecting it?

Because she wouldn't have gotten far. Not with his men at their checkpoints. He'd cleared them from their individual stations for this exact exercise. She'd been biding her time, waiting for him to hand her this opportunity on a silver platter. She probably figured out he would clear a path for her. Hide his men, essentially giving her the opportunity to go invisible once she left the room and cut the cameras. And it wouldn't take more than an educated guess to place Ivan, his head of security and four of his technicians in a room together.

"Keane," Ivan said calmly. "Check the door."

Keane frowned, then strode to the door and tried to open it. Exactly as Ivan feared it was locked from the outside. Ivan dropped his head and for the first time since the entire fiasco had begun, for the first time in years, he grinned. He had vastly underestimated his prisoner. It was actually laughable how much he had underestimated her. In fact, as emotion poured through him, he realized he was proud and extremely turned on by her; as though he sensed a worthy foe and was finally giving himself permission to take her as a mate.

He was also extremely relieved. If she had planned this well, it was highly unlikely she would hurt herself. She was showing far too much forethought and skill. When he'd been worried about her, he thought she was simply frantically trying to escape.

Ivan looked toward Keane who was trying to force the door with one arm, muscles bulging as he strained and shouted instructions to his men over the radio. "The doors are electronically controlled. All the offices and security are in this wing. She probably has the entire area on lockdown." He nodded toward the guys sitting at the consoles. "Let them work on getting us out. There's no point in you trying to break it down, it's meant to withstand a bomb." Keane stepped away from the door, clearly seething now that he was on the receiving end of Jaya's tricks. "Not so cute now, is she?"

"When I get my hands on our canary, I'm going to fuckin'..." Keane snarled.

"No one touches her," Ivan repeated his earlier order. "That includes you."

Keane fell silent for a moment and then nodded respect-fully. The men had worked together for years. Ivan wouldn't call him a friend; Ivan wouldn't call anyone a friend. But he did trust in Keane's loyalty. He'd bought the Irishman's mercenary contract from a group that had chipped him with a deadly explosive that would kill him if he either turned on them or went off the grid. Expecting similar treatment from Ivan, Keane had been shocked when his new employer had immediately had the chip removed and offered him an extremely generous compensation package if he agreed to work for him.

Keane had thanked Ivan by punching him in the face,

beating up some of his best men and then drinking himself stupid in the nearest town. He then attempted to impregnate half the single female population of the same town before returning to Ivan and accepting his offer. After Keane had signed on the dotted line, Ivan had returned the Irishman's right hook to the jaw, knocking him flat. Then he'd stood over his new hungover second and very succinctly explained the chain of command.

"Where do you think she'll go?" Ivan asked quietly so only Keane could hear. They'd run through the scenarios already, but he was no longer confident that he'd chosen the most likely outcome.

Keane looked a lot less confident too. "Still think she'll hide and try to wait us out until she finds a way off the island."

Ivan shook his head. "No, she's fast and she thinks on her feet. She'll look for a way off right now, while she has the advantage. We need to stop underestimating her and start believing that she can actually pull this off."

"Fuck!" Keane snarled, clearly thinking ahead. He started to speak into his radio and then stopped, making eye contact with Ivan. "What's it gonna be, boss? We're starting to spread the men too thin. Do they cover electrical panels, come find a way to get us out, or cover the boat dock, airstrip and helicopter pad?"

Ivan closed his eyes and shook his head. This is what she wanted. Him locked in a room and his men scattered and scrambling. "What a fucking beautiful mind," he murmured. "Genius."

"I'll say," one of the guys from the monitors said, his voice stunned. "Look, she just hacked her way through the security gate to the helicopter pad. She couldn't possibly know how to..."

Ivan walked toward the monitor, his gut clenching in fear.

He was trapped in a room watching a shitty security feed that cut out intermittently and his captive bird had just found her wings. He watched as she reached up on her toes for the door of the helicopter and wrenched it open, then hauled herself up inside. She had to reach way out in order to grasp the handle and get the door to close again.

A hush fell over the men in the security room and no one dared to even breathe as they waited to find out if Jaya could actually fly the thing. Seconds later the blades whirled to life. Minutes after that, just as Ivan's security team crashed onto the helicopter pad to stop her, she lifted off and headed for the mainland.

"Well I'll be goddamned," Keane said from beside him. "I guess she found a way off the island after all. Did anyone actually lay odds on the hacker?"

One of the technicians cleared his throat. "Uh, Jimmy did."

They looked down at the floor.

CHAPTER THIRTEEN

It felt so good to be in control again, to have technology back at her fingertips, that Jaya could almost feel the flow of happy sparks flying through her as she quickly looked over the helicopter controls. She mentally sifted through every flight simulation game she'd ever played where she'd had to fly using similar instruments and began pushing buttons. She let out a gratified whoop when she heard the helicopter blades roar to life over her head. She knew flying an actual helicopter wouldn't be the same as gameplay, but she didn't have much choice. And she'd spent hours upon hours learning how to fly in virtual reality simulators. It was how she got exercise and learned what she needed to know to keep her in business.

The best game designers in the world used systems that exactly matched reality. And Jaya had made sure she connected with those designers when using the simulators. In theory, she should be able to fly all sorts of different aircrafts. She glanced over the controls while the rotator blades picked up speed. She recognized most everything she would need to fly the helicopter.

"Okay," she whispered. "I think we can do this."

She reached behind her and pulled the seatbelt over her head, latching it around her middle. She glanced over at the squirming bag on the co-pilot seat. There was no way to buckle Haty in, though she wished she could figure something out.

"Hang on to something, kitten, this could be a bumpy ride."

Letting out a slow breath Jaya opened the throttle and pulled the lever gradually up so she could ascend. As the pitch increased she pushed the left pedal. The helicopter started to move to the right. She shrieked and immediately let go of the throttle, afraid she would hit the security perimeter fence around the heli-pad. She forced herself to take a deep breath and try again. She had to get moving. Ivan would know where she was by now and his men would be on their way to her position. If she wanted to leave the island she needed to do it now.

She took hold of the throttle and tried again. This time she was able to leave the ground without the helicopter pulling too far to either the left or the right, though the controls were extremely sensitive and she had a difficult time leveling out. She broke into a sweat as the aircraft rose. She glanced down, her heart racing. Ivan's men were attempting to get onto the platform, but she'd locked out the security codes.

She used the extra time it took them to get onto the heli-pad to calmly level out the helicopter and lift it higher. By the time they broke through the fence the helicopter was too high to reach and it quickly became clear that they had orders not to shoot her down.

"Now we head to Jakarta," she whispered, manoeuvering toward where she hoped Indonesia was. She'd taken the vague information Ivan had given her on the island's location, cross-referenced it with what she knew about this part of the world and the navigation instruments on her dashboard. "Let's hope we have enough gas, Hatyarra, or this is going to be a very short flight."

The most terrifying moment of her entire escape came when she flew the helicopter over the cliffs toward the open ocean. "Oh, holy shit!" she shouted, sorely tempted to squeeze her eyes shut. But she needed her sight, which included the breathtaking drop directly below her.

Then she made the first of a series of colossal mistakes. She decided she wanted to fly lower so she wouldn't die in case she accidentally crashed. Which she probably wouldn't have done if she'd just stayed level and kept flying toward Indonesia. She was still pretty close to the island when the helicopter started to jerk to the left. She over-compensated by pulling too hard on the throttle, which is when the helicopter began spinning. It jumped up and down then plunged toward the choppy waves.

Jaya was thrown around in her seat. She gripped the throttle, but it seemed to lock in position. Nothing she did made a difference. She was going to crash!

She reached for the bag on the other seat and clutched it against her chest, feeling the warmth of Haty seeping through. The cat seemed to sense their predicament. She used her tiny claws to cling to Jaya through the sack. Jaya sobbed against the bundle. "I'm so sorry, baby," she whispered. "Oh god, please don't die."

Seconds later Jaya was jerked hard to the side and then flung back in her seat as the helicopter hit the water. She screamed, her voice echoing through the small space. The whirling blades slashed the water and forced the helicopter sideways. She watched in horror as one of them bent and snapped off. A rush of water hit the window in front of her.

The helicopter was completely sideways in the ocean and sinking fast.

She took Haty out of the makeshift bag and very carefully dropped her the few feet to the other side of the helicopter. Then she braced herself as best she could so she wouldn't fall and unbuckled her seatbelt. Standing on the edge of the opposite seat she tried to reach over her head and push the door open. Tears streamed down her cheeks, but she still forced her brain to move, to work through the problem. There wasn't much she could do for herself except stay with the helicopter and hope a boat came before she drowned. But maybe Haty could swim back to the island. She had to climb on top of the dashboard and use the throttle for a foothold in order to finally get a good grip on the handle. Just as she threw the door open a big wave slapped against the side of the helicopter, sending it listing further to the side. Jaya was thrown back against the opposite door.

"Ouch!"

Haty landed on top of her just as another wave hit the helicopter, soaking them through the now open door. Haty screeched and burrowed into Jaya's neck. Jaya curled onto her side, the kitten cuddled against her. She sobbed helplessly. She knew she needed to get up, keep moving. Check to see if someone was coming for them. Urge Haty to start swimming, but she was too frightened to move.

She was jarred from her momentary pity party with a gasp when water rushed over her. She lifted her head. Water was coming rapidly through the open door. Looking around she stared out the front window and realized the helicopter was now swiftly sinking. This galvanized her into action. She didn't want to be trapped inside when it finally went down, though she was screwed if she was out in open water. She couldn't swim.

She crawled toward the opening, a shivering Haty clinging

to her shoulder. "Okay, baby, when we get out that door, you need to just start swimming. Go to the mainland and find Ivan. I'm probably not going to be able to go with you. Humans aren't like cats, we aren't born with the ability to swim, oh god!" The biggest wave she'd seen yet hit the helicopter, swamping the entire thing and flooding the interior almost completely. She sputtered and clung to the seats while Haty clawed her shoulders in a desperate attempt to hang on.

Jaya reached for the edge of the helicopter and dragged herself toward the door, resisting the swirling water attempting to suck her back in. She grabbed Haty, kissed the wet, squirming kitten and flung her out the door. "Swim, Haty! Go, go, go!"

The little grey and white body hit the water, bounced, sank then came up screeching angrily. She immediately turned around and headed straight back for Jaya. Jaya sighed and reached for her. She was pretty sure that was exactly what Haty was going to do, but she'd had to try. "Okay, sweetie, you're okay," she said soothingly. She reached out to scoop up the yowling mass as it hurtled toward her. She tossed the bedraggled kitten back up on her shoulder where it burrowed in Jaya's hair. "Not much of a killer now, are you?" Jaya muttered as she attempted to grip the side of the helicopter and pull herself up on top before it sank completely under the waves.

She slipped and lost her grip, falling off the side and sinking into the water. Panic hit as water engulfed her. She opened her mouth to scream but salty water rushed into her mouth and nose, choking her. She waved her arms and kicked her legs, trying to push herself up. Images of nothing but endless dark blue ocean stretched out beneath her flashed through her brain scaring her. Her heart felt like it was bursting in her chest. Haty finally let go of her. Jaya accidentally kicked the helicopter. Pain rushed through her leg, but she was able to reach out and take hold of the edge of the door and haul herself back up.

As soon as her head broke the surface, Haty launched herself back at Jaya, tucking her body beneath the heavy, wet curtain of Jaya's hair. Jaya coughed and gagged as water streamed down her face. She cried, her tears mixing with the sea water, and pulled herself against the front of the helicopter, resting her face against the windshield. She was utterly exhausted.

"Haty," she said, her voice rough from swallowing too much water. "You're going to have to swim once this thing goes down. J-just promise if you see I-Ivan..." Her teeth chattered so hard, from either fear or cold, maybe both, she could barely speak. The helicopter sank steadily until only the tiny portion Jaya clung to was above the surface still. "P-promise you'll bite his nose off if you can. J-just wait until he's asleep then you get him good. Okay, baby kitty? Revenge for mama?"

Jaya cried out in despair as the helicopter sank below the surface completely. "Oh god!" she yelled as she kicked and thrashed in an attempt not to get dragged under with the sinking machine. "Go, Haty!"

CHAPTER FOURTEEN

Jaya was just lifting off from the helicopter pad when his men managed to get Ivan through the first door. It took two minutes to get him the rest of the way through the security wing, which she'd locked down tight. Keane was bellowing into his radio, sending men to the docks and the airstrip.

"Where do you want to go, boss?" Keane asked. "Boat or plane."

"Dock," Ivan snapped grimly without further explanation. He stalked through the building toward the nearest boat dock. Given the sloppy way she'd taken off in the helicopter he didn't think she was going to make it far. Nothing in his background checks on her or his experience with her told him she was a pilot. He highly doubted her ability to make it to the mainland in one piece. He just prayed she wasn't badly injured if she did crash.

When he arrived at the dock, it was to find one of his fastest boats prepped and ready to leave. Ivan leaped onto the craft, Keane right behind him. Something crackled over Keane's radio that made them all freeze.

"She's down. Bird's in the water and sinking fast."

"Move out!" Keane shouted.

The boat shot forward, the man piloting it smart enough to use full throttle without being told. Keane took up post by the captain and gave him instructions while Ivan scanned the water for wreckage. The boat flew, skimming the salty waves of the Java Sea as the men frantically sped toward Ivan's sinking captive.

"There." Keane was the first to spot her. He pointed toward the horizon. Ivan whipped his head to the side, shading his eyes. He saw the black of the helicopter as it struggled against the battering of waves. "We're not going to make it in time, she's going under."

"We better," Ivan said grimly, gripping the edge of the boat in both hands. He kicked off his shoes and waited, tension thrumming through his muscles. "Get close, but not close enough to overwhelm the thing with fresh waves. We'll only sink it faster."

"Too late," Keane pointed out. "It just went under. Can see your girl though, she's waving her arms around like a damn fish on dry land. What's wrong with her? That's not how you swim."

"I don't think she can swim," Ivan growled. He'd never in his life felt more helpless than he did in that moment when he watched a wave hit Jaya. Her flailing arms disappeared beneath the choppy white-capped waves. "Cut the engine," he snarled.

The second the engine stopped he was in the water and swimming toward her in powerful strides. Relief shot through him when he saw her head break the surface again and her arms wave weakly. She turned and looked at him, her dark eyes, which had been dull and hopeless, lit up with a relief to match his. "Ivan!" she cried and tried reaching for him. Unfortunately, her lack of flailing sent her back under.

"Jaya!" he shouted, forcing his body to cut through the waves faster. He could hear someone in the water behind him. He reached her just as her hand breached the water in one last desperate flail. He took hold of her wrist and yanked, pulling her right out of the water and into his arms.

Ivan decided that he'd never seen anything as beautiful as Jaya spitting water out of her mouth, coughing, her eyes and nose streaming. She flung her arms around him and sobbed as though she were dying. He wrapped an arm around her waist and tread water with the other.

"H-h-haty," she cried brokenly. "I lost her!"

"Got 'er," Keane grumbled from beside them and held a limp bedraggled kitten up by the scruff of her neck.

Jaya reached out and snatched her cat, pulling her in between hers and Ivan's bodies and hugging her tight. She lay limp against Ivan as though she had no more energy left to either fight or swim. She was simply allowing him to hold her up while his men pulled the boat closer. He was stunned that she was trusting him to keep her alive, though she'd been in danger in the first place because she'd tried to escape him. He couldn't understand what was going through her mind.

The boat was now close enough to finish the rescue. His men reached for her, but Ivan refused to give her up. They'd just have to pull his heavy ass out of the water with his bedraggled burden. This was why he paid them the big bucks. When he tried to tug Haty from Jaya's arms, the kitty lifted her head and hissed at him, which woke Jaya from her half stupor.

"No!" Jaya protested, squeezing Haty tighter against her neck.

Ivan growled and looked toward Keane who was keeping pace with them. "I guess we're all going up together. You can help lift from the bottom if you can get a good grip while the others pull from above."

Keane grinned, showing his teeth and said, "Okay boss, but if I touch something of yours I shouldn't, don't shoot me later."

Ivan grunted in response and wrapped his arms firmly around Jaya. Two of his men gripped him beneath his arms and lifted, bracing themselves against the edge of the boat. He could feel the whole thing rocking under their combined weight but could only concentrate on the woman in his arms. He had one arm wrapped around her waist while she snuggled against him, protecting her kitty. He shifted his hand to protect her head just in case she fell as they were lifted over the side.

As soon as he was on his feet in the boat he shrugged his men off and knelt with Jaya in his arms. The cat crawled weakly up her neck and snuggled into her hair. Jaya kept her arms around Ivan's throat as though she were still in danger of drowning if she let him go. Her legs were bent back beneath her. Her delicate feet were bare, the toes curled against the cold. Her shoes must have fallen off and sunk into the ocean depths while she fought desperately for her life.

"I've got you, sweetheart," he murmured, smoothing the hair back on her forehead.

She nodded and leaned her head against his chest. Once again, he was amazed at the way she seemed to trust him. For now, at least. "Let's move," he snapped, not looking up. He needed to get her home and start warming her up. Shivers were wracking her body and though he was certain it wasn't entirely from the warm waters of the Java sea, he knew she would feel better once she was dried off and the terror of nearly drowning was behind her.

She tilted her head back and looked at him, her eyes dull with exhaustion. He expected accusation and anger but saw none of that. She licked her lips and then made a face when she tasted saltiness. The edge of his lip quirked up. She looked adorable, even half drowned. He covered her head with a protective hand and pulled her against his chest. She didn't resist. In fact, she seemed to wholeheartedly accept the comfort he was offering. She gripped the edge of his shirt in one hand and held on tight while they raced back toward the island.

If he could have held on to that moment he probably would have, only he would have had to somehow shut his men out of the picture. He loved the way Jaya clung to him, helpless and seeking comfort, grateful to be alive. He wanted her dependence. He wanted her life in his hands and he wanted it willing. He was beginning to realize in the short time that he'd spent with her that his icy heart, dead since the age of fourteen, was beginning to beat again and it was beating solely for the woman shivering against him. Now he wanted her locked down tighter than ever. Hidden from all danger, including any she could cause herself. And he wasn't willing to compromise. He was a man used to getting what he wanted. His single-minded pursuit of profit had taught him exactly how to attain the things he wanted, and he would succeed with Jaya. Whether she liked it or not.

Until he met her, he'd been content to face a lifetime alone, an empire beneath his feet, the world his playground. Now he wanted more. He wanted the soft, keenly intelligent woman in his arms to walk at his side. Even if he had to chain her to him and force her compliance. Eventually she would weaken. She would have to. Her heart was capable of so much more than his. Even with a mind tainted by her past, causing her to hide herself in basements and connect only through the virtual world, her heart was still beautiful and whole. He would prey on her weaknesses until she bent to him and him alone.

"Ivan," she said hoarsely into his chest.

He smoothed some of the drying strands off her forehead

and tipped her head back so he could see her face. It was streaked with drying tears. "Yes?"

"Thank you for saving us," she whispered, her lips inches from his, fresh tears sparkling in her eyes. "I didn't want to die."

Ivan nodded and, ignoring his men, dropped his head to her ear, skimming her cheek with his lips along the way. "You belong to me. I won't let you go, not even death gets to take you." He knew his words weren't comforting but they were the truth.

She jerked in his arms and narrowed her eyes at him. "That was very Heathcliff, Ivan. No wonder you don't have any friends."

He frowned and then chuckled at her audacity. Here she was sitting on her kidnapper's lap, speeding back toward his home, and she was accusing him of not having any friends. He leaned back to see her facial expressions better, glad that she was still clinging to his shirt, though he wasn't sure if she was aware of her action. "What makes you think I don't have any friends?"

She glanced over at Keane and said, "Hey, asshole, do you like this guy? Would you call him a friend?"

Keane raised a thick red eyebrow and let out a booming laugh. "Awe, fuck no! That fucker'd kill a guy as soon as look at him. And I never seen him drink a beer. Can't fully trust a man that won't sit and have a pint with me."

"Fuck you, Keane," Ivan said in a dignified voice and dropped his chin against the top of Jaya's head.

She giggled and held him a little tighter. Something within him relaxed a little. He felt less frantic as they reached the dock, though he insisted on lifting her into his arms and holding her against his chest as he stepped off the boat. She didn't complain or try to push him away. He knew this was a temporary thing, but he would still enjoy the submissive Jaya while he had her.

"Make sure no one disturbs us," he said to Keane, who kept pace with him as he strode toward his private wing. "Do what you have to do to get things running again."

Keane nodded sharply. "Yes, boss." He veered to the left and headed for the security wing giving Ivan and Jaya their privacy.

Ivan carried Jaya the rest of the way to his private quarters and entered the code, allowing them access. He pushed the door open and carried her over the threshold. She lifted her head and looked around.

"I feel like I could sleep for a week," she said with a yawn.

"Soon," he said, carrying her through to the washroom and setting her on her feet.

She stared up at him with wide eyes, caught somewhere between trust and wariness. Ivan reached for her neck and gently extracted the slumbering kitten who immediately woke and began protesting. "Take off your clothes," he instructed in a voice he hoped was both commanding and gentle at the same time. He carried the rapidly drying critter, her striped fur spiked up in every direction, into the bedroom and settled her on her kitty bed where she curled up and closed her eyes with a deep sigh of contentment. When he returned to the washroom Jaya was still clinging to the edge of the counter fully clothed.

Ivan gently pried her fingers from the edge of the granite counter and lifted her hands between their bodies. "Jaya, you're shaking like a leaf," he said calmly. "We need to get you out of these wet clothes and into the shower. Trust me, you'll feel much better once the salt is washed from your skin and you feel warm again."

Her teeth began to chatter, and her eyes filled with tears.

She looked down and away from him, avoiding his eyes. "I'll be fine, Ivan."

"You need to shower, Jaya," he said firmly. "Either you take your clothes off and do it yourself or I do it for you."

Her eyes snapped to him and narrowed. Ordinarily, resistance and argument irritated him. Gave him cause to assess and, shortly thereafter, terminate whatever relationship or person was resisting him. But Jaya was different. He was enjoying her fire. He wanted more, was relieved to see that it hadn't been extinguished in her near-death experience.

"Don't you dare." She crossed her arms over her chest and glared at him.

"Then take your clothes off and get your ass in that shower."

She looked as though she wanted to argue, to deny him. But she'd come to know him well enough to realize he would indeed strip her down and he wouldn't be nice about it. She glanced around, looking for an escape. Of course, there was none. He was standing between her and the only door. Her shoulders slumped a little and she uncrossed her arms and reached for the hem of her shirt.

She paused for a moment. "Can you please leave?" she asked.

"No," he denied her request. "Now get moving, Jaya."

"I hate you so much, Ivan." She dragged the T-shirt over her head with shaking arms and let it go, slamming her arms over her torso.

He frowned at her timidity. He wasn't completely surprised given her solitary existence, but he wasn't going to tolerate it for long. "That's not what you were saying when I was pulling you from the ocean. Now the rest, Jaya," he insisted.

She hooked her fingers in the waistband of the black leggings she almost always chose to wear when he didn't insist on a sari and dragged them over her generous hips. She had to lean against the counter and bend over to get them off her legs. She was so weak from her ordeal that she couldn't get her feet untangled and started to fall. Ivan caught her before she could hit the floor. He nearly groaned out loud when his fingers sank into her smooth, plush skin. He pushed her back against the counter and knelt at her feet admiring the rounded expanse of her soft, smooth stomach in front of his face.

"Let me," he muttered roughly, sliding his hand over one calf, lifting her leg and pushing her leggings off first one foot and then the other. She stood uncomplaining, her hands gripping the counter behind her. When he looked up, he nearly came in his pants at the sight. She wore nothing, but a skimpy pair of bikini cut panties, dark pink with purple lace around the edges. He really couldn't help but follow the path of the lace to where it disappeared right between her plump thighs. She wore a matching bra that clung so lovingly to her full breasts he decided that she should always wear whatever shape, colour and size this bra and panty set were. The perfection was blowing his mind.

His mouth watered and his brain flashed over every scenario that had her bent over the counter with him pounding into her from behind, or her sitting that full, curvy ass on the same counter with him slamming into her while she wrapped her arms and legs around his body, like she'd done in the water when he was saving her life. She owed him. She was his slave. He could do whatever he wanted with her.

She made a small sound of distress and his gaze snapped up to hers. Her eyes were round and worried. He realized that, without thought, he'd gripped her waist so hard, sinking his fingers deep, she would likely have marks. He looked away from her and reminded himself that she'd just been traumatized and, while he fully intended to have her, now wasn't the right time.

He moved his fingers from her waist to the edge of her panties and tugged them down her legs in one swift move. She jerked back against the counter and made a strangled sound. "Stop, Jaya," he said gruffly. "I'm not going to hurt you."

"Th-that'll be a first," she snapped between chattering teeth.

He chuckled. "There's my girl."

He stood up, towering over her and spun her around so she faced the mirror. She grabbed the counter again and held on for dear life. He unhooked her bra and tugged it down her arms, uncurling her stiff fingers from the granite top and pulling her arms through the straps. She grabbed for the counter again. Unable to resist, he leaned over her and placed his hands next to hers as he buried his face in the crook of her neck and breathed in, inhaling the scent of ocean and Jaya. Her unique scent drew him, drove him wild and called to him. It was warm and spicy with a hint of honey. He couldn't explain it. But he knew it was there. It had lingered in his bedroom since she'd been moved.

His lifted his gaze to look at her in the mirror. He ignored the wide, frightened eyes, not wanting the shreds of his conscience to wake up too soon. Her long, dark brown hair streamed in drying strands over her shoulders, covering most of her gorgeous breasts. He reached up and pushed the section over her right shoulder, revealing one breast. She made a strangled sound and lifted her hand to cover herself. He captured her wrist and pressed her hand back against the counter. She shook in his arms, the movement now having nothing to do with cold.

"So perfect," he said, his eyes caressing her in the mirror. Her nipple was stiffly peaked, the aureole a rich brown, almost black colour. Her breast was smooth and brown like the rest of her, but plump and perky at the same time, proclaiming her youth. Another point for his conscience to mull over at a later date. Though he didn't know her exact age, he did know she was much younger than him. Possibly as many as fifteen years separated them.

"How old are you, Jaya?" he asked, his tone still gentle but demanding.

"Twenty-four," she whispered.

Yes, fifteen years difference. And for a split second he contemplated the years she had ahead of her. The bright things she could do with her keen intelligence if not tied down by a man intent on holding her so tight the world would never get to see her light again. Then he rejected the thought. She belonged to him.

"I-Ivan," she whispered, her voice shaking. "What are you going to do?"

His eyes drifted down her rounded belly to the thatch of soft pubic hair. The rest of her was blocked from view. He wanted her more than words could describe. Blood was pumping hard and fast through his veins, proclaiming the woman before him his naked prize, urging him to take her. He bit down on her shoulder, sinking his teeth into the soft flesh, tasting sea, salt and Jaya. She cried out and flinched, trying to squirm away from him. He yanked her back and wrapped his arms around her, allowing himself the luxury of simple touch since that was all he could have at the moment.

He kissed the mark, then lifted his lips from her shoulder and whispered in her ear. "Nothing for now, my Victory. But soon... everything."

CHAPTER FIFTEEN

Jaya watched warily as he walked away, leaving her alone in the washroom to shower. Given how strangely protective he'd been acting since pulling her from the water, she was a little surprised, but grateful to have a moment to herself. Deciding to take advantage before he came back, she opened the shower door and stepped inside. She could barely stand once she was inside the cocoon of big frosted glass, a combination of aftershocks from her near drowning and her encounter with her captor sweeping over her. After a moment under the warm spray she was forced to sink to the smooth tile floor. She leaned her back against the glass and sat with her knees against her chest, her forehead on her knees, the hot water streaming over her. It felt amazingly good, though her mind was in turmoil.

The way Ivan had looked at her, touched her, it made her feel intensely alive and aware of her own sexuality. It also made her feel jittery as a grasshopper being chased by Haty. Her hand crept up to her shoulder where he bit her. She felt the slightly sore spot and the indents where his teeth had left marks; it was like he was branding her. She was reminded of when she'd called him an animal. It felt like weeks ago instead of only the night before.

"Better get my ass up or he'll come looking," she muttered to herself.

She finished her shower, weariness rocking her limbs. She could barely lift her arms to wash her hair and she decided to skip the conditioner altogether, despite knowing she'd regret it later when the inevitable tangles sent her to hairbrush hell. But it wasn't worth the ache and burn every time she moved her arms. She'd forced herself to more physical extremes today than she had in her entire life, especially her upper body.

She shut the water off and reached for a fluffy towel, squealing in shock when she was enveloped in one and lifted off her feet. Ivan set her on the bath mat and began drying her vigorously, despite her protests. Then, ignoring her heated arguments, he wrapped the towel back around her and carried her to the bed.

When she saw where he was taking her, Jaya tried to stop him and climb out of his arms. She gripped one of his biceps and twisted sideways, but he just shifted his grip, his hand sliding under the towel and enveloping her bare thigh. "I want to go to my cage!" she yelped desperately.

He didn't answer, just grunted in annoyance when her elbow connected with the side of his head. He dropped her on the mattress and when she tried to roll off the other side, he grabbed her wrist and twisted until she yelled in pain and held still. He dropped onto the mattress on his knee. "Stop fighting and lay still."

She froze and stared up at him, a question huge in her eyes. The towel had slipped sideways, revealing most of her upper body. He gripped the edge and tugged it the rest of the way off, tossing it to the floor. A shiver rippled through her, jiggling her breasts. She tried to cross an arm over her chest while groping for a blanket with her other hand. He took both of her wrists and flattened them on the bed beside them.

"This is happening, Jaya," he said quietly. His voice wasn't vicious or hard. In fact he was being surprisingly gentle.

"I'm not ready," she replied quickly, arching to the side. He blocked her with a knee. He was still fully dressed, though her own nudity made her feel so vulnerable it didn't matter that he was still clothed.

He shook his head. "We've spent weeks together, you're as ready as I'm willing to allow."

She frowned, her body still tense beneath his. His fingers curled around her wrists, chaining them. She could feel aggression thrumming through his body, ready to strike out at her. Her own body responded with confusion; part of her warmed and melted for him, her pussy beginning to dampen as though it was trained for this moment while her heart hammered and her muscles tensed, preparing for flight. She felt that he was holding himself tightly in check, rather than simply falling on her and fucking her.

"I've been your captive, Ivan," she whispered. "I still am. Having sex under these conditions isn't right. The power imbalance is too much."

His lips thinned into a grim line and he moved his thumb to her face, dragging her hand with him. He ran his thumb over her jaw and then down the side of her neck, drawing a cascade of shivers form her. "There will always be a power imbalance between us, sweetheart. Your captivity has nothing to do with that."

"And you'll always make decisions for me!" she snapped at him angrily, straining her body against him. "At least until you decide I bore you and it's time to get rid of me."

"That will never happen," he snarled down at her. "I'm never letting you go."

Her mouth fell open and the fight drained from her. She collapsed into the mattress. The savage truth written on his face, the strength in his fingers as they pinned her hands to the bed, told her he meant what he was saying. He'd decided to keep her, forever, without her consent. "No!" she gasped.

He didn't respond verbally. Instead he bent his head and crushed her denial under the storm of a kiss meant to seal his promise of a lifetime together. Though she rejected him with her words, her lips softened and opened under the onslaught of his kiss, giving him access to the sweet depths within. He released her hand and took her head in one enveloping palm, tangling his fingers in the wet strands of her hair and tilting her head back. He took her mouth in a ravaging kiss, sweeping his tongue over her teeth and tongue, nearly gagging her with the heavy oppressiveness of his attack.

She lifted her free arm and clung to his shoulder, gasping for breath when he finally lifted his head for moment. He buried his face against hers and groaned, "You're mine now, Jaya."

A high, choked sound escaped her. Her thoughts scattered as she felt him reaching back over his shoulders. Her confused mind couldn't comprehend what he was doing until she felt the bare skin of his chest pressing against hers and realized he was removing his shirt. Before she had a chance to process his loss of clothing, he was capturing her lips in another searing kiss that stole her breath and sent her heart pattering crazily in her chest. She clung to his shoulders as though she were still in the ocean and needed him to save her from drowning.

He lifted his hips from hers and reached between them. She whimpered at the loss, as her mind also kicked into gear, reminding her that he was preparing to take their already seriously messed-up relationship to the next level. She broke the kiss, turning her head to the side and tried to twist her body underneath his.

"Ivan!" she cried out.

He brought his arms down on either side of her shoulders, trapping her squirming body. He kicked his jeans off the bed and slid one long, muscular leg between hers. Taking her jaw in one hand he forced her head up to his. "Are you a virgin?"

"No!" she gasped, digging her nails into his shoulders. She wanted to tell him that she wasn't very experienced and it had been years since she'd been intimate with anyone, but the words caught in her throat. She knew her eyes were huge on his face, pleading for mercy, pleading for release, pleading for things that Ivan wasn't capable of giving her. His own face was set into implacable lines, yet still she felt safe in his arms, despite the quakes of uncertainty still rocking her.

He pressed his body more firmly against hers, dropping his weight. Excitement and fear flooded her. His grip on her face remained firm, his voice was deep and strained when he spoke. "I've wanted this since Athens, Jaya. I won't be able to stop. Do you understand?"

She tried to nod, but his fingers, biting into her chin, held her still. "I think so," she whispered.

"I won't be gentle."

He didn't give her any more warning. He released her face, reached between them and touched her. She gasped, turned her head to the side and automatically tried to close her legs. His hips, settled firmly between her thighs, stopped her. He used her own lubrication to glide one long, thick finger inside her, no finesse, no hesitation.

"Ahh," she groaned, clinging to his arms, digging her nails deep where the muscles bulged.

"You're so fucking wet, woman," he growled, lifting his finger between them and showing her. He rubbed the moisture between his thumb and forefinger and then stuck the finger in his mouth before returning to her pussy.

This time when he touched her, sliding his finger along her folds and back inside her welcoming passage, she lifted her hips as much as she could while trapped beneath him, meeting the delicious touch, the forbidden pressure he was treating her too. She decided to let her exhausted mind take a break. Physical Jaya was taking over. The woman who craved the touch of her captor, who wanted to know what would happen next in Ivan's bed.

He dipped his head, taking one of her nipples deep in his mouth and sucking it against his teeth, mercilessly torturing the small bud until she was crying out and wrapping an arm around the back of his head. She held him against her, both begging him to keep sucking her while tugging at his hair and screaming at him to stop. Her pussy flooded and her legs jerked in response. She lifted her hips, a silent invitation that he took without further preliminaries.

Ivan slid an arm around her waist and lifted her against him. Her back arched and her head lolled back. She still clung to his head, her hand threaded through his dark hair. She felt him widen her thighs and press himself against her entrance. The touch, the brush of something against her felt so good it set off a small set of white hot explosions throughout her body. She cried out hoarsely and gripped him, holding him against her.

"You are such a good girl, Jaya," he groaned harshly. "Keep holding on, sweetheart."

She tightened her grip just as he entered her, his cock sliding into the depths of her tight pussy, forcing unused tissues to accept his invasion. She shrieked as intense pleasure turned to streaking pain. Before she had a chance to adjust, Ivan gripped her waist in both hands and sliding himself most of the way out, slammed back in, sending her spiralling upward once more, gasping, then reeling in pain again. He thrust over and over, finding a barbaric rhythm. She understood what he meant. He wasn't gentle, not even a little. But he wasn't selfish either. He was just spinning out of control, now that he was finally inside her, possessing her.

His hands tightened, his hold becoming brutal as he slammed into her body, his hips bruising her soft flesh. Yet something was happening to her, something in the way he was forcing himself inside, touching her, he was pushing all the buttons just right. She went rapidly over the edge of pain into ecstatic oblivion. While he pinned her upper arms to the bed, his eyes roving over her face, she flung her own head back, straining to reach the sacred place he was dragging her ruthlessly toward.

Each time he slammed into her, he sent her spiralling higher. She tilted her hips up slightly, meeting him thrust for thrust as much as she could. Finally, after what seemed an eternity she reached the peak, gliding over with one glorious thrust. She screamed her pleasure, her hoarse cry echoing in the room. She slitted her eyes and watched the gritted grin of satisfaction he gave.

Ivan continued to fuck her, his hips hitting the cushion of her thighs, his cock sending sparks of orgasmic waves through her vagina with each hit. She stretched beneath him as though reaching for more, glorying in peak after peak as he handed it to her. He let go of her arm and took her face in one big hand, covering half of it with his long fingers. "Mine, forever," he grunted.

She didn't say anything, couldn't say anything. Her breath was completely stolen away by what he was doing to her. He let go of her other arm and took her head in both hands, completely enveloping her, blocking her sight. She felt his lips cover hers just as he thrust savagely into her one last time sending another wave of pleasure crashing through her.

"You are mine," he growled against her lips, flooding her pussy with his seed.

CHAPTER SIXTEEN

Jaya yawned and then untangled her hand from the blankets to smother the yawn well after it was already finished. Someone nearby chuckled which prompted her to open her eyes. She tried the left one first since she was laying on her right side. Ivan was propped up on an elbow, his naked chest directly in front of her, his eyes on her face. The vision of his rippling, muscular torso was enough to prompt her to open the other eye, though she wasn't a morning person so the whole eye-opening thing was a pretty big sacrifice.

"Good morning, beautiful," Ivan said, his deep voice more relaxed than usual.

She tilted her head back on the pillow to give him a good looking over. The lines around his eyes and mouth seemed smoother, less severe. She licked her lips and blinked some of the sleep away. "Coffee?" she asked hopefully. Since coming to the island, she rarely woke up until her breakfast was served. What was the point? With an entire day of staring at walls and teaching Haty to spill the blood of their enemies, Jaya didn't really feel the need to rise early.

"Here," Ivan replied, reaching behind him for a cup.

Jaya sniffed the air and immediately perked up. She fought with the blankets for a few seconds and then shoved her way into a sitting position. As soon as she was up she remembered that she was naked. She grabbed for the falling cover and yanked it back up to her armpits, tucking it firmly into place. When she reached for her coffee, her eyes met Ivan's amused gaze. Her cheeks heated under his look and she squirmed a little, feeling the soreness between her thighs.

This prompted her to glance sideways down at her arm. Sure enough, fingerprint bruises were beginning to show against her dark skin. She chewed on her lip a little and then gave the other side a quick glance. Yup, there too. She knew she should be upset, but oddly the visible marks of his possession caused creeping warmth in her belly that swept lower.

She accepted the coffee and took a sip, watching him over the rim. The look he was giving her held a wealth of masculine possession. Even in her relative innocence, she recognized it. But there was something else there, something that sent an arrow of concern through her. Men like Ivan, men with more wealth and power than they could possibly use in several lifetimes, held the things they considered precious close.

She was about to ask him about the cage and her prisoner status when the sound of an airplane flying low overhead startled her and made Ivan frown. "What the fuck?" he snarled. He leapt to his feet and reached for his pants, yanking them on without underwear. He buckled his belt and pointed at her. "Stay here."

Jaya nodded, her eyes wide and guileless as he slammed out of the bedroom, leaving her alone and naked in the middle of the bed. She quickly remedied the latter by pulling on a long brightly patterned skirt and white blouse. Then she sat on the edge of the bed, sipped her coffee and did her best to calm her heart rate. She fully expected Ivan to return quickly. It wouldn't take him long to figure out what was happening and why there were suddenly aircraft flying over his private island. A private island with a military no fly zone order and a communications scrambler.

"Are we under attack?" Ivan demanded, throwing the door to his security room open. Keane was already present along with two other men.

"Not yet, sir," Keane was quick to supply. "But this bird is not friendly. This is definitely reconnaissance. Next step will be a strike team and if they're organized they'll be here inside of ten minutes. With half of our security systems still down from the canary's escape attempt yesterday, we need to get the fuck out of here."

Ivan nodded. "Give the order, clear the island. Walk with me." Keane fell into step with Ivan as he strode down the corridors, retracing his steps toward his private quarters. "We'll go with exit plan Delta since Jaya took out the helicopter."

Keane cleared his throat. "Hate to say it boss, but the first thing the girl did up on the roof was black out our communications. Must've been her that sent a signal."

Ivan stopped walking and looked at his second-in-command, his eyes cold and flat. "Do you think I wouldn't have realized that the moment I heard the UFA?"

"Sorry boss," Keane grunted.

They continued moving. "Don't waste my time again with useless speculation. Jaya will be questioned and dealt with appropriately. I want you to make sure all sensitive information is taken care of and the island is abandoned. You have seven minutes. I'll deal with the prisoner."

They split off. Keane jogged back toward the communications and security wing while Ivan threw open the door to his room. She was sitting cross-legged on the middle of his bed, her feet tucked under a long frilly skirt, her kitten curled in her lap and her book balanced on a knee. She looked up at him as he strode into the room, her dark hair streaming over her shoulders. Her eyes were speculative and wary but not curious. Absent was the question that should have been there if she'd been innocent.

"Did you reach the part where Cathy betrays Heathcliff?" Ivan asked, bitterness leaking into his voice. He knew he had no right to feel this way, knew that she wasn't actively trying to betray him by leaving or sending a signal for help. But the irrational part of him wanted her to pay. She was his, belonged to him. She'd touched something inside of him, mired herself within the blackness of his heart, and dammit, he wasn't going to let her claw her way out.

Jaya carefully slid a piece of paper between the pages, a torn page from another book she used as a bookmark, and closed Wuthering Heights. She tilted her chin up and stared at Ivan. "Yes, I've reached that point. But I don't see Cathy's seeking the comfort and luxury of another home as betrayal. Heathcliff left her to the dubious and abusive care of her older brother. She couldn't possibly stay where she was, waiting for him to come rescue her."

"He loved her, would have done anything for her," Ivan said, staring back at her, searching her face for answers. Something was off. She was more relaxed, more confident than he'd seen her since he'd taken her from her home. As though she knew something. "She should have waited for him."

"Why?" Jaya snapped, her brows drawing together in

annoyance. "She had no guarantee that he would come for her. She only knew that her situation was bad and going to stay that way unless she went with the best opportunity in the neighborhood. It's the same story for women all over the world."

Ivan made an impatient sound and reached for her arm, dragging her off the bed. Haty hissed and leapt off Jaya's lap, bounding off the edge of the bed and onto the floor. "We don't have time for this. I need to know right now who's coming to this island and what they're planning. Don't bother denying you had anything to do with it. We already know you sent a signal out when you knocked out our communications."

"I wasn't going to deny anything," she snapped, shoving against his chest. "Of course I did!"

Ivan didn't check his strength, he released her arm and as she tried to straighten, he slapped her. His open palm caught her hard on the side of the face spinning her halfway around and sending her back into the side of the bed. He dropped to his knee next to her and lifted his fist again but realized if he hit her like that with his full strength he really would cause damage. But fuck, she was tearing him apart. He wasn't used to these emotions, wasn't used to caring what another person did to him. If anyone near him got close enough to cause such harm, whether it was warranted or not, he would not hesitate to put that person down.

Ivan pulled the gun from his holster and pressed it against her temple. He expected fear. Complete and utter terror, like he'd seen on her face the day he'd killed the waiter in front of her. Instead, when Jaya turned her face to him, her cheek burning bright from his slap, her eyes held a maniacal fury. As though she were inviting him with her eyes to go ahead and shoot her in the head, because she would get the last laugh. And she would. Because Ivan knew, no matter how many more years he lived, he would not find another woman like Jaya. Even if she'd spent half their time together acting, lulling him into complacency. It just proved she was an even worthier partner than he'd ever believed.

"Tell me who you contacted and what the plan is," Ivan demanded, pressing the gun harder against her.

She didn't flinch or speak. It became clear that she wouldn't. Ivan knew he could get it out of her quickly, but the methods he would have to use would be brutal and she would be damaged beyond repair. He weighed his options while staring into the face of the beautiful, treacherous woman that had come to mean too much to him. Since he wanted her intact, he would have to get most of the information he needed later when he could use less invasive methods for extraction.

For now, he would earn her hatred another way. He pointed his gun at Haty, who was busy cleaning her fur a few feet away from the bottom of the bed. "Speak now, tell me the attack plan, or I kill your cat." Her mouth fell open and she lunged forward. Ivan slashed an arm around her middle, flinging her back and trapping her against the bed. "Speak!" he shouted in her face. "You have three seconds."

"Okay," she relented, staring at Haty, who was still oblivious to their fight. "I don't know the exact plan. He said he would come rescue me when I sent a message and try to capture you. I don't know anything else. Honest!"

"Who, Jaya?" Ivan demanded. "I want a name."

"I can't tell you!" she cried desperately, staring at her cat with wide, terrified eyes. "I don't know his name."

Ivan shoved a frustrated hand through his hair. He believed her. He stood up, reholstered his gun and hauled her to her feet. She stumbled and then stood staring stonily past him. She sniffed and swiped at her eyes. "I always knew you were going to use her against me," she whispered stiffly.

"We'll discuss this later, and Jaya." He shook her until she looked at him. "You will tell me everything I want to know."

She stuck her chin out and gave him a coolly blank look. He didn't like it. It reminded him too much of soldiers he'd worked with; people sent to do the work of men who had programmed them for certain jobs. Jobs that didn't necessarily require their survival. He gritted his teeth and pushed her toward her cage where Haty had taken refuge. "You have thirty seconds to grab whatever items you want to keep, we're leaving and we won't be back."

She didn't hesitate, she bent to grab her book, which had fallen to the floor when Ivan had hauled her off the bed and then she lunged toward Haty. She ran toward the bed, tipped one of the pillows upside down and shook the pillow out. Then she shoved her book and the protesting kitten inside. Ivan reached for her wrist and pulled her out of the room just as he heard the first plane approach the island.

"Motherfucker!" he shouted.

Jaya's eyes went wide and she stared at Ivan, her mouth opening in shock. As if she couldn't believe Armageddon was about to fall upon their heads while she was still in the compound. "Hang on to that pillowcase," he snapped and scooped her up, tossing her over his shoulder.

The first explosion hit the west wing, taking out his security rooms. The entire castle shook beneath his feet as he ran. Jaya clung to his back but thankfully didn't struggle and didn't make a sound. She just hung on as he hurtled through the deserted corridors. He hoped Keane and the rest of his team got out before the missile strike. He trusted his orders were being carried out swiftly and the men were waiting in the caverns with the submersible boats.

Another explosion hit the servants' quarters seconds later, rocking the building and sending a flash of heat over Ivan's head. Jaya let out a yelp as fire licked their backs. Ivan growled and dropped to his knee cradling her against his chest while they waited for the heat to abate. She clung to him, her arms snaking around his neck. Her lips found his throat and she mumbled something over and over.

Ivan dropped his head to listen. "I'm sorry, I didn't know," she whispered hoarsely. "I didn't know. I killed them all."

Ivan shook his head, took her hair in his fist and tilted her head so he could see her face. "Shh, sweetheart," he whispered against her. "No one's hurt, they all got off the island. Don't worry about them." He didn't know if everyone was safe and, at the moment, he didn't care. He just needed Jaya to hold her shit together long enough for him to get her to safety.

She shook her head, tears dripping down her cheeks and chin. "No, no, no!" she cried. "They're all dead, all blown to pieces. I should've died too. I should die with them. It's my fault."

Ivan realized then that she wasn't there with him, that she was locked in the horrors of her past. That the confrontation with him in the bedroom and the subsequent explosions were throwing her into a panic or a PTSD episode. He gripped her face between his hands and kissed her forehead then held her close against his chest. He had to get her out of there while they were still in one piece. Whoever she had sent a message to either thought she'd managed to escape or didn't give a fuck about her. If they survived the siege on his property Ivan was going to find out who the fucker was and dismember him. If it turned out the bastard knew Jaya was inside the castle when he started bombing, then Ivan was going to find new and creative ways to prolong his suffering.

"Time to go," he said gruffly and lifted her in his arms, making sure her wiggling suitcase was still cradled in her arms.

"I'm s-sorry," she mumbled and turned her head into his neck as he began to run again.

"I know, sweetheart."

The next explosion took out his guard station on the outside of the building. The percussive force rattled the castle and nearly knocked him off his feet, but he stayed upright and continued running. The next boom he heard came from the island and the one after that from over the island. He grinned and shouted, "Ground-to-air heat-seeking missiles!" as he approached Keane, who was standing at the end of the hallway, holding open the door to the underground tunnels.

"Thanks to the Saudis, these motherfuckers won't know what hit 'em," Keane said returning Ivan's grin. "What a beautiful sight that was." Keane nodded toward Jaya. "Get what you needed?"

Ivan shook his head. "We'll find out soon enough. Let's get the fuck out of here."

Keane grunted and let the giant fire door slam shut behind them. He locked it and set a timer so no one could follow them through. Now that they'd knocked the enemy bird out of the sky, it was a fair bet the island would soon be overrun with foot soldiers. They ran for miles through the subterranean tunnels until they reached the caverns where Ivan kept several submersible boats. Keane used to tease him about how Bond villain-esque the keeping of such contraptions were. Now they were all breathing a little easier as they had a guaranteed escape route that was highly unlikely to be blown out of the water.

Ivan climbed on board the nearest one with his package held firmly in his arms. She didn't even try to struggle, just sat quietly with her bundle on her lap. As the boat sped away from the island he turned to watch his home go up in flames just before they submerged.

"I'm sorry," Jaya whispered again, her head under his chin. The pillowcase was held firmly in her arms. It had finally stopped struggling but was still shaking.

Ivan nodded and kissed the top of her head breathing in her delicious scent. "You don't need to be sorry, my love," he said quietly, for her ears alone. "I'll fix everything so this this doesn't happen again."

CHAPTER SEVENTEEN

They arrived in Jakarta in a flurry of action. Jaya assumed that most of the activity was in securing Ivan's non-island residence. She wondered how many homes he had around the world, island or non-island. She herself had nothing to do with all the chaos as she was too busy sitting in a corner handcuffed to a chair. There was a guard whose entire job was to stand nearby and watch over her. At first she thought it was to make sure she didn't escape, but then she began to wonder if it was a safety thing as Ivan had stopped in to check on her welfare several times during the hours she was left sitting. He uncapped a water bottle and tilted it against her lips each time he came in for a visit. Once he gently touched the side of her face, his eyes lingering over the bruise on her cheekbone where he'd slapped her. He frowned, regret burning in his cool gaze for a just a moment before he turned away to leave her still chained to the chair.

So weird considering she'd essentially betrayed him and caused his beautiful castle to get blown up. She tried to suppress a shudder at that last thought. She still couldn't deal with the destruction caused by any type of bomb. Being so close to one was almost more than she could bear. She had to believe her adoptive father had no idea she was still on the island when he gave the order, that he believed she'd managed to escape as her message had implied. She didn't want to believe that his desire for revenge outweighed his feelings for her.

Ivan strode back into the room and nodded toward the guard, indicating the man could leave. He left without a word. She marvelled at how well Ivan's people were trained. Like dogs. And the ones that didn't fall into line quietly disappeared. Would she die? Would he finally kill her? She didn't really get why he was being so nice to her. He had slapped her, but it had been a heat of the moment thing, right after she'd essentially confessed to bringing him down. Or trying to anyway. Now he was back to being her lover, as though she was precious to him.

He pulled up a chair and sat opposite her. She straightened a little, though it didn't do much good. Ivan was still a half-foot taller than she was, even sitting. And though not uncomfortable, her hands were cuffed behind her back. She was at a definite disadvantage.

"I need you to give me some answers," he said, speaking in a slow, clear voice.

Again, it seemed strange. She had grown used to his coldness, his terrible, mechanical mind, his bleak intelligence. It was as if her escape attempt and near drowning had changed something in him. Something that not even finding out about her duplicity could shake. She didn't want to call it love because that wasn't an emotion she could associate with Ivan. She didn't think it was an emotion he even knew how to identify. But something about his obsession with her was taking a weirdly tender turn. She didn't like the way her body was reacting to his sudden caring, the way she softened around him. She needed to remember who he was and the things he'd done.

She called upon all of her training and stared past him, her face blank and her emotionless. She did her best to clear her mind and make sure her face didn't betray her. Ivan sighed and shifted slightly. "Okay, sweetheart," he said quietly. "That's what I thought. I was hoping you might be in more of a sharing mood since I've saved your life twice now."

She blinked at him skeptically. "Really? Because I'm pretty sure my life would never have been in danger if you hadn't kidnapped me in the first place."

He growled and leaned closer, getting in her face. She leaned back, but he followed her. "And I'm pretty fucking sure you were always a plant, my love. Someone meant to get your ass kidnapped and placed within my organization." Jaya had to swallow her gasp. It took everything she had to clamp her mouth shut and stare past him as though he hadn't just guessed her every move. He grabbed her jaw and forced her face up so her eyes were level with his. "You play a hell of a game of chess my beautiful slave. And you almost won that round."

She kept her gaze blank and said in an even voice, "I don't know what you mean." But her lips were trembling in fear. Would he kill her now that he guessed? Would the fledgling emotions she'd brought out in him be crushed under the weight of her betrayal?

Ivan pulled his lips back in a feral grin. She'd never seen him look at her that way, as though he were about to lose control but enjoying himself at the same time. The look terrified her almost more than the bombing. Maybe he was going to torture her. Maybe she had overestimated his regard for her. Maybe he'd only saved her from the castle and the bombing so he could torture her slower, more horribly later on, when he had the time.

"Now it's my move," he said and reached into his pocket. When she looked down she saw he was holding a needle. She frowned and tried to jerk back. He shook his head and smoothed her hair back, then dropped his hand to her arm, holding her still. He pulled the cover of the needle off with his teeth. "I tried asking nicely. Now you'll give me the answers I need."

He sank the needle into her arm.

Jaya let out a scream of outrage and squirmed in his arms while he held her. He continued to run his hands over her hair and body. She knew she should fight whatever he gave her, but she found his touch soothing. Finally, anger gave way to tears and she asked, "Wh-what did you give me?"

"Sodium pentothal," he told her immediately.

"You've drugged me," she moaned, trying to twist away.

"This is the best way I can think of to get the information without hurting you in the process," he explained.

She went limp against him. There was no point in fighting, he wasn't letting her get away from him and he wasn't going to let her hurt herself either. She turned her head to look at him with a frown. "Why are you even explaining this to me? In fact, why are you worried about hurting me at all?" she asked, confused. "A week ago you were all kinds of threatening. You even hurt me a few times. Now you can barely stand for me to bruise. What gives?"

"A week ago I hadn't watched you almost die in a situation I had a direct hand in creating," he said quietly, his voice threaded with a steel determination to make her understand something. "I don't care if you fell into my hands by my design, by yours or by someone else's. I've decided that you belong to me and that I don't want you harmed. It disturbs me greatly to see you suffer, so I will attempt to minimize the things that upset you."

Her mouth fell open and she stared at him. Unfortunately

she realized that she was staring for far too long and his edges were growing fuzzy. Damn, the medication he gave her was taking effect. But their conversation was extremely important. It sounded like it might have a direct impact on her future.

"B-but doesn't that mean that you only do nice things for me so you don't have to be uncomfortable yourself?" she asked blinking heavily. "That's insane, like a psychopath or sociopath or something."

He shrugged and continued to hold her against his chest, mindful of her hands, still chained behind her back to the chair. "I've never adhered to a label before, never been diagnosed by a doctor. But yes, to some extent my feelings and reactions were largely stamped out and twisted when I was a teenager. I observe the feelings of others. Usually if someone makes me uncomfortable I eliminate the feeling. But you're different, Jaya. You make me want to feel, want to pursue the comfort you can provide."

"How is this possible?" she whispered, desperately wishing she could touch the features that were now swimming in and out of her vision. "You've kidnapped me, taken my freedom. And you know I will betray you again, just as soon as I can."

He smiled down at her and smoothed his thumb over her mouth. She frowned and tried to move her head. When he wouldn't let her she bared her teeth and snapped at him. "I think you're ready to answer some questions, sweetheart."

"Okay," she whispered and smiled sleepily back.

"When you escaped, you sent a message. Is this correct?" he asked.

"No," she said immediately, enjoying the way he sifted his fingers through her hair.

"You didn't send a message?" he asked, sounding confused.

"Yes, I did, but I didn't escape." Was that her voice? It

sounded all garbled, like she was trying to force it through a long hollow tube. "You let me go. Remember?"

She felt a vibration run through his chest and thought maybe he laughed. "Okay, sweetheart. I let you go. Fair enough to say you ran amok and caused some damage. Now, please tell me what the message said."

She tried to reach up and touch his face. It was such a handsome face, with a gorgeous chiselled jaw, meant for fingers to slide along when it wasn't knotted in anger or concentration. She pulled on her hands, but they were restrained. She frowned and tried to look behind her only to discover that her head was swimming and unable to swivel back the way she wanted it to go.

"Whoa!" she gasped.

He readjusted his hold on her and gave her a little shake. Her gaze snapped back to his face and locked on his fascinating jaw. "Focus, Jaya. What did the message say?"

"Riiight..." She thought about it and then said, "They were coordinates to your location and a message that I was attempting to get off the island."

"So you knew about the strike?" he asked sharply.

"No," she denied and wiggled in his arms trying to touch him again. "Would never want all those people to die. But I knew he wanted you dead, thought maybe he'd find a way to come himself."

"Who is he, Jaya?"

"Father," she whispered.

He gripped her jaw and forced her head up so she was looking right at him. The storm in his eyes was brewing up to something big, something terrifying. "Your father is dead. Who is the man that sent you to me? Give me a name," he demanded.

"Father," she said again, her voice drifting as the dark fuzz surrounding him began to take over her vision.

His fingers clenched into her cheeks, hurting her. She whimpered and shifted her shoulders wanting to push him away. His grey eyes bored into hers as if trying to reach into her skull and yank the answers from her brain. She couldn't even remember what they'd been talking about. It had been a pleasant conversation until he got all intense and annoyed. She frowned, Ivan was always intense and annoyed though, he needed to loosen up, take some of whatever he gave her. She was drifting on clouds and he was leading her, talking way nicer than usual.

"Am I going back in the cage?" she asked, her voice wavering and her eyes closing.

Just before she fell asleep she heard him say, "You will always be my caged bird, Jaya."

CHAPTER EIGHTEEN

Jaya moaned and rolled over. Her head felt like someone was beating it from the inside out. She reached up and grabbed it in both hands to stop the crazy spinning. It helped a little, but then she realized her hands were free of restraint. She pried an eye open, slid her arms down to eye level and double-checked. Yes, she was no longer handcuffed. She shoved a fistful of thick, dark hair off her face and looked around. She was laying on a king bed, filled with fluffy blankets, located in a big, airy room. It was similar to the one on Ivan's island, except there were dark red hangings covering the balcony door, which she figured must be open since the hangings were fluttering in the breeze.

Jaya pushed herself up and sat. Her wrists jingled. She looked down and saw several gold bands interwoven together and wrapped around both of her wrists. She held her left one up and examined it. The bracelet was beautiful, intricate and barbaric. Very much an Ivan gift. And there didn't seem to be a visible latch.

"Hello Ms. Jaya," a soft voice said from near the door.

Jaya nearly jumped out of her skin. She glared suspiciously

at the newcomer, an older woman, probably in her early eighties, sitting in a chair. She had dark brown skin, darker than Jaya's and steel grey hair, pulled back in a low ponytail. She wore a blue dress with an orange and red scarf wrapped around her thin shoulders. On her lap sat a content looking Haty.

Jaya narrowed her eyes at the kitten. "You'll go to anyone that cuddles you," she grumbled and said under her breath, "Lap slut." She scanned the room, cataloguing escape routes. The woman was definitely no obstacle. She was fairly surprised that Ivan hadn't tied her down or put her in a cage. Hadn't she proven to him on the island that she was dangerous when left to roam free? Oh well, his bad. If he couldn't learn, then he'd have to deal with the consequences.

Jaya was in the process of sliding off the bed when a slight pain hit her arm, jolting her. She hissed and grabbed her arm over top of the bracelet. Her quick mind instantly figured out what had happened. Her gaze snapped up to the woman who was calmly holding a device in her hand. It looked like a smart phone. Jaya's mouth fell open and her eyes bulged.

"Why you sadistic old bitch!" she snarled and lunged out of the bed, intent on grabbing her kitten and taking the frail looking octogenarian down. The lady zapped her again, harder this time, hitting both arms. Jaya growled and grabbed her other wrist. "Stop doing that!"

"You need to sit down, young lady, and start listening," the woman said calmly. She placed Haty on the floor, who ran to her mistress and began frantically jumping at her, not at all pleased with the shouting. "Mr. Ivan was very clear that you were only to be disciplined in extreme circumstances. He will not be pleased about this at all."

"I don't give a flying fuck what Mr. Ivan wants," Jaya yelped, cradling her wrists against her chest, the kitten held firmly under her chin. "You're both insane. Everyone he associates with is insane! You fucking electrocuted me! What will his evil mind come up with next? That's it, back to plan A, stab the shit out of him and get the fuck out of this madhouse."

The woman nodded sympathetically. "You are understandably upset, I can see that." Jaya rolled her eyes and opened her mouth to start shouting again, but the lady held her hand up. "But let's not make it worse with words and plans you cannot take back. Please keep in mind that you are holding precious kitty, who will also get the zap if you must be brought to heel."

Jaya saw red and nearly lunged for the woman despite knowing she was in for a nasty shock if she did. The old woman seemed to sense Jaya's precarious mood because she took a firmer grip on the device and put a soothing hand up. "I am not here to harm you, Miss Jaya, simply to ensure you adhere to Mr. Ivan's rules. This way you will not be able to escape and bring harm to yourself again. Nor will he have to cage you anymore." Jaya opened her mouth, then closed it and lifted her wrist, shaking it significantly. She raised an eyebrow. The woman sighed. "You believe your cage has merely changed, perhaps become crueller even."

Jaya growled and stalked to the windows, shoving the hangings viciously to the side. The bright Indonesian sun streamed through the open doors, flooding the room. Jaya blinked several times, her face smoothing into a look of awe as she faced Jakarta from what, as far as she could tell, was the top of an extremely tall luxury high-rise. Looking down, she saw two more tiers before the high-rise seemed to drop off. Men that clearly belonged to Ivan were patrolling the floors below her. He must own at least three of the top floors of the building if not the entire thing.

She stiffened as she felt the woman come to stand beside her. "Ivan can be a cruel captor. In fact, from what I have heard, he usually is," she said softly. "But you are different. And it's not his captivity that is the problem, but the cage you've built within your heart and mind. He only seeks to protect you."

Jaya turned away and let the hanging fall back into place. "That's some kind of steaming pile of shit. You don't know me." She glared down at the old woman before shoving past her and stalking toward an open door she suspected led to the washroom. At least she hoped it did and wasn't about to get her ass shocked again. "The second I find a way to electrocute that psycho, we'll find out just how much he enjoys a dose of his own protection."

Jaya made another awful discovery while she was showering in the ensuite washroom. She was running a bar of soap over her shoulder when she touched a sore spot. "Ouch!" She frowned, set the soap in the tray and explored the tender spot with her fingertips. She wasn't totally surprised given the way she'd been tossed around by Ivan, the helicopter crash and the exploding castle. But this didn't feel like a bruise, it felt like a small cut with a bump underneath the skin. A suspicion took root in her mind and she decided to find out if she was correct.

She rinsed, turned the taps off and stepped out of the beautifully carved, stone shower stall. She wrapped a bath sheet around her body and swiped her hand over the condensation obscuring the mirror. Turning, she balanced her ass on the counter and tried to look at the back of her shoulder. When she couldn't quite see it, she tried gathering her wet hair around one hand and wiggling closer. She yelped in dismay when her hair tangled painfully in her new bracelet and she started to fall into the sink.

Strong hands gripped her waist, stopping her fall. Her eyes flew up to meet Ivan's clear grey gaze. She opened her mouth to yell at him, to tell him how much she despised him for everything he'd done to her and was continuing to do to her. He bent his head and captured her lips, thrusting his tongue into her open mouth. She made a sound of outrage and tugged on her hand to shove him away but ended up pulling painfully on her own hair. He held her by the back of the head and continued to kiss her while using his other hand to extract her hair from the bracelet. As soon as the strands were free she tried to give him a push but he took her wrists in his hands and pulled them behind her back, holding them firmly in one hand.

She tore her lips from his. "I hate you," she growled angrily. "You're a monster."

"I know," he said and swooped in, shoving her head back against the mirror so she couldn't retreat from his kiss again. His lips were warm against hers, his tongue like hot, smooth steel forcing its way into her mouth and conquering the territory within. She wanted to deny him, but her resolve began to melt as arrows of heat shot through her, stealing her breath and her denials.

She could feel the familiar swirls of heat swooping and curling within her belly, begging her to open up to him, to accept his kisses, the sweep of his hand across her body. She moaned and tried to jerk her legs closed when he stepped between them, shoving his hips in, and forcing her legs wider. It was like magic, the way he could touch her, seduce her and make her forget the horrors he could play out with his hands and his mind. He kissed a path down from her mouth to her throat, to her chest. He tugged the bath sheet until it fell away, revealing her breasts. He latched onto her nipple and sucked.

"Ahhh," she moaned and relaxed the tense muscles of her legs, resting them against his muscular thighs. "I-Ivan," she gasped wiggling on the counter, trying to get closer. She accidentally hit her shoulder against the mirror. Pain streaked through her and she cried out.

He lifted his head, frowning. "What is it?"

"It's the goddamn tracker you put in my back, asshole," she snarled, tugging to get her wrist free so she could feel the bump again. "It hurts!"

Some of the heat from his eyes cooled. He kept his grip on her wrists, holding them tight behind her waist. He tilted her forward, into his chest, pushed her hair to the side and examined the wound. "It's healing. You'll be fine."

"Fuck you!" she yelled up at him, her face inches from his. "I'm not fine. You're an evil murdering monster, and every move you make just proves how fucking bad you are."

He stared down at her, his eyes glacial. She could tell that he was affected by her words, even though she was certain he'd been called much worse in his life. She knew that very little affected Ivan, yet it seemed she had a substantial effect on him. Her words were like poison darts. She opened her mouth to keep up her tirade, to threaten him, but he cut her off.

"I may be a monster to most people, but I'm also the man that holds your life in his hands, Jaya," he said quietly. "I believe that someone placed you in my organization, close to me. Perhaps even conditioned you to hate me. But, sweetheart, the important thing is... I don't hate you. Because if I did, you would be dead."

She flung her head away from him, glaring. She didn't know how he could possibly know the things he did about her. She was positive she hadn't told him these things, not even when he'd drugged her. It was like every step they took was a chess move. Stalking each other across a board, one move forward, a step to the side and then pounce. How could he know that Father had been spewing venom about Ivan

Vogel as long as she'd known him? Somehow Ivan had guessed.

"I don't think my little Victory hates me as much as she professes," Ivan said, his voice deepening.

"Don't call me that!" she snarled, jerking in his arms.

"I'll call you anything I want," he said, his voice a deep purr. "You belong to me. My prize, my victory."

His hand dropped down to the rounded curve of her belly, through the patch of hair at the center of her thighs and into the soft folds. She jerked against him but was forced helpless, knees splayed wide by his hips. She felt a blush steal across her face as his fingers found the wetness he sought. She tried to close her legs, buck him away from her, but he leaned closer, pushed his fingers further down the inviting folds of her dripping pussy. "You are so very wet for me Jaya. Hate me all you want, sweetheart, your body isn't lying."

She yelled curses at him but opened her knees wider when he continued to glide his fingers over her, flicking her clitoris with his thumb. He spoke words of endearment to her in different languages, assuring her of his intent to hold and protect her. She alternated her angry tirade with moans of pleasure until she could feel her orgasm begin to build and she abandoned her anger, begging for the peak that seemed just out of reach. Ivan released her wrists.

Jaya immediately reached to shove him away, but Ivan held up the zapper. She glared at him and held her hands up. He tucked the device back in his pocket, took her hands and placed them on the counter. He took her by the hips and pulled her to the edge of the counter with her feet still up. She tried to wiggle back, not liking how exposed she was, but he gripped her by the waist and yanked her back.

"Don't move," he ordered.

"Or what?" she asked, her voice acidic. "You'll zap me?"

"No, you'll miss out on a life-altering orgasm," he said

matter-of-factly, dropping to his knees between her legs. The breath whooshed from her lungs and she tried to look down at him, but the moment she did he went to work. Her eyes rolled back, along with her head and she no longer cared about escape, locator chips or electrocution bracelets.

She felt him slide long fingers inside her vaginal passage. More than she could comfortably take, three at least. It was nearly painful at first, but as soon as she felt his hot, rough tongue glide over her clit she forgot her own name, along with the discomfort of too many fingers inside her body. Her legs began shaking and sounds she was pretty sure she'd never made before erupted from her throat. Just before she could leap off the cliff of her orgasm, he tore it away, like the meanest Santa ever. She shrieked angrily and reached for his head, determined to shove him back between her legs.

A jolt shot up her arm and she immediately slammed her hand back down on the counter, shouting, "You evil bastard!"

He chuckled and continued the pressure within her pussy, rubbing and pressing until she was ready to jump out of her skin. He alternated whatever he was doing with his hand and fingers with his tongue, swirling and gliding it over her clit and sucking at the juices that were flowing freely from her. A part of her brain, still fairly innocent and inexperienced, wanted to cringe in horror at the decadence he was introducing her to. The purely sexually selfish part of her wanted to take hold of this mind-blowing orgasm he was treating her to with both hands and hug it forever.

She approached the peak of wherever he was taking her so many times she was a sobbing mess by the time he allowed her to have the shiny rainbow-coloured super orgasm. He pressed something hard against her g-spot, nearly making her tear a chunk off the counter with her fingernails.

"Now, Jaya," he commanded and flicked his tongue hard against her clit while pressing into her g-spot.

Jaya came with a shriek, her body bowing off the counter, a rush of fluid soaking the hands and tongue of the man beneath her. He caught her as she fell, supporting her back and head so she wouldn't get hurt on the way down. He cradled her neck and held her for a moment, their eyes meeting. She expected softness. She was wrong. She met only glacial iciness and determined possession.

"Tell me who you belong to, Jaya," he demanded.

She opened her mouth to deny him, but her lips were shaking and no sound came out. Every part of her was still shaking. She licked her lips and shook her head. He growled and lifted her off his lap, standing with her. He turned her around and bent her facedown over the counter, holding her with a hand on the middle of the back. He unbuckled his pants and pulled the zipper down. She looked at herself in the mirror and saw a face flushed with hunger. She looked up at him and saw another face filled with determination and the need to stamp his dominance. A part of her wanted to deny him, to tell him she belonged to no one. But she knew it wasn't true. She'd always been a commodity. Besides, every particle of her being was screaming for his possession. She wanted to feel him inside and all over her.

He bent his knees to accommodate her shorter height, lined himself up behind her and pushed into her. She gasped as his thick cock pushed its way deep inside her body, filling her completely. Despite her orgasm and the wetness that coated her pussy and thighs, she still felt the burn of his entry. It felt beyond amazing. She pushed back against him, the plush curves of her ass hitting his carved abdominal muscles. He groaned, gripped her waist and began stroking himself inside her, using her silken passage to find his own pleasure.

"Oh god, yes!" she hissed reaching up to push against the mirror so her ass could press more tightly against him.

"You feel so fucking good," he growled. He took a fistful of her hair and forced her head up so they were both looking in the mirror. "Look at yourself. So beautiful while you're fucking me. Who do you belong to?"

Jaya bit her lip and shook her head.

He tightened his fist in her hair until she cried out. The streak of pain somehow heightened the sensations in her pussy until she was sure she was about to come again. She began panting. He twisted her head to the side and slammed harder into her, knocking her belly and hips into the counter. "Whose slave are you?" he grunted.

She couldn't shake her head, couldn't move. Just lay with her chest pressed down, the orgasmic sensations flowing through her body. When she still refused to acknowledge his demand he slapped her ass hard. She yelped, absorbing the pain and taking pleasure from it. He picked up the device that would sent a current through her and held it up to the mirror. "Last chance. Speak now."

She narrowed her eyes and widened her legs, taking his ever more brutal thrusts. She closed her eyes and breathed just as he hit her with a current of electricity. Instead of feeling pain, she felt intense exhilaration. She shrieked as she came, her heart slamming into her ribcage and her legs turning to jelly.

"Fucking beautiful," he growled. He leaned over her, his fist still in her hair and growled in her ear. "Talk, Jaya. Whose slave?"

She opened her eyes to look into his, seeing the stormy possession. "Yours," she sighed. His face reflected satisfaction. She heard the device hit the floor as Ivan thrust savagely into her. He pulled out and she had seconds to feel the loss before he was turning her and forcing her to her knees. She dropped before him in a daze. He held her hair in one hand while stroking himself with the other. Seconds later he bathed her chin and breasts in hot jets of cum.

"Whose are you?" he demanded, looking down at her.

"I'm yours," she whispered as he cupped her chin and tipped her face up to look at him, his thumb and fingers smearing the fluid into her skin.

"Mine."

CHAPTER NINETEEN

"This silence has to end."

Jaya turned to glance back at Ivan as he stepped out on the balcony to join her. She ignored him and continued to watch Jakarta at night, sure she would never get enough. It was by far the most breathtaking sight she'd ever seen. Though she was a millionaire many times over, Jaya was not actually well travelled. Well... that wasn't actually true. She'd travelled and lived on most of the world's continents. But she'd lived mostly in basements, in out-of-the-way backwood hovels where no one would think to look for her. Or find her if they were looking. Until Ivan.

"I will be forced to use unsavoury methods if you don't start talking, Jaya," he said impatiently.

This time when she refused to speak he grabbed her arm and swung her around to face him. She frowned and glared up at him, finally acknowledging his existence with a derisive snort. "Like what?" she asked. "Drug me? Hit me? You already tried those things. I'm not impressed, Ivan. Do your worst. I've been trained to withstand you."

He laughed, though the sound wasn't pleasant. "You have

no idea what I can do to you, little girl. You're the one person in the world I would hesitate to harm. Otherwise you would've already given me everything I wanted by now and been irreparably harmed in the process."

She shuddered but lifted her chin and refused to back down. "You don't scare me."

"You sound like a child," he said derisively with a shake of his head. "You were sent to me on purpose, a meal to a lion. Your so-called father could not have thought you would survive the experience of meeting me, yet he sent you anyway." She opened her mouth to reply, to deny him, but he shook her, squeezing her arm in a tight grip. "Do not bother to deny what we are both intelligent enough to know is true. You must simply look past the brainwashing."

She gritted her teeth and yanked on her arm. He refused to let her go, instead taking her other arm and forcing her back against his front. She struggled, but he simply waited her out. There wasn't much she could do. The only clothes he'd supplied were a selection of saris so she was already limited as her limbs were bound by flowing scarves and a long skirt. She wanted to scream and shout, but finally just huffed an annoyed breath and decided to stand stiffly in his arms. Unfortunately, her exertions made her breathe heavily and each intake of breath brought with it an inhalation of his delicious scent, tantalizing and teasing her until she was ready to scream.

Ivan Vogel was her enemy. Had been her enemy for twelve years. Since the moment Father had rescued her. Yet... Ivan was determined to keep her. To give her pleasure. To twist her against Father, to make her spill her secrets. The ones she was supposed to guard with her life. She was so confused.

He dropped his face against her neck and kissed her. "I don't want to hurt you anymore, sweetheart," he murmured. "Something is happening to me, to us. I can't stand the idea of hurting you. But if you don't give me something else, I'll have to hand you over to Keane. He doesn't have the attachment I've developed. He'll be able to get the information we need."

She jerked against him, her heart speeding up until she thought it would leap out of her chest and run away like a scared little rabbit. She and Keane had bonded a tiny bit but she was under no illusion that the giant Irishman wouldn't torture her for information. A sob erupted from her throat. "I don't want that," she whispered shakily. Of course she didn't. No one wanted to be fucking tortured.

"Then give me something," he said, resting his chin on her head. "Tell me something to stop me from handing you over. Because we need something, Jaya. I'm not trying to upset you needlessly, but this is a matter of your safety. Whoever is targeting me has shown a willingness to harm you as well and I won't have that. You are the key to finding this individual."

She gasped and twisted her head up to look at him. "Father would never hurt me!" she insisted trying to make him believe her.

He shook his head. "I think you're wrong."

Tears filled her eyes. "I don't know what to say," her voice took on a panicky edge. "I don't want Keane to torture me! But I can't betray Father either. He took me under his wing when I was vulnerable. He trained me, made me his protégé. He took care of me when no one else would."

Ivan's eyes gleamed in the darkness of the balcony and she realized that her words, as innocuous as they were, were exactly what Ivan wanted. He said as much, taking her by the shoulders and turning her to face him, the lights of Jakarta at her back. "You don't have to betray your adoptive father, Jaya. Just answer my questions as best you can. If you do that much, with as much honesty as you can, then I won't give you to Keane."

She thought about it for a second, a tear escaping her eye and streaking down her cheek. "It still feels like betrayal," she whispered. "Like I shouldn't be here with you. Touching you. H-he hates you so much. But you confuse me, Ivan."

Ivan's expression melted into something close to pity. He wrapped an arm around her and held her close. For once she accepted his comfort without putting up a struggle. She tucked her head beneath his chin and wrapped her arms around his waist. She felt a slight jolt of surprise go through him at her acquiescence, the first time since they'd met. Then he tightened his grip on her and gave her all the warm strength she could hope for. When they surfaced from the hug, he led her back into the room and sat her down on the bed.

"Answer as best you can, as truthfully as you can," he said gruffly, his voice softer now.

She nodded.

"When did you meet your adoptive father?"

She thought about it. There was no reason to withhold the information. "When I was thirteen."

He nodded and winced a little before smoothing his expression back to its usual granite. "Shortly after your family was killed then," he said. "You met him in Mumbai?"

She nodded, her gaze following him as he paced the floor of the bedroom.

"How did you meet him, Jaya?"

The uncompromising way he said her name told her Ivan wasn't going to give her a pass on this question. That he wanted to know the answer and she wasn't going to get away with the so-called silent treatment she'd been giving him. She bit her lip and tried to rapidly sift through information in her head so he couldn't identify Father through the story of how they met. It was a unique story, yet she didn't think it would immediately identify the man that adopted her off the streets of Mumbai.

"Speak, Jaya," Ivan demanded, stopping in front of her, his hands on his hips, his glacial eyes laser-focused on her.

She knew Ivan was giving her this one chance to have a conversation with him, to earn his trust, to find their way toward a mutual understanding that didn't include a lifetime of distrust, torture and cages, at least until she found a way to leave. She nodded and took a breath, then released it and began speaking. "After my family died, I was left penniless, homeless and completely without family. Within days I was shunted onto the streets and then days after that I was dirty and starving." Ivan made a sound as though he would interrupt so she shook her head. "It doesn't matter, I wasn't the only child to face a situation like that in India. At least I was smart and resourceful. Before long, I was running with a gang of thieves and pickpockets."

He nodded and sat beside her, picking her hand up. He remained quiet allowing her to continue the story. She glanced at him curiously. He was such a strange man, so driven, so brutal. Yet when he decided he wanted to make her part of his life, there was no hesitation. He softened a part of himself for her. She knew from his actions and words that it wasn't a usual occurrence for him to soften himself for a woman, or for anyone for that matter. She was special, an anomaly.

"I was a highly intelligent child, so picking pockets became a skill I rapidly adapted too," she said with a smirk. "Until I picked the wrong pocket. He noticed right away. Grabbed my scrawny wrist and shook it. I was holding his new phone in that hand. He threatened to cut my arm right off if I didn't give it back, which if course I did. He looked like the bogeyman on steroids. I hit the pavement, bowing and scraping and swearing never to steal anything from anyone ever again."

"Lies," Ivan chuckled.

She smiled a little and ducked her head with a shrug. "Of course. I wasn't about to starve in a gutter somewhere. Besides, I wasn't after his actual phone."

Ivan nodded, his eyes gleaming with pride. "Clever little girl, weren't you? Tell me what you did then."

Her slight smile turned into a full grin. "I cloned his phone, specifically the apps for financial institutions and credit cards. I usually targeted marks that looked wealthy and technologically advanced for the time."

"And what year would that be?" Ivan asked. "2005?"

"2006," she corrected him. Then gasped, slapped a hand over her mouth and scooted back on the bed. She shook her head and looked horrified. "I didn't mean to say that!"

Ivan placed a hand on her knee and wrapped long fingers around her. "It's okay sweetheart, calm down," he instructed, his voice firm. "There's no way we can identify Father from what little information you've given us. I'm a master at interrogation and you haven't betrayed anyone. You need to just relax."

She nodded, but she still felt torn up inside at what she'd accidentally said. Apparently the expression on her face told Ivan as much. He wrapped his arms around her and hauled her into his lap, rubbing his hands over her. He unwound the brightly patterned scarf from her shoulders and placed a kiss on her breastbone.

"Sweetheart, I really just want to hear more about what a clever child you were," he said, tilting her face up so she could read the honesty in his clear grey eyes. "You are a remarkable woman. And I want to know how such a woman was created. Please continue your story."

After a moment of thought she nodded and sniffled. "The

population of Mumbai in 2006 was around twelve point four million people. The odds of you tracing Father from what I've told you so far are pretty astronomical."

Ivan chuckled. "Indeed, I'd be at it for a long time if I tried to sift through the individuals. Please continue, Jaya."

She glanced up at him sharply to see if he was making fun of her. "Well, I cloned the phone and then I took the clone back to my makeshift home. Basically, a box in the slums with some stolen computer equipment. I ran a program that quickly cracked the passcodes and then I emptied his accounts, easy as pie." She said smugly. "Of course, I was too young to do more than set up a shell account to pour my stolen funds into. Didn't have ID and wasn't old enough to get any, but as soon as I turned sixteen my plan was to get some ID, transfer some money around and live like a queen in the Bahamas somewhere. At the time I didn't have all the kinks worked out of that plan, but I would've figured it out."

"I believe it. So what happened?" Ivan asked.

"He was smarter than my usual marks," she admitted. "Figured out what happened, how it happened and who did it. He watched the marketplace where I targeted him and caught me in the act, doing it to another rich mark. He dragged me right off the streets and into his fancy car. I seriously thought I was about to die, then and there. Instead, he offered to mentor me for a warm place to stay and regular meals."

"And you agreed?" Ivan asked skeptically.

"Of course not!" Jaya made a derisive sound. "A white dude offers a little Indian girl a place to stay and some food? Are you serious? No fucking way! I ran away so many times in the first few months, it makes what I did to your little island look like child's play."

Ivan started laughing. He couldn't help it. The way she spoke, the look on her face as she spoke, the solid belief in her own intelligence and abilities, she was his perfect match. He just wished she would wise up and realize it.

"Fuck. My. Life!" she snapped.

"What?" Ivan asked, still laughing.

"I just told you Father is Caucasian," she said with an annoyed sigh. "I may as well just draw you a map to his house and give you a family picture."

Ivan sobered quickly, his gaze caressing her beautiful features. "Yes, you really should, sweetheart. Because this is going to end in one way only. The death of the man you call Father. His threat to me has become a threat to you and that can't be allowed."

Her eyes took on a haunted look. "Ivan," she whispered. "I don't know what to do. I think I'm becoming attached to you, but I owe him so much."

He shook his head and smoothed the hair back from her face. "Don't worry about it. I'll take care of everything for you."

CHAPTER TWENTY

Ivan stopped next to Keane who was standing guard on one of the wide, tiered balconies a few levels down from the master room where Jaya was being kept. Keane didn't bother acknowledging his boss with more than a slight shift of his body. He kept his sharp gaze focused on the Jakarta skyline twinkling with life well below them. The semi-automatic rifle held firmly beneath his armpit looked more like an extension of his body than the deadly weapon it actually was.

"Thought I gave you the night off," Ivan chided, his voice cool. "I need my head of security in top shape and you've had a long day between the evacuation and setting up temporary residence here."

Keane grunted but ignored the comment. Ivan understood and let the disobedience slide. Keane was damn good at his job. He wouldn't trust anyone else to patrol key points on the perimeter their first night in the city. Keane was also good enough to know exactly how much sleep he needed to do his job effectively. Ivan would just have to trust him to be alert and functioning when he needed him.

"Did our wee canary start singing yet?" Keane asked while continuing to scan the high-rise buildings across from them.

Ivan snorted. He didn't enjoy the familiarity with which Keane spoke of Jaya, but he didn't correct the Irishman. He knew Keane did it partially to irritate Ivan and any reaction Ivan gave was a point to his asshole second-in-command. Ivan also recognized an admiration from Keane toward Jaya, and Keane didn't tend to admire anyone that couldn't either arm wrestle him to the ground or drink him under a table, preferably both. Hell, Keane was still on the fence about Ivan because he refused to drink himself stupid with the men. His admiration toward Jaya might keep her a little safer while under their care, which is why Ivan allowed the offensive familiarity.

"A little," Ivan said shortly.

Keane chortled. "Very helpful, boss. Considering I'm supposed to find the bastard that blew up your island. Feel like elaborating?"

Ivan felt like telling his man to go fuck himself. He didn't enjoy any type of conversation unless he was talking to Jaya. He sure as hell didn't explain himself to others. He gave instructions and issued orders, which were then immediately carried out. Now that Jaya was under their care the dynamics were beginning to change. They had to work together to ensure her safety and the security of Ivan's holdings.

He nodded and leaned against the edge of the balcony. "She calls him 'Father.' He's Caucasian, though that doesn't tell us much except that he's not native to India. She's been with him since she was thirteen and believes that he rescued her from life on the streets. I don't think the relationship was physically abusive, though it was damn sure emotionally abusive."

"Brainwashed," Keane muttered succinctly.

Ivan pushed himself back. "She hasn't said much, but it

would seem she's torn between a lifetime of being told I'm an evil prick who needs to be destroyed and seeing for herself that I won't hurt her."

Keane snorted his laughter. "Except you are an evil prick and you've hurt the girl several times since you've had her. What? You plan on brainwashing her the other way now? Convince the girl that life as a caged bird is preferable to the hate her so-called father was spewing? Good luck with that."

"Fuck you, man," Ivan growled, but there was laughter in his voice. He couldn't deny Keane's observation. The Irishman had a knack for cutting straight through bullshit. Ivan was convinced if he hadn't employed the man, he would've eventually ended up dead by saying the wrong thing to the wrong slaver.

"She say anything useful at all?" Keane pushed.

"She was grabbed while picking pockets on the streets of Mumbai. Her so-called father snatched her after she cloned his phone and emptied his accounts," Ivan couldn't keep the pride from his voice as he recounted the story. "She was still a child when she was fleecing grown men out of their gadgets and scamming all their money."

Keane forgot to keep his laser focus on the opposite building. He threw his head back and laughed. "That's our girl!" he chortled. "Can you imagine the things she could do for us if she were brought to heel? God damn!"

Ivan suppressed the grin threatening to break through his icy exterior and simply nodded. Yes, the thought of how much Jaya could help him grow his empire had certainly crossed his mind when he'd seen exactly how powerful her brain really was. But he'd also been given a taste of the devastation she could cause as well. Unfortunately, Jaya's mind was twisted with the hatred of another person and until Ivan was able to trace the source of the man who called himself her father, he couldn't risk allowing her free reign in his organization. Perhaps never. She was like dynamite; small, hot, unstable, unpredictable and ready to go off if placed in the wrong spot. No, Ivan was going to have to be very careful with this woman. She was too important to risk.

"For now, we protect her. Forget any thoughts of using her," Ivan said, his voice hardening. "There's no doubt that this Father person is willing to sacrifice her to get to me."

The humour drained from Keane's expression and he shifted back to guard mode, scanning the evening for threats. "Of course, boss. Nothing happens to the woman."

Ivan turned away and strode back across the deck. He stopped next to the pool and looked down at the water, backlit by blue lights beneath the surface. It was an inviting prospect on a hot and humid Indonesian evening, though he rarely swam. It seemed he was often too busy working to make time for leisure pursuits unless they were directly related to physical training. While swimming was a physical activity, he preferred to work out with his men. Not for the social aspect, but to make sure the regime was tough enough. He wanted his men in top physical shape, able to take on any type of combat threat that came at them. He and Keane worked with them until they could handle themselves with ballistic weapons and in hand-to-hand situations.

Ivan stepped back from the pool and glanced up, as if drawn to look toward Jaya's room, though he wasn't expecting to see her. He stopped moving the moment his eyes landed on her. She was watching him, had probably been watching him for awhile, a slice of light from the bedroom behind her giving her a halo. She was sitting on the top of the balcony, her arms crossed over her chest, her bare thigh curled over the edge. She was wearing one of his T-shirt's, probably the only thing she could dig up besides a sari.

Anger surged through Ivan as he watched Jaya carelessly place her life in danger yet again. From the way she lifted her brow and the stubborn set to her shoulders he could tell she was doing it on purpose, bucking her new cage. Ivan took the stairs two at a time as he headed toward the master bedroom, intent on dragging Jaya off the ledge and spanking her ass. Would he now have to lock her away from the balcony too? Fuck, she was a handful. And fuck if he wasn't enjoying every move they made across the chess board. Even the small ones.

He unlocked the bedroom door and strode inside. Siti met him at the door. She was wringing her hands, apologies spilling from her lips. "I tried to get her to come down, Sir, but she is very stubborn. I couldn't use the discipline as I feared I would shock her right off the ledge."

Ivan's fury nearly boiled over at the thought of this woman, whom he'd hired and instructed to watch over Jaya, using the bracelets to keep her in line. He'd hoped the woman would bond with Jaya, act as a mother figure to her. He'd given her control to the bracelets as a last resort, to stop Jaya from leaving. Not to shock her at will.

"Get the fuck out," he snarled, positive that if he spent another moment in her presence he would murder her. The only thing stopping him was his need to get Jaya off the ledge quickly. That and he didn't want Jaya to have to see another dead body just when she was getting used to a softer side of him.

Siti ran toward the door. Ivan grabbed her wrist, held it up and removed the device from her hand. "How many times have you shocked her?" he asked coolly. He was beginning to suspect Jaya was partially out on the balcony to escape the old woman's presence.

Fear flashed across her wrinkled face. "I truly don't know, sir. You told me to discipline the young Miss if she tried to escape and she had many thoughts of this kind. I tried to keep the setting low and only punish when she truly deserved."

Ivan kept his thoughts well shuttered so as not to alarm the woman. He released her wrist so he wouldn't be tempted to snap it. "I want you to go find Keane and describe each time you were forced to discipline your charge. Please be precise. He will want details."

Keane had a good stomach and he wasn't picky about his victims. He also had a strong sense of poetic justice. There was a good chance Siti was about to find out exactly how electroshock jolts felt while she was detailing her brief time with Jaya. He watched dispassionately as she scurried from the room, glad to escape the psychotic boss and his feral woman.

Ivan continued to the balcony, pushing the hangings back. He wasn't worried about startling Jaya, she knew he was coming the moment she spotted him by the pool. She didn't bother looking back at him, though she must have heard him approach. He stepped up to her, wrapped a hand firmly around her upper arm and held her. He wanted to haul her off the ledge, shake her and demand she stop putting herself in dangerous situations. But he also desperately wanted to understand what made Jaya tick.

"How many times did Siti shock you?" he asked quietly.

She turned to look at him, a frown creasing her lovely features. "Who?"

"The old woman."

"Oh her," Jaya said dismissively, turning her face away from him again.

"How many times?" he demanded sharply, his fingers tightening on her arm.

She shrugged. Instead of saying anything, she rubbed one of her wrists over top of the bracelet. Her actions were almost jerky, as though involuntary.

"Are you hiding out here?" he asked. "Sitting up on the ledge so she can't shock you again?"

Jaya blew out an annoyed breath and shrugged her shoulders again, this time trying to push him away. "I don't know," she said impatiently. "Maybe. She was getting on my nerves and Haty didn't like the tension so I decided to come out here. She tried to make me go back inside using the phone thing. I sat on the ledge to stop her. I thought she was going to use it anyway, but I think common sense stopped her." Jaya snickered. "I'm guessing your orders were for a lightly fried prisoner, not a pancake."

Ivan's need to immediately go and disembowel Siti warred with his need to check every inch of Jaya to make sure she was uninjured. Since he knew Siti was in Keane's sadistic hands, he decided to stay with Jaya.

"Enough of this nonsense," he said darkly and hauled her off the ledge, careful to pull her into his chest in case she struggled and accidentally threw her weight toward empty space. She didn't struggle. She let out a small sigh, turned and slid off the concrete barrier and into his arms.

"Did you send her away?" Jaya asked hopefully.

"Yes," he said firmly. "She won't be back."

"Thank you," she whispered, gratitude leaking into her voice.

He felt like a bastard. He didn't want her gratitude. He should have kept her safe. Siti was meant to be a measure of protection and comfort for a young woman who'd spent a lifetime away from the company of women. Instead he'd fucked up and chosen badly. He knew nothing about caring for the damaged woman he was falling in love with and he feared he was only making things worse for her.

Ivan led her off the balcony and sat her on the edge of the bed. He took both of her wrists in his hands and pushed the bracelets back as much as they would go so he could examine the delicate flesh beneath. What he saw made him grit his teeth and take several deep breaths to calm himself so he wouldn't do something stupid that might frighten Jaya. The skin of her arm, usually a smooth medium brown colour was red and chafed. It was beginning to bruise with dark purplish-blue marks. He ran his thumb over the tender, slightly swollen skin and felt like the worst sort of asshole for coming up with this method of controlling her. He touched a tiny mole on inside of her wrist and lifted it to his mouth, placing a gentle kiss on the mark.

"I regret that I was the cause of these injuries," he told her, trying to infuse sincerity into his voice. "I didn't mean for you to be so heavily punished, simply deterred from escaping."

She stared at him for a moment and then asked, "You don't apologize often, do you?"

He chuckled. "Never."

"So I'm special then."

"Very," he affirmed.

"Huh," she said, her voice taking on a tone that suggested she'd just learned something she could take advantage of.

"You're still wearing the bracelets, sweetheart," he pointed out. "Perhaps you shouldn't push your luck."

She lifted a shoulder and dropped it carelessly. "I think you'll only zap me for sexual titillation and that seems to float my boat too. I'm also guessing you're about to make that old bitch very uncomfortable for spending the entire day electrocuting the shit out of me, which also floats my boat. Now you'll have to think of something else to contain your captive since your cages aren't very effective anymore." Her voice ended on a purr and she dropped her eyelashes, looking at him from beneath the dark fringe.

He growled and reached for her, wrapping an arm around her waist and hauling her onto his lap where she was forced to straddle him. The T-shirt slid up her thighs exposing her panties. She wiggled until she was able to wrap her legs around his waist. He fisted his hand in her hair and tilted her head back so he could see her face.

"Your brain is so fucking beautiful," he said, his voice deepening. "Even as you plan to escape me, I crave your intelligence, crave to know what you're thinking every moment that you think it. You are so perfect, my lovely Jaya."

She whimpered and moved against him, her pupils dilating as passion began to ride her. He ran a hand down her back and cupped her ass, pulling her against his erection. Holding her head firmly in place he licked a path from her ear down her shoulder and back to the place where her neck met her shoulder. He bit down and sucked hard, marking her, claiming her. Her hips began moving, back and forth on top of him as she sought pleasure against the ridge of his cock, hard against the zip of his pants.

"You can try to fly away, baby," he growled against her, reaching between their bodies while she cried out her pleasure in his ear. "But you'll never escape. You belong to me now."

CHAPTER TWENTY-ONE

Jaya waited. One, two, three, four, five seconds passed. Finally, Ivan looked up. She grinned and waved at him from where she was sitting cross-legged on the ledge of the balcony. The look of deep concentration that had been stamped across his features twisted into a fierce scowl. He straightened from where he'd been bent over, grappling with one of his men in what she could only assume was some kind of fake combat situation; though the punches, elbows and kicks they slammed into each other's bodies looked real enough. She'd been enjoying her bird's eye view, watching the sweat drip from Ivan's hair, down his naked, rippling torso to soak into the low-slung waistband of his workout pants.

Ivan pointed a finger at her and growled something completely inaudible. Jaya laughed, swung her leg over the ledge and blew him a kiss. His opponent took advantage of Ivan's momentary distraction, driving a fist into Ivan's stomach. Ivan barely flinched, instead swiveling around, grabbing the man's head and bringing it down sharply onto his knee. Jaya winced as his nose shattered, spraying blood all over the beautiful tiles surrounding the pool deck. The guy dropped to his knees but bravely kept his hands down while Ivan spoke to him, presumably explaining where the guy went wrong.

Jaya's hand twitched to her face and she wrinkled her nose in sympathy. In a mock deep voice, she said, "If you manage to land a punch on your victim then you finish him. Don't wait for him to turn around and break your nose. We like to break shit around here. You're lucky I didn't stab you in the throat, I like doing that too." She switched her voice to a nasally falsetto when she noticed the bloody nosed guy speaking. "Yes sir, anything sir. I enjoy broken bones. Should I lick the shit off your shoes now, sir?"

Someone giggled from behind Jaya. She glanced over her shoulder catching sight of her new keeper, a young woman around the same age as Jaya. Her name was Ndari. The woman had been shadowing Jaya since the disappearance of Siti two days before. Jaya had tried hating the other woman on sight, but Ndari was oddly endearing. She chattered nonstop, enjoyed modern conveniences, laughed at her mistress's shenanigans and, best of all, didn't zap Jaya.

Jaya found it completely incongruous that Ivan would hire such a woman to care for her. Yet, he'd also felt really bad about the whole Siti-electrocution situation, though he hadn't removed the bracelets yet. She glared down at them darkly.

"Oh my holy mother!" Ndari exclaimed, taking a peek over the balcony. "I don't know what I did to deserve this post, but I will thank the gods when I die and go to heaven because nothing beats the treats in this place. Oh my god, Jaya, look at that one," she squealed, nodding her head toward the pool patio in a direction which could easily indicate any one of the dozen of half-naked sparring men. "I swear to god his six pack has a six pack. Is that even legal?"

Jaya burst out laughing. She'd been finding it difficult not to laugh in Ndari's presence. Her arrival had been a burst of much needed fresh air in a seriously oppressive atmosphere.

"I don't think there's anything legal about any of those men down there," Jaya replied, her own eyes glued to one man. He still watched her, but continued to spar, mindful of the distraction she created.

Ndari nodded seriously and then leaned more heavily against the concrete barrier for a better view. "So true. Arms dealing is dangerous work I suppose. They need to keep in top shape." She watched happily for a few moments, then her brows knitted together. "Oh shit, is the Master looking up here?"

Jaya laughed, "Not sure he's stopped looking up here, Ndari. I'm actually pretty impressed with his ability to kick ass while not looking at his opponent."

"Holy crappola! Quick, pretend you're being scolded!" Ndari turned to Jaya with a concentrated frown and began wagging a very dramatic finger in her face while still side-eyeing the guys. Jaya burst into laughter again and slapped a hand over her face. Ndari groaned. "He'll never believe I'm trying to get you down from there now. Quit laughing!"

"I'm sorry!" Jaya snorted trying to look like she was being properly chastised. "But seriously, where on Earth did Ivan find you? So far I haven't met a single person in his organization that hasn't had the personality beaten out of him."

"He can try, I suppose. But then he'd have to contend with my brother, his royal highness, Prince Sal Kamala," Ndari huffed, still frowning and waving her arms around while checking out the men at work. "Sally isn't super fond of me on the whole, but he wouldn't like to hear that I'm in pieces either."

"So your brother just handed you over to Ivan?" Jaya asked curiously. "To work as my keeper or something?"

She shrugged. "More like a companion. And yes, Sally was a little annoyed about the whole swimming naked in the Sea of the Ancestors thing, so he needed an expedient solution after my arrest. I'm actually not sure if it was the naked thing I was arrested for or being drunk as a skunk in a sacred place. Neither is acceptable behaviour for a female member of the royal family. Or a female. Or a human person in our country. Apparently, Ivan was looking for a new companion for you rather immediately and Sally needed to get me out of the country for a while. Things worked out well, didn't they, new friend of mine!"

Jaya stared at the other woman as though she were a unique creature that one didn't experience often in the wild. From the outside Ndari appeared to be everything the companion to a rich man's mistress should be; demure, conservative, somewhat pretty but not extraordinarily beautiful. But once she started chattering she lit up like the sun and revealed all sorts of interesting secrets. Her dark brown eyes sparkled with curiosity, and dimples flashed in her round cheeks when she smiled. She had even, white teeth, and small hands painted in henna. Her dark hair was cut to just past her shoulders and clipped behind her ears. She had a brightly patterned head scarf, but at the moment it was pushed back onto her shoulders. She wore jeans with rips in the thighs and knees and a Ralph Lauren polo shirt.

"Oh my god, look at that one, over there by the cabana! Does he not look like a god of war with all those muscles and that long rippling mane of hair, like a lion?" She made a growling sound. "The things I could make that man do once he was acquainted with my skillful tongue."

Jaya erupted into loud giggles again, drawing the attention of not just Ivan, but several of his men who glanced up at the watching women. As soon as Ivan realized his men were looking toward Jaya's bedroom, he snapped something that brought their attention quickly back to combat training. He pointed at Jaya, telling her silently to get off the ledge, but she refused, crossing her arms over her chest and lifting her chin defiantly.

Ivan snarled something at his sparring partner, who nodded sharply and stepped back. Ivan turned swiftly toward the penthouse, his long legs quickly eating up the distance. He seemed utterly careless that his men knew exactly where he was going, that he was drawn by his rebellious woman. It surprised her that he didn't care about his reputation. Was he that much in control of himself and the men around him?

"Well, I think it's around my break time," Ndari said quickly, backing away from Jaya, toward the safety of the bedroom and the doors beyond. "Not that you aren't perfectly wonderful to spend time with, but the thunderous expression on the Master's face doesn't bode well for the future comfort of anyone in this room."

Jaya swung her leg back over the ledge and hopped back onto the patio. She waved at Ndari as the woman made a beeline toward the exit. "See you later! Maybe take the east stairwell. Ivan will be coming up from the west."

"She is as smart as she is lovely," Ndari exclaimed before dashing out the door and running full tilt down the hall toward the east stairwell. Jaya was still laughing when Ivan slammed the door against the wall and strode into the room seconds later.

"Not even fucking locked," he snarled in disgust, throwing the door shut again and twisting the lock. He turned toward Jaya, a glower marring his ruggedly handsome face. "What're you looking so pleased about. I intend to blister your ass for continually putting yourself in danger. Maybe if you can't sit down, you won't sit on the fucking ledge."

She bit her lip in an attempt to look more serious but knew her dancing eyes were giving her away. His gaze swept over her, a habit that he seemed to enjoy each time he saw her after a few hours' absence, taking in her bared belly in the light green and gold sari she'd chosen. She'd left the wrap laying across the end of their bed. "Sorry, Ivan." She tried to sound chastened.

"No you aren't," he growled, taking a step toward her. Jaya's pulse sped up in anticipation of his touch. Whether rough or gentle, her body wanted him exactly the way he was right now; annoyed, half-naked and glistening from his morning workout.

"I could pretend I was sorrier than I really am," she said in a sultry voice, looking at him from beneath her eyelashes.

He stiffened, catching the drift of her thoughts. "Don't try to distract me," he snapped. "That's the second time I've caught you up there." *That he knows of*, Jaya thought, but wisely kept the thought to herself. "What the fuck were you thinking?"

"Oh, that's easy," she said, licking her lips. She stepped toward him and wrapped her arms around his waist. He reacted quickly, gripping her ponytail tightly and pulling her head back until she was forced to look up into his face.

"What are you doing, Jaya?" he asked, his voice dropping, the anger ebbing away. She enjoyed their sexual encounters, but so far, she hadn't initiated anything yet.

She smiled up at him and traced a finger across his jaw, teasing the days growth of whiskers there. "I'm showing you what I was thinking while I was sitting out on the ledge." Her voice dropped to a husky whisper, "Trust me, you'll like it."

He grunted and loosened his hold on her ponytail but didn't let go. She leaned forward, her hair sliding through his fingers, and licked him. She placed her tongue flat on the bottom of his pectoral muscle and ran it in a path over the tip of his nipple, which peaked and hardened, up to his shoulder where she stood on her toes and bit down, sinking her teeth into the muscle. Ivan groaned deep in his throat and slid his hand to the back of her neck, cupping her and holding her hard against his chest.

"Fuck, Jaya," he growled. "Were you really thinking about tasting me?"

"Yes," she whispered against him, her lips brushing his skin and sending a cascade of goosebumps across the smooth flesh, save for a small pucker inches away from her nose. She brought her hand up to touch it, dragging her nail across the scarred ridge.

"Bullet," he grunted, sifting his fingers through the fine hair of her ponytail. "Do you really want to taste me, Jaya?" he asked huskily, his grey eyes searching her upturned face. "All of me?"

She nodded and licked her lips, staring up at him wide-eyed. She lowered her lashes and then looked back at him, giving him her best hit of sultry. Apparently it worked. One hand tightened in her hair while the other wrapped around her waist and dragged her into his body for a quick, stinging kiss.

He released her lips and growled, "On your knees, sweetheart."

Her breath caught and her system flooded with sexy signals, urging her to do exactly as he commanded because the treats would be so worth the effort. She sank to her knees, his hand still wrapped in her hair, guiding her down. When her knees touched the floor, she placed her palms next to them too steady herself and looked up at him for his next instruction.

"Good girl," he growled and sifted his fingers through the ends of her ponytail. "Now take my cock out."

Jaya reached up eagerly. The bracelets jingled on her wrists, reminding her of her current incarceration. Instead of feeling anger though, she felt warm stimulation flood her system. Though she wanted to despise her captor, he was getting to her. The way he looked at her, touched her, protected her. Even the way he commanded her.

He wore sweat pants for his morning workout so she was able to easily roll the top down a few inches, reach inside and grasp his already rigid cock and pull it over top of the grey material. It bounced against his flat abs before she could properly grasp the hard flesh. The moment her fingers touched his penis, wrapping around him, he gasped, his fingers tightening in her hair.

"Now what?" she whispered.

He cupped the back of her head and urged her gently forward. "Now lick, sweetheart."

She happily complied, leaning forward on her knees, pressing her toes into the stone tiles beneath her for balance. She placed one hand on his thigh to steady herself while the other one remained firmly wrapped around his cock. First she licked her lips, anticipating licking, tasting, fucking him with her mouth. The thought made her mouth water.

She licked around the top edge, savouring the salty, masculine taste. She breathed him as she did it, wondering what kind of Ivan aphrodisiac seeped from his pores to drive her so wildly crazy. She could feel herself growing wet, her heartbeat pattering within her chest, picking up speed as her excitement grew. She flicked her eyes up and watched the heavy-lidded predatory enjoyment on his face. His granite jaw knotted and relaxed with each lick and swipe of her tongue. The hand at the back of her head just rested there, touching, not guiding or forcing her. She loved the comforting feel of his touch against her hair as she pleasured him in the most intimate way possible.

"Fuck, not going to last long like this," he grunted.

She glanced up and grinned around her mouthful of hardened cock. She could feel his gradual loss of control in the tightening of his stomach muscles, thighs and ass. In the way his nails scratched against her scalp around her ponytail as though he was holding himself back from grabbing her and forcing her down his length until she gagged and choked.

She slid her hand away from the base of his cock, giving herself more room to take him into her mouth. She choked a little, saliva pooling in her mouth and spilling out. He grunted as she bobbed up and down, further and further, using her now lubricated hand to explore his testicles. They were big, hairy and tight to his body. She felt them pulse as she raked her nails gently down them, sliding her forefinger along the seam.

"So fucking good, baby," he groaned, widening his legs.

"Mmmm," she murmured around him, vibrating him in her mouth. She lapped luxuriously at his cock and smiled again when it grew bigger, hardening further in her mouth. She loved the velvety feel of it gliding along her tongue and touching her lips. She loved playing with him, experimenting, sucking in her cheeks and seeing how he would react. Licking the ridges and then pretend swallowing while watching the ecstasy on his face.

"Going to come, can't stop." His gripped the back of her head in both hands and held her, but still he didn't force her.

She rolled her eyes up to watch him. He was staring down at her through half-closed eyelids, his eyes a stormy cauldron of heat. The look on his face was savage and beautiful, completely untamed. It was stunning. It stole her heart.

The first salty jets of liquid hit her tongue. She closed her eyes and swallowed, savouring the taste. Then she opened her eyes, moved her head back a little, opened her mouth and stuck her tongue out, taking the next hit across her lips and tongue. She licked her lips and swallowed the rest.

Ivan dropped next to her, dragged her onto his lap and took her mouth in a devouring kiss. She was surprised at first, but quickly wrapped her arms around his neck and accepted him into her mouth, enjoying the glide of his tongue over hers, rough compared to his cock. When he finally released her lips, she sighed happily and smiled.

He swiped a thumb over her slightly swollen lips and murmured, "Thank you, Jaya. That was a gift I won't soon forget."

"You're welcome," she whispered. "I hope it was good. I don't have a lot of experience."

His arms tightened around her and for a moment she thought he might get upset. He was such a possessive man when it came to her, she wouldn't put it past him not to get jealous over the two times she'd given blowjobs years ago and demand the men's names and current addresses.

"It was incredible, sweetheart," he told her. "But I must confess, it was my first time." She stared up at him in shock, speechless. She *knew* she was inexperienced, but she never in a million years would have thought Ivan lacked experience. He was just so... powerful and sure of himself. It didn't seem possible. He smiled grimly and continued to smooth his thumb over her lips and chin. "I've had plenty of opportunity, maybe a little desire. But women have always been a nuisance, a commodity, easily disposed. I haven't fucked the same one twice in years, I don't care if they get off, and I don't stay much longer than it takes to ejaculate into a condom."

Disgust began to replace the harmony that had filled Jaya. This was the man Father had warned her of, the Ivan that used people and discarded them, murdered them. She tried to push him away, but his arms locked around her, forcing her to stay on his lap.

"I've never trusted a woman enough to allow her to touch me with her mouth," he growled down at her, his steel grey eyes penetrating. "Never wanted that kind of vulnerability or loss of control. Only with you, Jaya."

"But you can't trust me," she blurted out, wanting to set him straight.

He smiled, his face hardening into its usual mask. But his eyes... they remained a heated liquid. They told her that she was wrong and that she belonged to him.

CHAPTER TWENTY-TWO

One of the worst things about Jaya's plan was tricking Ndari. She'd spent almost a full week in Ndari's company and she absolutely adored the little psycho. She was full of funny anecdotes, great advice and she loved Haty almost as much as Jaya did. And that was the second part of Jaya's plan that nearly tore a hole through her heart. She wouldn't be able to take Haty without causing suspicion. If she left without the kitten then Ivan would believe she legitimately planned to come back.

"What has your panties in a twist?" Ndari said from her upside-down position on the floor. She was laying on her back with her legs straight up against the side of the bed, her bare feet in the air. She was tossing Haty up above her head and catching her like she was a human toddler. The weird thing was every time the kitten landed or Ndari let her go, Haty came scrambling back for more.

Jaya turned on her toes and paced back across the room, glancing down at the strange pair as she passed. "Nothing, I just hate being cooped up like this all day, every day," she said, carefully controlled impatience leaking into her voice. "She's going to claw you in the face one of these times."

"I always wanted a nose piercing," Ndari said, tossing the kitten straight up. Haty twisted in the air, stretching her paws out in all four directions like she could fly, before allowing the woman underneath to catch her.

Jaya shook her head at the weirdness. "I don't think you'd get to choose where she puts the hole."

"And I don't think you're telling me the truth about your restlessness," Ndari grouched, throwing Haty up on the bed and rolling over onto her stomach. Haty leapt off the bed, jumped on Ndari's back and began kneading and purring. "For days you have paced this room, back and forth, too annoyed to stand still, yet unable to settle into a game or a decent conversation."

Jaya lifted an eyebrow at the other woman. "Are you complaining about my lack of companionship? Because last I checked, you were hired to keep me occupied, not the other way around."

Ndari snorted and tugged the playful kitten from its nest in her hair. "And last I checked I wasn't getting paid for this shit show of a job. I was just given to you as a happy alternative to jail time. But I can work harder at keeping you pleased if that's your desire." She pushed herself off the floor and made a show of dusting off her jeans and top. "Yeah, I heard what happened to your last companion. I have no interest in disembowelment so let us try to keep you happier than she did, oh depressive one."

Jaya's mouth fell open for a second and then she started laughing. "Yeah, you aren't sadistic like she was. And holy crap, I was kidnapped! I'm allowed to be annoyed about my circumstances."

Ndari shrugged and began pacing opposite of Jaya. "Meh, I think you should get over it and start enjoying life."

"And how exactly do you suggest I do that?" Jaya asked sceptically.

"Well, the man that holds you and has become enamored of you is also very rich, correct?" Ndari pointed out. "Start spending his money. I guarantee, there is happiness in spending. I very much enjoyed spending my brother's money before he sent me here."

"I have plenty of my own money," Jaya grumbled. "I was a world class hacker before he took me. I have bank accounts in countries all over the planet."

"Uh huh, well save it for a rainy day and start spending his dough. I bet it would make him happier too. He might see it as a sign that you're finally settling down and accepting all that he has to offer."

Jaya tipped her head to the side and thought about it for a moment. "Good point. Alright, Ndari, how do you suggest I spend his money? Usually I would shop online, but there's no chance that Ivan will let me near a laptop. And I doubt he's willing to let us go shopping the old-fashioned way. So, how else?"

Ndari grinned. "Don't be so pessimistic. I bet he'll let us go out with the proper escort of bodyguards with rippling muscles and a penchant towards protectiveness. You need a healthy excursion and he needs to see that he can trust you."

Jaya chewed on her bottom lip and then nodded slowly. "Alright, I think I agree with you. It's time I get out of this penthouse and into Jakarta."

"Perfect!" Ndari exclaimed brightly and gave Jaya a shove toward the door. "Now go convince Ivan we want to go shopping. I'm bored out of my mind and this companion needs a new pair of shoes."

"Why do I have to ask him? Isn't he more likely to say yes to you?" Jaya balked.

Ndari shook her head. "My goodness no! I prefer my guts

to stay exactly where they are. Off you go now love of Ivan's life."

Jaya blinked as she reached for the door and exited into the hallway. She gave the guard a half smile and explained her need to see Ivan. Since there were standing orders that she be allowed to see the boss whenever she wanted, he simply nodded and waved her ahead of him. As she and the guard walked away from the safety of her suite toward Ivan's office Jaya wondered if she had just been royally played by her royal highness, Princess Ndari instead of the other way around. The woman came across as both intensely flighty and uncannily intelligent.

Jaya was more than a little surprised when Ivan agreed to her request with very little argument. He seemed to believe that she could use a change in scenery and he was happy to indulge her sudden need to spend money in the bustling city. His only stipulation was that she and Ndari be escorted by his five most skilled men, including himself and Keane. Jaya was stunned that Ivan was willing to take her out on something so trivial as a shopping trip and waste such precious resources as his top men. But that was his choice and she wasn't about to argue. She virtually flew back to the room to tell Ndari about her success.

Ndari's jaw dropped. "You have got to be shitting me!" she said in shock.

Jaya narrowed her eyes. "You thought he'd say no?"

"I thought he'd lock your ass up tighter than the crown jewels I once paid a cat burglar to steal from my brother," Ndari replied and then threw a scarf at Jaya's face. "Here wrap this around your head. He's not going to want your face seen in public. I can't believe we're actually going out!"

"So you sent me into Ivan's office believing he would reject our plan and possibly freak out at me for suggesting a trip into the city? What the fuck, Ndari, you are seriously the worst friend!" Jaya grabbed the scarf and pulled it over her hair. She let it hang down and rest on her shoulders. She would pull it over the bottom half of her face later.

Ndari made a pssshhh sound and waved her hand through the air. "Pretty sure I'm your only friend, hacker chick."

"I have friends!" Jaya protested.

Ndari took her arm and pulled her from the room where half of their escort waited for them in the hall. "Uh huh," she said sceptically. "Friends don't let friends get kidnapped. Where were these so-called friends when you got your ass captured and caged?"

Jaya could feel the curious eyes of their escort all over the two women as they walked. Any conversation with Ndari was usually bizarre, plus they made a striking pair. Jaya wore a deep pink Sari edged in silver lace with a silver scarf while Ndari wore a pair of ripped up skinny jeans, red stilettos and a Sons of Anarchy T-shirt. Her beautiful black hair was covered with a patterned head scarf and she wore a pair of chic sunglasses.

"My friends have no idea what's happened to me. And I don't see you trying to bust my ass out of the gilded cage," Jaya pointed out.

Ndari goggled at her as they rounded the last of the stairs and stepped out into the bright sunlight. "I like you a lot, girl, I really do. But your ass is not worth getting my ass dismembered and mailed back to my brother in pieces over. Nope, let us just stick to the companionship part of our arrangement and forget about flying the coop. Oh look, the males are going to go shopping while armed with some very interesting weapons. Oh my, is that a grenade on the Irishman's belt?"

Jaya stepped up to Ivan and Keane who were waiting by the penthouse elevators. They were indeed well-armed for their excursion. Ivan was wearing a suit without a jacket, his shoulder holster clearly visible. Keane had at least three guns and a massive knife attached to his body armour as well as at least one grenade on his utility belt. The other guards were wearing similar amounts of weaponry. She was beginning to feel as though she were being escorted by a small army.

As they stepped onto the elevator she turned to Ivan and asked quietly, "Don't you think the bodyguards and weapons will draw attention to us?"

He glanced down at her and lifted one thick eyebrow. He didn't say anything. He didn't have to. That one look told her that he didn't care. His men were going with them and they were going armed to the teeth, no negotiation. She had no idea if the precaution was for her safety or to prevent her escape. She really hoped it was the former. She decided to just ignore the weapons overkill and try to enjoy her day. Though she didn't know how Ivan was planning on taking her shopping without drawing a whole lot of notice.

She soon discovered that it wouldn't be a problem. Ivan had no intention of frequenting the type of places where an armed escort of five men would draw notice. Instead he took Jaya and Ndari to only the most upscale stores in the high-end sections of Jakarta. While Ndari had a blast, spending Ivan's money like it was water, Jaya was disappointed. She wanted to see more of Jakarta. Not just the rich-rinsed, sanitised parts of the city.

Store after store happily paraded their wares in front of Jaya, Ndari and their bodyguards. It became quickly apparent that Jaya's plan to cause a scene and get herself lost in a crowd of marketplace shoppers wasn't going to happen. But she was highly intelligent and resourceful, she assessed the situation and came up with a new plan.

"I'd like to go to that jewelry store over there," she said, pressing her finger against the tinted window of the car they were in. They'd just finished shopping in a clothing store a street over. She would have liked the chance to wander the streets, looking at the different shops, but Ivan flat out refused to allow their party to do anything but drive from store to store.

"Ohmygodyes!" Ndari squealed as she leaned over Jaya to get a better look at the Tiffany and Co. jewellery store. "I definitely need a replacement tiara for the one that got stolen that time the cat burglar didn't listen to instructions correctly."

"And what do you need, Jaya?"

She swivelled her head to look at Ivan who was sitting across from her. His eyes were intent on her face and the tone of his voice was speculative. She lowered her lashes and glanced at his jacket and the bulge beneath where his gun was. He'd put his suit jacket on, covering his broad shoulders and the holster and weapon beneath while patiently escorting the women on their shopping spree. He looked relaxed, at ease, in the back of the car, but she knew he was ready for anything, including any move she might make to flee.

"I like to look at pretty things," she told him, trying not to betray the excitement in her voice. "I rarely went out when I lived on my own. I would shop online and almost never spent money on frivolous items. I upgraded my computer systems, shopped for necessary items like clothes and food, and I bought state-of-the-art tech equipment, but almost never found the time to shop for girly stuff. I find... I like to look at pretty and expensive things. Who knows, maybe I'll find something absurdly overpriced to spend your fortune on. Perhaps you'll decide I'm not worth the effort of keeping around."

"Hmm, I doubt it," he said, his eyes lingering on her face. He turned to address the driver. "Pull over up here, we're going to Tiffany's."

Ndari breezed into the store as though she'd been born and raised in a Tiffany's. She snapped her fingers at one of the sales assistants and asked where they kept the tiaras. Keane found the security officer, had a brief chat and shortly thereafter helped the man clear the store of any other customers. Ivan took Jaya by the arm and steered her toward a case. She took one look, shook her head and backed up, completely forgetting her plan for a moment. She hadn't been trying to get him into a jewellery store so they could peruse engagement rings together. He gave her another gentle tug forward.

"Just have a look," he murmured for her ears alone.

She narrowed her eyes at him as she took a step toward the counter, glancing around them to make sure the exchange wasn't witnessed. A salesperson hovered nearby but the icy persona Ivan projected stopped him from approaching. Smart decision.

"What part of our *relationship* makes you think we're ready for engagement rings?" Jaya hissed sarcastically tugging on her arm. "The part where you lock me up in cages or dungeons on a regular basis, put electrocution bracelets on my wrists and tracking chips in my back?" She glanced around again to make sure no one was looking at them. "Oh, I know! It must be the part where you keep threatening me and calling it love or whatever twisted emotion your hideous brain thinks this is."

His already cold grey gaze turned glacial and she shivered in his hold, wishing she'd kept her mouth shut. But Jaya had never been one to keep her mouth shut. Mostly because she lived a solitary life and hadn't learned the value of keeping silent around dangerous international arms dealers. And this one was beginning to look seriously pissed off. Well, if he didn't like this part of the Jaya show, he was definitely not going to like act two.

He leaned closer, until his lips brushed the tip of her ear. She noticed he did that when he was mad and really wanted her to hear the terrible thing he was about to say. She flinched, but his grip on her arm became tighter and he pulled her closer into his chest. "Perhaps, it is the part of our relationship where I refuse to let you go." He turned her in his arms until she was standing directly in front of the counter gazing down at row after row of indecently expensive sparkly diamond rings. "Ever." He tapped the glass hard with his left index finger. "Pick something, Jaya."

Jaya began sweating almost as soon as the rings came out. Not because of the symbolism, she could pretend the ring meant nothing to her. And since she was going to be long gone before it ever touched her hand, choosing one didn't really matter. Not because of the price tags on most of the beautiful solitaire diamonds; she could afford any one or all the rings herself if she wanted them. Hell, she should choose them all just to spite Ivan and his evil plans. No, she was freaking out because she was about to throw her plan into action and she was completely terrified. She was losing focus, constantly glancing at Ivan while he was encouraging the salesperson to bring out more rings for her to try on.

The salesman made the mistake of mentioning that it was store policy to bring out only one ring at a time. Ivan lifted an eyebrow and said in an arrogant drawl, "Change the policy. I want to see all the rings. If you have a problem with that then I'd be happy to speak to the owner. Though I promise you, if Miguel is forced to speak to me at this time of night in Brazil, he'll have your head."

The man swallowed audibly and stammered something unintelligible while reaching hesitantly for another tray of rings. Ivan reached for the ring on the counter and pulled Jaya's hand forward, pushing it gently on the third finger of her left hand. She glanced down at it. A shudder rippled through her frame as she stared at the huge gaudy diamond, set in a gold band and surrounded by two rows of tiny diamonds. She didn't even have a chance to reject it before

Ivan was pulling it from her finger and tossing it back on the counter.

"Next," he said coldly.

"Jaya!"

She twisted around and glanced toward the back of the store where Ndari was trying on tiaras. Despite the anxiety flooding her system she couldn't help but laugh at the woman. She'd shoved her head scarf back onto her shoulders and was now wearing a ridiculous amount of diamonds perched on her shiny sable head. It looked pretty funny with her rocker T-shirt and jeans.

"Gorgeous," Jaya announced.

"Get your depressive ass over here and try on some crowns," Ndari shouted turning back to the alarmed looking salesperson. "I think we will require a matching set. Or perhaps a best friend set. You know, like those friend bracelets where each friend gets half a heart and then we're friends forever. Only with tiaras instead of bracelets. And not half a tiara, because I'm not willing to compromise and give up half my crown since I am, in fact, a real-life princess."

Jaya burst out laughing and tugged at the hand that Ivan still had firmly in his grasp. He'd pushed another ring onto her finger. She didn't even glance at him. Instead she said pleadingly, "Just for a minute, Ivan. I really think I want an indecently expensive best friend tiara."

Something about the happiness shining in her gaze and her spontaneous smile must have swayed him. As though he knew he'd finally done something right in engaging a companion of an appropriate age and temperament. He nodded indulgently and released her hand, allowing her to cross the store. She held her breath half expecting him to follow her, the possessiveness he felt over her and his wariness of taking her out in public urging him to keep close, but he continued to linger over the engagement rings only his eyes following her as she crossed to stand at Ndari's side.

She let out a slow breath and barely noticed as the other woman perched a jewel encrusted tiara on her head, chattering away while fluffing Jaya's hair around her shoulders. "Absolutely perfect! Just look at you." She spun Jaya around, nearly knocking her into the glass case until she was facing a long-suffering salesman who was helpfully holding up a mirror. "It's not exactly the same as my tiara, but I think the sapphires in this one really bring out your skin tone."

Ordinarily, Jaya would be enjoying herself while choosing outrageously priced, useless jewellery and sparring with Ndari but she had other things on her mind. Like calculating the exact distances between the security gates when she brought them down. She was nervous and unhappy and torn about the decision she felt she had to make. A part of her didn't want to leave Ivan. Okay, a big part of her. But she knew she had to. She'd been trained for half her life to believe he was an evil villain and he'd done very little to prove otherwise. She believed he was becoming attached to her, and his attachment was intoxicating, but she owed her loyalty to someone else. With that last thought, she set her plan into motion.

She yanked the tiara from her head and said to the salesman, "I don't like it, show me another." When he reached for it she tossed it just out of his reach. His eyes popped wide in horror as the precious item sailed past his outstretched hand and hit the floor. Jaya barely stopped an eye roll from slowing her down. The jewelry was hardier than the glass cases they were showcased in. Which she fully intended to utilize to her benefit. The second he bent over she grabbed Ndari and yanked her around the counter with her, shoving her down. Then, before anyone could stop her, as all eyes in the store were now on her, she grabbed one of the smaller earring cases, picked it up and slammed it into the big display case, shattering the glass.

"Holy mother of all that is not good!" Ndari gasped, jumping back from the flying glass and covering her face.

Jaya let go of Ndari's wrist, her eyes glued to Ivan as he lunged toward her, his face twisted in fury. He was too late. Security gates all around the store fell into place cutting them off. He was locked in the front of the store with a salesman and a security guard while Keane was locked in a separate section with another security guard. Jaya, Ndari and the other salesperson was at the back of the store behind the heaviest gate, locked in with the computer system, exactly where she'd been hoping to be.

The rest of Ivan's security team were locked outside the store. She had to work fast if she wanted to escape before he managed to organize them. Men shouted all around her, but she ignored them, put her head down and worked, her fingers flying across the computer's keyboard. She quickly and easily hacked into the Tiffany's security system and made sure all access to the building was denied to Ivan's men while checking on her own escape routes, then catalogued a plan B and C just in case she was cut off. She was in the process of hacking into the security systems for the other shops in the building when she was wrenched away from the computer. She lost her balance and fell hard against the counter, cutting her arm when she reached out, touching the jagged glass.

She looked up in surprise. She'd completely forgotten about the salesman. He'd jumped out of the way so quickly, she hadn't thought him brave enough to step in when she began reigning chaos. He was frowning and wringing his hands at the mess she'd made, his wire-rimmed glasses askew on his long nose, his suit somewhat ruffled. She was about to slap him silly and get back to her hack job when a shot rang out. She shrieked and jumped back, slamming into a stunned Ndari as the salesman went down in a spray of blood.

Jaya whipped around to stare at Ivan whose gun was now aimed at the store security guard. The guard's face was leached of all colour and he was holding his hands up, no weapons visible. Though the gates separated them, they didn't stop bullets from flying around the store.

"No one touches her," Ivan growled, his furious gaze still glued to Jaya. "Are we clear?"

No one answered for a moment as stunned silence continued to hold everyone immobile. Then Keane said, "Yes, boss." He reached toward the shaking store security guard, who he was locked in with and took the gun from his holster. "I'll just be taking this so you ain't tempted."

Ndari continued to clutch Jaya's arm, her fingernails digging into the skin, her breathing harsh in Jaya's ear. Jaya could feel blood dripping freely down her arm from where she was cut but she couldn't seem to move. Couldn't tear her eyes from Ivan's cool, angry gaze. In one rash act she'd changed everything. Now there was nowhere to go but forward, because if he got his hands on her he was going to lock her up tighter than ever. Tracking chips, electrocution bracelets and armed guards would be the least of her problems.

"What next, Jaya," he said coldly, setting his hands on the counter next to the engagement rings. The gun clicked as it hit the glass. She could almost see the vibration go up his arm as fury ripped through him, but he held it in check, knowing there was nothing he could do to her now while they were separated by the gates and he was unwilling to put a bullet in her. "It's your move."

CHAPTER TWENTY-THREE

Jaya ignored him and turned back to the computer, typing as fast as she could, knowing that she was losing precious seconds. Ivan was just as quick witted as she. The more time he had to work the problem, the less likely she would be able to escape. She glanced up to see him speaking rapidly into his phone, his voice short and clipped. Another glance through the Tiffany's window showed his men separating, one going left and the other right to cover the other exits. It was a fair bet that he would have more of his men on their way from the high-rise.

"Oh my god, Jaya!" Ndari exclaimed weakly. "Look at your arm."

Jaya didn't respond, instead hunching her shoulders over the store computer. She pounded her fist against the counter in frustration. "Come on you piece of shit!" She glanced at the other salesman, the one Ivan hadn't killed yet. "Tell your boss, that guy Miguel or whatever, that he needs to upgrade your system. This one is slower than a turtle racing to its own death."

The guy opened his mouth to respond, but when Ivan's

head swiveled toward him, he ducked behind the case of engagement rings and hid. Ndari pulled the scarf from her neck and began wrapping it around Jaya's arm, tucking the ends in. Jaya ignored her, gritting her teeth against the pain as she continued to work. Seconds later she got what she wanted. A hiss sounded from above them and water began spraying all over the jewellery cases. She laughed out loud at her success, only mildly annoyed at how long it took to hack the system. She cocked her head to the side. Yup, she could hear screams and shouts coming from the other stores. She'd tripped the fire system across the entire building.

"Very clever, Jaya." Ivan's deep voice reached through the misty spray.

She glanced up and gave him a cocky grin. "Have a nice life, Ivan. Hopefully we won't run into each other again." She turned on her heel and sprinted for the side door that would now grant her access to the inside of the strip mall. She'd tripped the release when she hit the fire alarm. It was a safety precaution so no one would get trapped in a burning building.

"Don't you touch that fucking door!" Ivan shouted after her. She heard the sound of shattering glass just as she rounded the corner to the back office and assumed he must have finally lost his temper.

She was reaching for the door when she heard Keane yell, "Go with her Princess and don't you let her out of your sight."

"Okay, but I refuse to take responsibility when she's like this. Like a feral cat or something, you just can't please her. I mean I thought the tiara looked amazing!"

Jaya peeked through the side door and didn't see any of Ivan's men running. She hadn't expected them to be on the inside of the shopping centre anyway. He would have sent them to cover the back entrance, not expecting this escape route. She'd hadn't seen it on the building blueprints but had been relatively certain it would exist when they'd passed the outdoor shopping centre. She'd helped Katie Pullman, cat burglar extraordinaire, and many others pull off enough heists that she knew how most buildings were set up.

She tried her best to blend in with the crowd, which wouldn't have been easy, due to Ivan's insistence on her always wearing traditional sari's, except everyone around her was soaking wet. No one paid any attention to her, despite her strangely wrapped bleeding arm and the shouting tiara-wearing princess trailing after her.

She stumbled against a good-looking man who was trying to shelter under the awning of an upscale sandwich bistro. Sliding her hand into his jacket, she lowered her lashes and murmured an apology, making sure to thrust her soaking wet cleavage and swath of bared belly out. He was polite enough to glance down at the assets she was so kindly putting on display. He grinned and assured her that he was perfectly fine. He opened his mouth to say something else but Jaya spun away from him, running in the opposite direction, an irate princess hot on her heels.

The lovely high-end stores were now pretty much empty. She would be quickly caught by either Ivan or one of his men if she didn't leave the vicinity immediately. She took about five more steps when Ndari caught up with her, careful to take hold of her good arm. She was smart enough not to stop Jaya. Instead, she simply held on for the ride and ran with her.

"Where are we off to, my dearest tiara buddy?" Ndari puffed from beside her, nearly losing her footing as the heel of her stiletto skidded along the wet marble floor. Jaya caught her and then, thinking fast, pushed Ndari into another store. Swarovski's jewellery store. Apparently Tiffany's had some competition in the shopping complex. Ndari gasped and reached out to grab hold of something. Unfortunately, she took hold of a display case full of diamond bracelets, which went crashing to the floor in a shower of sparkles. Two security guards converged on her while Jaya mouthed 'sorry' and began running.

She knew that the main exits were going to be monitored by now, so that left the roof or the parking garage. She decided against the roof since she wouldn't be able to get off quickly enough. She would have to go to the parking garage. She hurtled toward the stairs leading down, hitting the door so hard it hammered against the wall. There were no sprinklers in the stairwell because the heavy doors were fire resistant. Her waterlogged shoes squished as she ran down the stairs and she had to remind herself to slow down lest she slip on the concrete and hurt herself. Then who would Ivan murder in bloody revenge for hurting her? She snickered hysterically at that thought as she shoved the basement door open and ran into the parking area.

Perfect! There was a nice selection of fancy cars to choose from and no uppity owners to get annoyed with her need to steal one. Though she dearly wanted to go with the aqua blue Lamborghini, she decided perhaps something a little more understated would be more likely to help her escape. So, channeling her ex-employer's wife, Riley Hart, she set about hot-wiring a cute little Maserati. She didn't have any practical experience, but after getting to know Katie's little pack of misfits, she'd decided to learn. It didn't take her long to get into the car and disable the alarm. Though it did take several precious minutes for her to overcome the electronic operation before she finally got the engine to turn over.

"Yes!" she shouted, sitting upright in the seat, her arm shaking with weakness. The scarf was soaked through with blood. She put the car in gear and hit the gas, racing forward through the dim tunnel-like underground garage. She was about to reach for the seatbelt when a shadowy figure stepped out in front of the car.

"Fuck!" she shouted slamming her foot down on the brake. She wasn't used to driving a vehicle of any kind, but especially not standard transmission and she stalled the car. She was thrown into the steering wheel, the impact knocking the breath from her. She pushed herself back and glanced fearfully up, knowing exactly who would be standing in front of her stolen car.

Ivan stood tall and solid, his legs spread, his eyes focused entirely on Jaya through the windshield of the Maserati. He'd discarded his suit jacket. He looked breathtaking, his soaking wet shirt plastered to the muscles of his chest, his dark hair slicked back like he'd run a frustrated hand through the wet mass. His thick eyebrows were lowered as though permanently set in a frown. What stole Jaya's breath wasn't the sheer masculine beauty she faced with. It was the empty holster tucked against his side, the gun held in his fist, ready to fire and the look in his eyes that told her that her latest escape attempt would end in severe punishment.

Next to Ivan, held tight with his hand wrapped around her arm was Ndari. His gun was pressed against her temple. Gone was the usual playfulness on Ndari's face. There was now only terror and the acceptance that a very dangerous man with the intention of murdering her held her. Jaya's eyes met Ndari's and tears spilled from her lashes. They both knew Ivan could reach Jaya and get her from the car if he wanted. There was no way she could start the engine again before he was able to get her out and back into his custody. No, this was punishment for her flight. He'd tested her and she'd failed, leaving the moment the cage door opened.

She screamed and reached out for her friend, begging him not to do it. She turned to claw at the door, attempting to get to them, knowing it wouldn't be in time.

Something banged against the car making Jaya jump. Her eyes flew open and she stared up at the horrific tableau in front of her. Ivan still held Ndari, but he'd dropped his gun hand and slammed it against the hood of the car. His face was ice cold, but his eyes were a raging inferno of anger.

"Get the fuck out," he snarled.

She reached for the door with shaking hands, pushing it open. She glanced down at the blood that flowed freely from her arm to drip onto the doorframe and the concrete below. As she gripped the door with her good hand and pulled herself out, she wondered exactly how bad she'd cut herself. She'd been too preoccupied with escape to really pay attention before. But now that the garage was beginning to swim around her, she thought perhaps the blood loss was somewhat significant.

Something else caught her attention, something that sparkled for a second in the dim lighting of the underground tunnel. She forced her darkening vision to focus on her left hand as she carefully rounded the car toward Ivan. She was still wearing a beautiful diamond solitaire engagement ring. She let out a weak, bitter laugh. It was perfect. A large, beautifully cut square diamond set in a simple claw with a white gold band. Somehow the ring he'd thrust onto her finger just before she'd unleashed chaos in the jewellery store was exactly the ring she would have chosen.

As soon as she was close enough Ivan gripped her shoulder and dragged her around the front of the car, pushing her back against the hood. He pinned her, his fingers wrapping around her neck. Even in his anger, his grip wasn't overly tight, his fingers not hurtful. She could feel the tension thrumming from his body, his arm and through to his hand. He fought with himself, struggled to maintain his cool.

"Tell me why," he snarled.

Jaya blinked up at him, trying to stave off the black fuzziness that ate at the edges of her vision. She licked her lips and shook her head sadly. "I w-was always going to run," she said quietly. "You knew that, Ivan. A part of you wants to test me, see if I'll finally stay, but deep down you know I'll always run. Because you can't keep something that doesn't want you unless you keep it locked up."

His fingers squeezed just a little tighter, a reminder of her fragility. "I know," he growled, acknowledging the truthfulness of her words. "That wasn't what I was asking. I want to know why I didn't shoot her to punish you." He flicked his gun back toward Ndari who squeaked and jumped back a step. "We both know I would have. There's no conscience stopping me."

Jaya studied him, feeling her consciousness begin to slip away. She blinked a few more times, forcing herself back to wakefulness. She glanced at Ndari who was hovering with a look of deep concern on her face. Jaya wanted to tell her to run, to save herself in case Ivan changed his mind and killed her in bloody retaliation for Jaya's escape attempt. But she needed to stay awake long enough to have this conversation.

"You can't love me... can you?" The words burst from her lips in a denial, but as soon as she saw rage morph his features for a split second she knew she was correct.

He stood, looming over her, his stormy eyes taking her in her sadly bedraggled state. There was no sympathy evident in his gaze. "Anyone else would be well past dead for the things you have said and done to me."

Her lips parted as she took in his words. The intensity, the meaning. "You love me," she whispered.

"Of course," he snarled. "Only a sadistic fuck like me would fall in love and do what I've done to you. Would lock up a woman and throw away the key. Which is exactly what I'm doing, Jaya. This thing between us is forever. Consider it as good as a marriage."

"Dear god," she whispered.

She should have run farther, faster. Should've just run him

over when he stepped in front of the car. Because now he knew her thoughts, her desperate need to escape and return to Father. Now he would never trust her, would watch her every move. It could be months, years even, before another opportunity to leave arose. She was well and truly fucked.

He said something else, his hands tightening on her, but she didn't hear. She finally allowed herself to succumb to the swirling blackness that had been threatening to swallow her up. It was safer than contemplating a future as Ivan's wife.

CHAPTER TWENTY-FOUR

It occurred to Jaya, as she fought to swim back through the currents of her fuzzy mind toward wakefulness, that she'd never in her life been unconscious until she met Ivan. She'd never needed surgery, never been knocked out or hit in the head. Her luck had definitely taken a turn for the worse when she met the evil arms dealer with a penchant for drugging her and placing her in extreme situations. Perhaps, she would mention this when the shitstorm of his inevitable anger came down upon her head.

His was the first voice she recognized as she began to wake up. His deep baritone was a sharp reprimand that she couldn't escape, though she didn't think she was the recipient of his displeasure this time. She tried to lift her lashes, tried to move her limbs as she waded toward the low murmur of voices, but couldn't seem to get her own body to respond to her commands. As though he knew she was surfacing, Ivan's voice drifted closer, his lips brushing against the edge of her ear, his voice taking on a quieter tone, though she still heard the dark promise within, the need to deliver pain as he spoke. "Take it slow, Jaya. You lost a lot of blood."

She tried to speak, but no sound emerged. She sucked her lips in, wetted them, and tried again. "Ndari..." she whispered.

Jaya could sense Ivan's disappointment. His hand fell on her body, ran down from her shoulder, where his thumb briefly caressed her collar bone before falling to her arm and wrapping around it possessively as if to remind her to whom she belonged, of her current fragility. That she shouldn't be asking for someone else while at his mercy. She wanted to explain her desperate need to make sure that the other woman still lived, that he hadn't punished her while Jaya was asleep. She didn't trust him. But she was too weak to do more than murmur for her companion and pray that he would comply.

He shifted on the mattress next to her and turned to say sharply to someone, "Get the princess."

"Yes sir." The voice belonged to Keane. She heard a door shut. Jaya let out a sigh, happy her friend was still alive.

As the seconds ticked by, silence weighed heavily in the room. Ivan's hands felt like chains, pinning her to the bed beneath her back, though his hold wasn't hard. Somehow the intent within his heart bled through his veins, making the air around them stormy and sinister. Though the last thing Jaya wanted to do was face him, she forced her eyes open and turned her head. What she saw chilled everything within her. His face was like granite, much the same as when she'd first met him. Except for his eyes; his eyes were on fire. They held possession, love, anger and punishment. He didn't even attempt to hide his truth from her. He wanted her to know everything he felt.

She shivered and looked away, glancing around the room. She was back in the bedroom she shared with Ivan, tucked carefully beneath the covers. She looked down at her arm, resting on top of a pillow. It was wrapped in a thick bandage from wrist to elbow. She asked in a tentative voice, "How bad?"

"Sixteen stitches," he said coolly. "You didn't need a blood transfusion, though it was close. I had the best plastic surgeon in the city brought in to make sure the stitching was flawless."

She nodded and flexed her fingers then curled them as though about to type on a keyboard. Pain shot through her arm. She winced and relaxed the muscles, allowing her arm to drop back onto the pillow. Ivan watched dispassionately. "I-is there any permanent damage?" she asked hesitantly.

He didn't answer for a moment. She glanced back at him, studying his face. She knew exactly what he was thinking; the same thing as she. He was replaying each moment of her escape up to and including the moment she got hurt and then every minute after until he recaptured her. His face darkened as their eyes met and his hand fell on her good wrist, tightening while he thought about how close he came to losing her.

"No permanent damage," he growled.

She stared up at him helplessly and watched the storm brewing within. She knew something awful was coming but didn't know what. He'd admitted to loving her. But he was not a good man. So what did being loved by a man like Ivan Vogel mean? She suspected she was about to find out.

"You betrayed me," he said, ice and fury clashing in his voice. She could feel the barely leashed vibrations running through him.

He was well and truly pissed at her. "I've betrayed you before, run away before, remember?" she said. She twisted her wrist in an attempt to pull it from his hold. He tightened his grip, pressing the metal of her bracelet into her flesh.

"Not like this," he said coldly, his grey eyes flickering

down her body outlined beneath the covers. "I've given you every chance to settle down. I've given you more chances than I would have given any other person. You knew better and yet you did it anyway."

She sighed and lifted her injured hand, wincing as she did, and pushed a swath of hair from her forehead before letting her arm drop again. He made an annoyed sound and lifted her wrist back onto the pillow, elevating it. "I had to... had to get to Father," she said quietly. "I don't belong here anymore."

He took her chin in a hard grip and forced her to look at him. "You aren't going anywhere, ever," he said. His words were said with such quiet decisiveness that she had no choice but to believe him. "If you make any more attempts to leave I will kill someone you love. Starting with the princess, then your precious cat, then your American friend, Katie Pullman."

Tears filled her eyes and she shook her head. "I-I don't believe you." She tried to call his bluff, though every part of her screamed that he wasn't lying. She knew what this man was capable of.

He stood and leaned over her, placing his hands on either side of her body and caging her in with his tall body. He blocked out the bright Indonesian sunlight and any comfort she might have found in the open balcony doors with the hangings thrown wide, allowing a breeze to flow through.

"You know the dreams that I have, the night terrors?" When she nodded, he continued. "They aren't about my family, not really. In them I'm reliving what I did to the families of the men that mowed down my village. How I stalked and hunted them. How I maimed and murdered, not just men, but women and children... elderly... everyone. I killed them all, and Jaya, I enjoyed every moment of it. If I could go back, I would. Just so I could relive those moments, spill the blood that runs through the veins of my enemies. Only this time, I would utilize the patience I've learned over the years. If I could go back, I would prolong their suffering, explain to them why they were dying with such bloody brutality."

"Stop!" she gasped, trying to wrench her chin from his grasp. The horrors of what he was describing were playing out vividly in her mind. He refused to let her go.

"Never." He leaned closer, until his lips brushed against hers in a soft parody of gentleness while his words hit her like bullets. His icy grey eyes pinned her to the bed with maniacal fervor. "I will never let you go, Jaya. And you will never again underestimate me or I will make you regret it."

She shivered helplessly, pressing back against the pillows. "How can you want to keep me this way? Doesn't it matter to you that you'll never know my love?" Her words came out in a plea.

He shook his head. "It would seem we are past the point where I can force your love. Now I will have to keep you any way I can have you." He leaned forward and pressed his lips against hers again. As always there was a jolt between them as currents of attraction passed from one to the other. He leaned back far enough to whisper, "Remember, I will kill the things you love if you betray me again."

She nodded, a tear leaking from the corner of her eye and spilling across her cheek to drip from her chin. She gulped back the sobs that threatened to burst from her lips. He released her and stood back, watching her coolly as she struggled to collect herself. When she finally had her emotions under control, she looked up at him and said, "What now? Will you put me back in a cage?"

He shook his head. "No, I think you understand how serious I am. I'm hoping I won't have to make an example out of any of your friends. If you agree to my terms then I can allow you the freedom of my property and limited excursions into the city with the appropriate permissions and an armed escort."

"If I agree to your terms?" she repeated with a bitter laugh and pushed herself up into a sitting position on the bed. He reached out to help her. She wanted to shove him away but held herself stiffly in the circle of his arms while he fluffed the pillows against her back and settled her once more. She closed her eyes and tried to enjoy the strength in his arms and the clean, masculine scent that lingered in the air around him. "You haven't given me any choice. Of course I agree that you shouldn't kill any of the people I love."

He nodded and gestured toward the door. "Then you'll have the freedom to move around at will."

She stared up at him angrily, chewing on her lips for a moment, before finally snapping, "I always fucking knew you were going to use Haty against me. I wish you'd never given her to me, you bastard!"

He lifted a shoulder in response, his gaze never leaving her. "That was never my intention when I made her a gift. But your safety is more important than anything else and I will use any and every method at my disposal to get you to settle down and accept your situation. If that means using your cat against you, then so be it."

Jaya opened her mouth to shoot back another furious response, but a short knock cut her off. Ivan strode to the door and allowed Ndari entrance. Keane stood at Ndari's back, his gaze unfocused and unfriendly. He didn't step into the room with the princess. Ndari glanced hesitantly at her boss, who stood tall and imposing by the door, before walking to Jaya's beside with Haty clutched in her arms. She dropped the kitten on the bed and sat gingerly beside Jaya. She refused to look at Jaya though, tears filling her eyes. Jaya understood. She'd used Ndari to escape and nearly gotten her killed in the process. She probably wouldn't be so forgiving either. Still,

Jaya wrapped her good arm around her friend and finally allowed the tears to fall freely. It was with a great deal of relief that Jaya heard the door close and saw, when she glanced up, that Ivan had left the women alone in the room.

After a moment, Ndari loosened up and hugged Jaya back. They cried together for a few minutes, the intensity of their shared experience making words difficult to find. When they finally separated and made eye contact Jaya was the first to speak, bursting into an anguished apology, "I'm so sorry, Ndari, so fucking sorry. You nearly died, and it was all my fault!"

"No, I'm sorry!" Ndari exclaimed, choking on the words. "I should've been a better friend. I should've been more serious, should've found a way to help you leave. I r-really thought he was going to kill me. Then when he got hold of you I thought he was going to kill you too. Jaya, I've never been so scared in my life."

Haty, who had been sniffing the sterilized bandage on Jaya's arm became disturbed by the intense emotion swirling around her. She meowed loudly, ran up Jaya's chest and burrowed under her hair. Both women laughed, releasing some of the tension. The kitten had grown bigger. Now her grey and white striped butt poked out from beneath Jaya's chin when she tried to hide.

"You don't have to worry that Ivan'll hurt either one of us again," Jaya said sadly, reaching up to stroke Haty soothingly. "I'm not going anywhere. He's convinced me never to try another escape attempt again."

Ndari's face, already drawn and serious, became even more so. She nodded slightly, staring down at the bed for a long time, a faraway look in her eyes. Finally, she said, "I have always fought for the concept of free will and when I couldn't have free will, I insisted on free thought. The man that professes to love you, my friend Jaya, nearly took my free will, my free thought and my life from me today." Angry tears filled her eyes. The dark orbs focused and moved to Jaya's face. "My brother is a powerful man. If and when we decide we want to leave, there is not a soul on this planet that will stop us."

CHAPTER TWENTY-FIVE

How did they get the pool such a deep, lovely strangely unnatural shade of blue, Jaya wondered? She tilted forward a little more and squinted at the bottom, marvelling at, not only the colour, but the gorgeous brightly patterned orange, red and purple underwater tiles. It was like a lovely sunset built into the bottom of the swimming pool. She leaned over so far on her crossed legs, trying to trace the pattern with her eyes to see if there was an actual picture that the tips of her dark hair touched the water, turning from dark brown to black.

"Chemicals." A hand came down on her shoulder, stopping her forward momentum. "Watch yourself. Boss doesn't want you in the pool yet, canary."

Jaya twisted her head to look up at the towering redhead and then winced when she looked directly into the intensely bright sunlight. She lifted her good hand to shade her eyes and pulled an exaggerated face. "Boss doesn't like much, Keane."

He grinned at her, then had a quick look around to make sure no one saw him touching Ivan's woman. He wisely took his hands off her immediately after she was safe from taking an unauthorized swim, then squatted next to her, settling on his haunches. "No, I don't s'pose he does. But at least he cares enough to keep you safe."

She shrugged and leaned back on her arms, making sure to put most of her weight on her good arm. She uncurled her legs and dipped them in the water ignoring the fluttering hem of her skirt as it soaked up the water. It had been nearly a week since her escape attempt and true to his word, Ivan had given her free run of his Jakarta home. Though she did *not* have free access to technology, she had found the week oddly relaxing. She'd seen very little of Ivan, except for at night, when he'd insisted they share a bed. He hadn't made any sexual advances while she'd been recovering from her injury. He had simply held her, his chest to her back, while they slept, then slipped out in the morning before she woke, though she'd felt the ghost of his kiss against her temple before he left.

She giggled as she watched the hem of her skirt swirl in the water and thought maybe it looked a little like a fish swimming around her ankles, especially in the lovely unnatural chemically induced cerulean water. She couldn't wait until her arm was healed enough that she could go swimming. Though she wondered how that would work. First of all, she would have to learn how to actually swim, and second, she couldn't imagine Ivan being okay with his men seeing her in a bathing suit. Yet he wouldn't want her to swim unguarded. Then again, he wouldn't want her to swim without a bathing suit.

"He'll swim with you himself," Keane's amused voice answered what she thought had been an unspoken musing. "The men'll stay close, but not too close."

"Did I say that out loud?" she asked, shading her eyes to look over at him again.

"Indeed," he chuckled. "How're them pain meds treating you?"

"So good!" she said enthusiastically, grinning up at him. "Never been sick or hurt or anything before. Prescription drugs are pretty awesome." She frowned and lifted her injured arm, wiggling her fingers. The pain was gradually diminishing each day. "But getting cut and having stitches sucks. I don't think I'll do that again."

"Good plan, canary," Keane agreed easily. He glanced around with interest. "Where's your princess at?"

"Hiding," Jaya said honestly.

Keane's gaze sharpened, and he frowned. "Yeah," he said gruffly. "What from?"

"Not what," Jaya answered, kicking her feet out and spraying water in a wide arc. "Who."

Keane didn't say anything for a moment. He studied the rooftops across from them, his practiced eyes taking in every detail with militaristic precision. Jaya tried to follow his gaze, tried to see what he saw, but her brain was slowed down by the pain meds and she wasn't trained to take in every possible danger, every possible scenario. She looked at everything through innocent eyes, curious what he could be seeing that was different from what she was seeing.

"Who's she hiding from?" he finally asked, as though the words took effort. Because he already suspected, but he wanted her to answer out loud, tell him why a relationship between himself and a woman like Ndari would be impossible.

Jaya blinked and glanced at the giant tattooed redhead out of the corner of her eye. She hadn't expected Keane to care about her off-the-wall companion, but he seemed to harbour a soft spot for the nutty princess. "She's a free spirit," Jaya said softly. "She's spunky, fun and a bit wild. Ivan put a gun to her head and threatened her life because of me. She's not going to get over that quickly. She doesn't want to see men with guns right now." Her eyes flickered down to the semi-automatic tucked under Keane's arm. "Can you blame her?"

He grunted and shifted a little. "Guess not," he sighed.

His facial features hardened a little. As though he was realizing he had no hope with someone like the princess. Too bad. Keane didn't seem like such a bad guy. Then again, neither did Ivan when he was kissing her on the head, gifting her with kittens and saving her from drowning. It was all the other horrific things he did that made him a terrible person. She shifted on the patio tiles suddenly uncomfortable with her thoughts. She wanted to hate Ivan. She didn't want to think about the things he did for her.

She cleared her throat and lifted her legs to the side as though about to get up. Keane surprised her by putting a broad hand on her knees and stopping her. His long, work-roughened fingers curved around her, holding her in place. She didn't feel threatened exactly, but she didn't feel at ease. She knew she couldn't leave in that moment, even if she wanted to. Keane was too much like his master. She was sharply reminded of the time Ivan threatened to hand her over to Keane for questioning when she refused to tell them anything about Father. Her heartbeat picked up and she had to remind herself that she was safe, that Ivan would never allow any harm to befall her. She glanced quickly around to make sure they weren't alone and was gratified to see other men patrolling the pool deck. Then she felt foolish. Keane had been nothing but solicitous of her all week while she'd been healing, while his boss had been absent. She forced herself to relax and look up at him curiously. His own gaze was uncannily knowing, as though he knew every single thought that had flickered through her brain and was patiently waiting for her to sort through her emotions.

She nodded her head. "What's up?" she asked a little breathlessly.

He moved his hand. Touching her was a definite no no, but he still did it. As though he believed it was worth Ivan's wrath to make that connection with her. She respected him for the effort, though she wished he wouldn't. He unsettled her almost as much as his boss.

He took a deep breath and looked around the patio area, then shifted to a more comfortable position. She frowned and stopped kicking her feet in the water. The rugged Irishman looked directly at her when he spoke, his accent was still strong, but his words more pronounced than usual. "You ever heard of brainwashing before? Like when a person has been taken by another person or group and spent years told something until they believe it?"

It was like being hit by a bucket of ice water. Jaya wasn't stupid. She knew what he was getting at. She gritted her teeth and stared hard at the water between her feet, concentrating on the bright colours. But they no longer mattered, no longer seemed cheerful. The drugs that floated in her system no longer carried her on a happy cloud. She suddenly crashed back to reality.

"I have no idea what you're talking about," she said dully.

"Then you're stupider than I thought," he shot back.

Her head snapped to the side and she glared at him. "Fuck you!"

"Calm yerself, I'm trying to help," he growled low, for her ears only. "I like you and I been around for awhile. I can make sure you survive the boss intact, canary. Now listen up, you need to hear what I have to say, cause I know all about this brainwashing bullshit."

She yanked her feet out of the water and twisted her knees to the side trying to escape Ivan's persistent second-in-command. "Stop!" she snapped. "I don't have to hear this, Ivan would be pissed if he knew."

Keane shrugged. "Maybe. But you'll be alive." He leaned back and casually placed one long, muscular arm behind her back, trapping her where she sat. The curve of the pool on the other side made it difficult for her to get up and leave unless she wanted to go for a swim. She tried to lean away from him but her injured arm wouldn't take the weight. She had to settle for glaring. He smirked and continued speaking. "When I was a young man I used to compete in strongman competitions. Won 'em all. Fame went to my head. I would drink and whore and gamble until I spent all the winnings."

"No surprise there," Ndari said haughtily, plopping down on Jaya's other side. She tugged Jaya's injured arm into her lap and scooted right up against her side. Jaya smiled in relief at seeing her friend out and about. "You are the biggest man-whore I've ever had the misfortune to share a rooftop with."

Keane snorted and eyed Ndari with interest, taking in her bare legs in a pair of short shorts. She dropped her legs into the pool next to Jaya's. "And how exactly would you know that?" he asked. "You're the only two women up here besides a sixty-year-old house cleaner and I haven't touched any of you."

"Just look at you," Ndari said accusingly, waving her hand toward him. "It's pretty obvious that you like to stick your wick in anything that moves. There isn't a discerning bone in your body, obviously." The note of disdain in her tone was impossible to miss. Jaya thought Ndari was just asking for trouble, especially if the look on Keane's face was anything to go by.

"Anyway..." Jaya interrupted, rolling her eyes, "you were saying."

"Yes, as I was saying," Keane murmured, eyeing Ndari as though she were his next meal. "When the money ran out and I was between competitions, I had to find work. Weren't much I was good for. Just fighting and fucking." They both ignored Ndari's 'ah ha!' as he continued speaking. "Soon I was picking up mercenary contracts. They were high-paying and I enjoyed the travel. Eventually, after a few years, I picked up a contract with the wrong boss, a mean son-of-a-bitch that preferred his soldiers a little more docile."

Jaya held her breath. She suspected she knew what was coming. She's spent enough time on the dark web to know what sort of contracts he was talking about, what sort of terrible work was out there for men and women willing to do anything for money.

"He drugged you," she whispered.

"Some of the guys were willing when he offered up enough money. Those of us that tried to leave were dragged back by his soldiers and drugged forcibly." His teeth clenched so hard Jaya could hear them creak. She wanted to reach out and touch him now, despite her earlier fear. No one deserved his fate, despite his youthful arrogance. "He drugged us, used mind control and detonator chips in our necks to keep us in line. I worked for him for seven years. He thought he had my loyalty. Like a beaten dog, forced to eat from his master's hand."

Jaya held her breath, tears burning behind her eyelids. She could feel Ndari's hand clenched around hers. It was Ndari that spoke in a hushed, choked voice. "What happened, Linton?"

For a moment Jaya had no idea who Ndari was talking to and then she realized that Keane's first name must be Linton. She hadn't known. He looked up, his sharp aqua blue eyes resting on the princess. After a long, thoughtful moment he answered. "The moment that chip was out of my neck I tracked the fucker down, wrapped my hands around his neck and choked the life out of him."

Both Ndari and Jaya held their breath for a few seconds. Ndari's hand jerked against Jaya's and then she said quickly, with conviction, "Good."

Jaya was reminded sharply of the times Ndari had talked of free will, free speech, free... everything. Ndari had never really thought herself free. She was a princess, trapped by a country, trapped by philosophy, trapped by law, trapped by family and a brother. She'd envied Jaya her supposed freedom before her capture. But she hadn't known that Jaya had never been free. The image of Father flashed through her brain; his frowning visage, his anger at her every failure to find and destroy his one single enemy.

Jaya jerked her hand away from Ndari's, pulled her legs from the pool and stood. She looked up across the rooftops, lit up in the bright hues of another gorgeous sunset. She closed her eyes against the beautiful serenity, turned on her heel and stalked away.

"Jaya..." Ndari called to her.

"Let her go." Jaya heard Keane say. "Her cage is getting bigger and she doesn't know how to fly yet."

CHAPTER TWENTY-SIX

Instead of going back to her room, Jaya stormed toward Ivan's office. One of the guards gave her an alarmed look and jumped in front of the door. She stopped abruptly and stepped back with a frown. "What exactly are you doing?" she demanded, hands on her hips.

"We have orders not to touch you, Miss Jaya," he said quickly and with authority.

"Uh huh," she said, quirking a brow and taking a step forward. "Sounds good. Get out of my way."

"I-I'm also under orders not to let anyone in to see the boss," he stammered, pressing himself into the door so he wasn't at risk of touching her.

"Riiight," she drawled. "Well...." She quirked her head to the side and thought about it. "Not to come across as immature and all... but..." she reached out and placed her hand on his chest, splaying her fingers wide, "get the fuck out of my way."

He jumped to the side breaking contact with her. The second he cleared the door, she wrenched it open and hurried inside, slamming it shut behind her. She sort of instantly regretted her impulsiveness when she was met with the barrel of a gun pointed directly at her forehead and Ivan's furious grey gaze. He reholstered the gun when he saw who had entered his private sanctuary, lifted a thick eyebrow and pointed imperiously at a chair as if to tell her she'd better sit or he would bring the gun back out. Jaya took her time sitting, as though it had always been her decision.

Turning back to his desk, Ivan spoke as if Jaya hadn't just entered the room and interrupted his work. "Is Valdez aware of your interest in the Carlo Cignani?" Ivan asked coolly, though there was an edge of warmth to his voice. "I won't move on the transaction without his final approval."

"Fuck you, Ivan!" a woman's voice said furiously over the speakerphone. "What I say or do to my husband is none of your business. You sold me to him in exchange for a good friend. I'm only doing you this courtesy because the painting will show up on your radar as soon as it goes missing and we both know you'll trace the heist back to me."

Jaya's mouth fell open and she lurched out of the chair, reaching for Ivan's desk. "Katie!" she yelped. "Is that you? Are you okay, my friend? Last I heard this bastard gave you up to the Valdez cartel. I was so worried about you, kitty cat!"

"Oh my god, XSource! Holy shit, is that you?" Katie shouted, excitement clear in her voice. "I'm doing okay. Just married to Roman Valdez, very much against my will. What about you, I heard everything! I thought Ivan was going to kill you when he got his hands on you!"

"While this reunion is very touching, I'd rather you ladies do it another time," Ivan said coldly, raising a hand when it looked as though Jaya wanted to speak again. She pressed her lips into a thin line and swore at him silently instead. "Katie, I'm fine with your procurement of Cignani's Madonna and Child. Do what you like with it. Consider it a wedding gift."

Before she could reply, he pressed the disconnect button. His cool, assessing gaze lifted to Jaya.

"Why are you here in my office, Jaya? You've never been here before, so it must be important if it can't wait." His cool gaze ran over her curves and then warmed as he took in the way her skirt clung wetly to her legs.

She crossed her arms over her chest and glared at him. "Why *am* I here, Ivan?" she asked, frustration heavy in her voice. "I don't get it! I've never really gotten it. I'm a hacker and a damn good one, but you've never even tried to use my skills to your advantage. You could kidnap any pretty face and keep her locked up, but for some stupid reason you chose me. I would understand this situation way better if you actually tried to use my abilities to your advantage, but you don't. It makes no sense. It's like buying a fancy car and keeping it locked up in your garage and going in to touch it and look at it but never taking it out for a drive."

He studied her for a moment, a slow, lazy grin spreading across his face. Slowly, deliberately he began stalking her around his desk. The look on his face was different, more relaxed than usual, darkly mischievous. Her eyes widened and she backed away from his advance until her ass hit the edge of the wet bar. Liquor bottles and glasses rattled, making her jump. She tried to edge to the side but he brought his hands down on either side of her. She was reminded of those soap opera villains from the 70's and 80's that would trap women in their offices and take advantage of them. She used to put old episodes on for background noise while she was hacking, finding them titillating while she worked.

"But I do want to drive you, sweetheart," he murmured, bending until he could run his lips along her jawline. She turned her face to the side, intending to move away but instead giving him easier access to her vulnerable ear. She shivered when he pressed his nose and then tongue against the tender spot just behind her ear. "I want to fuck every vulnerable part of you. Hold you down and take you over and over until you're finally helpless, until you know nothing but me. Until you want no one else but me in your life." His deep voice penetrated her, while his tongue brushed against her skin, wrapping her in a fog.

Her heart beat heavily within her chest begging her to obey him, telling her he wanted only good things for her. She turned her head to the side and looked up at him, searching his steel grey eyes for a hint of softness. "Why haven't you asked me to work for you?" she whispered, pressing her lips delicately, helplessly against the edge of his chin, feeling the beginning of his day's whiskers rasp against her. "Why won't you use me? Is it because you think I'll use my knowledge to escape, to leave you?"

His hands tightened on her arms. The bar rattled at her back. "I know you will," he growled, his voice back to its usual coolness.

She blinked and looked past him, ignoring the clench of his hard hands on her body and the possessiveness of his hold. She was looking inward, trying to figure out what she would do if she did manage to get her hands on a computer. More and more Ivan was pulling her into his world. He was confusing her with his crazy concern every time she got injured or put herself in danger. His possessive love was beginning to take its toll on her. But she owed her loyalty to someone else... didn't she? The man that called himself her Father, the man that fed, clothed and provided her with shelter for years.

"Let me go," she whispered.

"Never." His answer was instant.

She looked up at him, dark eyes pleading with light. "I just need some space."

"I will never give you that," he said, his words falling like hammers. He was relentless. This was Ivan. The man who built an empire from nothing, the man who conquered everything around him.

Tears sparkled in her eyes. "Why?" she asked desperately. "What do you want from me? You don't want my hacking skills, you don't want me to help you make more money, what could you possibly want from me?"

He lifted a hand and cupped the back of her head, caressing her, before clenching his fingers in the strands, controlling her by forcing her to look up at him. Tears spilled from her lashes as she took in the terrible storm of emotions he was always so careful to keep at bay. No longer. Now he wanted her to see what he kept from the world. The grey wrath that, once unleashed, could cause devastation. "I want your love," he said simply, his cool voice at odds with the war going on in his gaze.

She opened her mouth to speak but a sob emerged instead. He tilted his head and kissed her, despite the salt of her tears tainting the taste. His kiss was gentle at first, but quickly turned to a devastating assault. What he once might have asked for, he now demanded. He gripped the back of her skull in one hand, his fingers twisting in the strands of her hair, holding her immobile, while his other hand wrapped around her waist and yanked her firmly against him.

She clutched his shoulders, twisting her fingers in his shirt and holding tight while she continued to sob wildly in his arms, the echo of his words hammering through her brain. She didn't participate in the kiss, couldn't participate in her current state. It didn't matter. He took over completely, thrusting his tongue into her mouth, showing her who was master. White lightening streaked pleasure through her brain, sizzling every part of her body. She moaned in his arms, giving herself up to the experience.

Finally, he tipped his head back, releasing her lips. But

only by a few centimeters. When he spoke, his words rushed hotly over her wet mouth, swollen from his brutal kisses. "I'll be everything to you, sweetheart. I promise, I'm keeping you forever."

She stared up at him, the emotions so overwhelming she could barely speak. Her lips shook when she opened her mouth. How had he come to mean so much to her, so quickly? Finally she whispered, "I think I want that too."

His hands tightened, almost unbearably and his eyes snapped grey fire down at her. "Then choose to stay with me, choose to stop running."

She reached up and wrapped her arms tight around his neck, clinging to him as though he were her lifeline. "Okay," she whispered.

And she meant it. The ties to her past started to loosen and fall away. The misplaced loyalty that had bound her to Father meant less and less. Logically she'd always known he hadn't really cared for her. That the sterile room he'd kept her in during her early teen years, the food he provided, the equipment he'd given her hadn't been the same as love. But without anything else to latch on to, without any other comparison she'd allowed the man who'd rescued her from the streets of Mumbai to fill her mind with hate. Now it was time to let go of Father and embrace the man who professed to love her. Right or wrong, this was the path she wanted to take.

The look of intense relief on Ivan's face told her she'd given him something precious, something far better than all the riches he could have conquered on his own. Despite the tears still wetting her cheeks she smiled. "It's too much work to hate a man determined to love me even when I blew up his island and caused thousands of dollars of damage to a Tiffany's store."

"Hundreds of thousands," he corrected her. "The money

doesn't matter. I'll buy you a hundred islands and a dozen jewellery stores. Blow them all to hell if you want."

They stared at each other, feeling the sizzle in the air as their undeniable attraction raced between and around them. It had taken them several weeks to get to this moment of perfect synchronicity. Months even as Ivan had chased her across the globe intent on capturing the tech genius that teased him.

His fingers clenched against her. "How's your arm?" he asked huskily piercing her with his uncanny eyes.

She caught her breath and enjoyed the sensations swirling in her belly. He wasn't really asking about her arm. She could feel the shift in tension between them from loving to sexual. He wanted her and he wanted her right now. She licked her lips and glanced at him from beneath her lashes. "It's better, doesn't really hurt anymore."

"Is it better enough?" he demanded, a hard edge to his voice. He wanted her bad, but he wasn't willing to take any risks.

She looped her good arm around his neck and pulled herself boldly up against him, pressing her breasts against his hard chest. Heat swirled between them, flaming higher with each touch. This was the first time Jaya had gone into Ivan's embrace without hesitation. She pressed her lips against his throat, tracing first the hollow with her tongue and then his Adam's apple when it bobbed against her mouth. He groaned and clenched his hand against the back of her head.

"I need you to touch me, to make love to me, Ivan," she whispered into the flesh she'd just licked.

His hand tightened in her hair until his hold was nearly punishing. He tipped her head back against the bar, his eyes devouring her face seconds before his mouth took hers in another sweeping kiss. She shoved her tongue back against his, tightening her fingers against him and pulling him hard against her. Heat sparked through her body, raging higher and higher, an inferno that threatened to burn out of control now that she was giving herself permission to have this man.

Ivan's response to her wholehearted enthusiasm was to take her harder than ever before. He gripped her face in both hands, pulled her against him and lost every ounce of the prized control he'd spent a lifetime cultivating. She moaned into his mouth, reached up and slid her hands into his hair, holding him close while he fucked her mouth with relentless strokes. She jumped when she heard a smash, but he refused to release her. Another smash told her they were rattling the bar so hard bottles were dropping to the floor.

Ivan wrapped an arm around her waist, lifted her off the floor and turned them around in a sweeping circle. He strode to his desk and shoved everything aside, heedless of what it was. Everything that got in his way went crashing to the floor. As her ass touched the surface she lifted her legs and wrapped them around his waist. He growled appreciatively and reached back to shove the sandals off her feet. Once they were gone he shrugged his holster off. Her eyes flew wide when his gun hit the floor with a thud. He didn't seem to care. He gripped her neck and pulled her back up into his embrace, his lips meeting hers again, the rasp of his chin scraping her flesh with the desperation of each kiss.

They clung to each other as though it were their last moment. As though discovering each other for the first time but unable to slow down long enough to explore. Jaya wanted to touch him, wanted to run her hands over masculine shoulders and broad muscles, but he kept knocking her hands aside in his furious assault on her senses. She heard the tearing of fabric but had no idea whether it was her clothes or his. She felt his fingers between her legs, strong and sure, stroking and pressing with relentless intent.

There was no build up, no foreplay. Suddenly he was

there, shoving his fingers relentlessly inside her. She threw her head back against the desk with a shriek and pressed her knees to the side lifting her hips in desperate supplication. He shoved her panties to the side and removed his fingers, flicking her clit on the way out. She cried out again, this time in disappointment.

"Look at me," he demanded, reaching between them and unzipping his pants.

She tilted her head up in time to see the piercing look of desire and blatant possession just before he pressed himself against her and then leaned forward, using the hardness of the desk to thrust full-length inside her. Jaya gasped at the fullness of his intrusion, reaching up to grip his shoulders, digging her nails into his shirt.

He took her with long, fierce strokes, his eyes never leaving her face. She locked eyes with him and refused to look away, understanding that this moment meant something. This was the first completely consensual coming together. She was giving him her free will and agreeing to stay. Equal ground.

He leaned over her, gripping her so tight the space between them virtually disappeared. His strokes became shorter, shallower and more brutal as his hips slammed her into the desk. She wrapped her arms around his neck, buried her face against him and held on, clinging to the man determined to take everything from her, but give her more in return. He turned his face into her neck and bit down on the flesh between her shoulder and neck. Pleasure burst through her and she came in a wild rush of colour and hot, sizzling sensations. Her head fell back and she opened her eyes to stare into the bright sunlit sky through the window behind them while he continued to wring every last lingering bit of orgasm from her body.

With a savage, satisfied grunt he tipped over the edge of

orgasm, joining her in the blissful, floating world he'd sent her spiralling into moments before. He dropped his head and buried it into the thick cloud of her hair, spread out all around them on the desk.

She tilted her head and looked down. "I think you might need a new laptop," she said breathlessly.

He chuckled and said, his voice muffled, "It's a good thing I know someone who's great with computers."

"Excuse me?" she said disdainfully. "First of all, I am not a computer repair person, I am an elite hacker. There is a big difference! That's like asking Scarlet Johansen to star in Sharknado. Just no. And second of all, since when did you decide to trust me near a computer?"

He pushed himself up, his hands splayed on either side of her head. She couldn't help herself, she just had to tilt her head to the side and watch the play of muscles through his dress shirt as he moved. Despite the impressive orgasm he'd just treated her to she could feel the tingles begin to spark back to life in her tummy and lower in her pussy. Especially when he pulled out of her. She gasped and pressed her knees together as he moved back. She wanted to put her hand between her legs and continue what they'd just started and finished but she didn't think that was fair to him. Not that he would mind the show.

"I have to start trusting you sometime, and I choose to believe you when you say you want to be with me. Now, tell me, what's with your obsession with the American actress?" he asked with a chuckle, straightening his clothes and then reaching to help her sit up on the edge of the desk.

She stared at him in astonishment for a moment before saying in a rush, "Are you serious? How can you not have a thing for her? You're a guy for god's sake, you have no excuse! She's the freaking Black Widow, plus she's amazing in virtually everything she's ever been in. *And* she was married to

Ryan Reynolds. Yes, it was for like a minute. But it must have been the best minute of her life. Can you imagine being married to the guy that played Deadpool? Epic!"

He simply watched her while she spoke, his expression softer than usual, more indulgent. "I have no idea what you're talking about, but I must admit, I enjoy watching you when you speak this way. Yet another facet of your character for me to fall in love with."

She grinned at him and pushed herself off his desk allowing her skirt to fall the rest of the way down to cover her legs. She wiggled until her panties were back in place. "Good, because we're going to be spending a lot of time on your nerd education in the near future mister Vogel if you intend to hang out with a Master hacker."

"I will do as you command, watch whatever you think I must," he opened the door and, ignoring the man guarding the hall, pulled her against him for another kiss. "But let's be clear, sweetheart. There is only one Master around here."

She grinned up at him and whispered, "Master Vogel." She swore she felt his cock twitch against her right before she pulled away and left him standing in the door of his office.

CHAPTER TWENTY-SEVEN

"I think my kitten has decided to move in with you," Jaya said accusingly, settling herself next to Ndari on the bed where she was curled on her side playing with a string toy that had feathers on the end. Haty was doing her best to murder the feathers, scattering the pink, red and yellow fluff everywhere. "What did you do, promise her a lifetime supply of chin scratches and those treats that she's addicted to?"

Ndari shrugged a shoulder and glanced up. "Just the blood of our enemies, starting with the Irishman. He stepped on her tail yesterday and she now wants his heart in a box."

"Sounds like her," Jaya agreed with a laugh. They both watched the adorable, chubby kitten with her too-big paws continue to roll around on her back and bat the toy while Ndari bobbed it in and out of reach. When Jaya looked back up it was to find the other woman's eyes intent on her face as though studying her.

"You're happy here now, truly happy?" she asked suddenly, her tone serious.

Jaya thought about it, wanting to give Ndari an honest answer. After what the two women had been through, she deserved that. "Maybe it's the pain meds, but I think so. And I don't know about happy exactly... not yet anyway. But I think it'll come eventually. Once we work out the kinks." She smirked, thinking about what she'd just said, specifically remembering the time Ivan'd zapped her while they were having sex. She tilted her head to the side. "Well, maybe not all the kinks."

Ndari sighed heavily and reached behind her, into her back pocket. "Then this belongs to you." She handed a phone to Jaya. Specifically the phone Jaya had lifted from the guy at the mall right before hotwiring the Maserati. She gaped at it for a second before looking up at Ndari. "I thought I'd dropped it while I was running!"

Ndari shook her head. "You shoved it down the front of your shirt. Ivan put you on my lap while we were waiting for his men to arrive in the garage. He was pacing back and forth like a madman, not paying any attention to me, just watching for them. I felt the phone while I was checking your pulse and put it in my purse when he wasn't looking."

"And you've had it ever since and haven't said a word." She tried to keep the accusation from her voice, but she had trouble imagining someone as open as Ndari keeping such a big secret.

"I'm sorry," Ndari said, her own voice anguished. "I needed it close, like a security blanket. It was going to be our out if you decided you wanted to leave or if he did anything else horrible, like putting a gun to my head again."

Jaya felt like a terrible friend at the reminder. "Of course you wanted it," Jaya replied, softening her tone. "And so you should have a phone. I'll talk to Ivan about getting you a legitimate one of your own now that he's decided we're going to try the trust thing. It shouldn't be a problem."

"Really?" Ndari said, excitement shining through. "Because I've been dying to call the palace. I can't even tell you how boring that place is when I'm not around to shake things up. I need to make sure my half-sister, Alissa, stays out of my closet. That skank has terrible taste in clothing, yet she still borrows my shit."

"Wow, I've missed you," Jaya laughed and reached out to hug her friend, ignoring Haty's outraged protest when she ended their game and sent the kitten scampering. "We've been much too serious this week."

"Agreed," Ndari said, squeezing Jaya back.

Once they settled back onto their opposing sides of the bed, Ndari studied Jaya with a calculating twinkle in her eye. "What?" Jaya demanded, becoming quickly acquainted with her friend's penchant toward mischief.

"Well... you know how our last shopping trip got interrupted?" Ndari said. To her credit she didn't say it in an accusing tone, as if she didn't blame Jaya for reining chaos down upon Ivan and therefore everyone in his vicinity. Jaya rolled her eyes, nodded and twirled her finger, as if to say get on with it. "Anyway, I was thinking we should try the shopping thing again! Your man still has the big bucks that need spending and, honey, not that you don't look adorably quaint in that never-ending parade of saris you keep wearing, but it's time to update your style."

Jaya giggled and defended herself. "Okay, the saris aren't my choice. Ivan saw me in one once at a ball and was smitten! Can I help it that I'm gorgeous in traditional gear? I'm usually a T-shirts and leggings kind of girl. In fact, I'm a hacker, I'm usually a pyjamas-unless-I'm-absolutely-forced-to go-out-in-public kind of girl."

Ndari made a face and shook her head. "No girl, we definitely need to work on your style then. You're about to become the wife of one of the world's most notorious businessmen. Legit or not, Ivan Vogel is known internationally. You need to look the part."

"This conversation is pointless anyway. He might trust me a little more now, but I doubt his trust is going to extend to another shopping trip the moment he stops threatening to murder everything I love."

Ndari gave her a pointed look. "You're pretty thick for a genius. Did he not just give you access to an entire world of online shopping and a princess who has spent her entire life as a professional shopper?"

Jaya's mouth fell open.

"Exactly," Ndari said smugly. "Do you suppose he has limits on his personal credit cards or do you think he's one of those super rich guys like my brother who has unlimited funds?"

Jaya barely noticed when a shadow fell across her, blotting out the intensely bright sunlight. After a moment she forgot about the distraction and continued to pound away on the keyboard, her brand-new laptop perched precariously on her crossed legs where she sat on one of the pool lounge chairs. She wore a bathing suit and a pair of shorts. It had been a long, hard fought argument with Ivan to wear even this little out on the pool deck with his men around, but she'd finally won him over by promising to purchase a modest swimsuit, which she did.

"More packages've arrived."

Jaya jumped and barely managed to grab her laptop before it took a nasty spill off the end of the lounger and into the pool. Her head swivelled up and she found herself staring at an amused Keane who stood towering over her. She wondered how long he'd been standing there. Now that she was back online she noticed that Ivan's men seemed to enjoy sneaking up on her more and more often. She frowned. Maybe she should tell Ivan to put bells on them.

"The princess is opening them in her private quarters. Says she'll put your stuff away in your room for you." He drawled the word *princess* like it was offensive. Jaya wasn't exactly sure what was going on between Keane and Ndari, but the tension between the two was becoming explosive. They came from two completely different worlds and though there was a definite attraction, Jaya didn't see how any kind of relationship could be possible.

"Thank you for telling me," Jaya murmured, a hint of sarcasm in her voice. There was absolutely no need for him to interrupt her to tell her about the packages. "What do you really want?"

"What're you doing there?" he asked, nodding toward the laptop.

She eyed the computer then glanced back at him. After a moment she decided to tell him. "I'm locking a certain dictator who's slowly starving his people and inflating the currency in his country out of his personal accounts so he can see what it's like to go hungry. I mean, I'm sure he'll gain access to funds somehow, but he'll be uncomfortable for a few days."

Keane chuckled. "Bravo, canary." He shook his head. "Dangerous though, if you get yourself caught."

"They won't catch me," she said confidently.

"We caught you, canary. And put you in a cage." His blue eyes turned serious, piercing her with a warning.

She nodded and closed the laptop, setting it aside. "Yes, and now I have you and Ivan to protect me. Trust me, Keane, I won't do anything stupid."

"Like keep an unauthorized phone on the premises," he said coolly, his gaze flattening.

She gasped, shock hitting her. She could feel adrenaline

rushing through her limbs, screaming at her to run away. She had to force herself to sit still. She wasn't under threat, not yet. If Keane had told Ivan about the phone, this would be a very different conversation. Why hadn't he told Ivan about the phone? First though, she needed to know how. "How did you know?" she asked, her voice quivering.

"Saw you in the security feed at the mall," he answered easily, dropping to his haunches beside her, his head now level with hers. "Boss asked me to see if you'd knocked them all out when you assaulted the system back at the jewellery store. It looked like you had. Wasn't until a few days ago that one of our tech guys found a camera in the food court that hadn't gone down."

"Wh-why haven't you told Ivan?" she asked breathlessly, her mind racing ahead to every possibility. Keane could still tell Ivan. Ivan could still freak out and decide to punish her through his worst threat, murdering someone she loved. She had to warn Ndari!

"Have to be honest here, canary. If I'd seen that tape a week ago you'd've been up shit creek. I would've handed you over to the boss and let him sort it out. But I only saw it two days ago. Which means you've had the phone for a week and haven't done shit with it." His voice was low. He didn't want their conversation overheard. "I'm curious about your intentions, if you have any at all. Could be, you took it in the heat of the moment and now you don't know what to do with it."

Jaya took a deep breath. She didn't want to drag Ndari into this mess, but she needed to be completely honest. She needed Keane to trust her. She believed it was going to keep the two women safe in this situation. She told him exactly what'd happened with the phone from start to finish. She also promised to give him the phone, relieved that she wouldn't have it hanging over her head any longer.

When she was done telling him her side of the story, he

nodded and said, "Good girl. I'll be having a wee chat with the princess to make sure she corroborates what you're saying. If she does, then this need go no further than the three of us. I'll make sure the tech guy forgets what he knows as well."

Though Jaya was relieved she also desperately wanted to run to Ndari and tell her to tell only the truth when talking to Keane. She suspected Ndari was going to either clam up or spout off at the unpredictable, potentially violent man and either scenario wasn't going to be in her best interest. As if reading her mind, Keane stood up and grinned down at her. "Oh no you don't. You best be leaving her royal highness to me."

CHAPTER TWENTY-EIGHT

Weeks passed and the trust between Ivan and Jaya grew. Jaya was seeing Ivan as a different man than the one who kidnapped her and kept her locked in cages. A different man than the one she'd spent half a lifetime hearing described to her in gruesome detail. But at the same time, Ivan was still the same man she had been attracted to from the very beginning. He was cool, in control and completely, unbearably dominant. He only warmed for Jaya. He only unbent for the woman he loved. If anything, his newfound love made him more unapologetically vicious to the world around them.

Jaya tried to point this out to him, tried to get him to soften his approach to others. Especially his poor secretary, Anna, who flew in from Athens for a three-day business meeting. But he would not be swayed. He simply looked at Jaya as though she should know better and carried on with business as usual; murder, mayhem and arms dealing on an international scale. Or so she presumed. He didn't involve her in his work and she was glad he chose not to.

Ivan *had* given Jaya a few restrictions when he'd given her a laptop and access to the internet. If she wanted to work, then she had to run her contracts through either Ivan or Keane before she agreed to them. She could shop at will and she had to keep a low profile while chatting. Under no circumstances could she tell anyone where she was or who she was with. Ivan was to have access to her internet and chat history at any time if he chose to look.

So when she finally felt brave enough to contact Father, she had to do it completely in code and she had to strike a perfect balance so she wouldn't tip Ivan's tech people off. She decided to contact him in a chat room on the dark web, which would automatically arouse Ivan's suspicion, but could be easily explained once he read the transcripts. She thought it might arouse too much suspicion to try a regular web connect given that most of her work was conducted through the dark web. If she put the suspicious stuff right out in the open, Ivan would most likely sink his teeth into that instead and ignore the deeper subtext. Or so she hoped.

As usual, Ivan left early that morning, kissing her on the head before rolling out of bed and leaving for his morning workout. She knew she likely wouldn't see him again until that evening and felt safe in pulling out her laptop and settling on the balcony to their room. There was no point in wasting a gorgeous morning breeze while planning subterfuge. She turned the laptop on and quickly got to work, bringing up the restricted site she used to contact certain clients. It came up with a notice saying it had been shut down and users were to contact the administrator for further information. She clicked on the unhappy face icon which brought up username and password boxes. She filled them out and was taken to correct site; simply called Buy and Sell Web Services. But it was so much more than that. This was *the* website, where the world's elite hackers convened to bid for jobs. Or if they were really good, like XSourse, the clients vied and bid for her attention.

Jaya grinned in relief when she saw exactly what she was looking for, an ad looking for a specific hacker. Her. She saw that the ad had been put up repeatedly every week since she went off the grid. It said:

Daddy is looking for his lost cat. The cat is small with dark hair and sticky paws. He's good at getting into spaces he shouldn't. Contact me if you've seen him, I just want to know that he's safe.

Jaya wrinkled her nose and rolled her eyes at the 'Daddy' reference, but they'd agreed that Father should place a lost cat ad, so she was pretty sure it was him. She supposed he didn't want to call himself Father because she and his other foundlings called him Father so maybe it was too recognizable, but still... she glanced at Haty who was lolling on her back on the warm paving stones.

"That just sounds dirty," she told the cat. "And I'm so not going there with a man that's actually like my father figure. Ugh, nope, need some mental bleach."

She replied to the ad:

XSource: Found your lost cat. He's fine and looking for work.

She brought up another tab and began searching other sites, checking in with friends, expecting it to take time for Father's reply. She was surprised when a chat window popped up right away.

Daddy: Glad you're good. I have a job for you.

XSource: Drop the 'Daddy' bullshit and I'll think about it. Can't work while choking on vomit.

Daddy: Do you want the job or not?

XSource: It's. Just. So. Wrong.

Daddy: ...

XSource: Dude, you're really going to make me call you daddy? Fine. Where, when and how much?

Daddy: That's Big Daddy to you kitten.

XSource: I hate you so much.

Daddy: The job's in Atlanta. Tomorrow. Four million. Will send the exact job details once you've accepted.

Jaya gasped and sat back in her chair with a thump as the image of his words burned in her brain. He'd answered all three of her questions quickly and succinctly, unwittingly piercing her heart in the process. She actually rubbed a hand over her chest, trying to soothe the ache within. Atlanta meant he knew where she was and he was extracting her tomorrow. Four million meant he was bringing a team of four. Reading between the lines she would guess it wasn't an entire assault team, since four men against Ivan's entire well-trained army wasn't going to end well for Father. So, he must have a different plan for her extraction.

Still, the thought of anyone on either side getting hurt because of her stole her breath and made her feel faint. Some of the men that Father might bring were people she'd practically grown up with. He'd always been careful to maintain distance between the talented children he collected. But lonely kids, starving for affection found ways of being together. She'd lost her virginity to one of those boys at the age of sixteen in a mango grove behind the barracks. Thank goodness she hadn't become pregnant. Father, while occasionally benevolent, was overall a brutal leader, especially with the men he conditioned to follow him. Jaya had been special, his intelligent genius pet. The weapon he might one day use against his greatest enemy.

She set the laptop aside and stood, taking two restless steps away from the chair and then back. If she was honest, it was mostly the thought of anything happening to Ivan that nearly brought her to her knees. She knew on an intellectual level that Ivan could take care of himself, but the thought of a bullet finding his flesh, the thought of Father finally winning vengeance, and all because of her... it gutted her. She blinked back tears and dropped back into the chair, lifting her hands to the keyboard and typing.

X Source: Job rejected. Not enough time to plan.

Though she knew it was just her overactive imagination, she swore she could feel the heat of Father's anger through the laptop. She knew what he was probably thinking. Betrayal. It was what she would be thinking in his place. Standing up, she began pacing again, guilt eating at her. This man had tried to raise her after her family died. He'd rescued her from the streets, an ugly situation that had been rapidly deteriorating for a vulnerable young woman. She owed him better than to turn her back on him. But did she owe him her entire life, her happiness? Did she owe him the life of the man she loved?

She heard the message box pop up again. Tears pricked her eyes because she already knew what it was going to say. She turned on her heel, grabbed the edge of her skirt and sat. She narrowed her eyes at the screen.

Daddy: Unacceptable. You are needed for this job to go forward. Be ready.

She shook her head and lifted her hands to the laptop, about to refuse again. But then dropped them. What choice did she have? Somehow Father had a lock on her location. Probably the jewelry store thing. It had her signature all over it. From the outside it would look like a regular heist gone wrong. But anyone looking closer would see the necessary skill involved in the way she'd manipulated the security and fire systems. Father probably had an algorithm running the world over searching for her digital fingerprints in hopes of picking her up somewhere. He would be coming to Ivan's

Jakarta penthouse tomorrow, with or without her cooperation. Perhaps if she agreed to go with him, there would be less of a chance of anyone getting hurt.

XSource: Alright. I want 6 million, wired to my Bahamas account. Half now, half after the job. Give me the details.

Daddy: Five million. Check your account, 2.5 transferred now.

Jaya checked her account, knowing there was an excellent chance Ivan's people were monitoring her chat. Sure enough, two and a half million dollars had just been transferred to her account. She sucked in a quick breath. Father meant business. He wasn't messing around in his intention to get her back. Or to kill Ivan. She just hoped she could prevent one of those from happening. Actually, she hoped she could prevent both. She was beginning to think she'd finally found her place in life. She was cautiously optimistic that the Ivan thing was going to work out for her.

XSource: Deal. Now the job details?

Daddy: I'll send tomorrow at noon. Be ready, kitten.

The nickname finally clicked. He'd called her kitten twice now and she'd been too grossed out to think about the code word. That, and when she lived with Father at his compound, she'd rarely trained with him and his men. The word 'kitten' was code for rooftop. He was trying to tell her that the extraction would take place on the roof. Which made sense since there weren't many other places he could do it. Unless he had a key to the extremely locked down elevator. And then he'd have to somehow get off the elevator without getting mowed down by Ivan's people. He was also giving her the time for her extraction. 10am, two hours before the stated time. She logged off the chat site, closed the laptop and stared sightlessly across the downtown skyline.

Ivan stood next to his tech guy, watching Jaya's online conversation in real time. It had taken about a minute for his guy to catch up to her. At first they were simply looking at a replica of her screen, but she somehow managed to black them out. Once they figured out what she was doing, the tech guy began retracing her footsteps. When he'd tried to log onto the chat site she was using he was instantly rerouted. Finally, after some fast and fancy typing they were in. Ivan watched, far more impressed with Jaya's skills than those of his own people. If they had half the talent she did, they would at least be able to keep up with her.

It wasn't until he began reading her conversation that admiration swiftly turned to rage. He wasn't exactly sure what part of the conversation enraged him more; the part where she thought she was duping them through a badly coded conversation, her use of the term 'Daddy' while speaking to another man or her blatant betrayal of him while knowing he was most likely somewhere nearby reading a transcript of her conversation. Did she really think he was so stupid that he couldn't read through this weak attempt to connect with her Father or one of his disciples?

The love he felt for her burned and churned in his gut, made him wish he could hate her. But then, hatred was a feeling too. And Jaya was the only person capable of pulling any kind of emotion from him.

"What're we gonna do?" Keane grunted from beside him. "Canary going back in her cage so she don't get caught in the crossfire?"

Ivan wanted to nod his head, wanted to agree with the man. But he was smarter than that. If he wanted to finish with this threat on his life, the same threat that was also putting Jaya at risk then he needed her involvement. Though her move to connect with Father angered him, he knew it was a good move, he could use it to their advantage. Flush the enemy out, invite him to Ivan's doorstep and then take him apart piece by piece.

"No," he said coolly. "We'll use her to bring Father in. Make sure she's visible, then get her to safety. It's your job to make sure nothing happens to her."

Keane snorted. "I think I'll request compassion leave. My auntie is sick and I need some time off. Think my odds of survival are higher that way."

Ivan ignored him, turned and left the room.

CHAPTER TWENTY-NINE

"Anything you want to tell me?"

Jaya glanced up at Ivan, positive that guilt was written all over her face. They were walking side-by-side down the wide hall toward their bedroom. They'd just shared their supper meal and Ivan had decided to spend the rest of the evening with her rather than go back to work. Her heart had leapt at the suggestion since she might be leaving the next day. Who knows if he would want her back once she left? If he would understand her reasons. She was going to soak up as much of his attention while she could.

She shook her head, dark hair swirling around her shoulders as she tilted her head to look up at him innocently. She could tell from the gathering storm in his grey eyes that she was failing. He knew something was up, had probably followed her earlier chat and wasn't happy about it. She bit her lip and walked into their bedroom when he opened the door and held it for her. The moment she cleared the threshold he slammed it shut and locked it, clearly taking out some of his anger on the heavy door. She flinched and stepped back.

He turned to look at her, his eyes sweeping over her from head to toe, warming slightly but not losing the boiling anger that had seethed just below the surface from the moment he'd picked her up for their evening meal. She'd chosen something completely different to wear, wanting to make an impression on what was possibly her last night with the handsome arms dealer. With the arrival of her new wardrobe, thanks to a spendy princess, she had plenty of choices. She was now wearing a Stella McCartney mid-thigh length black lace dress that covered her from wrists to neck. But the sheer fabric hinted at lush curves and complimented her dark skin. Ndari had insisted she wear the dress with a pair of 'killer' black heels, which Jaya began to take literally after a few hours of practicing in them. But the overall effect of the outfit was worth it. Even angry, Ivan couldn't take his eyes off her.

"Tell me who Daddy is?" he demanded, his voice hard, though his gaze still lingered on her breasts and hips.

She shook her head a little. "He's no one important."

"He's obviously important enough that you're planning on doing a job for him without permission," Ivan shot back. "Now start talking unless you want to discuss who exactly you'll be calling daddy in the future. And trust me, if we have that conversation, you'll be doing it on your knees."

Jaya couldn't help it, despite the stress she was under, she giggled at the thought of Ivan forcing her to call him daddy. She covered her mouth quickly, but not before he caught her amusement. He, of course, was less than amused. His eyebrows came down in a glower and he took the steps separating them. She jumped back quickly, hitting the edge of the bed, and nearly fell backwards. He caught her arm and jerked her upright.

"You think this is funny?" he growled.

"No," she whispered, and then the image of him telling

her to call him daddy while she went down on him smashed through her brain again. She laughed out loud. "I-I'm sorry! I can't help it."

His lip twitched and he dropped his forehead against hers. He gripped a handful of her hair and wrapped it around his fingers, allowing some of the smooth strands to escape, while others stayed caged in his grip. He used his other arm to pull her in close against his hard chest. She snuggled against him, his willing captive. He forced her head back a little and dropped a gentle kiss against her lips. "I love you so fucking much, even when you're actively ripping my heart out," he murmured against her.

She shook her head, wrapped her arms around his waist and stared up at him. "If I rip your heart out then I'll keep it safe, I promise." It was the best she could give him. She wasn't going to promise not to betray him, not to rip out his heart, because she was going to do both. But she was going to do her best not to hurt him too badly.

He stared down at her, his eyes steely. Finally he dipped his head in a single nod, picked up her hand and pressed a kiss into the palm. "All I ask is that you be safe, Jaya, my love. If anything happens to you…"

She felt a lump in her throat at his words and had to blink rapidly. She almost couldn't believe that she'd found this kind of love. A man that she could fall in love with, a man that had fallen in love with her, flaws and all. A woman both with and without a history. And she was going to walk away from him, the man promising her love and family; the things she'd never had and always yearned for. A sob of despair escaped her throat and a tear dripped straight down from her eye to her cheek.

Ivan swiped his thumb over the apple of her cheek. "Tell me," he said huskily. She sensed that he wanted her to speak, but he wasn't curious. It was like he already knew.

She opened her mouth to confess, to tell him that Father was coming to take her away, that she didn't want to go. That she wanted to make her life here, with Ivan, on top of the world in Jakarta, where they were safe. Only it was false. They weren't safe and never would be. Though difficult, they could both eventually be tracked. Especially by a man with the resources and determination Father had. It had taken many years, but Father had eventually found Ivan through his cat burglar, Katie Pullman, and then used her to get to Ivan by putting Katie and XSource in touch with each other. Now it was up to Jaya to go to Father and talk to him, find out if she could convince him to give up his life-consuming vendetta against a man who didn't even know who he was. For that matter, Jaya didn't even really know who Father was. He'd always been just a shadowy man that'd asked favours of his foundlings, utilized their talents in return for a roof over their heads and food in their bellies.

But it was more than that, her brain whispered.

Father had used his own hatred to somehow twist the children he rescued. He'd done it subtly, using words and images until Jaya could barely remember a time when she hadn't hated and feared Ivan Vogel. Only when he was sure that Jaya was a good, obedient little minion had Father let her loose in the world to run amok. To build her own empire using her hacking skills. All he asked of her was that she occasionally fuck with Ivan's arms deals and insinuate herself in the life of his protégé, Katie Pullman.

She realized that Ivan was waiting for an answer. Her lips quivered as she whispered the words that came out before she even knew what she was saying, "Ivan, I think I love you."

His hands tightened on her and his eyes grew fierce. He nodded, his own lips thinning right before he spoke. His voice was hard. "I won't forbid you from doing this job tomorrow, Jaya, but you promise me you'll be safe."

"I... I'll try," she said, her words stumbling as she choked on a sob.

He shook her. "No, you will do it," he said roughly. "You will not put yourself in any kind of danger or I will put you in a cage for the rest of your natural life, sweetheart. I'll make your cage on the island look like luxury in comparison. You understand?"

"Oh god," she sobbed, clinging to him. Neither of them acknowledged what they weren't saying out loud. That she was going to betray him and try to find a way to leave with Father and that he knew. That he knew and forgave her. "Ivan!"

He bent his head and took her lips in a desperate, passionate kiss that she returned full measure. She dug her fingers in his hair and anchored herself against him, meeting his tongue thrust for thrust. She was surprised when she tasted salt and then realized that she was crying, sobbing into his mouth. She didn't care and she didn't stop, she continued kissing him with everything she had, using her body to show him how much she loved him.

She felt his hands fumbling at the back of her neck and shrieked, "No!" into his mouth just as he took her dress in both hands and shredded it right down the back. She reared back in his arms, only a few inches since he wasn't willing to let her go far and glared up at him. "This was a $3,400 dress!"

"Tell the princess she has excellent taste," he said, yanking the dress right down her body. He lifted her from the puddle of badly torn material and swung her around to face the bed. "My god," he growled with appreciation, taking in the black thong, thigh highs and demi-cup bra set. "Excellent taste in everything. She can definitely stay."

Jaya looked at him over her shoulder and bit her lip then smiled. She couldn't help herself, the look of sheer lust on his face as he stared at her nearly bare ass, the release of tension from moments before, she simply had to say it. "You like what you see, Daddy?" she drawled in a husky voice, trying to sound sexy. Then she ruined it by giggling and clapping a hand over her mouth.

He growled at her and shoved her forward, face first. He caught her by the hips before she could do a complete face-plant and urged her onto her hands and knees. Excitement went zinging through her, pooling in her belly and sizzling outward until she was panting, waiting breathlessly for his next move. She didn't have long to wait. He tugged the ends of her hair in one hand and wrapped it around and around his fist until her head was forced back. He leaned over her, his eyes glinting with purpose. He reached into her bra and cupped her breast, squeezing the supple globe with just enough strength to leave her gasping but unhurt.

"You want to play with me, do you, baby?" he asked, growling in her ear.

Jaya tilted her head in a tiny nod. "Yes, please," she moaned, licking her lips and staring up at him, begging him with her eyes. She'd never known Ivan in this kind of mood. Had never really seen him any other way except serious. She knew deep in her heart that only she could bring out these facets of his character. It warmed her and made her want to push the beast, push him until he broke and showed her everything he was capable of; good and bad. It all belonged to her.

"Such a good fucking girl," he groaned, and then brought his hand down on her ass, spanking her. Jaya jumped and then automatically lunged forward trying to get away from the unexpected pain. He wrapped his hands around her waist and held her still until she stopped struggling. "Don't move."

She held still and after a moment, when her brain was able to separate from the heat of the spanking she could feel the sizzle and spikes of heat streaking outward from her ass and lighting her blood on fire. She dug her fingers into the bed and held on as he lifted his hand and brought it down on her ass several more times in quick succession, spanking each cheek alternately. She jumped with each strike, unable to suppress the instinct, but pain turned to pleasure and bloomed within her. Her pussy quickly became wet and felt unbearably empty. She wiggled beneath him as he ran a broad hand over the heated globes of her ass.

In one swift move he gripped the waist of her thong and dragged it down her legs, stretching it over her spread thighs and yanking it off her legs. Jaya lifted herself, helping. As soon as her knees were back on the bed he slapped her again, sending her heart and her libido soaring. She shrieked and tossed her hair back but dug her hands into the bedding, refusing to move under his harsh treatment.

"Such a good, obedient girl," he snarled over her.

She groaned, his words making her even wetter, even wilder to have him inside her. It was everything she could do not to shove herself back into him and beg him to fuck her. She wanted him worse than she ever wanted anything.

She tossed her hair back again and glanced back to see what he was doing, why his hands weren't on her, in her, fucking her. He was busy pulling his tie off and wrenching his shirt open, his smouldering eyes caressing every inch of her body, lingering on her upraised ass. He kneeled on the bed next to her and drew his hands gently down from her shoulders, to her arms, circling her wrists. The silk of his tie caressed her arm as it slid down her skin and she shivered at the sensation after the beating her ass had just taken.

He pulled her hands behind her back, pushing her forward until her shoulders were resting on the mattress and tied her wrists with his tie. She immediately tested the bond to find out if it was secure. She whimpered as it tightened around her, digging into her flesh a little. He placed a hand over her wrists and squeezed his warning. She stopped struggling.

"You said you wanted to play," he said, his voice deep and thick with passion. He moved back behind her and used his thigh to push her legs further apart. She moaned as another rush of heat hit her belly, sending more fluid to her already dripping pussy.

Her breath caught and then scattered as he ran two long fingers through the folds, dragging them from front to back, over and over, around and around, before pushing them inside her. He did this with slow laziness, as though exploring her, but with confidence. Like he knew exactly where to touch, how to touch and with how much pressure. She closed her eyes, feeling the slow build-up of another exquisite orgasm at the hands of her captor.

Then he pulled his fingers from her body, wrapped his arm around her waist, and dragging her closer, placed his fingers at the entrance of her ass. Her eyes flew open and she tried to wiggle out of his grip. But with her arms tied behind her back and his grip on her waist, she was helpless. She opened her mouth to deny him access to the most private part of her body, when he used the lubrication from her pussy to push forward, breaching the virginal ring of her ass, slowly filling her.

Jaya cried out, her voice a strangled moan, muffled by the bedding beneath her head and the hair that had fallen into her face. Was he trying to punish her? Maybe he really was angry with her still. But, while the burn hurt, it wasn't unbearable. She felt full, too full and the sensation was foreign. She felt as though she needed to push back against him. He kept forcing his fingers in, pushing them deeper and then twisting them within her. She yelped and dropped her bottom onto her heels, trying to escape him, but he released her waist long enough to give her ass cheek a sharp slap, the hardest one yet.

"Back up on your knees," he snapped.

She lifted her ass again and realized the pressure in her anal passage was much more bearable now. In fact, it almost felt good. He continued to work her ass, using more wetness from her slick pussy to ease his way, while she moaned and whimpered underneath him. After a few minutes, the burn morphed into a sizzling heat that merged with the warmth that'd been building in her pussy. A different kind of orgasm began to build, one she never expected, never thought to experience.

He leaned over her and said in a low voice, "We're going to play a different sort of game now, my love."

She stiffened, hearing the dark intent and the anger in his voice, still simmering from when they first entered the room. "What kind of game?" she gasped.

"The game where you tell me what tomorrow is really about," he growled against the side of her head. "And I don't punish this ass even more than I want to right now." He twisted his fingers to the side, pushing them deeper. Jaya lunged against him, caught in his steely grip. She tried to catch her breath, but it was a losing endeavor.

"I-I don't know what you mean," she moaned, her voice thready.

"You know exactly what I mean!" he shouted, losing his cool. He jerked back from her, his hands leaving her body.

Jaya flinched and closed her eyes, afraid of what he was going to do to her. She could feel the heat of his anger rolling off him. She knew it wasn't directed entirely at her. That it was their circumstances, it was Father, Ivan's own feelings, both their pasts, everything that brought them to this moment. He slapped her ass so hard she screamed. She felt no pleasure in the strike and knew he'd done it to hurt her.

Knew he'd probably done it so he wouldn't do worse. Ivan was losing control.

She felt his hand on her pussy and flinched, afraid he would hit her again. But he only ran his fingers through her pussy, collecting the fluid and smearing it over her ass. She twisted around on her shoulders to look at him. He scooped more of her juices and, unzipping his pants, he pulled his hard, thick penis out and used her own wetness to lubricate himself. Her mouth began watering as she watched him stroke his hardness, his hand wrapped around his cock, using her vaginal fluid to glide back and forth, his smouldering, angry gaze chained to hers.

He moved to her, lining himself up with her. She stiffened when she felt the velvety head of his penis caress her anus. Tears pricked her eyes and she pleaded with him silently, begging him to reconsider. His jaw stiffened and he took her bound wrists in one hand and her hip in the other. Then he began pressing himself into her, forcing his thick cockhead into her virgin anal passage.

Jaya let out a yell and buried her face into the bedding as unbearable blazing heat tore through her ass. He grabbed a handful of her hair and forced her head up. "You will look at me," he growled. Through clenched teeth.

Tears streamed down her cheeks, but she did as she was told. She looked back at him as he took her ass, sliding relentlessly forward until he was buried deep inside her. She shook beneath him, feeling as though she was being torn in two. Her heart beat so frantically she was positive she was having a heart attack. He stayed that way for long minutes, leaving her in agony until finally her body began to stretch and relent, accepting his invasion.

As soon as he felt the gradual relaxing of her muscles he reached beneath her and began caressing her clit. She moaned and arched, pressing herself more fully on the cock buried deep within her ass. The dual sensation between her ass and her clit were lighting her on fire. She thought the bed would combust and go right up with them. She didn't care. She began rocking her hips, encouraging him to caress her, to push her into the mindless oblivion she knew he could treat her to.

"No, sweetheart," he growled. "You've been a bad girl and bad girls have to wait."

She cried out when he took his hand away from her clit. But then he moved, sliding his hips back, moving his cock and then pushing it back deep inside her ass. She cried out and arched low, trying to get away from the painful heat tearing up her insides. He smoothed a finger over her clit, playing the nub like an instrument, gifting her pleasure before slicing her with pain. He did it over and over until she couldn't separate one from the other, until she cried and begged for both, uncaring of which he gave her. He pressed fingers deep inside her pussy and used the heel of his hand against her clit while he thrust forcefully into her tender ass.

She felt a final streak of unbearable pain bolt through her as his cock flared wide in her ass, followed by the sweet gift of pleasure as he finally allowed her to leap over the ledge of her orgasm. His hand wrapped possessively around her bound wrists and he grunted his own release, thrusting deep inside her and flooding her anal passage with hot semen. As his hips moved she felt it drip down the crease of her ass to her pussy.

He pulled out of her, careful not to move too quickly and hurt her. She still cried out, tears pricking her eyes. She moved her head, wiping the wetness on the bed. Ivan placed a hand underneath her and helped ease her flat on her belly. She thought he would untie her wrists, but he didn't. Instead he climbed onto the bed and gathered her in his arms. He turned her so she was laying next to him. He brushed her hair from her face and looked down at her, his expression fierce and deadly.

"If anything happens to you, Jaya. If one single hair is bent or broken," he said, his voice a low promise. "I will crush this world until there is nothing left. I won't stop until everyone pays. Including you."

CHAPTER THIRTY

Jaya was so wrapped up in her current state of nervous tension it took a few minutes for her to notice the look of absurd scepticism written all over Ndari's face. When she finally did glance over at her friend she couldn't help laughing out loud. Ndari was sitting primly on the lounge chair next to Jaya, her super wide-brimmed sun hat shading her face but doing nothing to hide the look of utter consternation she was giving her friend.

"What?" Jaya asked, still laughing. "What are you looking at?"

"Are you serious?" Ndari asked haughtily. "Where should I start? Uh, how about with the clothes you chose to go swimming in." They both glanced down at Jaya's outfit of black leggings and fitted long-sleeved top. Her hair was tied back in a tight ponytail. The outfit wasn't very appropriate for a hot Indonesian morning.

"I said I *might* go swimming with you, I'm still not sure," Jaya murmured, defensively.

"Uh huh," Ndari said, sceptically, then jerked her chin

toward the edge of the building where Ivan and Keane stood about ten feet apart. "And what about the deadly duo? Granted the Irishman is usually hanging about, creeping on us, but your stalker over there can normally be found locked up in his office waving the hand of God at this time of day. What gives? Why are they hovering like hawks over a weirdly dressed baby chick?"

Jaya rounded her eyes innocently and shrugged, leaning back on the lounger. "I have no idea what you're talking about."

"So you have no idea why everyone is so tense that I'm thinking I'll probably get my ass shot if I so much as look at you funny." Ndari crossed her arms over her breasts. She was far more appropriately dressed in a revealing one-piece bathing suit with a sheer wrap that did nothing to hide her incredible curves. Like the princess she was, she completed the outfit with black stilettos.

"No idea," Jaya assured her and then glanced at the time on her laptop, which was open on the small round table next to her lounger. It was eight minutes to show time. "Do you think you can go inside and find my sunscreen? I think I'm starting to burn."

"I don't see how," Ndari snorted. "You're covered from neck to toe."

"My face is burning," Jaya insisted. "Please go find it. I think I left it under the sink in my washroom."

Ndari lifted a brow and then took the hat off her own head and plopped it on Jaya's head. She bent over at the waist and glared at Jaya from the brim. "I'm not going anywhere, girlie. If you're about to rein chaos again, then you're doing it with me by your side." She whispered so no one else could hear.

Jaya blinked back the tears that suddenly prickled in her

eyes. She leaned forward and hugged Ndari tight, not caring what Ivan or his men thought. "I promise you, I'll be fine. But I need you to go inside now. Please do this for me?"

Ndari shifted and looked at Jaya, took in her anxious expression, the plea on her face. Finally she nodded and stood, breaking contact with Jaya. "Alright," she said, loud enough for some of the men to hear. "I'll go find the sunscreen and some snacks. Be right back." There was a tiny hitch in her voice, but otherwise nothing noticeable was off as she took her hat back from Jaya, turned away from where the two women had been sitting and strode toward their private suites.

Jaya sighed in relief when her friend disappeared through the doors. Now if only she could keep everyone else safe. She had no idea what was coming, what kind of assault or extraction plan Father might be setting up. She did know that he wasn't usually worried about casualties, especially where Ivan Vogel was concerned. His lack of concern toward human life was one of the reasons she'd felt compelled to leave Father when she became old enough, when she was seventeen. Five years in his compound, living his hatred, learning how to survive had given her both a deep sense of gratitude and a desperate need to get out on her own and spread her wings.

Minutes after Ndari disappeared through the condo door, about three minutes after 10am, Jaya finally heard what she'd been expecting. A disturbance. Shouting from the west side of the building made everyone turn. Gunfire shattered the stillness of the morning, making her jump where she sat. She stared hard toward the sound, but of course couldn't see anything. They were blocked by the residence section of the tower. Her head came up and her gaze clashed with Ivan's. His speculative look told her he'd also been expecting something like this. He turned and said something sharply to Keane who grabbed a couple of his guys and left.

Jaya stood, but Ivan turned to her swiftly, pointing a finger imperiously. "Get your ass back down," he snarled. "I don't want to see your head above the edge of that chair."

She nodded and hit the patio, curling up against the edge of the lounger. She gripped the metal railing as though her life depended on it. She couldn't figure out what was going on. She twisted her neck around and stared up, trying to guess where the assault was coming from. She thought they must be coming for her in a helicopter because nothing else made sense. But she hadn't heard the blades of an approaching aircraft. But how else would men that didn't belong to Ivan be getting on his roof?

Her thoughts scattered when the lounger next to her was shredded by bullets. She screamed and covered her head with her arms as the shooter hit the patio tiles all around her sending shards of marble and concrete flying in every direction. She felt something slice into the back of her hand, which was covering her face. When the shooting stopped she whipped her head up to see what was happening.

Ivan and his men were standing in positions around the pool, all eyes on her. As soon as the shooting ended, Ivan lunged forward, clearly intent on getting to her. As soon as he took a step forward bullets began hitting the water two feet in front of her, spraying drops several feet into the air and soaking her. It quickly became clear that no one was to approach her.

Jaya shook her hand, hissing in a breath at the pain slicing through her. Blood dripped from the tips of her fingers. She pulled the sleeve of her top down over her hand and swiped at the blood, soaking it up. Ivan caught the action and glared murderously. She could see his thoughts, see his fury over her injury, no matter how minor. "I'm sorry," she mouthed. His lips thinned and he shook his head, the glint in his eyes dangerous.

Her gaze drifted past his shoulder and landed on something behind him. A man had just climbed over the side of the 50-story building and was standing several feet behind Ivan. Although his face was covered by a helmet she knew exactly who he was. Father had come for her. He looked past Ivan and beckoned to her, signalling that she should walk around the pool toward him.

Jaya stood on shaking limbs and began walking. She glanced sideways at Ivan as she started to pass by him, and though she wasn't very close, she could still see the fury that ripped across his features. The devastation as he realized he was about to lose her and there was nothing he could do. Apparently the thought broke him. He lunged forward, intent on getting to Jaya before she could get to Father. The rooftop gunman opened fire, shooting so close to Ivan that patio chips were thrown up in his face, cutting him. He was thrown backwards. His men grabbed his arms and yanked him out of the path of the bullets, while two more dropped to their knees and returned fire, aiming for the top of the building.

Jaya screamed and tried to run to Ivan. Father got to her first, wrapping long arms around her waist and pulling her against his solid body. She slammed a fist into his shoulder and tried to see around him to make sure Ivan was okay, but her view was blocked. He yanked her back toward the ledge of the building, ignoring her frantic struggles.

"What are you doing?" she yelled. "Please, just let me go. I don't want to go."

He turned to her and without a word slapped her so hard the entire world spun, going black for a few seconds. She felt herself lifted up onto the ledge. With quick, efficient movements she was strapped to his body. She blinked several times, mentally screaming at herself to wake up and fight. She swam her way to the surface, opening her eyes in time to see Ivan back on his feet, a look of horror on his bloody face right before she tipped over the ledge of his high-rise building wrapped in the arms of his enemy.

CHAPTER THIRTY-ONE

Jaya glared at the man who had spent twelve years protecting her and providing for her. Even once she'd moved away from him and his disciples, learned to fly on her own, she'd still come back to him for advice, for a home. She wiggled her fingers. It was hard to feel at home when she was zip-tied in the place where she had once shared meals and companionship with the man sitting across from her.

Over the past weeks, distance and perspective from this man had brought the realization that she was pretty sure Father was willing to sacrifice her for his vendetta. Now, with her butt and fingers numb from being tied to a chair and her cheek bruised from his rooftop abuse, she was feeling even more certain. She wondered why he hadn't finished his assault on the rooftop. Why, if he was willing to sacrifice his only adopted daughter to the cause, hadn't he just killed both her and Ivan when he had the chance?

Because he knew he wouldn't get away with it? No, Father didn't care if he lived or died, as long as he took Ivan Vogel with him to hell.

"Because I need to know what you mean to him." Father answered her question, reading her easily. He'd always done that. In fact, when she'd finally left his compound at the age of seventeen, it had been his suggestion. He'd read her thoughts, known she was no longer happy living among him and the rough, violent adopted men he raised.

He was sitting across from her in his simple home, a home built for calm meditation. He leaned forward, elbows on knees and studied her. He looked greyer than the last time she saw him two years ago, his beard now fully white. He reached for her, ignoring her flinch and pulling her arm forward a little, pushed the sleeve up. It was uncomfortable since her hands were zip-tied behind her back. He tapped a finger against the thick wrist cuff.

"This is pricey, my dear," he murmured, twisting her wrist around, examining it. He ignored her pained yelp of protest. "And it doesn't come off, does it? Only a possessive rich bastard would do something like that." He looked into her eyes, his dark brown ones filled with insane glee. "One very much in love with the woman he's marked. He also went to tremendous effort, not once, but twice, to have you returned to his care when you managed to escape. I was more than a little surprised after your first attempt that I didn't find your mangled corpse on that island. Vogel isn't known for his patience with such antics."

She narrowed her eyes at his matter-of-fact tone when it came to the possibility of her demise. "I have no idea what you mean. Ivan simply saw the use in having me around."

He looked sad for a moment and then the look was replaced with resignation. He ran a broad hand over her forehead, smoothing it over her hair and down her ponytail. He leaned forward and kissed her on the top of her head then sat back in his chair, crossing one leg over the other. He studied her critically for a moment.

"And just like that my enemy steals your loyalty," he said coolly.

"Maybe you would still have my loyalty if I ever had yours," she cried out, unable to hide the bitterness from her voice. "I know why I'm here, I know what you intend."

"And what is that?" he asked, his dark eyes glinting viciously.

"You're going to use me to get to Ivan, to kill him." Her breath caught as she thought of her lover dying at the hands of this man. A flash through the years made her realize how very little she actually owed Father. He didn't have her loyalty, not really. Yes, he'd fed and clothed her in her early years, but he'd demanded so much more in return. That wasn't how relationships worked. Family and love wasn't a transaction. It was caring about the safety, health and comfort of the other person, like Ivan's care for her.

"Do you have any idea what that man has done to me?" Father asked, in a final attempt to turn her back to his side. Back to the seething hatred he'd carried with him for decades. She understood the need to have her on his side. And this is probably why he'd taken her from Ivan's penthouse, rather than used her as a shield while murdering Ivan. If he could turn Jaya against Ivan before killing him, then the death of his enemy would be that much sweeter.

"You're finally going to tell me?" she asked quietly. "After all of these years, all the chances you had to tell me why you wanted us to hate this anonymous enemy of yours, now you'll give up the goods?"

"Yes, my dear," Father said, nodding. "You deserve the truth."

"Too late, I already know," she said derisively.

His mouth dropped open and he stared at her in shock. "He knows who I am?" he sounded almost impressed, as though he'd been recognized by a rock star.

"No," she snorted. "Of course not, you've been very good at hiding yourself from both him and us, your loyal foundlings. No, I figured it out on my own. You see, Ivan is less reticent about discussing his past. I put two and two together."

"And came up with what?" Father snarled.

"He murdered your family," she said unemotionally. "He hunted them down and killed them one at a time. If I had to guess, he probably killed your wife and kids."

He moved so fast, she didn't have a chance to get out of the way, couldn't even if she wanted to since she was tied down. He slapped her across the face, first one side and then the other. Her head rocked back and her ears rang. He gripped her jaw and dragged her forward in the seat, his fingers biting into her cheeks. She felt the tender skin on the inside of her mouth cut into her molars and winced. He leaned in so close she thought for a second, with her now scrambled senses, that he was about to kiss her.

"He murdered my wife," he snarled, spit flying from his lips to land on hers. "Strangled her in her bed and then cut out her heart, left her for me to find. Then he went down the hall to my kids' rooms and killed them too. He showed no mercy, not even for my babies. I was only following orders, was only a soldier back then. It wasn't my fault his family was killed, yet he didn't care. He just... killed them all."

Her heart broke for him, broke for the man that he used to be, the man that found his family viciously murdered. But it also broke for the fourteen-year-old boy who returned to his village after hearing rumours of a massacre, discovering his family missing and then digging up a mass grave to find them. Though horrifically unfair, unjustified and awful, she understood why a young Ivan had savagely turned against the soldiers and their families. He was too young to deal with the horror of the situation, the sadness and emotions ripping him apart. He was a youth with knowledge of weapons and warfare and he turned that knowledge against the people that had hurt him. His youthful vengeance shattered the lives of dozens and shaped Ivan Vogel into the man he became, a deadly arms dealer with a reputation for ruthlessness. Father released her jaw and stood.

"I'm sorry," she whispered.

He turned his back to her and dipped his head in a nod. "Nothing will bring her... them back."

"You're right," she agreed. "Nothing will, but there is more to live for than hate, Father."

He turned when she said his name, responding to the softness in her voice. His gaze was remote, as though he'd already made a decision. But then, he'd made the decision years ago when he'd pulled the trigger on Ivan's family. Everything after was just a series of domino events related to that single event.

"I wish that was true, my daughter," he murmured. "I wish you were loyal to me once more."

Pain blossomed in her chest and threatened to choke her. A part of her wanted to dive into his arms and beg him to accept her again, accept her as the daughter she should be. She closed her eyes and took a breath, shoving the pain away. "And I wish you cared more about me than you do about murdering Ivan Vogel."

This man wasn't her father. Jaya's father would never use her against her lover, no matter what. Jaya's father had loved her unconditionally and he had died horrifically in a bomb attack. Just like she wasn't Father's daughter; his daughter had died in her bed. Jaya had never been able to replace her. Father had always held Jaya at a distance, never hugging her close, never giving her the tender words a teenager needed to hear as she grew. She'd been a useful tool and now she was about to bring him his greatest gift, the thing he'd been waiting for.

"I assume he's tracking you," Father said.

There was no point in denying the obvious. Father had already guessed how much she meant to Ivan and denying an attachment would be pointless. Besides, she might be able to use her unique position to negotiate a truce between the two men. She had to try; both men had feelings for her, she had the best chance of getting them to stand down. "There's a chip in my shoulder," she admitted.

He nodded his head absently, his eyes calculating. "He'll be here soon then. Probably started tracing your whereabouts the moment we parachuted off that roof. His tech capabilities will be sophisticated, so he likely tracked us while we were flying. Bastard might be here within the hour."

Jaya tilted her head back and glared. "Count on it. If there's one thing Ivan's good at, it's finding me."

CHAPTER THIRTY-TWO

From the outside Ivan knew he looked his usual icy collected self. He wore the same clothes as his men; combat fatigues meant to blend into a jungle environment since Jaya's captor had led them to Thailand during rainy season. He sat in the back of the military aircraft he'd purchased for bigger operations, leaning forward, arms bent loose across his knees. Though he appeared calm, even speaking to Keane about logistics, on the inside he was a boiling cauldron of fear, fury and smouldering rage. He intended to bury Father's operation until it was nothing but a pile of rocks.

"We can land the plane in Bangkok and drive in, it'll take maybe three to four hours to get to her location," Keane said pointing at a location on the map. "The region is dense. I suspect the going'll be slow once we're on the ground and in the mud."

Ivan shook his head and stabbed the map with his middle finger. "Here. She'll be half hour out, max."

Keane growled his displeasure. "We can't land this fuckin' thing in the middle of a jungle, boss. Bad idea."

Ivan turned icy eyes on his second. "Didn't say anything about landing. And I'm not asking your opinion."

Keane frowned and then, when he realized what the boss was saying, turned an interesting shade of green. "Awe, fuck off. Fucking hate jungle jumps."

Ivan grunted. "Assholes got onto my roof that way. Figure we can return the favour."

"Sure," Keane snarled, swallowing audibly and reaching for the parachute over his head. "Hey," he shouted down the plane toward the pilot, "when was the last time these things were safety inspected?" No one answered, but everyone around them began putting on their parachutes and checking each other's harnesses. Keane pulled his on and latched the harness around his chest and stomach. He glared at Ivan. "Fuck you."

Ivan followed suit, ignoring his irate second-in-command. Once he was strapped in, he twisted around to glance out the window. He pointed. "See that, we'll meet on the west edge of that town. Organize the men."

Keane nodded and stood, reaching for a strap over his head to steady himself. "Oi, listen up!" he shouted down the length of the plane. Two dozen heads swivelled toward him. He explained their plan in short, succinct sentences. Moments later, the co-pilot was opening the door and they were preparing for the jump. One at a time his men jumped from the plane without hesitation. He wasn't surprised, most of them were ex-paramilitary or guerilla. They were all trained for this. Keane turned to glare at Ivan before tucking his arms across his chest and stepping out the door. Ivan nodded at the co-pilot and took his turn, following his man through the door.

He'd jumped many times in his life, both while training with his men and when the need to parachute into certain countries to make a deal arose. He always enjoyed the rush of a good freefall. The feeling of air and space flying past him, caressing his hair and face, cooling his skin. It was like the wide-open solitude of the sky matched the permanent iciness of his heart. But today he felt none of that, just a desperate need to put boots on the ground, get to his woman and ensure her safety. Then beat some damn sense into her for putting them both in this goddamned situation. A situation she could have prevented if she'd been honest with him.

He looked to his right and then his left. Parachutes were opening all around him and men were drifting gently toward the trees below. He could tell his guys were aiming for the small clearings in between and hoped they were accurate, he needed them largely unhurt for the operation. He knew he should open his own chute, prepare for landing. But the over-whelming desire to land fast, get to the village and plan the assault was replacing his need for safety. He waited, glancing at his watch and counting down until he knew he was reaching critical velocity. He felt, rather than saw, Keane's anxiety. The Irishman was shouting, but he was too far away for Ivan to hear.

Ivan deployed his chute and braced for landing, bending his knees for the impact. He hit the ground seconds later, much harder than he would have if he'd stayed in the sky longer. He allowed his body to collapse and rolled, tangling in the parachute as he went. "Motherfucker!" he snarled as his shoulder jarred against a rock. As soon as he stopped moving he was back on his feet. A quick inventory proved that he was fine except for a few bruises.

Rather than waste time pulling his parachute in, he pulled his blade from its sheath and severed the lines, detaching himself from the billowing fabric. He dropped it and walked away, heading swiftly for the village. He got to the meeting point within minutes, the first to arrive. Men began jogging up to him moments later, hunkering down, waiting for their next order. They'd been working for Ivan for long enough that, even without job specifics, they knew exactly what to expect from him.

Keane strode toward Ivan, a look of savage disgust on his face. Ivan understood when he caught a whiff of the guy's breath. Apparently the Irishman *really* hadn't enjoyed his jump or his landing; maybe both.

"Report," Ivan demanded. "Is everyone here?"

"Quinn broke his right arm landing in a tree," Keane said right away and then did a quick head count. "Everyone's here."

"Can he shoot left-handed?" Ivan asked.

"Yes, sir." A man stood up.

Ivan glanced at him. He was holding his arm stiffly at his side, but he looked tough enough. He should be, Ivan only hired the best of the worst. Quinn appeared ready and able to join the strike team. "Stay on the periphery, lay down cover fire. Don't engage directly unless you're ordered to. If you're lying to me about your ability to shoot left, it'll be the last thing you do."

"Yes, sir," Quinn acknowledged quickly.

Ivan laid out the plan for his men, allowing Keane to interrupt occasionally with logistical suggestions. Though Ivan had decades of field experience and was a deadly opponent, Keane was a true man of war. His ability to wage all out battle was what made him the only man worthy to stand at Ivan's side and why Ivan tolerated him, despite his toe-over-the-line approach to his boss. Finally, Ivan looked up from the map he'd been tracing with his finger.

"Any questions?" The battle-hardened men just looked at him. His plan was simple. Go in, get the girl with as few casualties as possible. And once she was out, burn the place to the ground with everyone in it. "Let's move out."

The trek through the forests of Thailand was hot, humid

and deeply uncomfortable. Ivan set a gruelling fast pace that would put them in Father's encampment in less than twenty minutes. Keane should be thanking him for forcing them to jump into the middle of the jungle rather than travel bumpy, muddy roads for hours and then go by foot.

When they arrived close to Father's base camp, Ivan's men scattered at his silent order, taking position according to his instructions. He and Keane had developed their strategy based on real time satellite images sent to him every twenty minutes during their three-hour, twenty-two-minute flight from Indonesia to Thailand. There were several men scattered throughout the jungle guarding the encampment. Ivan's people would take them down one at a time. No doubt they were expecting his arrival, were expecting an assault, but they could have no clue how swift or skilled his men were. They were about to find out.

Once they were in the camp, they would attempt to do as little damage as possible until they reached Jaya's position. The last message he got from his secretary, five minutes ago, indicated that she was being held in a house at the centre of the tiny village, according to her locator chip.

Trusting that his men had done their job without complication, he walked boldly into the encampment without pause, Keane at his side. Two men came running toward them. They looked around Jaya's age, maybe a little older. Keane made quick work of them, putting a single bullet in each man, headshots. Ivan turned to glare at his man.

Keane shrugged. "They're probably under orders not to kill you. Fuck if I'm gonna die in this stinking mudhole."

"I should drop you back in the desert where I found you," Ivan said coolly, shaking his head as they made their way toward the hut where Jaya was supposedly being kept. He was surprised she wasn't out in the open, where it would be easier for Father to plan an ambush.

"Better than jumping out of airplanes into this fucking bullshit," Keane grumbling, lifting his semi-automatic and waving it at a man who stepped out of one of the small houses. The man looked startled but dropped his weapon a few feet away from his boots and then followed it to the ground, his arms over his head. The move might save his life.

Ivan's men began descending on the village from their jungle positions, moving in one at a time, covering each other. They took the village with militaristic ease, working together like a well-oiled machine, each cog doing its job with precision. Father's men were young, and while they tried valiantly to protect their home, they couldn't match the skill and brutality of Ivan's force. According to orders, Ivan's people took the village with as few casualties as possible, quietly moving in, striking with swift ease, making it clear that Father's men either complied or died. Most laid down their arms and gave up.

Ivan grabbed a man near the point where Jaya was being held and, gripping him by the hair and twisting viciously, asked, "Where is Jaya?"

"Who?" he asked, his eyes wide with fear. The stench of urine indicated his bladder had released. The dead body of his comrade at their feet probably didn't help his confidence.

Ivan unsheathed his knife and held it to the man's throat. It was a wicked looking blade with deep serrations along the sharp edge. His eyes took on the death chill that usually convinced those that knew him it was time to take a long walk in the opposite direction. "Where is the girl? The hacker?"

He tried to speak, but nothing came out. Ivan's patience was beginning to ebb. He was considering disposing of this nuisance and moving onto fresh prey when the guy finally lifted a shaking hand and pointed at a home, slightly nicer than the one's surrounding it. Ivan nodded, lifted the guy, turned him and slammed the knife into his belly, gutting him. The man screamed, a chilling sound. Ivan hoped his enemy heard and knew he was coming.

"How come you get to kill them and I can't?" Keane asked, nudging the dying man with his foot. "Doesn't seem fair."

Ivan ignored him and bent to wipe his knife. Resheathing it, he stood and strode toward the house containing Jaya, intent only on collecting his woman. When he got to the door he turned and looked at Keane.

"Got your back," the Irishman grunted.

CHAPTER THIRTY-THREE

Ivan had come for her.

She sensed him well before Father's men warned him that Ivan and his men were near. It was as though her heart knew the moment his feet landed on Thai soil. It started beating faster, the blood speeding through her veins in anticipation, rushing in her ears, distracting her. Soon she would be safe in the arms of her lover. She closed her eyes, forcing herself to take deep breaths, forcing back the nausea that swelled in her gut at the confrontation to come. It was inevitable, she could do nothing to stop it, so she might as well calm herself. As Ivan would urge her to do. Nerves could get someone killed. She'd heard him yelling this at his men while training with them.

Conversation between herself and the man that professed himself her only family became stilted. There was less and less point in trying to reach a madman. As his life's goal approached, his ability to listen to reason drifted away, if it had ever been there. Perhaps if she'd known his reasons for hunting Ivan years earlier she might have been able to reach him, but not now. Still, when the first bullets rang through his encampment, Jaya tried one last time to plead for his life, never once doubting who would leave victorious. Ivan never failed. And she had a plan to help him.

"He's coming for you Father," she said calmly. "And he won't let you live. Not after you took me away from him. It was bad enough that you blew up his island, but he might have forgiven you that at my insistence. If you'd given up this vendetta." Father approached her and looked down, his gaze as cold as hers. She was wasting her breath. But still, she had to try. For the sake of the child she'd once been. The child who had desperately needed rescuing and had clung to this man for support and affection. He had only given her one of the two, but it was worth something, worth his life if she could do something to save him. "Please, just go. Go away and save yourself! He'll kill you and he'll do it slowly and viciously. You don't understand!"

He grabbed her arm and dragged her from the chair, positioning her in front of him. He turned so that they were facing the door and then he bent to speak in her ear. "I understand perfectly, my dear," he murmured. "I never intended to leave here alive. I died the day he took my family."

"Then why are you doing this?" she cried.

"I've watched and waited for years, trying to find something he loved so I could take it away from him." His voice dropped to a whisper. "And I handed him the one thing he could love on a silver platter. Now I get to take her away while he watches. It will be my sweetest victory."

A chill slithered down her spine as he lifted a gun and pressed it against the side of her skull seconds before Ivan stepped through the door. She was reminded sharply of the time Ivan had held a gun to her head, when he'd hugged her after dreaming of his family, of murdering Father's family. Only she'd felt safe in Ivan's arms, had known on a visceral level that he wouldn't hurt her. Father intended to kill her, to use her to avenge himself.

"Jaya," Ivan said, his voice cool, his eyes devouring her, starting at her feet and lingering on her face where bruises were beginning to show. "How are you, sweetheart?"

She took a few quick breaths to steady her voice and then said calmly, "I'm fine, Ivan. Though the hospitality here leaves something to be desired. I'm about ready to leave on the first flight out. I'm just shocked it took you so long to get here, I was about ready to pawn my bracelets to get out of here."

"Enough!" Father snapped, waving his gun at Ivan before returning it to Jaya's head. "On your knees, throw your gun away." Ivan immediately did as Father demanded, tossing his gun to the side and kneeling on the floor. A detached part of Jaya's brain noted that even in that position he was still the most commanding man she'd ever been around. He filled the space with his brutal, coolly dominant personality. Even in such a perilous situation it made her shiver, made her want to fly to him, snuggle against him and beg him to hold her.

"Do you know who I am?" Father demanded.

"Borjan Tadic," Ivan said without pause. "Born 1964. You were among the men that came to my town of Rekovi in 1992 and massacred 77 people, my family included. I returned the favour by killing yours. I've known who you were almost from the moment you started hunting me."

For a moment no one said anything as they absorbed the impact of Ivan's words. Finally, Jaya whispered, almost to herself, "Borjan," saying Father's birth name out loud. Somehow it took away some of the impact of his importance. The man that had built himself a jungle compound and filled it with semi-loyal followers, then spewed his hate at them, insisting they follow him. Giving him a name took the teeth from his hate a little. His fingers tightened around her, as though it angered him to hear his given name on her lips.

"If you knew who I was then why didn't you kill me?" Borjan growled, anger making him careless as he pulled his gun from Jaya's head and waved it toward Ivan. She edged her hands, which were still tied behind her back toward him and took a fistful of his shirt. He didn't seem to notice. "If you've been tracking me all these years, why haven't you brought me down sooner?"

Ivan's eyes glinted as his focus finally shifted away from Jaya for the first time since entering the hut. A savage note entered his voice when he responded and his accent became more pronounced. "Same reason you didn't kill me on that rooftop. You'll suffer more alive than dead. Every day you spend without your loved ones is one more day that I am victorious over you."

Jaya froze, her hands stilling in their quest to find Borjan's bare stomach. She stared at the man she'd fallen helplessly and completely in love with. This was him, the vicious animal, the beast in all his glory. She was deeply and utterly glad he'd fallen in love with her, because she had no doubt that if he hadn't she would be in little pieces by now, shipped back to the man now holding her, using her as both a weapon and a shield.

Ivan spoke again, his stormy, ice cold gaze now returning to Jaya. "I give you one chance only, Tadic. Let her go. I intend that you die here today, but your manner of death is still in question."

"I don't care about death," Borjan snarled, spit flying past Jaya's face to land on the ground in front of Ivan. "I will take her with me and enjoy the look on your face as she falls. I will gladly spill the blood of my adoptive daughter if it means crushing what is left of your soul. Fuck this mortal body. I don't care what you do to it."

He lifted the gun against her head. Jaya pressed her wrists against the bare skin of his stomach and closed her eyes, waiting for the jolt. At least she hoped that's what she was about to feel, because she'd take electrocution over a bullet to the head any day of the week.

A powerful, sharp vibration hit her, stabbing her arms and running right through her body. Jaya's knees gave out involuntarily and she tumbled to the ground at Borjan's feet. Though she knew the electrical current had hit him too, he somehow managed to stay standing. Probably because he didn't take the bulk of the electricity that Ivan hit them with. As she tumbled, Jaya's head snapped back and she saw something fly over her head and bury itself deep in Borjan's shoulder. She lay on the ground, still within reach. She tried to crawl away, but her limbs wouldn't obey, Ivan had probably hit them with the maximum jolt of electricity the bracelets were capable of.

Borjan hit the ground next to her, collapsing to his knees. She searched for his gun but didn't see it. He must've dropped it when Ivan zapped them. She rolled her head up in time to see Ivan climbing to his feet and talking a step toward them, the dam finally breaking on the fury within.

Borjan didn't see Ivan, wasn't looking at him, he was so intent on killing Jaya. So utterly focused on destroying the one thing Ivan loved. He crawled over top of Jaya and wrapped shaking fingers around her neck.

"It's over, Father," she whispered.

He didn't even get a chance to tighten his fingers around her throat. Ivan stood behind him, looking down at Jaya over top of her captor's head. He took the knife he'd thrown into Borjan's shoulder and yanked it out. Blood sprayed across Jaya. She tried to turn her head to the side, but her head was being held immobile. Ivan lifted the blade and sank it into Borjan's other shoulder, weakening his grip on Jaya.

She wiggled in his arms, desperately wishing her hands weren't tied behind her back, until his grip, weak now and slippery from blood, finally gave way. She crawled out from under him and sat a few feet away, hunched over and gagging. She spat out some blood, maybe hers, maybe Father's. She looked over at the scene in front of her; Ivan standing over the man that had once rescued her from the streets of Mumbai. She could see Father's fate written all over Ivan's face.

"Please, Ivan," she begged, trying to plead for a swift death. "Please just finish it."

His gaze became glacial and she knew what his answer would be before he even spoke. "He took from me." Ivan shoved the man away and knelt down next to Jaya. He took her chin in his hand and he ran a thumb over her bottom lip then her cheek, brushing gently over a tender spot. She couldn't suppress a flinch. "He hurt you." Tears filled her eyes and she met Borjan's shadowed gaze where he lay on the floor watching the pair. "Now I'm going to hurt him more."

CHAPTER THIRTY-FOUR

"I don't understand," Jaya whispered.

She was standing in a gorgeous hotel room in Bangkok, wrapped in a big fluffy bathrobe, the horror of the past day having finally been washed from her skin. She gazed blindly out into the waking dawn of the city below not really seeing the splendor. Her brain was still frozen on the terrors of her kidnapping at Father's hands, his death and their wild ride back through the rainy jungle at night. Ivan hadn't wanted to linger in Father's encampment after dispatching him. Though he hadn't listened to her plea in regard to Father, Ivan had allowed some of her fellow disciples to live. The ones that had dropped arms and walked away from the conflict, agreed to train with Ivan and his men. Ivan had told Jaya if they survived training and he was convinced they weren't brainwashed by Borjan, he would give them the same choice he'd once given Keane, employment or freedom.

Ivan came to stand behind her, wrapping his arms around her waist and drawing her against his solid heat. She closed her eyes and breathed deep, taking in his familiar, comforting scent.

"What don't you understand, sweetheart?" he asked, gently sweeping the wet strands of her hair aside and kissing the skin behind her ear.

A shiver ran through her in response and her breath caught. She forced herself to step away from his seductive touch so she wouldn't be distracted. She needed an answer. She turned to look at him. He was so tall, so solid. He was dressed in only his combat pants, having taken his shirt off and thrown it over a chair. Her chest ached with the knowledge that this beautiful, hard man loved her. That he would do anything to keep her safe. Except... would he?

"If you always knew who Borjan was... why didn't you go after him when you realized you l-loved me?" she had to force the words past stiff lips. She knew this conversation was important, but at the same time, part of her didn't want to know. Not if he gave her the wrong answer. "Was playing with him, making him suffer just a little longer, that important? That you were willing to put my life in danger?"

Pain blossomed in her chest. Two men had been willing to use her in revenge against each other. The thought was awful, untenable. She didn't think she could survive knowing Ivan was willing to let her get hurt, or possibly even sacrifice her to Borjan. She'd wanted so badly to believe in all of Ivan's words of love. But they meant nothing if he'd been willing to allow his enemy to live, putting her life at risk at the same time.

Ivan turned Jaya in his arms. His grey eyes liquid as they looked down at her. "There is a very simple answer to your question, my love. I may have known who he was, but I didn't know where he was."

"You didn't?" she asked, surprised. "All these years, and you couldn't find him?"

Ivan shrugged. "He would come across my radar once in awhile, but no, for the most part, I had no idea. He kept himself well hidden. Who set up the electronic perimeter defences around Borjan's encampment? Who installed his state-of-the-art security system? Who ensured that every time an interested enemy of Borjan's went looking for him, they would think he lived first in China, then in Canada, then Australia... you get the picture."

"Oh!" she said, her eyes rounding. "I did that."

"Yes, you did," he said, admiration clear in his voice. "And you did such an excellent job of his security that you frustrated my every attempt to discover his whereabouts over the years. About two years ago I'd decided that Borjan had become enough of a nuisance, that I was done keeping him alive for my amusement. I tried hunting him, but every time I turned around, I hit a digital roadblock. Then I became curious about the person setting up the blocks. Sweetheart, I didn't know where to find him. If I knew, then the moment he became a threat to your life, I would've taken him out."

"Ivan..." she whispered.

"I'm so sorry, Jaya." His deep voice held a wealth of sincerity. "If I'd known you were going to get tangled up in my vendetta, if I'd known what you would come to mean to me, I would find a way to turn back time and change my decision to murder those people. I would have walked away from my burned-out village and dead family and found another way to survive the pain."

Jaya stepped forward, wrapped her arms around his waist and pressed a kiss against his chest. "Thank you for saying that. I believe if anyone could turn back time through sheer strength of will, it's you." She turned her head and listened to his heart beating against her ear. "I'm so sorry about your family, Ivan. If I'd known Borjan's history, I probably would've handed him over myself."

Ivan hugged her close, tucking her into his body and enveloping her in his naked warmth. She sighed and pressed herself against him. Jaya had never felt safer in her life. She turned her face up and ran her lips along his jawline, kissing him whisper soft. She felt the clench of his biceps against her as he crushed her into his body, holding her so impossibly close she could barely breathe. She wasn't going to complain. She loved his possessive need to keep her close. She'd grown up without a family, without connection and love. She trusted Ivan to give those things to her.

"I need you, sweetheart," he growled against the top of her head. "Need to feel you under me, around me."

Jaya's body responded instantly, softening for his possession with wet heat. She licked him where she'd been kissing him. His fist clenched in the bathrobe at her back and he yanked, pulling it from her body. She started to stumble backwards at the force he used, but he grabbed her before she could fall and lifted her off her feet. Jaya gasped and gripped him tight around the neck.

"Legs around my waist," he ordered.

"Okay," she said breathlessly, wrapping her legs tight around him.

She stared in helpless fascination at the way his arms bulged as they held her up. He backed her right up until her ass hit the window behind her. She squealed as the cold touched her bare skin and tried to arch away from it. He held her up with an arm around her waist, reached between them with his other hand and unzipped his pants. Jaya's mouth began to water and she tried to lean forward so she could see his cock. He pushed her back with a hand between her breasts.

"Don't move," he growled. His steely grey eyes burned into hers as he lined himself up with her dripping pussy and slammed himself home.

Jaya cried out and arched her back, gasping at the sudden fullness inside her. He slid his hands underneath her, holding her up by the ass and giving himself leverage to slide even deeper. He growled and pushed her further into the unyielding window, not moving, just enjoying the feel of her sex clamped around his cock, taking him deep.

"So fucking good, Jaya," he said against the side of her head. "Could stay here forever."

She slid her fingers into his hair, touching the dark strands, caressing the skin of his neck. This man belonged to her, nothing could change that. He wouldn't allow them to be separated.

He began moving inside her, taking her with long, deep strokes that sent her senses reeling. Pleasure rocketed through her body as each stroke brushed against her clit and struck her g-spot. She dug her nails into his back and held on for the ride, giving herself up to him.

Desire swamped her and she cried out. "I'm coming!"

"Good girl," he grunted, squeezing her tight.

He slammed into her, taking her over the edge, revelling in her cries, praising her beauty, the way she looked as she came and everything about her. Jaya floated on a cloud of bliss as he continued to stroke himself within her dripping pussy. His cock flared hot and wide inside her and she screamed as another orgasmic wave took her.

"Love you so fucking much," Ivan growled against her, biting her shoulder. He came seconds later, his hot semen bathing the walls of her pussy while he held her tight in his arms. Before she could respond, he took a fistful of her hair, turned her face to his and kissed her hard, bruising her lips in a passionate kiss.

CHAPTER THIRTY-FIVE

One Month Later

Jaya closed the book and set it on the table next to her lounge chair, her hand lingering for a moment. The dark, wild and tragic tale of Catherine Earnshaw and Heathcliff still called to her even after she'd finished the story. A shiver of appreciation ran down her spine and she closed her eyes on a sigh. This was her second time through and this time she was able to absorb so much more from the story. The deep abiding passion of the characters, the rich scenery, the sense of mystery and awe surrounding the entire story. And though it had ended badly for some, it still finished on a positive note, finished with a love that had sprung out of hate.

She stood up and gazed out at the sun setting on the city of Jakarta. In the past few days she'd begun hoping Ivan would agree to make their home here. She knew he was considering all the security angles. He thought the high-rise city setting was riskier than another island or a remote country somewhere off the grid. Jaya had argued that it would be easier from a work perspective if they stayed in the city. He'd given her 'the look' as she was coming to call it. Now that she no longer feared him, she just ignored it and did her own thing anyway. Which was picking up new jobs at will and playing with her internet friends.

Ivan had tried to enforce his rule of picking and choosing her jobs for her, but since neither he nor any of his people came anywhere near her tech capabilities there was no way for him to know what kind of jobs she was accepting. He quickly became aware of her rule breaking when she had to sneak out of bed one night to do a particularly time sensitive job that was in a different time zone. Ivan had responded by taking away her laptop. Jaya had then stolen Keane's smart phone and hacked into the penthouse security system, locking everyone in until Ivan promised to negotiate with her. Since then, she'd agreed to run her jobs by him as long as he agreed to allow her unilateral decision-making on which jobs she chose to take.

"After all, I am a multi-millionaire," she'd murmured against his lips, allowing him to wrap his arms around her when it looked like negotiations were going her way. "I've been taking care of myself for several years now."

"And look where that got you," he pointed out, kissing her lips, then her nose and forehead.

"Where?" she asked, breathless.

"Kidnapped by a villainous arms dealer who caged you up and ravished you," he growled, picking her up and striding toward the bed.

She laughed as he dropped her and then came down on top of her. "Maybe so, but I'm happy with the outcome. And if this horrible crime lord arms dealer guy plays his cards right I *might* consider selling him some of my fancy hacking services."

He looked down at her, a frown creasing his forehead as though he were thinking about it. "I said villainous, not horrible," he finally said. "You need to get your terminology correct if you intend on getting that laptop back. Remember what happened to the last guy that made me an enemy."

She gasped and smacked his arm. "That's so awful, Ivan! No wonder you never make jokes, you're really bad at it." She giggled and pulled his head down, meeting his lips in a searing kiss. Her heart soared, bursting with the freedom and happiness he'd gifted her.

That conversation had been a few days ago and he'd given her laptop back. True to her word Jaya had told him of every job to come along and detailed the ones she intended to take. She'd enjoyed the look of astonishment he couldn't quite conceal from her as she described the intricacies involved, the reason she didn't take jobs for completely monetary gain. Sometimes she took jobs for political reasons, sometimes for charitable and sometimes for the sheer challenge. She felt gratified when she saw admiration reflected on his face.

Since their discussion, Ivan had created an office work space for her right next to his, designed with only the basics. He'd explained that he wanted her to order exactly what she wanted in both tech and office equipment to make her office its most optimal for her use. She'd nearly started crying when he'd shown her. Instead, she'd slammed the door shut and thrown herself into his arms hoping he got the message. He did. They made slow, sweet love on the floor of her brand-new office. A place she'd always dreamed of, but never dared hope to have. A room filled with space and light and all the best and newest equipment. But best of all... the man she loved right next door.

"Hey, daydreamer, get your ass down here." Jaya looked down at the pool where her two best friends were laughing and waving at her. She waved back and assured them she'd be down in a minute.

Ndari and Katie had taken to each other like ducks to water. They were two very confident women with a taste for the finer things in life. After a little bit of circling and sizing, they'd finally settled on the side of becoming instant friends that air kissed and Snapchatted their exploits every few hours. An amused Jaya had instantly hacked their Snapchats and added a beagle in sunglasses and a santa hat to every picture. They could usually be found arguing which princess from which country had the best crown jewels, and which online store they would raid next with Ivan's credit card. Though both Katie and Jaya had plenty of their own money, it was agreed that Ivan's credit card had the best likelihood of being unlimited. Though no one had proved it yet.

There had been some tension between Katie and Ivan upon Katie's arrival, though it was completely on Katie's side as Ivan was cool as always at meeting the former protégé he'd given up to get his hands on Jaya. Sensing the tension between his lovely wife and a very powerful international crime lord, Katie's husband, Roman Valdez, had immediately stepped in. Silent, tense, angry, and tattooed from head to foot, Roman was the epitome of every badass gangster Mexican movie villain rolled into one. Jaya was in awe and possibly might have been a little in lust if she weren't so totally enthralled by her own badass antihero.

Jaya had stepped in and broken the tension by throwing her arms around Katie, hugging her tight and exclaiming over how beautiful the tall blond was. They'd never actually met in real life, though Jaya had, of course, seen Katie many times over surveillance. Katie had never set eyes on Jaya before, hadn't even known the real name of the hacker genius that had helped her time and again through her many heists. So the two women had plenty to catch up on. Once this was pointed out to her, she was happy to leave the room with an excitedly chattering Jaya, throwing one last pointed glare over her shoulder at Ivan.

Jaya rifled through her drawer coming up with a black

one-piece bathing suit. She grinned as she held it up, then tossed it on the bed, quickly disrobing. Once she was dressed in the bathing suit, she stood in front of the mirror. "Well, he insisted no bikinis. He wasn't super specific otherwise." She shrugged, a gleam of mischief in her eyes as she surveyed the deep plunge of material that ran all the way down to her belly button. The sides were held up by a thin see-through mesh. She pulled on a long, silky robe and bent over to kiss Haty's soft head where she was slumbering upside down on Ivan's pillow. The cat stretched out a paw, purr-meowed, yawned and went back to sleep. Then Jaya left the suite to join her friends.

"Hey, bout time you joined us, lazy bones," Ndari sent a wave of water slicing toward Jaya as she walked toward the pool.

Laughing, she dropped her robe on the nearest lounger. It had taken some work, but she was now able to spend time at the pool without thinking about that awful day when Borjan's men shot up the pool area. It helped that Ivan had the entire area renovated to look completely different and insisted it be done shortly after their arrival from Bangkok. Ndari had also dragged her outside almost daily, insisting she spend time in the sun, socializing and learning how to swim with her wacky friend as a tutor.

"Do you think Katie should try stealing my princess tiara?" Ndaria asked, swimming to the edge of the pool and pressing herself against the ledge, leaning her arms on the warm pool tiles, her breasts swelling over top as she bobbed up and down in the water. A quick glance to the side confirmed that Keane was on duty near the balcony perimeter. His eyes were glued to the trio, or more specifically, the princess. "I don't mean one of the tiaras I've picked up in a jewelry store, but the real deal. My crown jewel. The thing that makes me a princess."

Jaya laughed. "A tiara isn't what makes you a princess!"

Ndari rolled her eyes. "Well obviously it was the accident of birth thing, but in the mean time, the tiara is pretty freaking awesome, why wouldn't Miss Blond-thing stick-up-her-ass want to steal my tiara? She's stolen everything else of value in this place."

"Okay...!" Katie started, lunging toward Ndari, clearly intent on doing some damage.

"Is there a problem here?"

Jaya twisted around at the deep voice, Katie and Ndari stopped their pool sparring match. Roman Valdez, tanned Mexican God, strode up to the pool, his eyes on his wife.

Katie swam immediately for the edge and lifted her arms. "Roman." Her voice was breathless, her eyes hot with longing, room for no one but her husband. Heedless of the water dripping from his wife, Roman reached for her, placing his hands beneath her armpits and lifting her from the pool. Jaya and Ndari stared in fascination as Roman kissed Katie, uncaring of their audience. She pressed herself against him and, when he finally released her lips, whispered, "No problem here, baby."

"Jaya."

The spell was broken, Jaya blinked and turned to look at Ivan. He wasn't looking at Roman and Katie. His gaze was on her. Though his eyes were grey: steel, silvery, light... they also held such unreachable darkness. She didn't know if it was the tragedy that befell his family or if this was just Ivan. But there was always going to be a part of him she couldn't reach, couldn't know. She would just have to be comforted by the thought that he knew her. He could reach her, he knew how to touch her heart.

"I love you," she whispered knowing he was too far away to hear.

He strode toward her, reaching for her robe and picking it

up off the lounger as he approached. He opened it over her shoulders, covering the bathing suit she'd known he wouldn't approve of when she bought it. He bent to capture her lips in a lingering kiss, then wrapped his arms around her waist, trapping her against his hard chest. She lifted her hands to hold on to him, clinging to his solid frame.

"I love you too, Jaya. My Victory," he said huskily and reached to bring her hand forward, pressing his lips against the ring on her finger. The same ring they had found together in the Tiffany's store before Jaya had tried to escape. Sometimes she wondered if he'd given it to her both as gesture of his love and a promise that he would always find her.

Her gaze flicked up and she nearly stepped away from him. Though his voice was soft and gentle, his eyes told a different story. One of darkness. One of a man that had done anything and everything to attain his position of power. A man that knew how to hold on to what he valued. Ivan would always come for her; no matter where she was taken, where she fled.

He would never let her go. Especially now that he had her love.

THE END

ACKNOWLEDGMENTS

Dear readers,

Thank you for reading Capturing Victory! I would like to thank my lovely editor for always pushing me to work harder, sharpen my skills and for challenging me to do better. I also want to thank my favourite cover artist for not only creating the best covers in the business, but for throwing a few teasers and banners my way as well.

A very special thank you to the amazing readers that generously give their time for free to help me organize my releases and spread the word about my books. In particular, I would like to thank Sansa, Kimberly, Kristi and Barbie. There are many others as well that show their support in other ways, including conversations and kind words. It means the world to me and helps me continue on this dark and twisty romantic writing path.

Thank you again for reading,
Love Nikita

BONUS: THE PRINCESS AND HER MERCENARY

Read Keane and Ndari's story today!

He'd waited for the woman for four months, sixteen days and a handful of hours. Keane was fucking done waiting. Patience, his boss and friend, Ivan, had told him. Play the long game. Ivan wanted to make sure his second-in-command could extract the Princess without getting killed. What a joke. Keane had the luck of the Irish. He could hit a palace in some obscure country and be out in a matter of minutes. He had full confidence.

Still, he'd waited. And he'd burned for her. He'd known at their first meeting that she was the one, yet he'd still been forced to let her go. Now, he pined after her like some love-struck pussy. He wanted her in a way he'd never wanted another woman. Sure, he liked to fuck around, had his share of women to keep him occupied. None of them were the Princess. She was a class unto herself and he couldn't wait to get his hands on her for real. No more teasing, as she'd done to him while acting as a companion to Jaya. Ndari was about to become his for real.

Sure enough, minutes after he'd hidden himself in the palace, he heard the whisper of feet against the stone tiles, heading his way. He knew his woman, knew exactly where she would go if she thought the palace was under attack. Shouts halted the progression of the woman coming toward him and then he heard her voice filter through the door as she shouted back.

"Carry on, gentlemen. It's just a little power outage, I'll be fine."

Keane melted into the shadows as she pushed open the heavy door to the jewel room and slipped inside. Her dark head was turned as though she was concentrating on something on the other side of the door. Then she closed and locked it, turning to face the room. A slow grin spread across her face as she surveyed her surroundings. She was visible in the dim lighting of the various display cases.

She was fucking gorgeous, even more beautiful than he remembered. Her dark hair was loose and flowing down her back. Black with streaks of honey and brown. Her big eyes were a stunning, deep velvet brown. Her body was a mouth-watering picture of curves packed into a floor length blue dress with a slit right up to her thigh and running shoes on her feet. Loosely clasped around her shoulders was some kind of strange cloak with feathers. Trust the Princess to wear something completely inappropriate to a kidnapping. Of course, she didn't know there was about to be a kidnapping.

She approached the first display case, stepping right up to it and pressing her hands against the glass. "Greetings, my children," she murmured, tilting her head to get a better look. Keane smothered a chuckle at the way her eyes lit up. Woman sure did love her jewels. He would have to make sure she stayed showered in them. The way to his Princess's heart was through the shiny stuff.

She left the first display case and prowled around the room checking on all the others. She paused here and there but only for a few seconds at a time before stopping in front of a glass case off to the left, the one closest to Keane's position. She moved around the case until her back was to him, her hands on the glass.

"Here we are little darlings, did you miss your mama?" she asked, her voice bouncy with anticipation. She tapped one long lacquered fingernail against the glass.

"Don't know if those bits of coloured glass missed you, but I sure as fuck did." Keane stepped out of the shadows and into the light so she could see him. His heart pounded in happiness and anticipation as she whirled around, her hand clutching her throat.

Finally, his princess.

Now available for purchase! Click HERE

Get the latest updates at **nikitaslater.com**

BONUS: THIEVING HEARTS

Revulsion hit Katie like a punch in the stomach. It was everything she could do to search for the key to her old apartment in her coach bag, fit it in the lock and open the door. She wasn't sure who she hated more, her ex-husband or herself. She didn't understand how he could feel such disgust for her and her profession, yet summon her here month after month.

Oh, she understood the money. Blackmail for money was an easy concept to comprehend. It was the sex she didn't get.

She shifted uneasily in her knee length button up tan coat. Reaching for the belt, she knotted it tighter around her too slender waist. She knew she'd lost too much weight recently. Constant fear and agitation had taken its toll on her figure. She spent every waking moment terrified that the FBI were going to break down her door. All because of the man whose apartment she was about to enter.

Something didn't feel right. Usually she heard the sound of music or the TV blaring. The smell of food would hit her as she cracked open the door and stood nervously waiting for his summons. Colin liked to keep her waiting. Like a dog or a slave. Today she heard nothing.

She pushed the door open further and saw that the interior of his apartment was flooded in darkness. Had he forgotten about their appointment? Impossible. It was the same time every month. Since the day of their divorce a year ago. She would come to him on the 25th of the month at 8 pm, like clockwork. If she didn't, he would make the call that would end her life.

Something definitely wasn't right. Her legs began to shake. She wished desperately that she wasn't wearing four inch heels. Not that it was her choice. Colin chose her apparel for these visits. It rarely deviated. He liked the easy access of the coat, heels and nothing else.

She stepped further into the apartment, allowing the door to close behind her. The sound of the muffled slam made her jump. Her heart pounded in fear and her palms dampened. She smelled something metallic.

Blood.

She bit her lip to hold back a whimper. "C-Colin?" she whispered. Then realized he wouldn't possibly be able to hear her unless he was standing right next to her.

"Colin!" she called in a stronger voice.

When he didn't answer she took a few more steps closer to what used to be her kitchen before the divorce. Before Colin had taken everything from her and then demanded more every month after. A $25,000 payment and her on her back with her legs spread, a willing vessel for him to use as many times as he wanted before kicking her out like some dirty whore. Something he liked to call her during their hours together. She shuddered.

With shaking fingers, she reached for the light and pushed. The bright overhead light blinded her for a moment. She blinked and then turned her head toward the metallic smell, forcing herself to brave the possibility that something might have happened to Colin. She gasped in horror as she took in a pool of blood that was far too big for someone to simply walk away from.

She whimpered and backed away from the kitchen, intent on reaching the door, her eyes glued to the blood. It was almost perfect in its shiny depth, the way it was spread across the floor. No smears, or prints to mar its glassy surface. She forced herself to blink and continue moving toward the door. She would call the police as soon as she got down to the lobby.

Her heels were the only sound in the apartment as she shuffled slowly backward toward the door keeping her eyes on the blood, as though it would somehow attack her. Before she could reach the door, her back hit a solid wall of muscle. She opened her mouth to scream and would have jumped away, but a hand clamped over her lips and another around her waist, pinning her arms to her side. She was dragged backwards into the heat of a very hard, very male body.

She knew instantly the man holding her wasn't Colin. Her ex-husband was the same height as her when she wore heels. And he wasn't near as hard as whoever was pressed against her back. This man was rock solid. Was this man responsible for the massive pool of blood on the floor? Of their own volition, her eyes fell to the crimson lake. She tried to struggle, but the man held her so tight, all she could do was wiggle helplessly against him.

He groaned and pushed his face into the back of her neck, nudging his nose into the short blond hair and breathing deeply. W-was he actually smelling her? He tilted her head to the side and forward a little so she was forced to look down. He ran his nose down the exposed arch of her throat from her ear all the way down to her shoulder. He was definitely inhaling her scent. His lips teased her shoulder and he tugged the sleeve of her coat a little until it moved toward the edge of her shoulder exposing more skin.

Oh god, what was he doing? Was this man going to rape her in her ex-husband's apartment? Had Colin's depraved mind come up with some new kind of punishment? But how did that explain the blood? Somehow, she *knew* deep inside that the blood belonged to Colin. Just as she knew no one could survive the loss of that much. She whimpered against the hand.

Her fear seemed to penetrate his fascination with her skin. He straightened to his full height, which was still several inches taller than her, even in heels. Though his broad palm remained firmly over her mouth, he used his thumb to rub her cheek soothingly as though to calm her. She blinked rapidly as his thumb brushed too close to her eye, her eyelashes sweeping over the rough pad. He groaned again from behind her and tightened his arm in response, pulling her further into the cradle of his thighs. She gasped into his hand, feeling the rigid length of his cock through the back of her coat.

Then she caught sight of the tattoo that ran along the edge of his forefinger. His trigger finger. It said, "For Dexter."

Her dead brother's name. She stiffened in his arms, anger suffusing her as she realized exactly who held her. She didn't bother struggling. There was no point. He was too tall and outweighed her by a lot. The bastard also had a ton more street fighting experience than she did and wasn't afraid to fight dirty.

He chuckled darkly from behind her. He knew the exact moment she realized who he was. He dropped his hand from her lips, no longer worried that she would scream bloody murder, and slid it down the front of her body. He wrapped both arms around her waist, still keeping her arms pinned to her sides and dragged her tightly back against him. He thrust his erection into her ass.

"What are you doing here?" she hissed angrily.

"Think that's pretty obvious," he growled, bending his head to speak in her ear. "Come for you, pretty lady."

She shivered against him, her eyes falling on the blood. "Wh-what did you do to Colin?" she asked, her voice both a plea and a hope.

His body became rigid, his arms so like steel bands around her that they hurt. He didn't speak for a moment. She got the feeling he was controlling himself so he didn't say or do something he might regret. She frowned, her breath catching in her throat. Roman would never hurt her. Would he?

"You don't have to worry about him anymore."

Katie opened her mouth to argue with him, but he brought his hand up to cut her off, pressing his palm against her lips once more. "You don't want to talk to me about your husband right now, Katie. Nod if you understand?"

She shivered and nodded quickly. She wanted to know what he did to Colin, but Roman was like a wild animal. He'd always been dangerous and unpredictable. There was no telling what he was going to do next. Until she was in a better position. Like on the other side of a locked door, her questions could wait. He moved his hand again.

"What happens now?" she whispered, hoping that one question would be okay. Was he going to let her run back to her life now that he'd done whatever he'd come to do?

"You come with me, like you should have years ago when I asked you to."

She gasped and jerked in his arms. "Impossible!" she told him.

She had a job in Milan in just a few days. She absolutely couldn't go with Roman. She knew the odds of his letting her out of his sight. The man had an eerie way of tracking people. The only way she'd managed to escape him all those years ago was because she'd begged him to let her go. And for some reason her opinion had always mattered to the street hardened criminal.

"Not impossible, Katie," he growled at her. "In fact, it's a fucking promise. You're coming with me this time. I'm done living without you."

"No!" she gasped out, lunging in his arms. "You can't do that, Roman. I have a life. I won't go with you!"

"I've been watching you, Katie, my love," he growled at her, lowering her struggling body to the floor as she twisted in his arms. He took her elbows and locked them behind her in one strong grip. He pulled something from his pocket with his other hand. "You live a half-life. I'm done watching from the shadows while you slowly kill yourself. It's time to start living again."

"With you?" she spat out, glaring at him over her shoulder.

"With me," he confirmed.

When she realized what he held, she begged him to stop. She threatened him and tried to kick him with her sharp heels. He ignored her threats and her pleas. He pinned her to the floor, lifted her coat to her thigh, baring the smooth naked skin. He froze when he realized she was completely bare underneath. Then he shoved his hand roughly into her coat to confirm his suspicion, cupping her bare breast.

She gasped and surged up into his hands. He slammed her back into the floor, treating her with a lack of care she'd never felt from him before. He leaned over her, his breathing finally as heavy as hers and growled in her ear, "Knew the fucker was blackmailing you. Had no idea you liked it enough to spread your legs. Maybe I should've let him live and just walked away from your mess."

She screamed and fought to get away from him. He cut her screams off with a heavy hand over her lips and plunged the syringe viciously into her thigh while she beat at his chest. After a few seconds, she stopped fighting, her body gradually going limp beneath him. He pulled her across his lap, cradling her head against his arm, and smoothed the coat over her nakedness.

She watched his dark, sinister face as she drifted into unconsciousness. The only man she ever truly loved. The man she feared above all others. He'd finally come for her.

Now available for purchase!

"Fuck," Riley grumbled, twisting to make sure she was correct. Nope, she didn't have the right tool.

It was late at night and all the guys had gone home so she couldn't call out to one of the other mechanics and ask them to hand it to her. Damn. With an aggrieved sigh, she pushed herself out from under the car. Shoving her long ponytail out of the way, she crawled toward the toolbox and rifled through until she found what she was looking for. Loud, thumping music filled the garage from where her iPhone was plugged into its port on top of one of the tool benches.

Turning back toward the '69 Camaro, Riley adjusted her lamp and prepared to slide back under. This baby was a thing of beauty. It called to her from the moment it entered her shop, which is why she was still working on it at 2:00am. If she did it up right she'd be able to turn a pretty profit on this little sweetheart and take Cilia on vacation. They desperately needed some bonding time.

The music switched off and a deep voice reverberated through the darkness of the garage. "I'm looking for Mr. Bancroft."

Riley froze for a few precious seconds before her head snapped up, judging the distance between a shadowed man and the gun in her toolbox. He stepped forward into the circle of her light, closing the distance between them. Riley's heart slammed against her ribs as his face became visible and she recognized the most ruthless man in the city. Soloman Hart, mafia kingpin, was standing in her garage, staring down at her with cold intent. He now stood directly between her and her gun. Not that she thought it would do any good against a man like him.

Riley felt incredibly small and grimy next to his large, well-dressed frame. She sat crouched on the concrete beneath him, wearing her usual tank top and grimy, oil-stained overalls with the top left to hang down. Her shiny, dark brown hair was pulled back in a messy ponytail and she wore no make-up.

He seemed to be looking her over, taking in every inch of her with interest. Her eyes narrowed in return. She was used to guys staring. She was a thirty-year-old female mechanic, working in a garage full of men. She looked younger than she was and knew she was attractive. Definitely fantasy material for some guys. Which is why she tended to work in the office and on cars in the back, well away from the clients. Very few people knew who actually owned the garage.

"How did you get in here?" she demanded, pushing herself up and standing to her full height, which was still several inches shorter than him. She crossed her arms in front of her chest and glared at him. She had a damn good security system or she wouldn't have been alone in the shop blaring music in the middle of the night.

He ignored her question and raised a dark, thick brow. "Mr. Bancroft?" The single question sent a chill down her spine, letting her know that the next words out of her mouth better be an answer, because Soloman Hart was not a man known for patience.

Riley pressed her lips together for a moment and wondered how best to answer him. The truth of 'Mr. Bancroft' was complicated. And Riley was starting to suspect she may be in some danger. The likelihood of a man of this caliber showing up in her garage for any reason was slim. Which meant something not good was going down. Soloman had men to deal with his car issues, he didn't deal with things like this himself.

She moistened her lips and then stopped when his sharp eyes followed the movement. Taking a breath, she said, "Mr. Bancroft is dead. He died two years ago."

His brows drew together in a frown that made Riley shiver from head to toe. Yeah, he didn't want to play games with her. His next words confirmed this thought.

"Don't fuck with me, little girl," he growled. "Everyone knows Alan Bancroft is dead. I'm looking for the owner of this garage. Alan's son, Riley Bancroft."

"Okay," she whispered. "Why are you looking for Riley?"

Holy shit, she was going to die! The look on his face suggested that the last person that questioned him instead of instantly giving him the answers he was searching for had died a really extra terrible death.

Surprisingly, he answered, his deep voice clipped as he spoke. "Someone stole one of my vehicles yesterday. It was my favourite and I want it back. Thought it might show up here."

Shock flickered across her face. Who would be stupid enough to steal one of Soloman Hart's cars? Well, that explained why he would show up on her doorstep himself at 2:00am looking for answers. She ran the biggest chop shop in the city. Only very few people knew she ran the garage. She had a very good team of mechanics, mostly inherited from her father, that helped keep her safe behind the scenes. Few people even knew the name Riley Bancroft. Except, somehow Soloman did.

"Wh-what kind of car?" She asked hesitantly, hoping like hell it hadn't gone through her shop. She usually did her homework and found out where the vehicles came from so this kind of shitstorm didn't come down on her head, but that didn't mean things didn't get under her radar once in a while.

"Koenigsegg Regera." His voice held no inflection as he named one of the most expensive vehicles in the world. A car that would be one of a kind in the United States.

Riley took a few seconds out from her terror to be impressed. Damn. Soloman must like him some nice luxury racing automobiles. Too bad the man was such a cold-hearted, ruthless bastard. Under different circumstances she wouldn't mind getting under the hoods of his fleet, see what he had going on up in there.

She breathed a sigh of relief. "Nope, I definitely would've noticed one of those. Never even seen one in person, let alone had one in here."

He nodded, still studying her carefully as though taking in

every minuscule expression that crossed her face. Finally, he said, "I'd still like to have a conversation with Mr. Bancroft."

Fuck. That was going to be a problem since there was no Mr. Bancroft. Instead, she nodded her head.

"Sure, no problem. I'll have him call you tomorrow." She'd get one of the other mechanics to call and reassure him that his car was never there and if it showed up he would be the first person they called.

He reached out and took her hand before she realized what he was about to do. He held her fingers in a grip that told her she shouldn't pull away from him. He had tattoos over his hand and knuckles. He looked down at the black, chipped nail polish and rubbed his broad thumb over the tops of her much smaller nails. She shivered at his touch. Based on his reputation and the few glimpses she'd had of him she'd always considered Soloman Hart cold, but his hand was surprisingly warm.

"What's your name?" he demanded, his voice deep and compelling.

Riley tried to pull her hand away, but he continued to hold her. She turned her body away and said in a haughty voice, "None of your business."

He stiffened next to her and she bit her lip, worried that she was about to find out what made this powerful man so feared among their underworld set. He chuckled lightly, running his thumb over her knuckles. "I think you'll find I can make it my business."

She shivered and dropped her eyes, still refusing to answer. She did not want this man finding out who she was. For more reasons that the obvious. When he was alive, Alan Bancroft had taught Riley everything he knew, but he'd kept her existence on the down low in case they ever needed to pack up shop and run. There was also the complication of her mother. Cilia Bancroft, shady accountant to the super rich, was a handful and best kept out of the notice of men like Soloman Hart.

"You can fly, little bird," he said quietly. He looked down at her, capturing her brown eyes with his bottomless dark eyes. "I will let you go for now."

"F-for now?" Riley asked hesitantly.

He released her hand and stepped closer, towering over her, his chest nearly brushing hers. Riley gasped at his unexpected movement and tried to move back. Her leg bumped against the car she'd been working on and she was forced to stand still next to him. Her head swam as his subtle, masculine scent enveloped her. It made alarm bells go off in her head. He didn't immediately move away from her.

"For now," he confirmed. "I think the day will come that we will see... a lot more of each other."

Her mouth opened and she stared at him. Was that a threat? He was looking down at her with something she couldn't entirely define. Speculation? Possessiveness? But how was that possible? He didn't even know her. Though she'd seen him before, they were just meeting officially for the first time.

His eyes brushed over her one last time and she had a keen awareness that she was being granted some kind of reprieve. But it came with a time limit. One that would eventually run out. Her heart slammed against her ribs.

"Do you know who I am?" he asked.

She blinked and then nodded slowly.

"Say my name," he demanded.

Riley gaped up at him for a moment and then, desperately wanting the dark man to leave, she gave him what he wanted. She licked her lips and whispered, "Soloman."

He turned and strode away from her, resetting the alarm before leaving the garage.

Soloman slid into the passenger side of his second favourite vehicle. Turning to his friend and bodyguard, he said, "Did you catch that?"

Roman nodded. He had been standing in the shadows near the door where he'd disabled the alarm and unbolted the lock to allow his boss entry to the garage. Though Soloman didn't need back up, the two rarely worked separately, especially since Soloman's climb to the top had earned many enemies. Both knew it was better to have a loyal man guarding each other's backs than to go it alone.

"I want her," Soloman said quietly, not taking his eyes off the passing street lights.

Roman grunted, but didn't say anything. He already knew. The boss rarely pursued women, beyond having them brought in for a quick fuck. That he even asked for this one's name was surprising. "I'll find out who she is."

Soloman nodded. "I want to know everything. There's something about her... I think I might keep her for a while."

Roman grunted. He'd get their information guy out of bed and working on the problem of the chick immediately. Find out who she was so the boss could get laid. Soloman Hart wasn't used to being denied. No one needed to be around the man when he wasn't happy. Much better to just bring him the woman's information and then the woman herself all wrapped up and tied in a bow. Fewer people would die that way.

"And find out where the fuck Riley Bancroft is," he snapped, drumming his fingers restlessly on his leg. "I want my goddamned car back."

Now available for purchase!

ALSO BY NIKITA SLATER

If you enjoyed this book, check out some other works by #1 International Bestselling Author, Nikita Slater. More titles are always in progress, so check back often to see what's new!

SINNER'S EMPIRE

Book 1 - Sin of Silence - Preorder

Book 2 - A Silent Reckoning - Coming Soon!

Book 3 - Goodnight, Sinners - Coming Soon!

THE QUEENS SERIES

Book One – Scarred Queen

Book Two - Queen's Move

Book Three - Born a Queen

Book Four - The Red Queen (Coming 2021)

Alejandro's Prey (a novella)

The Queens 4 Book Box Set

FIRE & VICE SERIES

Book One – Prisoner of Fortune

Book Two – Fight or Flight

Book Three – King's Command

Book Four – Savage Vendetta

Savage Boss (a novella)

Book Five – Fear in Her Eyes

Book Six – Bound by Blood

Book Seven – In His Sights

Book Eight - Burning Beauty

Book Nine - Chasing Ecstasy (Coming soon!)

Fire & Vice 6 Book Box Set

THE DRIVEN HEARTS SERIES

Book One - Driven by Desire

Book Two - Thieving Hearts

Book Three - Capturing Victory

Novella - The Princess and Her Mercenary

Driven Hearts 4 Book Box Set

THE SANCTUARY SERIES

Book One - Sanctuary's Warlord

Book Two - Sanctuary on Fire

Book Three - The Last Sanctuary

Book Four - The Road to Wolfe

Book Five - Skye's Sanctuary (Coming soon!)

The Sanctuary Series 3 Book Box Set

LOVING THE BAD BOY SERIES

Loving Vincent

Loving Jared

Loving Rico (Coming Soon!)

STANDALONE BOOKS

The Assassin's Wife

Because You're Mine

Mine to Keep (a novella)

Luna & Andres

Kiss of the Cartel

Stalked

AFTER DARK

In collaboration with Jasmin Quinn

Collared: A Dark Captive Romance

Safeword: A Dark Romance

Chained: A Mafia Marriage Romance

Good Girl: A Captive BDSM Romance

Hostile Takeover: An Enemies to Lovers Romance

The After Dark Box Set

Visit **nikitaslater.com** for more information

and the latest updates!

ABOUT THE AUTHOR

Nikita Slater is the International Bestselling dark romance author of the Fire & Vice series, Angels & Assassins series, The Queens series and several standalone novels. Her favourite genre is mafia romance, the bloodier the better, though she loves to write about every subject under the sun. She lives on the beautiful Canadian prairies with her son and crazy awesome dog. She has an unholy affinity for books (especially erotic romance), wine, pets and anything chocolate. Despite some of the darker themes in her books (which are pure fun and fantasy), Nikita is a staunch feminist and advocate of equal rights for all races, genders and non-gender specific persons. When she isn't writing, dreaming about writing or talking about writing, she helps others discover a love of reading and writing through literacy and social work.

www.ingramcontent.com/pod-product-compliance
Lightning Source LLC
Chambersburg PA
CBHW071206210726
48293CB00002B/309